I0574586

Let Me Handle Your Heart
Josie Hunter

Josie Hunter

Edited by Megan Joseph

Book Cover by Ashley Santoro

Dedication

To the dreamers and visionaries who refuse to wait for
permission:
I pray you continue doing everything you can to give what has
lived in your spirit bone and breath.
Bless the world with your gift and your dream. We need you.

To those who have known rejection:
May you learn, as I have, that sometimes man's rejection is God's
protection and redirection.
Even when things don't go the way you hoped, please know that
He has something much better for you.
I pray God equips you with the mindset, discipline, and
resources to steward the amazing blessing He's sending your
way.

Author's Note

For a long time, in the back of my mind, I didn't think I could write a full-on romance novel, even though I always slipped in romantic subplots in stories I wrote. I didn't even want to admit to myself and others that it's my favorite genre to read and watch. I think I was afraid to claim and write romance for fear of not being taken seriously as a writer. Even though romance is the best-selling genre in the world, it's still often dismissed for not being "real" and/or "serious" literature. And because a lot of women love it loudly, sometimes people label romance fiction with what I consider a disrespectful term: chick lit.

But I am beyond *proud* to read, write, and enjoy a genre that centers connection, softness, and love in a world that is so divisive, hard, and hateful. And I'm even prouder when romance fiction is boldly and unapologetically *Black* as fuck!

Also, heads up: much of the dialogue is written in AAVE dialect—in case you think the misspelled words are mistakes!

—Josie

Official Playlist

This is the official sonic companion for the novel! I recommend you listen in order as it follows the story, but even if you don't, it's still a vibe.

If you're reading the e-book, click the image to access the playlist. If you're reading a print book, simply search Let Me Handle Your Heart in Spotify to find it.

I hope you enjoy!

—Josie

Table of Contents

1
You Have a Choice

Tuesday, August 15

Tim

Z ay Dubb$ is 30 years old today. This nigga wanted to party on his actual birthday. A *Tuesday*. Who the fuck parties on a Tuesday?

But he's also been in the rap game for over a decade, so he wanted to go all out. He had me rent a huge modern mansion overlooking the beach for this celebration. This place is packed, although some Hollywood types would call it "intimate." DJ Tone Def, one of Zay's homies, is blasting Zay's music and his other favorite songs, literally making the walls vibrate. The avant-garde chandeliers are dim in the great room where the main "dance floor" is. The event planners and I strategically rearranged the furniture to catch fucked-up guests for when they will eventually fall on their asses.

Zay and his crew are vibing out, drunk and high, thanks to the open bars and his plugs. Most of the guests—other household names, some industry folks, and some special ladies—are also cross-faded. Since I've worked these types of functions for years, I know some people have broken out other "party favors" to partake in a few quiet rooms. No judgement at all, but sometimes niggas get too fucked up and do something crazy, which means *I* have to clean up their messes.

I'm leaning against a wall near one of the bars. Cellphone in hand, I scan the crowd so that I can catch something if shit goes down. My presence is supposed to be observant and unobstructive. Basically, stay *out* the way until I need to get *in* the way to handle a situation. This job can be glamorous sometimes, like accompanying clients on private jets to overseas performances and rubbing elbows with music legends at industry dinners. But not today. Ensuring that Zay's party runs smoothly, he has a good time, and that he and his friends don't fuck something up is *not* fun. Babysitting rappers is never fun.

But what *is* fun and always brings a smile to my face is food—*especially* when it's free. And damn, does this job always come with good free food.

I was able to pull in a few favors to hire an in-demand celebrity chef to cater this party. The huge buffet table positioned between the kitchen and the dining room is calling my name. I'm low-key skinny, but a big-back at heart. If I didn't have to run behind some of these niggas, I'd definitely be fat as fuck.

I glance at my phone and see it's almost 11 o'clock. I've been here since four, getting this place set up and I haven't eaten since the Del Taco I crushed on the way here. Since I don't have any crisis texts, I head over to the buffet in the massive dining room to make a little plate before I don't get another chance tonight. I pile wagyu sliders, ahi tuna tartare, and some sort of crostini onto my plate.

But something funny-looking catches my attention. *Maybe it's a fancy tart?* I think. The filling is a mixture of something green and white. I frown as I lean forward to look at it as if the food will whisper to me what it is.

Out the corner of my eye, I see the silhouette of a woman sidle up to the other end of the table. She starts making a plate and to my surprise, she gets one of the tart things! My eyes damn-near bug out of my head and I have to see who she is to think, one, that tart looks good, and, two, it's something she actually wants to eat.

I glance up at her and do a double take. Literally.

She is absolutely gorgeous. In her heels, she's a few inches shorter than my six-foot stature. Long, middle-parted, teased-out curls frame her brown face, reminding me of how SZA wears her hair. Her makeup is gold and dewy, complimenting her two-toned nude lip gloss look. A scarlet dress with a plunging neckline clings to her hourglass figure like a second skin. Red is my favorite color and she's rocking the hell out of it.

I've been living in Los Angeles for six years, so I can tell when a woman's body is natural or bought. *This* woman looks natural.

Her nails are almond-shaped with white French tips. A gold clutch purse is tucked under her right arm. As she moves closer to me, her scent wafts my way—something sweet and warm. I don't know if she can feel my gaze, but I break away for a second and slyly skate down her frame. A high slit in her dress reveals a toned leg and gold heels. *And she got the French tips on the feet!* I don't necessarily have a foot fetish, but what man doesn't like pretty feet on a woman?

I clench my jaw to calm my racing heart. This woman is stunning—and I'm around beautiful women all the time. But it's not just her looks that have me stunned. Her wanting to eat this tart thing has stunned me silly. I have to get to the bottom of this.

"Have you eaten that thing before? Cuz I'm curious about it but it just looks suspicious." I point to the tart on her plate.

Camesha

Caught off guard, I turn to my left to face the man next to me.

I expected men to approach me tonight—and they have—but *not* like this. Not a man wearing a vintage San Antonio Spurs T-shirt, simple gold chains, and New Balances to ask me about the hors d'oeuvres. He sticks out—definitely more casually dressed than everyone else here who's dripping in designer brands and flashy jewelry.

I clear my throat and wipe on a slight grin, slipping into *the voice*: slow and light. "Uh, it's actually not bad."

"Ah-hah! It's not *bad*, but you ain't say it was good either. Ya know, I 'on't know if I can trust ya judgement," he teases with a smirk, shaking his head. He picks up a tart with his fingers, not the little tongs next to the tray, and inspects the food dramatically.

Despite myself, I smile faintly, amused by his antics. "You're really pressed 'bout this tart, huh?"

Still eyeing the fuck out of the food, he says in a low and focused voice, "What can I say? I take food *very* seriously." He tosses the tart into his mouth.

I watch his square jaw as he chews. *He's . . . got a cute face. Very proportionate*, I muse, inwardly cringing at the word. Most of the guys here aren't necessarily ugly, but they're definitely enhanced, whether it'd be veneers or hair transplants. But as long as the money's green and legal, it doesn't matter what they look like.

This man is slim and taller than me even though I'm wearing four-inch heels. Despite his stature, he seems unassuming. With brown skin the color of gingerbread, he looks like he needs a haircut as his curly top fade has grown out of his line-up and his chin hair is a tad scraggly.

To my surprise, I'm actually curious if he likes the tart. I can't tell as he keeps a neutral expression on his face until he swallows.

He nods. "Okay, not bad like you said. Tastes like broccoli and," he smacks his lips, "Gruyere cheese—if I'm not mistaken. But it's *definitely* not goat cheese so I'm safe." He wicks imaginary sweat from his forehead. "Cuz I've definitely been burned wit' goat cheese. Highly do not recommend." He cringes, before popping another tart in his mouth.

I just shake my head to stifle a laugh, but I'm unsuccessful.

What's wit' this guy? No one ever talks to me like this at events, especially not men. They ogle and compliment, and if they're bold, they proposition. But they *never* make small talk about appetizers. This exchange is weird, but it's nice, a welcomed change from having to perform for the guests.

I put my plate down on the buffet table. "So, what's ya deal?" I blurt out my intrusive thought. Embarrassed, my eyes widen a bit as my face gets hot. "I mean . . . why are you talkin' to me?" I ask, slipping back into *the* voice.

His eyes shoot to mine as he chokes a little while swallowing his second tart. His tongue licks cream residue from the corners of his mouth. "Why not? You're here, I'm here. Seemed rude not to say anything. I mean, my parents did raise me wit' *some* modicum of respect." He pinches the air to show me. "Plus, I was really curious and unsure 'bout that tart thing, and you helped me out."

Was it really that simple? Nothing in LA has ever been that simple for me.

The man glances around before leaning forward, keeping respectful distance between us. I can smell his woody cologne this close. A smirk is on his face as he says, "And it seems like you're the only person here not high or glued to their phone. So, you seemed like the safest person to talk to."

I'm not sure why, but my cheeks heat up a bit, so I slyly drop eye contact. He retreats into a standing position.

What does he really want from me? Does he know who I am? Is this *his game?* I can't tell, but I know what my purpose is at Zay Dubb$'s 30th birthday party.

I slip back into character: I tilt my chin down, narrow my eyes, wipe on a flirty smirk, and shift my weight to expose more of my leg in the slit. The man's gaze flickers a little, noticing the movement. *Bingo.* "Safe, huh?"

"The safest fa sho." He offers a lopsided smile.

I look him in the eye and drop my voice into my deep, sultry register, "Well, that depends on whatcha lookin' for. . ."

Then, surprisingly, he chuckles. Not like how some men do it to be smooth and sound unbothered. This guy's chuckle is warm and genuine. *I actually* made him laugh. "Oh, I'm sorry. I'm just here for the food." He lifts his plate to emphasize. "And to escape my job for a second. I'm fuckin' starvin'," he whispers the last sentence before popping a mini tuna tartare into his mouth. He shakes his head and chews like it's the best thing ever.

My smirk falters, confusion wrinkling my eyebrows. "Wait. Y-You work here?" I ask in my actual voice.

Speaking around the tartare in his mouth, he says, "How cool would that be—if I worked at this mansion?" He swallows. "But nah. Zay Dubb$ is one of my clients. I'm a handler and tonight, I'm specifically makin' sure he doesn't pass out in a pool of Hennessy."

"Oh." I chortle, relaxing a bit.

Okay, so, he isn't a guest tryna bait me into a job—albeit a quirky, unconventional bait, but still a bait. Men have said and done weirder things than talk about appetizers to get some pussy out of me.

This man is working, too. . . A funny, surprisingly down-to-earth man who, for some reason, is talking to me like I'm a normal party guest.

"Yeah. . . So, what's the deal wit' those shrimp cocktail shooters?" He points to the food. "They look good but has the shrimp been deveined?" he asks with a grimace.

Back to the appetizer talk, I guess. Now that I know he's not a guest, I feel more relaxed around him. And I don't hold back. I laugh. "Deveined? I 'on't know."

His eyebrows arch like he's shocked. "You know what that is, right? The *vein*," he puts in air quotes, "is the shrimp's digestive tract that runs along the back of its body. It . . . *contains their shit*," he whispers the last part.

I crack up, trying to keep my composure since I'm still working. "I 'on't know if it's been deveined or not. I haven't looked. But they're good. Better than the tarts."

"Okay. You weren't wrong 'bout that tart, so let's see if you can go two for two." He playfully side-eyes me before grabbing a shooter. "What's ya name, by the way?"

I almost choke on my own spit. Something about him makes me feel comfortable enough to tell him my *real* name. Which is new for me.

This man feels harmless, but feelings can be deceiving. And my feelings about people have *definitely* been wrong countless times before.

Still, I trust my gut. Mama always said, *"If you can't trust ya gut, how can you trust anybody?"* I clear my now dry throat. "Camesha."

"Camesha," he repeats like he's testing how it feels in his mouth. "Nice to meet you. I'm Tim. Starks." He squeezes his eyes closed and twists up his mouth at the pause he put in his full name before throwing back the shooter. He's so awkward, it's kind of cute.

A giggle escapes me like I was holding that bitch hostage. "Nice to meet you, too, Tim."

He grins, holding my gaze longer than expected. There's something steady in the way he's looking at me, like he's not in a rush to get back to working Zay's party. Like we're just two guests enjoying the event.

I glance at my food and next thing I know, he's leaning in again even though it's not that loud in here. "How are you tonight? You good? I 'on't know if you got a handler tonight, but if you need anything—*whatever* it is—find me, okay?"

His face is serious, but his tone is surprisingly warm. He's not being flirty or pushy. Just seems genuine. Like he could actually care about my wellbeing tonight. The handlers I've worked with in the past have never really treated me like this. They were all professional and nice, but Tim feels different. Kind.

Before I respond, Tim adds, "Oh—and in case you ain't know, there's a quiet bedroom downstairs that we turned into a break lounge. It's away from all'is." He motions to the great room behind us. "It's a good spot to breathe if it becomes too much out here."

Oh my God. Can he see how tense I am? Do I look *like I need a break? Because I would definitely like one.* But it's not because I've been here long—only two hours. I just always wish these events go by fast.

Just when I'm about to respond again, Tim's phone rings. He pulls it out of his jeans pocket to glance at the caller ID before his eyes return to mine. "Duty calls," he says before pursing his lips. "But seriously, Camesha, if you need anything, just holla. I'll be around makin' my rounds." He cringes immediately.

I laugh.

"I promise, I *didn't* mean for that to rhyme." He tucks in his lips.

"It's okay." My laughter falters. "But thanks. I'll let you know if I need anything, Tim."

He offers a tight-lipped grin and takes his plate before disappearing into the crowded great room.

With my heartbeat thrumming in my ears, I exhale a breath I didn't even know I was holding in. *What just happened?* Tim really talked to me like I'm not just supposed to be part of the scenery and enhance the vibe.

I retrieve my plate and pop a gold-dusted chocolate truffle into my mouth. I head over to one of the less populated bars and ask the bartender for some semi-sweet white wine. He pours and slides the glass to me. Hopefully this calms my anxiety so I can finish this night strong.

But the feelings Tim conjured up inside me linger. *Why did he make me feel so . . .* seen?

Tim

DJ Tone Def had called me when I was talking to Camesha, so I head over to him. He tells me that his power cable is fraying. He doesn't want his equipment to run out of juice and bring the party to a screeching halt. I understand because even though these motherfuckers are cross-faded, they *will* notice when the music stops. So, I run to the garage to retrieve extra cables from my all-black 2020 Jeep Grand Cherokee. I keep shit like that in my ride for just-in-case moments like this.

"You're the fuckin' man, Tim," DJ Tone Def says, dapping me up. His fat hands are a little sweaty.

Still catching my breath from all that running, I just nod and salute him. My slim ass is out of shape.

As I back away from the DJ booth, I scan the dancing crowd, searching for any signs of potential chaos.

But instead, I find Camesha.

She must've finished her plate as she's standing hands-free, her clutch still under her arm, near the floor-to-ceiling wall of glass. But she's not alone.

This young nigga with baby dreads is all in her face, cheesing hard as hell and chatting her ear off. She's smiling—well, sort of. It's the kind of smile I've seen hundreds of times in LA—hell, one I've given, too. The type of smile that's more polite than genuine, one you wear when you're enduring more than enjoying something.

The guy, a newer rapper I recognized but forgot his name, is gesturing wildly, his gaudy chains gleaming under the dim light. He's probably just happy to be at this party since I believe he was featured on one of Zay's most recent hits. And he's also probably giddy to rap to Camesha, one of the baddest—if not *the* baddest woman here.

She tilts her head, feigning interest in dude's story, but I can tell her attention is elsewhere. I'm not saying I can read her super well after just talking to her for the first time, but I felt her tense energy at the buffet table.

And then Camesha's sexy, melodic voice and her using her moves on me?! Sheesh! I'm not the smoothest nigga, but I'm kind of flattered if she thought that my small talk was game. Shit, I'm surprised she asked why I was talking to her in the first place. I mean, yeah, I had an *idea* of what her role is at the party, but she's not as obvious in her approach like some of the other ladies here. She's more subtle, reserved, and composed. But regardless, she's still a person. And we're both here by ourselves, so why not strike up conversation with a gorgeous woman?

Camesha's body is angled slightly away from the rapper. And if I'm reading her well, she has a contemplative look on her face as she shifts from one heel to the next. She's killing them in this outfit but I'm sure those heels are killing her feet.

Then her gaze flicks away from the guy. And our eyes meet.

I freeze. I don't want her to think I was staring or anything because that'd be creepy. But I kind of was. I'm simply drawn to her for some reason.

She tucks her chin down a little and I squint, trying to decipher her expression. Tightening my jaw, I give her a subtle nod in acknowledgment. Her mouth twitches subtly like she's about to grin but changes her mind before she returns her attention to the rapper who hasn't missed a step in his one-sided conversation.

I force myself to unglue my gaze from her and head to the nearest bar. Another handler I often collaborate with on large events like this, Benny Munz, is at the bar, typing on his phone while nursing what looks like a Negroni.

Benny's an older white man—probably almost 50—from Boston. He recently got a hair transplant, and he has a penchant for wearing shirts too small for him, the fabric screaming over his big belly. Benny originally worked with rockstars before he migrated to rappers because they showed him a "different kinda fun." Zay's not one of his clients, but some of Zay's friends are.

"Yo Benny, I got a quick question for ya."

"Shoot," he says without looking up. "What's up?" After sending the text, Benny puts his phone down and faces me with a raised eyebrow.

"That girl over there," I tilt my head toward Camesha without being obvious. "The one in the red dress. Ya know her?"

Benny's eyes follow my move and light up when they land on her. "Oh yeah, that's Cammie."

Ah, so Cammie is her professional *name. Camesha must be her real one. And she told me that.* My body warms up at her sharing that with me.

"She's, uh, you know . . ." He shrugs.

I want him to just say it out loud, to confirm it even though she basically did. "What?"

"A vibe model." He cringes. "Ugh, I hate that that's what they're called now. Back in my day, we just called 'em party girls. Kept it simple." Benny knocks the rest of his drink back in one swallow.

I never *drink*-drink while working but Benny is another breed. I guess because he's been doing this for so long, he can multitask—drink *and* do his job well. Or maybe he's just a nutjob.

"Oh, and she's an escort."

"Okay," I say, keeping my tone neutral. "So, whassup wit' her? She got an agency, manager? She solo?"

Benny furrows his eyebrows. "Are *you* interested or is this for a client, Tim?"

I deadpan him. "*Always* for a client. Just gimme the rundown, Benny." It's getting late. I've been working this party for hours and Benny's teasing and dumb jokes are grating on my nerves.

He nods, looking impressed. "Timmy always stays ahead of the game." I roll my eyes at him calling me Timmy while he asks the bartender for another drink. "Cammie's independent. I've *only* dealt wit' her. No agency, no manager. She, of course, only does high-end clients. Very selective though. Got a *shit-ton* of rules." He pauses and leans closer. "Like, if someone wants to fuck her, she always asks to see clean STD test results and if they can't provide it, then her price goes up since she's assumin' a risk."

My eyes widen at that, mentally noting everything he's saying. *Camesha's very professional. . . I like that.* "Really? And they go for it?"

"Of course they do. You see her! She's sexy as shit. They'll do anything to get a piece of her."

I nod in agreement. She *is* sexy as shit.

"And then she keeps everything really low-key. Shit, she doesn't even have social media, Tim." Benny makes a mind-blown gesture with his hands. "I mean, what young woman in the world—let alone in LA—*isn't* on social media? I mean, unless she's got a private account." He shrugs.

"Wow. So how you know 'bout her?"

"Another model named ZZ introduced me to her a few years ago. I was the first handler in Tinseltown to get her contact info. She obviously has a sexy look so I knew my guys would be interested in her fillin' events . . . or fuckin' her." Benny shrugs. "Anything to keep the clients happy, right?"

I nod, zoning out a little. I can't stop my eyes from drifting back in Camesha's direction. I can't stop thinking about the way she looked at me when I was talking to her, like I was the first person who actually *just* talked to her and wasn't expecting something from her. She looked like she was waiting for me to ask her "How much?"

The bartender slides Benny his drink. He slaps my arm, saying, "Well Tim, I gotta check on *my* girls." I guess that was his assignment tonight: hire vibe models and escorts. Rappers can't have a poppin' party without fine-ass women around.

Before Benny gets too far, he comes back and rasps in my ear, "Lemme know if you want her contact info."

I squint my eyes at the stench on his breath. "A'ight. Thanks, Benny."

When I'm certain that he's gone, I glance back in Camesha's direction. The rapper is closer, leaning down to talk in her ear. His breath is probably kicking something serious, smelling like the weed Zay and his friends are smoking. But Camesha's keeping a straight, unfazed face. He's probably saying something she's heard a million times in her line of work, but she giggles anyway. Still doesn't reach her eyes.

Her gaze flickers toward me again, making my heart stutter. Then she looks back at him. It's like she knew I'd be standing here, looking.

I huff out a breath and drag my hand down my face. *This girl.* I turn toward the bartender. "Hey man, can you hand me that plate I stashed back here—and can I get a bourbon, neat?"

Camesha

Outside on the balcony is nice. The night sky is cloudless and it's a full moon. The air is fresher. And it's quieter, even with the people occupying the pool area on the lower level. I can still hear the ruckus going on in the mansion, too, but the noise is dulled behind the thick windows. But still, I don't have to focus so much on the party. When I close my eyes and take a deep breath, I can smell the salt from the Pacific Ocean and faintly hear the waves crashing the shore.

I definitely needed a break after listening to Lil Hibb try to spit game for 20 minutes. He's only 21 and just getting some clout, so I'd cut him some slack but, my God in Heaven, he talks a lot. And about nothing! Bless his heart though. Shit like that is all a part of the game.

The quiet is a blessing. Although it's not actually calming my nerves. Even though I've been doing this for three years, events like this, where I know a lot of men will be looking to have sex, *always* make me anxious. I've learned how to wade the storms and put on a brave face, but sometimes actors get tired.

I lean forward, pressing my forearms into the balcony rail, and look down. All I see is darkness, but I know there's jagged rock and grass, eventually leading to the beach. This could actually be very dangerous should someone get too drunk or high and think they could fly. But I'll leave that worry to the handlers. Like Tim.

Speaking of, our eyes kept meeting after our first encounter. Listening to these men talk, it's easy to tune them out after a while. So that my eyes don't glaze over and I retreat into my head, I glance away. Keeps them on their toes and forces them to regain my attention, to impress me. Honestly, they all seem to like the game anyway. But I wasn't expecting to catch Tim's eyes several times when I did it. His face was always soft with a gentle focus, like he never learned to wear a mask. He was just . . . present.

The soft whoosh of sliding glass doors breaks the silence, making me turn around. As if I thought him up, I see it's Tim.

"Outside's not a bad spot to catch a breather either. Unlike inside, the air out here is fresher and cleaner," he jokes. He strolls to the railing and pauses a few feet from me. "Shit, I'm sorry. Did you wanna be alone right now?"

A slight grin touches my lips. It's nice that he asked. "You're good."

He nods, then copies my position.

"You needed another break, too?"

"Yeah, the help needs *multiple* escapes."

I laugh and look out toward the ocean.

"Seemed like you had ya hands full back there wit' what's-his-name," Tim says, but his tone is teasing and has a slight edge to it.

I chuckle, wondering what that edge in his voice is all about. "Nothin' I can't handle. Underneath all'at bravado he was projectin' was a shy, young man. He wanted *something*, but not that bad." I feel comfortable subtly talking about my hustle with Tim.

Tim nods. "Good. Cuz it looked like you were plottin' ya escape."

I smirk. "I mean, you're not totally wrong. A long night *is* still ahead of us."

We both laugh and look beyond the balcony.

"You do that often?"

My eyes widen as my body freezes, goosebumps erupting on my skin. "Do what?"

"Play nice wit' guys like him?—Shit, wit' guys like me?" Tim asks, slight humor in his voice, before he chews his bottom lip. He looks seriously curious.

Breath hitches in my throat. *Okay, so he for sure knows. . .* "It's part of the job," I blurt out, a jolt of honesty coursing through me. "And I'm not playin' nice witchu, Tim. You've been—," I stop myself, unsure if I should continue.

I take a deep breath. "You've been nice to me. Kind, actually. And warm." *Jeez, chill wit' all the compliments, girl.*

"Okay, cool. Glad you see me as bein' kind and warm. I was hopin' I ain't come off creepy or nuttn." He exhales a breath like a weight was lifted off his shoulders.

I chuckle. "Definitely not. I can tell the difference."

Tim nods repeatedly. "So, you like it?—Ya job, I mean?"

I pause, breaking eye contact. No one's ever asked me that—not in a way that felt like they genuinely cared about my answer. "It's, um, it's complicated." I'll just leave it at that. Out the corner of my eye, I take a peek at him, seeing him nod.

"I hear that. . ." Tim clears his throat and pushes off the railing. "Well, Camesha, I'll let you have ya alone time. If you need an escape route, just lemme know. I've walked this house all day, so I know the layout pretty well." His smile is lopsided.

I giggle, despite myself. "I'll keep that in mind."

He nods his head like he's jogging his brain to come up with a reply. "Good. I should pro'ly get back in there. Could be a level five crisis goin' on."

I look at him puzzled, my eyebrows scrunching. "There's such a thing as a level five crisis?"

Tim looks up at the sky briefly. "Nah. I just made that up."

I laugh—*really* laugh—head thrown back, the sound coming out unabashedly. I cover my mouth though before I get out of hand. After all, I'm still at work.

Tim stares at me, smirking and looking amused that he amused me. Or that I cackled like a gotdamn hyena. "I'll see you 'round, Camesha." He flashes a smile at me, making me feel warm.

I just grin, watching him shimmy back inside. I suck in a deep breath and face the ocean again. *That was nice*, I note.

Tim

On the edge of the great room, I'm chatting with Zay's manager, Reggie, and some junior executives from his label when the man of the hour staggers toward us.

"Yooo, lemme holla at Timbo for a minute!" he interrupts our pleasant conversation, both hands gripping my shoulders.

Reggie chuckles and gives me a knowing look as the execs smirk. They're all familiar with Zay and Cross-faded Zay so they offer understanding smiles before leaving.

I turn toward Zay. He's sweating bullets in a silk camp shirt with some crazy print on it. This nigga is wearing dark jeans and oversized sunglasses, too. He never steps out with less than 10 pieces of jewelry on—no lie. And from the looks of it, he's wearing all of that and a new piece he probably got made for his birthday: an iced-out "DTG" pendant which is his motto, "Dubbin' The Game."

"Whaddup, man?" I say.

Zay rips his glasses off his face. His eyes are bloodshot and languid, but he's wearing a goofy smile. "Yooo, I see you holdin' it down, man. This party is fuckin' fire. You and the other handlers really did y'all thing tonight. But you my man, Tim, so I *really* 'preciate you comin' through for a nigga. You always do."

While I cherish any time my clients appreciate my work—because dealing with their asses is never easy—Zay's flattery is a dead giveaway that he's about to dump something on me that's outside my current responsibilities.

"Glad you're havin' a great time, Zay. You deserve it. It's been an amazin' year for you."

"You gotdamn right I deserve this shit," he says a little too passionately and loses his balance, starting to sway.

To steady himself, Zay leans in and wraps his arm around my neck. His breath is so foul that I try not to blink as my eyes start to water. "Aye, y'all niggas got it right up in here wit' fine shit. *Especially* that one." He points a finger.

My shoulders tense up and my jaw clenches as I turn to follow his finger.

Camesha. He wants Camesha. *Of course he does. E'rybody would.*

She's chatting closely with one of the other handlers I don't know that well, a bald light-skin dude. *I think his name is Miles? Maybe he hired her?*

"O-kay," I say around my knotted-up stomach.

"Yeah, what's her name?"

I quickly remember the professional name Benny told me. "Uh, Cammie."

"Cammie," Zay says, like he's tasting it or something. "That's a cutesy-ass name for a sexy-ass bitch like her."

Yeah, well, nigga, I got the real name. Inhaling deeply, I coach myself to calm down.

"She bad as a muhfucka. I'm lookin' to slide up in that, Tim. I know you ain't hire her or nuttn but since I trust you the most out of these other niggas, could you handle that for me?"

And there's the request.

Out of my peripheral, I see Zay eyeing me, waiting.

I swallow over a growing lump in my throat. "Lemme see whassup wit' her."

An even goofier smile smears his face. "That's why I keep yo' skinny ass around, Tim." He's got nerve calling *me* skinny when we have the same build.

I try to keep my face neutral with a slight grin when we dap-hug. His cologne is wearing off and now he's smelling straight up like this party: liquor, weed, and sweat.

"A'ight, lemme know if shawty down or not." He slaps me on the back before he stumbles over to his homies.

I don't like this. At all. Zay has asked me to set him up with vibe models, escorts, and minor celebrities before. And I'm always friendly to everybody who's working these functions, but Camesha *feels* different. I don't feel comfortable coming to her with this. I know that's partly why she's here, so the request wouldn't be out of the norm for her. I just don't want to talk to her about this when our conversations so far have been just nice exchanges, not business ones.

But either way, I'm working just like she is, and it *is* a part of my job. Handle things for my clients. Even if I don't want to.

I look back toward the area where we last saw Camesha and I don't see her. I scan the great room and spot her near a bar on the other side of the house, near the buffet table. I make my way through the dancing crowd—mostly men humping women throwing it back on them and people hyping them up and videotaping it.

As I approach Camesha, I see she's sipping from a wineglass.

Camesha

I put my drink down on the bar and look toward the crowd, coming face to face with Tim again. I relax into my high-backed chair.

"Hey," he says lightly, like he doesn't want to alarm me even though I saw him coming.

"Hey. . ."

He motions to the bartender, and the man nods and leaves. *Ummm, what's this about?* I wonder.

"Can I sit?" Tim asks.

"Yeah, I'm not savin' it for anyone," I chuckle, even though I'm getting nervous, heart fluttering and shit. His energy isn't the same as it was before.

"Just wanna be respectful of ya space. Not sure if you wanted to be alone." He grins crooked.

That's polite of Tim. I love that he's been considerate this whole time. Grinning, I gesture for him to sit down.

He clears his throat. "So, uh, who hired you for tonight?"

Oh, he wants to talk about that. A pinch winds up at the base of my neck, so I sit up and roll my shoulders back. I clear my throat, too. "Um, Miles."

Tim nods, snapping his finger. "I *thought* that was his name. So, uh, I was just talkin' to Zay . . . and um—"

"Yeah?" The anticipation is killing me. I have a feeling I know where this is going, but it seems like Tim's trying to carefully pick his words. Adorable.

His eyes shift around the bar. "He was interested in you. Ya know, for later tonight?" I notice a bite in his jaw. *What's that about?*

"Really?" I say, hiding my sigh by tipping some wine down my throat.

"Yeah. . ." His jaw flexes again before he looks at me. "I wanted to check in witchu about it. This is entirely up to you, Camesha. If you 'on't wanna do it, I'll tell him you're not available."

Oh. I swallow the little bit of spit in my mouth as my heart quickens and my face warms. I shift in my seat and avoid Tim's now intense gaze.

He's giving me a choice.

Pushing some hair behind my ear, I mutter, "Thanks."

"Of course." He stands. "I can give you some time to think about it, but I will need to let him know soon before he starts houndin' me wit' that liquor and weed breath," he chuckles.

There's that Tim humor I've come to know throughout the night. "No pressure though." He holds his hands up in surrender.

Chortling, I drop my head, feeling slight relief in this grave situation. "Thanks, Tim."

"No pro'lem, Camesha." One side of his mouth quirks up before he drums the back of his bar chair and leaves.

I watch Tim drift away into the crowd. I turn around to face the bar as the bartender returns.

"Ma'am, would you like another glass?"

"No, I'm good. Thank you." I need to be clear-headed right now.

He grins and starts cleaning up his space. With his long hair in a bun and his calm demeanor, he doesn't match the vibes of this party. Makes me wonder what other events he works.

Honestly, I'm just trying to distract myself from what Tim said.

I'm used to propositions, but from him? It *feels* weird because of our nice little talks tonight. He asked for his client, but still. I get paid to be here regardless of if I fuck anyone or not. Miles already paid me half up-front and I get the rest after the party. Tonight, I'm primarily here to just add to the vibe, but should someone want to have sex with me, I have that choice to take them up on it.

Tim made sure to tell me I had a choice. He made it abundantly clear. And it's not like I don't know that—I know that I always have a choice, even if it is a part of my job. It's just never been *offered* to me. That's nice.

Tim

I plod away from the bar, hoping that Camesha says no to Zay's proposition. Maybe that's selfish of me considering she's here to work and that can be part of her job. Some of my clients, including Zay, pay women on top of their agreed amount in exchange for their maximum discretion, so I know she could also make additional income for her time. But I don't know, it doesn't sit right with me the way Zay was lusting over Camesha, wanting to end his birthday on her note. I've only spoken to her a few times tonight but, for some reason, I'm starting to see her as more than just another gorgeous face at these events.

I shake my head to get out of my feelings and slip back into work mode. I take a quick lap around the mansion to check up on things—glancing at the DJ booth, Zay and his crew, the bedrooms, guest lounges, and the pool.

Once I'm back on the main floor, I look toward the bar I left Camesha at and I don't see her. Instead of whipping my head around to spot her, I just drop down into one of the sofas.

I pull out my phone. It's now approaching midnight. Scrolling, I see recent texts from Mob, my group chat with my best friends, Jaquade and Bryan. I also see job requests, client complaints, and even my mom checked up on me not too long ago. *Why is she up this late?* Anyway, it might be time to separate my life with two phones.

Several minutes pass of me mindlessly scrolling through my Instagram feed before I hear my name being called, snapping me out of my trance. I look up and I see Miles, Camesha's handler for the night.

"Whaddup, man?" I stand up, seeing I have a few inches on him. I've seen Miles at other things, but never really had to work with him before.

"My girl Cammie said she wants to meet Zay tonight," he says all business-like.

Cotton fills my ears as he keeps talking.

She wants to do it. It *shouldn't* make me feel some type of way, but it does.

"Tim?"

I snap back to reality, seeing Miles arch an eyebrow, awaiting my response. "Yeah, man, I'll set that up."

He grins. "Cool. Just tell me where she should go. Here's my number, Tim."

I listen to Miles recite his digits as I program it into my phone.

Next thing I know, I'm telling Zay that Cammie is available. He cheeses hard as a motherfucker, rubbing his hands and nodding.

It bothers me, seeing how juiced he is to sleep with Camesha. I try to shake the thoughts about what could go down between them behind closed bedroom doors. I know how Zay gets down—because unfortunately, he's told me—and I don't want to imagine Camesha in that position . . . or *those* positions. But she agreed to do this.

I suck up any personal feelings and bite the bullet. I guide Zay upstairs to the suite I had roped off with security. I knew he'd probably want to fuck *somebody* tonight, but I didn't want it to be the woman whom I've enjoyed easily chatting with periodically.

Cross-faded as shit, Zay hobbles inside the room to get situated. Outside the door, I text Miles to let him know that Camesha can come up.

I tell the security guard what she looks like so he can be on the lookout. I don't want to be here when she saunters into that room, so I trudge down the side staircase. *Lemme go find some' to keep myself busy.*

Camesha

I'm in one of the first floor bathrooms, freshening up using the flushable wipes I always keep in any purse I bring to a gig.

Miles (11:54pm):

> Cammie, Tim said you can come up to meet Zay

Before I can respond, Miles sends me an attachment of Zay's STD results. My eyebrows shoot up at that, pleasantly surprised.

Miles (11:54pm):

> Zay likes to be clean, too.

Isaiah Ramsey is his real name? I think, skimming his clean results. Only a handful of clients have shared their results without me having to ask. I always appreciate that though.

I forward Miles my results as well so he can share them with Zay.

Me (11:56pm):

> Good. Coming up.

Miles texts me directions to the suite so I could walk up there myself. It's to not draw attention to the transaction. Everyone at these parties knows there's escorts, but it's typically discreet. Although some girls don't move like that.

In the hallway, I spot the security guard and slip my phone into my clutch.

I exhale in relief, glad that Tim isn't here. I didn't have the nerve to tell him that I *wanted* to take the job. I had a feeling he'd look at me a certain way. Not necessarily in a bad or judgmental way, but a way. And I didn't want to see his reaction and spend all night trying to decipher it. I'd rather just think about how unbelievably warm he's been to me.

After Tim left me with Zay's proposition floating in the air, I thought about it. I'm so close to making $500,000. So, I *need* that money. The quicker I can make this money, the faster I can start my dream life. Whatever that is.

Plus, I've heard from other hustlers at this party and groupies, who don't keep their mouths shut, that Zay tips his tricks. Heavy.

"Name, Miss?" The bodyguard asks in a gruff voice. He's a bald, Black man with the girth of a gotdamn tree trunk. I'm sure the things he's seen in this profession could fill a book. And so can I.

I slowly smile at him, and say in my practiced voice, "Cammie."

He nods and opens the bedroom door. "Thought so. Zay's inside."

"Thank you. . ." I leave space for him to fill in his name.

"T-Bone." His real name is probably something like Terrell or Tyrone.

As I slide past him to enter, I caress his massive bicep. "Thank you, T-Bone."

He looks down at me and smirks, careful not to lick his lips. "No pro'lem, sweetheart."

After what happened three years ago, I'm now always extra nice and sweet to security just in case I need them to help me if these men act up. Ever since that night, my Spidey-senses are always tingling and I'm always ready to kick my heeled foot in a man's dick.

I thank God every day for protecting me in this life.

Now that I'm standing in the suite's sitting area, T-Bone softly closes the door behind me. It's quiet in here, but not too quiet where T-Bone couldn't hear me if I scream.

I should be fine though. Though I may not be good at reading people in my personal life, professionally, that skill is now as sharp as an old lady with comebacks. I've been watching Zay all night and while he's obnoxious, I don't get dangerous vibes. He came up in the streets but left that life when he blew up.

To my left is the large bathroom and to my right is an anteroom that probably leads to the actual bedroom. I can barely admire the elegant décor before I hear some rustling.

Showtime. I take a deep breath, roll my shoulders back, tuck my chin down, and slip into Cammie like muscle memory. Confident. Flirty. Composed. I sashay into the bedroom with an extra swish in my walk.

Zay is sprawled out onto the eggplant-purple chaise lounge. He's kind of good looking, but drunk and high isn't a good look on him. His shirt's unbuttoned, revealing hard-to-see tattoos on his deep brown skin. A half-empty glass bottle of brown alcohol dangles from his hand. When he registers my presence, he lolls up. A lazy veneered smile smears his face.

"Dayuuummm, baby. You fine as shit." His half-lidded eyes drink me in from my heels to my face.

Smirking, I slowly strut toward him. "Thank you, honey."

Zay sits up straighter and moves his legs for me to sit next to him. I drop down as he takes a swig from his bottle and sets it on the floor. "Ya sexy ass enjoyin' ya'self tonight?"

"I am. Are *you* enjoyin' ya'self, birthday boy?" I ask, my voice low and sultry.

"Yeah, and I'm finna enjoy it even more witchu here." He leans in, biting his bottom lip.

I can smell his breath. And it *reeks* like Tim said, making me giggle.

Zay must think it's for him as he smiles and rubs my thigh exposed in my dress's high slit. "I ain't even gon' lie, baby, you the baddest bitch here. This ya real hair or a wig? It's long and pretty as fuck."

I want to roll my eyes as that's not the first time someone has questioned my hair before. Instead, I just smirk. "It's my real hair. Homegrown."

Zay's eyes open a tad wider. "Yeah? Shit, I can tell this body homegrown, too. You pro'ly from the South, huh? Done grew up on cornbread and shit. Witcho slim-thick ass."

I giggle and glance away like I'm shy. I really just want him to stop talking.

Zay leans in closer, and I hold my breath. "And you got the sexiest lips I done ever seen," he whispers, his right hand cupping my face as his thumb just barely touches my bottom lip. "So sexy that I'd love to see these shits wrapped 'round my dick. But I ain't even gon' hold you, I saw you was clean and shit, so I'm tryna fuck some' bad." With a pained expression on his face, he grips the front of his jeans.

I can see his print. And it looks like my clients' average size—about three to seven inches. I can handle that. "We can do that."

He grins wider.

Moments later, after I watched him roll on a condom, my dress is hiked up and I'm bent over the side of the bed as Zay hits me from the back, his hands gripping my waist, my ass slapping his pelvis as he grunts. He's not going too hard like I thought he would, but I'm also wet enough for it to be smooth. Thanks to me imagining one of my celebrity crushes.

It's hard to stay in character—moaning and yelping at the right times—as my mind's not in the room with Zay. My mind usually isn't when I'm with a client, but this time, all I can think about is Tim—his genuine concern and care in his voice all night. It wasn't the first time someone has checked up on me at a job, but it was the first time it didn't feel patronizing, questioning why I did what I did.

Some clients would call themselves giving me a compliment by saying that "I'm way too pretty to be escorting." I'd eat that remark with a smirk, but internally, I'd want to kick them in the dicks for saying that. The implication always rubs me wrong, like they think I should be grateful for their attention or that my beauty is currency that I'm wasting in this hustle. *I'm clearly not too pretty for you to pay to fuck me though, dumbass.*

Little do they know, this work is only a steppingstone. To where, I don't know yet even though I've had seven years in Los Angeles to figure it out.

Last year, I was able to use the hustle money to put a down payment on my first home, a condo in Inglewood! It was my first big "I did that!" moment since I moved to LA. Then this year, I bought a new car. Besides that, I save, invest, donate, and even send some money back home to my family in Columbia, South Carolina.

I want to do something else big for myself with the cash. . . I really enjoyed designing my sanctuary from scratch—watching YouTube videos and reading articles, then scouring thrift stores, estate sales, and eBay. Maybe that's something to pursue professionally?—But I don't know, it's just an idea that's rolled around in my head. Either way, I'm so close to meeting my ridiculous goal.

But I do know that I want to discover my purpose and gifts sooner rather than later. I felt like I could find some ground to walk on if I moved away from home. And with a lot of money, comes options. Choices.

Tim hadn't said anything like those past men. All night, he didn't look at me with judgement. He hadn't tried to save me.

He reminded me I have a choice. And I *choose* to fund my dreams—even if they're unknown right now—this way in the city where they come true.

"Damn, this pussy tight as fuck, shawty," Zay pants as he thrusts into me, bringing me back to the present.

Thank you, Kegels. "All for you, honey," I fake moan.

Tim

It's been almost 30 minutes since I left Zay in that suite. I'm fucking up, having a second bourbon to distract my mind from veering off into trying *not* to imagine what they're doing up there.

I keep wondering if Camesha is okay. I mean, I'm sure she is. She's a professional. It's *me* who's not okay as I knock back the rest of the drink I was nursing. *Dammit, I'm turnin' into Benny.*

Speaking of, I see him hovering over the desserts on the buffet table. The catering staff has been working diligently in the chef's kitchen on the other side of the mansion to keep cranking out a fresh spread throughout the night.

I stroll over to him. "Yo, Benny."

"Talk to me, Timmy," he says, eyeing the food.

I roll my eyes at him calling me that again. Only my mom is allowed to call me Timmy. But I need him right now, so I suck up my comeback. "Look, Zay seems to like Cammie, so he might want her at other things. Figure I should get her info."

Benny finishes making his plate, a mini pyramid of those chocolate truffles. He looks at me with a smirk on his face. "Tryna be proactive? Nice."

"Gotta anticipate the clients' needs—ya know that," I playfully hit his arm, when really, I want to ring his neck for making this exchange more annoying than it has to be.

I *could* ask Miles for Cammie's info, but he seems more professional and territorial. Benny doesn't gatekeep, freely giving folks information since he's been in the handling game so long. But he'll tease you when you ask for stuff.

"That I do." He throws a truffle into his mouth. Benny pulls his phone out of his pocket starts swiping.

My phone dings, and I retrieve it to see he texted me Cammie's contact.

"'Preciate it, OG." I slap him on the back as I back away.

Still chewing, he throws up a deuces as he tromps away to sit and enjoy his desserts.

I head to a couch in the great room. Rubbing my face, I think, *Three more hours before this party is over.*

2
The Hustle

Friday, August 18

Camesha

The Pacific Blue Notes, a local middle-aged jazz quartet who perform here at The Adonir Hotel every Tuesday through Thursday evening, is playing a slow, slinking song. Balancing the gold platter full of drinks with one hand, I weave through the tables in the hotel's restaurant and lounge.

I've worked at The Adonir for two years now. It's a boutique hotel, so it's smaller and quieter than some of the chain hotels where I interviewed.

After being a barista in Los Angeles for almost four years—albeit at different cafes and with promotions—it was boring and uninspiring. I didn't want to keep moving up in the industry. It was just supposed to be something to hold me over until I figured out what I really wanted to do.

Customers complimented me and some even offered me modeling gigs. That's actually how I built most of my early wardrobe: getting free merch after modeling for indie clothing brands' websites and their social media. And when my co-worker Zaria noticed that male customers kept flirting with me or asking me out, she suggested I do like her and "cash in on all'is male attention."

I would never tell her this and big her head up even more, but she started dropping so many gems on me:

"Knowin' what you don't want is as good as knowin' what you do want."

"Hustlin' lets you enter circles you normally wouldn't be invited to, plus you can travel."

"You can figure out ya purpose later. Get to the bag first. More money equals more options."

At this point, maybe I'm naïve and feel like my purpose is going to fall out the sky and knock me upside the head.

For weeks, we'd go out after work so that I could pick her brain about her hustle. How she got into vibe modeling and escorting. What she had to do at events to set the "vibe." Where'd she have sex with the guys. What her boundaries were. How much money men were willing to pay—which she said doesn't really matter. "If they approach you, they wanna pay. Trust me, no number is too high for the one who wants you," she said.

But Zaria *still* works at her café even though she's making so much bank from vibing and escorting. Hell, she told me that when videos of her spa treatments and lavish trips with clients went viral, she became a full-on content creator. She said her followers wonder how she's able to "afford" her lifestyle, but she keeps it mysterious, playing to their many theories: her family's wealthy, she's a sugar baby, or her favorite, she's a mistress paid to keep quiet. "It's fun," she said. And she loves having encounters with film industry folks at her café because her ultimate dream is to be an actress. But if that doesn't happen, she wants to be a "kept woman to live the luxurious life [she] was made for"—her words not mine.

When I decided to do this, I set a goal for myself, one I thought was impossible to achieve. Earn $500,000 and dip.

Now, I'm about $85,000 away from reaching that in three years. That is fucking insane!

Shame's sticky fingers crawl up my back whenever I think about it: how much money I've been able to make in three years just by partying and fucking rich men. No shade to the women who actually enjoy this work, but for me, it's always been a weird tug of war—a complicated mess I've been trying to wade and reconcile with.

Zaria said that for some women, sex work does what drug dealing does for some men. It's one of the fastest ways to make a shit-ton of money. . . And honestly, that makes a lot of sense to me. Besides, I like to dance with my friends and at home, but I didn't think I'd have the confidence to pole dance and strip in front of a lot of people.

So, no one forced me to escort. It wasn't my last resort. I chose to do this.

I just didn't think I could make that much money in such a *short* amount of time. And I'm utterly shocked at how *much* men pay to fuck me. Lust can be an irrational thing.

I figured fixing coffee wasn't sexy enough for me. The same men hitting on me at the café are *not* always the same men who would pay to have sex with me. Zaria mentioned that she once worked at a hotel, and that's how she met her first clients, so she prepped me for my job interviews.

Lo and behold, I meet a lot of my escorting clients at The Adonir now. Whether they're traveling for work, vacation, or here for a bachelor party—doesn't matter. But I *never* entertain a man who is clearly here with a woman. Because men are audacious as fuck, they definitely try to proposition me, but it's way too messy and risky. The goal is to be careful, to run a smooth operation.

Anyway, the jazz band announces that they'll be taking a break, and the small dining room applauds as they exit the stage.

I've grown to enjoy jazz. The soothing music eases me into the mood to become Cammie when I meet these men.

I arrive at my last table. A slender white man probably in his early 40s, wearing a slate-blue polo, gray slacks, and crisp white leather sneakers. His chair is scooted away from the round table so he can rest his right foot on his left knee as he scrolls his phone. A shiny, simplistic—yet most likely expensive—watch cuffs his wrist. His short brown hair is neatly swept to the side and back. *He's givin'. . . tech CEO or executive.*

"Another water with lemon," I say, my voice honeyed as I set his drink on the table.

He could be a client. When I took his order earlier, I noticed the way his gaze lingered on me. These men are never as smooth and clever as they think they are.

He looks up from his phone, a smile overtaking his face like I'm a happy distraction from whatever millions of dollars of business is stressing him out. "Thank you. Cammie, right?" He leans forward to pick up the sweating cup.

When I was a barista, I used Camesha, but as soon as I decided to hustle, I started going by Cammie professionally. The only people who call me Camesha are my family and friends. *Well, you also told Tim ya real name. . .*

"Yes." I offer him a slight smile.

He nods and sips his drink.

"Can I get you anything else, sir?" I slightly tilt my head and soften my gaze at him. He's not that bad looking. I like that his teeth look real and straight, like he had braces when he was younger, and he still diligently wears his retainer.

"Actually," *Here it comes*, I think, "I was wondering if . . . *you* could join me for a real drink later? I think your company would be a perfect ending to my very stressful business trip," he chuckles nervously.

I giggle, earning a twinkle in his eye. *They love that gigglin' shit.* "Very tempting, but *I'm* not on the menu."

The man sets both feet on the floor and leans forward. His blue eyes darken with lust as they dart around the room before he damn-near whispers, "Well, what about the *secret* menu? I mean, you are one of the most *beautiful* women I've ever seen in my life."

I grin bashfully, resisting the urge to roll my eyes at that tired line. Even men with gazillions of dollars, status, and power have terrible game. But having the gift of gab ultimately doesn't matter when they pay me.

"When do you get off work, Cammie?" he asks. "I'm in room 805—very large suite at the end of the hall. Lots of privacy and it's near the stairwell. I have a fully stocked minibar, too. And," he drops his head like he's going to drop a huge truth bomb on me, "honestly, it's been lonely these last few nights. I promise I won't take too much of your time." He's laying it on pretty thick and now, he's telling on himself: either he's saying he won't and *can't* last long or he *actually* wants me to join him for an innocent nightcap.

I'm sure this man is quite persuasive in whatever field he dominates, but here, I clearly have the upper hand. And I intend to use it.

I hold eye contact a little longer, making him sweat. Under my scrutiny, I clock his slight restlessness and the desperation swimming in his eyes.

He wants me. Bad.

"It's gonna cost you, sweetie—"

Eagerly, he cuts me off, "I have it. I can easily send it to you, no problem."

It always surprises me how quickly men like him shed their collected businessman façade for that of a desperate wealthy man.

"Okay. And you're clean?" My eyes dart over his face and hands for any signs of disease like herpes. . . *None. Good.*

He squints like he's not sure what I'm talking about. Arching my eyebrows, I tilt my head and his face lights up. "Oh, yes, yes. I-I've *only* been with my wife. We've been married for 12 years," his voice falters as if his wife is within earshot.

I subtly scan the room to see if a woman is looking. Even though I've watched him dine alone this evening, I can't be too sure.

"Oh, she's not here. We live in Bellevue, Washington."

O-kay, he's givin' me a lotta personal information. I clear my throat. "Can you show me *proof* that you're clean?"

"Nooo. . . Is that a problem? I promise you, I'm clean."

"I don't do promises, honey. I need proof," I say, my voice a purr.

He nods repeatedly. "I know. But I'm telling the truth. I'm clean, Cammie."

This man is putty in my hands as his desire ramps up to a dangerous level. He's consumed, all rational thinking thrown out the window to make room for his overwhelming lust. Pleadingly, he looks up at me, his blue eyes a pool of desire he's drowning in. He waits with quickened breath for any possibility of a yes with me.

I won't keep him sweating and guessing. "Price goes uuuppp—"

"Yes, I understand. You're taking a risk on me."

Good businessmen understand risk. "Okay, you can have my number, Misteeeerrr—"

"Eliot Novak, sorry. Where are my manners?" he chuckles with a big grin on his face.

Sounds familiar. . . Definitely a CEO or some', I think.

He urgently swipes to his Contacts on his phone and pauses. I smile, reciting my work number.

"Got it. I'll call—"

"*No,* only text me." I turn and leave his table, swaying my hips in my black uniform pants as my gaze trails over my shoulder.

Eliot's most likely entranced and pitching a tent in his pants right now as I head over to my service station in the corner.

Easy money's about to get made tonight. And I'll deposit all of it into the high-yield savings and brokerage accounts I opened just for my hustle earnings. Honestly, it feels weird using that word, but I guess it's correct: I earned it? *I mean, sex work* is *work*. . .

Anyway, I can't help but think about Tim. He's been on my mind a lot these last few days since Zay Dubb$'s birthday party. The way Tim looked at me—not with desire but like he was trying to understand me. I really don't need to be under that kind of examination right now, but it felt nice to be seen that night. It felt nice to not perform for him—I didn't need to be Cammie. I got to be Camesha—albeit a guarded version.

Honestly, his unique charm was beginning to slowly chip away at my wall that night. Why did he have so much care in his voice? Why did he offer me agency regarding Zay's proposition? Tim was different. And different can be good, but it can also be unpredictable. Being intrigued by him could be a distraction from earning the rest of that $85k.

I lean back on the service station and pull my phone out of the left back pocket of my work pants to check the time. 30 more minutes until my shift is over.

A text comes in at 6:58pm:

> Hi Cammie, this is Eliot. Room 805 if you're coming.
> I can send you all the money now or later. Up to you.
> Thank you.

A pleasant smirk dances on my lips at his concision and politeness. I like it when a client gets straight to the point. Some escorts, like Zaria, will indulge men in conversation, but if I can, I try to mostly listen in person. I definitely don't have the energy to entertain them in text.

I reply to Eliot, requesting my full fee now. *I mean, since he offered.* I always try to get all the money up-front.

Out the corner of my eye, I see that the host sits a couple in my section. Exhaling a deep breath, I close my eyes to slip back into work mode. By the time I open my eyes, I see a notification banner drop down: Eliot sent the money. *Oh, he's serious-serious. And I will oblige.*

I push off the post, shoving my phone back in my pocket before going to greet my new customers.

Tim

I've been on set for one of my client's, Aye Bandz, music video for hours. His new single "BADDIEZ" is blowing up, already a viral sound on social media.

Part of my job as a handler is to liaise between my client and the rest of their team to coordinate efforts. I'm an independent contractor, so there are some things I can do that the payrolled team can't, just because I might have a wider network since I work for and with so many different industry people. So, Bandz called me to help him capitalize on the virality of his song so he can put out the video as soon as possible. I was able to book a popular director and even scouted locations. We settled on a studio in the Valley to shoot the entire thing in one day.

The team and I are sitting in our own folding chairs behind the cameras, scanning the set for anything that could use our assistance. My job demands a keen eye for detail and the ability to anticipate fuckshit. So far, the video shoot has been smooth, a rare blessing in my line of work. But I know anything can happen, so I'm ready for that, hence my restless, bouncing leg.

The director calls "Cut" on this millionth take for a 10-minute break and the room erupts and buzzes with activity. The diverse, curvy video vixens surrounding Aye Bandz disperse to the bathrooms or to hair and makeup. Bandz's publicist beckons him for something, and he staggers over there. On the way, he tips his head at me, his freeform locs bouncing, and I salute him. Bandz is quiet and reserved in real life, the opposite of his loud and rambunctious public persona.

I use this break time to stretch. Standing, I hear my knees and back pop, sounding like Rice Krispies when you pour the milk in the bowl. Pulling my phone out of my pocket, I pace and respond to messages.

I've been mulling over contacting Camesha for three days since Zay's birthday party. A famous former child actor knocked over the buffet table when he was drunk, so I had to coordinate clean-up. Camesha and I made brief eye contact after her time with Zay, but we didn't speak. I wanted to see how she was doing, but I also didn't want to seem nosey and overbearing. I don't know, Camesha has just captured my attention.

And evidently, Zay's too. Finally sober, he called yesterday, telling me he wants Cammie to come to his album release party next week.

Again, I've done this sort of thing before, but this time feels different. My interactions with Camesha felt special that night. Since the party, I've found myself thinking about them with a smile. I mean, in the middle of the shitshow, she was delicious peace.

Like that night, whether I want to or not, I still have a job to do. So, because Zay wants her again, I have to see what I can do to handle his request.

I sit back down in my chair and type a text:

> Hey Cammie, this is Tim Starks. We met at Zay Dubb$'s bday party Tues night. He's having an album release party and he wants u to come. Lemme know if ur down. I can get u on the list and send u the details

I read it over and before I can send it, the smell of flowers and vanilla curl into my nose. I'm so familiar with the scent that I'm not surprised when I look up and see GiGi Savage sauntering over to me. She's wearing an orange halter bodysuit and matching knee-high leather boot heels, the color popping off her caramel-brown skin.

At just 27, she's been in the industry for seven years, vibe modeling and appearing everywhere from music videos like this to starring in beauty brand commercials. There's even rumors that she lets men hit for a price, but she doesn't confirm or deny them publicly. I don't even know if *my* clients have hit, but if they do, she somehow makes sure everyone keeps that shit to themselves. Keeps you guessing and keeps you on her profile. People love her mystique and sex appeal.

There's a whole lot of switch in GiGi's round hips. Her ass isn't completely natural like I suspect Camesha's is, but I remember seeing GiGi before the surgery and most of what she's toting back there is hers. Her hair is big today, a flourishing afro with defined corkscrew curls. Her hair product on top of her signature fragrance add to her aura. She smells delectable and I just *know* that's on purpose. GiGi seems very intentional.

"Hi Timmyyy," she drags out the last syllable, her voice syrupy sweet. Oh, I forgot, she calls me that, too.

I restrain myself from rolling my eyes as I sit up in my chair to entertain her. Because that's what it is with her: watching her show out.

"Whaddup, GiGi?" I lock my phone and slip it in my pocket. I saw her on set with the other ladies, but I didn't think much about it. Didn't think she was going to talk to me. Big mistake because I'm sure her little visit is about *something*.

"Please, Tim, I said you can call me *Gianni*," she says, pouting her glossy, plump lips. Natural. She lightly touches my shoulder, her pointy jeweled nails leaving an invisible line as she lets her hand fall off.

I give in so she can hurry up whatever game she's probably trying to play on me. "Whaddup, *Gianni?*"

She smiles wide, the jewels on her white canines shining under the bright lights. She's literally a star and she knows it. "So, I know that Zay Dubb$'s album is comin' out soon. And he's havin' an album release party. . ." she trails off.

I nod slowly, hoping she'd boldly ask for what she wants since she boldly came over here.

But that's her thing: GiGi is always flirting. And not just with me—with other handlers, managers, artists and even their homies. It works on some people, but not on me.

"Oh, c'mon, Tim baby, don't do me like that." She pouts again.

"Do you like what, girl?" I chortle, leaning back in my seat. If anything, GiGi is entertaining as hell.

"I wanna go-wuh," she whines. "Can you please get me on the list, Timmy?" she says lowly, inching closer. Her breath is minty, and I finally notice her slowly chewing some white gum. This close, her scent encapsulates me. She smells so good that it lures me in, but I know better than to fall into her trap.

She pretends to be distracted, tracing the thread on my black OutKast T-shirt's neckline.

I can't lie, GiGi *is* sexy. Like a siren. Dangerous, but gotdamn tantalizing.

GiGi glances up at me, finding me watching her. A slight grin smooths onto her pretty face.

And I snap out of it. Clearing my throat, I say, "I'll see what I can do, Gianni. Ya know I can't make any promises," I say just loud enough for only her to hear me.

She tilts her head and pouts again. "Just . . . keep me in mind, Tim. I know you'd look out for me."

My eyebrow quirks up. I can't place the angle she's coming at me with, but something's off. I'll have to keep an eye out on her.

GiGi steps back, her gaze trained on me, but unreadable. When she's several feet away, she twirls around and sashays toward the bathrooms, leaving a trail of clicks from her heels.

My jaw stiffens. No lie, her ass is jiggling too nice in that outfit. Some of the other men working on set crane their necks to admire the sight as well, refraining from whistling.

I'll have to deal with her later when the time comes. GiGi almost got me, and I'm not even totally sure what she really wanted. It can't be to *just* go to Zay's album release party. There's more to it, and I'll have to expend brain energy on that later.

Shaking my head, I pull my phone out to finish my text to Camesha. After a moment of deliberation, I add to the message:

Me (7:42pm):

> Hey Cammie, this is Tim Starks. We met at Zay Dubb$'s bday party Tues night. Anyway, he's having an album release party and he wants u to come. Lemme know if ur down. I can get u on the list and send u the details. It's chill if ur not interested. Just thought of u

And before I can psych myself out to *not* do it, I send it to her and shove my phone in my pocket.

It is true: I *have* thought of her. Not just for this job, but in general. I just hope my message isn't too forward or weird. I mean, I feel like we shared *something* that night. I'm only human to want to see if it was real or if my mind was playing tricks on me because I was hungry most of the time.

Camesha

I unlock the door to my condo. Once inside, I close and lock it, sliding the barrel into the bolt.

My shoulders sag at the warm feeling encapsulating me. Home. I rented my first solo apartment before this, but it still never felt like mine. I was never really comfortable nor felt very safe there.

I own this condo. Here, I can truly be myself.

And right now, that starts with getting clean. I plod over to my bedroom, drop my backpack and phones on my bed, then peel off my second uniform. I hop in the shower.

When I clocked out, I took my backpack from my employee locker and slipped into the customers' gender-neutral bathroom near the restaurant to prepare to see Eliot. I mean, after he paid me in full and with a quickness, I *had* to make good on my end of the deal.

I freshened up with some wipes and reapplied deodorant. I unrolled my little black dress and shimmied into it. I toed off my work sneakers and socks, flicked toe jam out of the crevices, and lightly lotioned my legs and feet before putting on red-bottom high heels. In the mirror, I touched up my makeup with concealer and lip color. Sometimes it's a lipstick kind of day and others it's a gloss moment. Tonight, I went with red lipstick. Seemed more like Eliot's vibe. I always pack a few roll-ons and wear one depending on the client's vibe. Eliot was looking at me like he wanted to devour me, so why not smell edible? Tom Ford's "Lost Cherry" it is.

That's my routine every time I meet an escorting client during my hotel shift.

And once my look was complete, I was ready to go see Mr. Novak. With my windbreaker hood on and head down, I boarded the elevator and strolled to his room. Upon knocking, the door opened immediately, like he was impatiently waiting for me. Eliot was now dressed in plisse lounge pants and a gray T-shirt. He smelled like he took a shower using the hotel's geranium and bergamot body wash. I appreciate a client who *tries* for me. It's hard to stay in character if a man's hygiene isn't up to par.

Eliot sheepishly apologized for "starting" before I arrived, referencing the drink in his hand. He asked me what I drink, then he made me a vodka soda. I watched him to ensure he didn't slip anything in it.

He indulged me with a little bit of awkward conversation before I gently encouraged him to make a move, to get what he paid for. After all, I've been on my feet, working for hours. I was tired so I really wanted to go home. He understood.

Eliot removed his shirt, and I was surprised that his skinny self had love handles. But when he pushed his pants and underwear down, his pink-ish penis sprang to life. He was probably a good seven inches hard. *Not bad.* I watched him roll on a condom before he asked me to strip tease.

With my clothes off, he was on me like white on rice. During the act, he asked me if something he wanted to do was okay or not. I texted him my rules after he sent me the money, but I thought it was cute that he still asked.

I can tell that he'd only been with his wife like he said. His sex was basic missionary. When he pumped into me, he repeatedly told me how beautiful I was. I, of course, said thank you, and scratched up his back, which seemed to make him thrust into me harder. And he sucked on my breasts and neck, moaning like I tasted like literal chocolate.

Eliot didn't last that long before he came hard, collapsing on top of me. I caressed him as he caught his breath. He thanked me, pulled out, and threw his used condom away.

My cooch still felt intact, unlike when I'm with some clients. Their hard pounding makes me feel like my vagina's in a boxing match. But with Eliot, he was fervent, but gentle. And like a gentleman, Eliot offered to "clean" me up, even though he didn't nut in or on me. I knew what he was asking and when I said yes, he was determined to make me cum with his lips and tongue. I ran my fingers through his neat hair as I gave *real* moans this time.

After I came, Eliot eagerly lapped me up like a good boy. *Golden retriever head-ass.* Admittedly, it felt good as fuck to orgasm, which I haven't been able to do in a while unless I had help with my toys at home.

Before I left, Eliot graciously thanked me for my time again.

If he hits me up again, I definitely *wouldn't mind lettin' him eat me out once more*, I muse as I step out of the shower and turn off the hot water.

I rub my body with plum and vanilla body butter. I slip my feet into furry slippers to trek to my kitchen so I can fill my water bottle with lavender-chamomile infused water. I'm tired, but not sleepy so this combined with an episode of *Abbott Elementary* should do the trick. With that, I return to my room, push my decorative pillows onto the floor, and climb into bed.

I turn on a random episode and sip my water, scrolling through my personal phone's texts I missed while I was working. It's a little after 10:30pm here so I keep the messages from my younger sister, Simonique, and my parents unread so I can respond to them in the morning.

Chuckling, I reply to some of the shenanigans in my best friends' group chat with Nikki and Oluchi, a.k.a. Lu. Some crazy long story about Nikki and the same lady at her job who's been having a one-sided beef with her for over a year. My friend texted that she'd "beat that old bitch ass off the clock" and I believe her, especially if the older lady hits her first.

I switch to my work phone and respond to a few people. I save all my clients' names under aliases. EC, or Edgar Clinton, a stand-up comedian, wants to fly me out to "celebrate" after taping his fifth special. My forensic accountant client, R2, or Ross Reynolds, asks for my availability in the next month since he'll be in LA for business. A handler I've worked with before, Chey, texted me about a vibe modeling opportunity in two months for a retired rapper's liquor brand launch party.

But one message in particular makes me sit up:

Unknown (7:42pm):

> Hey Cammie, this is Tim Starks. We met at Zay Dubb$'s bday party Tues night. Anyway, he's having an album release party and he wants u to come. Lemme know if ur down. I can get u on the list and send u the details. It's chill if ur not interested. Just thought of u

My stomach does a weird flip thing. And my cheeks heat up. Especially at the last part.

A thought pops up to distract me: *Tim musta gotten my number from Miles or Benny. I saw them chattin' multiple times that night.*

I immediately save Tim's number in my phone before considering his text. *He* thought *of me. . . For the job or just in general?—Doesn't matter, Camesha. Zay wants me to fill his party or he wants to fuck me again?* My mind zooms with more questions, causing a collision. I blink to unscramble my brain, my twitchy fingers ghost over the keyboard.

Me (10:46pm):

> Hey Tim. Can we talk about this on the phone when you get a chance?

My heart races after sending it. The job sounds straightforward enough, but I don't know, I *kind of* want to hear

Tim's voice? The delusional part of me thinks, *Maybe if I talk to him again, he'd leave my thoughts.*

Huffing out a breath, I lock the phone and drop it, the thing disappearing in my ecru comforter. I focus on *Abbott.*

Not even a whole minute later, my work phone chimes with a notification. My breath catches in my throat, startled by the unexpected sound. *Ain't no way. . .*

I pick it up and read:

Tim (10:47pm):

Yeah u can call me now

Really? My eyes bug out of my head as I pause the show. Unlocking my phone, I open up to our text thread. I click his Contact icon, my finger hovering over the call button for a moment. *Fuck it.*

"Hey," Tim answers on the second ring, his voice smooth and easy on speaker.

"Heeeyyy," I let out, slower and timid. *Why am I nervous? I spoke to this man in person. And callin' was my idea!* "I honestly didn't think you'd respond to my text that fast or pick up the phone when I called."

He chuckles, a warm, pleasant sound in my ear. Goosebumps dot my skin. "Damn, that's crazy. So, you thought I was just playin' on yo' phone? What kinda professional do you think I am, Camesha?"

I laugh, my body relaxing despite my effort to stay erect and alert. "I-I 'on't know, I just wasn't expectin' those things."

He chortles, "Well, what can I say? I'm reliable like that."

Double meanin' or am I lookin' too deep into that? Anyway, I gulp to calm my galloping heart rate. "I see that." I clear my throat. "So, tell me about this party. What would I have to do?"

"Right. So, Zay is throwin' a release party for his new album called *The One They Lookin' For* next Friday. He sobered up after his party," Tim pauses, "and he told me that he," another pause, "enjoyed his time witchu and wanted me to see if you were able to come out again." I'm almost positive Zay didn't word it like that, but I appreciate Tim summarizing his sentiment carefully.

"Hmmm, okay. So y'all would pay me to just vibe at the party? . . ." I don't buy it. Zay had a piece of me already, so surely if he wants me to come, he also wants to fuck me again. I mean, I'm down if he tips me like he did last time.

"Um, I-I 'on't know—I really can't say, Camesha." I hear what sounds like Tim walking somewhere, the air rushing and crushing through the speaker. "And by the way, how was last time for you?—Not that you have to, like, gimme details or anything. I just—I wasn't able to talk to you afterwards. Got busy handlin' shit," he releases a nervous laugh. "But I-I wanted to check up on you. See how you were doin'." He exhales like it took everything in him to voice all that.

A slight smile softly touches my face as butterflies flood my stomach. I avert my gaze to my lap as if Tim is standing in front of me. I don't think a handler has ever asked about my experience. Not even Miles asked me about that night! *Does Tim* actually *want feedback though?* I can't help but wonder if there's another reason he wanted to check on me.

Either way, it's rare aftercare, but always appreciated. And this all still aligns with who Tim was that night. Caring and concerned. We love consistency, even from our handlers.

I clear my throat to shoo away the nerves. "I mean, you checked in wit' me about it first, so that made the whole thing easier."

Tim exhales a sigh of relief.

"You gave me a choice, Tim. And I really appreciate that." I try to fight it, but a grin claims my face as my heart flutters.

"You're more than welcome, Camesha. And this time would be no different. I wantchu to be good and comfortable. I gotchu."

There goes that phrase again. It's a sincere punch to my gut. So simple, yet so powerful. People have said that to me countless times and it meant nothing. But with Tim, I *almost* want to believe him. He has a warmth and a genuineness about him. Or at least I feel like he does. I just hope my feelings about him aren't wrong.

"You 'on't gotta gimme an answer right now. His party ain't 'til next Friday and the guest list is still bein' finalized. Just lemme know as soon as possible."

"I-I wanna do it." I surprised my damn self with that quick answer. I'm sure the money will be good like last time. And knowing that Tim is involved and will be there makes me kind of feel . . . safe?

"Really?"

I giggle before I can stop myself. "Yeah."

"Cool." He exhales, sounding relieved. "A'ight, so I'll add ya name to the list. *Cammie*, right?" I swear I can almost hear his amused smile.

"Right." I tuck in my lips.

"Bet. I'll get everything squared away and send you the details. Address, time, which section Zay'll be in—all'at."

"I 'preciate that, Tim."

"No pro'lem." He pauses. "This day has been long as fuck and it's gettin' late, so, I'll get off ya phone."

A yawn fights to unfurl from my mouth. As hard as it is to admit it to myself, I kind of want to *keep* talking to Tim. . . "Yeah, it's been a long day for me, too. Goodnight, Tim."

"Goodnight—Oh, and, uh, this is my *personal* phone so if you need anything, text me. Sometimes I can't answer calls right away, but my notifications are always on so I will see ya text, *like I did tonight that you ain't think I was gon' see*," he jabs, sounding fake hurt.

I crack up. "I'll never question ya professionalism again."

He chuckles. "It's all good, Camesha—Or should I call you Cammie? I 'on't wanna be disrespectful or anything."

Awww. My face softens at that. "Call me Camesha . . . when it's just us. Cammie when we're 'round other people."

On his end, I hear what sounds like a snuffed *poof,* like a car door shutting. "Gotcha, I can do that," he breathes out. "A'ight, Camesha, *fa real* this time. 'Night."

I giggle like a little girl. "'Night."

We hang up and I stare at my phone screen with a crazy wide smile on my face.

Tim is . . . dangerous. Not in the way that hustling can be sometimes, but in the way that he makes me feel *things*. He comes off so warm and inviting, sweet and considerate. And when I don't catch myself, I almost feel comfortable letting him see the real me. Shit, Tim's the only handler who knows my government name! And as nice and different as all this is—not having to really perform—it's scary as hell. He *feels* genuine, but I can't be too sure. *God, I pray I'm not makin' another mistake.*

Sunday, August 20

Zaria called me out the blue this morning to invite me to work out with her at her high-end "health club" in West Hollywood. It's members-only but she's allowed to bring one guest a week. I usually exercise at Planet Fitness some mornings before work. But she knows I don't work on the Sabbath and neither does she, saying, "If God needed a day off, then I will follow Him. Can't nobody do more than the Lord!" That made me laugh but amen to that.

The alarm on Zaria's fancy sports watch sounds off, so we drop the 20-pound kettle balls we used for Russian twists.

Dramatically, she flops back onto her yoga mat, her sweat-glistened four-pack abs heaving up and down. Zaria used to be a sprinter in high school and college. But now she's traded in her spikes for high heels and her compression shorts for minidresses. She told me that some men ask her to sit on their faces and so she can squeeze her toned thighs around their heads while they ate her out. Wild stuff.

"Damn, girl, you worn out already? I thought you were the athlete between the both of us." I playfully tap her arm that's blocking the ceiling lights from her face. I blot my face with my sweat rag.

"Bitch, don't make me hurt you." Zaria rolls over onto her stomach to start a cobra pose for our cooldown.

I laugh and do her pose. "Hey, I wanna ask you some'."
"Yeah?"

There's very few people in here, but I still lean forward to speak lowly. "Are you familiar wit' a Tim Starks?"

Zaria's eyes dart around like she's trying to jog her memory. "I think so. What's he look like? Who is he?" A mischievous look crosses her face now as she whispers, "Wait, is he a client? Are you askin' me if I fucked one of ya clients?" Her mouth dramatically drops open.

I flow into a butterfly stretch and palm my face. *This girl.* I wouldn't care if she fucked one of my clients—ain't none of them my man—but I know some girls are a little territorial of their tricks. "Nooo. He's a celebrity handler. I was just wonderin' if you've ever worked wit' him before."

Zaria copies my stretch. "Oh, okay. . . Tim Starks, Tim Starks—you know what," she snaps her fingers, "I think I *did* work wit' him. It was for a Keyana Renay music video. She wanted a few bad bitches in that thang." She sticks out her tongue and rolls her body.

I smirk at her antics, "How was ya experience wit' him?"

She side-eyes me playfully. "Lotta questions, today, Padawan."

I deadpan her. "I met him at Zay Dubb$'s birthday party and he just offered me a job to work Zay's album release party on Friday."

"You vibed? Did you wear a skort?" When Zaria was mentoring me on the hustle, she told me the code words she uses when there are too many people around. "Wearing a skort" is escorting.

"Both."

She nods and waves for me to continue.

"Yeah, so Tim and I spoke a lil'. And he seems," I squirm, trying to think of the right words because I don't want to get Zaria excited because she swears she's finna have her *Pretty Woman* moment and wants other "escort girlies" to also have theirs, "nice. What was he like when you worked wit' him?"

"I mean, that was like—no joke—maybe four years ago. But I remember him bein' really nice. Very respectful." She transitions into a hamstring stretch and I follow her.

I nod. *So far so good.* "Did he, like, check up on you?"

"Girl, what kinda handlers you workin' wit'? They *check up* on you?" She sounds taken aback. Or maybe a tad jealous of this good thing.

I knew it was rare! But I just look at Zaria with a straight face. "So, that's a no?"

"Nah, he ain't check up on me, Camesha. I mean, he did in the way of, like, lettin' me know I can ask him for stuff. But that's it. He was professional."

"Oh, okay." I tilt my head, not sure how to feel about this. "Did y'all talk outside of that?"

"You want me to, like, have water-cooler discussions wit' these niggas, like we in the office? We talked 'bout the video shoot, girl."

This is why I can only hang out with her ass a few times a year. She's so damn dramatic, my head starts to hurt. I'm going to need her to get her big break soon so she can channel all that extra shit into acting.

"Okay, ZZ," I mutter, restraining from rolling my eyes. I move into a lunge since my hips need more opening.

She gets into that same position. "So, are you takin' the job?"

"I already did. Ordered my outfit. Should be here tomorrow since the party is Friday."

We both nod and I feel my hips stretch where I needed it.

"Well, lemme know how it goes cuz tomorrow, me and my boo flyin' out to Fiji. He wants me all to himself for an *entire* week." She rolls her neck and wiggles her eyebrows.

We sometimes discuss clients and trade stories, so I know that Zaria's *boo* is Marlon Reed, a 48-year-old former NFL star.

I offer a slight smile, knowing she's hoping that he'll quit playing and make her a kept girlfriend or wife soon. "That sounds nice, girl."

"Thanks." She's all shy now, poking her lips out and squirming.

For Zaria's sake, I hope Marlon makes his move. But Zaria and her two-year "relationship" with Marlon have no room in my head. My mind is zooming with thoughts about Tim.

He kept it *strictly* professional with Zaria, but he didn't with me. Besides him telling me Zay wanted me, our talks felt light, like I've known him for a while. Tim Starks seems to have a talent for making one feel comfortable and present.

He looked at and spoke to me in a way that clearly *isn't* required for him to do his job well. *So, why was he treatin' me that way?* It has plagued my mind. *Was I special or some'?*

Nope. Can't be. I immediately throw that thought out of my head. *Maybe he liked what he saw and is just butterin' me up to get some pussy outta me.*

Nah, that's not it either. Tim doesn't give me the vibe that that's the type of time he's on. But then again, I don't really know him.

At this point, I think I'm okay saying I need to see more of him to make an actual judgement.

3

The One They Lookin' For

Friday, August 25

Tim

Z ay Dubb$'s fourth album release party is in full swing at Club BLUR in downtown LA.

Three large VIP mezzanines on both sides are supported by thick steel columns. The chaotic dance floor and the stage are down below and to the left. The venue is all darting multi-colored lights, smoke, and shadows. The air is thick with the stench of various fragrances, weed, and liquor. Bodies are packed in here: women draped in their freakum dresses and sky-high heels and men dripping in designer and jewelry, all vibing to Zay's music. DJ Tone Def is spinning Zay's hits from his entire discography—three mixtapes and three albums—and his features. Zay will announce his new project at midnight.

Leaning on the railing of the event team's VIP section, I scan the crowd below. The lounge coves underneath the mezzanines are for fans, but that doesn't mean some won't try and succeed at worming their way into VIP. Security is prepared for folks to wild out.

I've been at Club BLUR literally all day. Got here this morning with Zay's team to check on the crew setting up, coordinate with catering, and assemble the VIP gift baskets. A bunch of shit. I usually don't drink energy drinks, but I guzzled two to stay alert. Details and crisis management matter at an event like this.

Zay arrived almost two hours after the party started to make a grand entrance. DJ Tone Def announced his arrival and the club went bonkers. Zay's entourage preceded him, but when he was revealed, I expected nothing less than what I saw. Sunglasses covered his face, but probably not to protect his eyes from the glare his entire jewelry collection was reflecting. He wore another loud-ass print shirt, pants that had a gazillion pockets on it, and the latest designer collab sneakers.

And when he came to the team's VIP section to thank everyone and make a toast, he removed his sunglasses. I can tell he pre-gamed. This nigga was gone.

My cellphone vibrates in my pants pocket and I stand up straight to pull it out.

Cammie (11:41pm):

> I'm here. Security just let me in

My heart skips a beat. It's my first time seeing her since Zay's birthday party. I can't lie, I'm a little nervous. And I may or may not have dressed differently tonight to look like I belong in her presence.

Me (11:41pm):

> Bet. Im comin down

I slip my phone back in my pocket before weaving through the section toward the spiral staircase, dapping up and cheek-kissing familiar faces. I steal a mint in a bowl on the bar, unwrap it, and pop it in my mouth before I descend the steps to the dance floor. Turning right, I walk toward the entrance through the dancing crowd.

I stop in my tracks, seeing her before she sees me. And man, what a sight it is.

My gaze lingers on Camesha from head to toe. Her hair is middle-parted again, her fluffy curls roll down her body. She's glowing under the darting club lights. She's wearing the hell out of a teal sleeveless corset top and a flouncy miniskirt. The thin straps of orange block heels climb up her toned legs. A matching tiny purse dangles on her shoulder and her phone is in her hand.

When someone accidentally bumps into me, I snap out of my trance. Can't be caught drooling over this woman. I'm a professional in Los Angeles whose around gorgeous women all the time. But man, there's just *something* about Camesha that's got me shook.

I lick my lips and set my jaw before approaching her. "Cammie."

She turns around, her hair almost hitting me in the face, a whoosh of some fragrant hair product. "Hey, Tim."

Sheesh. She looks unreal up close. Her makeup flawlessly enhances her natural beauty. Her lips are glossed similarly the first time we met: with two tones. And she smells so damn good, something syrupy sweet and spicy. It makes me want to lean in, but I straighten up. "Hey. So, you had no pro'lems gettin' here and gettin' in, right?"

"Not at all." A little grin lifts a corner of her mouth.

I nod repeatedly, trying to think of what to say like I'm technically *not* her employer for the night. "Uh, Camesha, you look absolutely, uh," I kick myself internally for stumbling, "amazin' tonight—You did the first time we met, too. I just-I," I grind my teeth to calm down, "I'm just sayin', you look gorgeous."

She flashes me a quick grin and pushes some hair behind her ear, revealing some feathery dangly earrings. "Thank you, Tim."

Did I peep her blush?!

Camesha

Get it together, Eesh, I coach myself after reeling from Tim's compliment, or should I say compliment*s*. *He's . . . cute when he's flustered.* That stuttering shit would annoy me with a client, but Tim's not a client. He's—*oh my God! I guess, he's my boss for the night?*

I subtly roll my shoulders back. *Be Cammie, Cammie, Cammie.* "And you look very nice tonight, too," I say, motioning to his outfit. *Well, that came from Camesha.*

But Tim *does* look really handsome. He appears to have gotten a haircut and defined his curls. *Okay, he takes care of himself,* I note. He even lined up his goatee—*Not* that I'm staring at that man's lips! *Although they look nice, too*—Anyway, he's dressed up compared to the last time I saw him: a black polo with two buttons undone and black slim-fit slacks with dressy sneakers. Looks like he's wearing the same diamond earrings and two gold chains, too: a shorter Cuban and a longer one with a dog tag-like pendant.

It's a simple outfit, but very, very effective. I swallow and pull my gaze to meet his. *Fuck! He pro'ly saw me checkin' him out.*

"Thank you, thank you." He offers me a warm smile, like he appreciates my compliment. Like I appreciate his. *Not* that I got dressed for Tim. I dressed for Zay since he's really why I'm here. But damn, it feels good to be seen by Tim again. And just to see him. *Ooof, get it together, girl!*

Tim clears his throat and leans in, his body radiating one of my favorite scents on a man: Tom Ford's "Oud Wood." It matches his vibe. "A'ight, so Zay's section is this way." He points up and to the right.

"There's only industry folks and special guests in VIP," he speaks near my ear, his breath smelling like a fresh mint. "There's catered hors d'oeuvres in the sections and, of course, a bar, too. Zay wanted open bars everywhere, but we convinced him to just have the one in his section. Ya know, save his money. Plus, can you imagine this whole place crawlin' wit' drunks *and* high muhfuckas?" His eyes widen at the idea of that nightmare.

I laugh a little too real. *Ugh, I devolve into a lil' schoolgirl 'round him.* "That would be insane."

"Fa real. Oh, and each section has two all-gender bathrooms, but the stalled ones are 'round the corner here." He points behind me.

"You got the lay of this place down, huh?" I smirk.

He smacks his teeth. "Shit, I better. Been here since 11 o'clock this mornin'."

My eyes bulge. "Really?"

"Yeah, had lots to do. I almost took a nap in one of the lounges while they were puttin' the final touches on everything, but I had to go back home to shower and get dressed."

Then I see it: the exhaustion swirling in his eyes.

I must've been staring at Tim too long because now, there's a certain something between us. Silent, but heavy.

I break away from his gaze when I get hot. "I guess I should go see Zay."

"Yeah, follow me." He starts walking and sticks his arm out so I can hold his hand. It's slightly clammy, but warm as his fingers gently clasp mine. *This is different. Feels like I'm lettin' my man guide me in a tight crowd and not my boss takin' me to my client for the night.* I shake that thought to get back into Cammie mode.

But dammit, it's hard from this angle. I feel much smaller and shorter than Tim, even though in my heels, he's only a few inches taller. He's not buff, but I can tell he's got some lean muscle, his broad back and shoulders shifting deliciously underneath his shirt.

I need a drink. . . And I probably need to Rose myself when I get home, I think.

Tim leads me up the spiral staircase to the smoky section, careful to go slow since I'm in five-inch heels. I don't plan on walking a lot tonight. I'm just supposed to be eye candy next to Zay and maybe be his candy later.

"Zay's over there." Tim stops walking and nudges his head in Zay's direction.

I lean forward to look for him. Tim turns his head. Our faces are now inches apart. My eyes seem to vibrate looking at his. I'm trying *not* to look at his full lips encapsulated in that immaculate goatee. But I notice his jaws are taut.

Feeling a little dizzy from our closeness, I back up a little. "Thanks, Tim."

He slowly smiles. "No pro'lem, Cammie. It's like last time—just holla if ya need me. If I'm not in here, I'm a text away. But I'll mostly be walkin' around checkin' on stuff, makin' sure nobody breaks *shee-it*."

A chuckle escapes me. I don't know if he's naturally funny or if he's purposely trying to make me laugh. But whatever it is, it's working. "I'll hit you up." Impulsively, I touch his bicep, feeling the muscle tense underneath my hand. *Shit! Did I cross a boundary?* With slightly enlarged eyes, I purse my lips before strutting further into the section.

I can feel Tim's eyes on my body. *I hope he likes what he sees*, I think before I could stop myself. A moment later, I quickly glance over my shoulder, seeing he's gone now.

Back to work for him. The start of work for me.

I earn a few leers from men and glares from working women. Three years into this thing, I've gotten good at being able to spot my fellow hustlers. I mean, every woman in here is dressed to the nines, showing off their goodies and hoping to score a big spender tonight. But us? We look like ornaments, shiny and shimmery, meticulously assembled to appeal to our clients. And purposefully unattainable to everyone else, even though some guys will still shoot their shots. Hell, I intentionally dressed like a peacock since Zay peacocks with his outfits.

Some women don't like seeing what they perceive as direct competition, especially in close quarters. They can be standoffish, like I'm finna steal their trick. And that is never the case with me. If anything, I want to talk to them to see if they also think we're crazy to do this—all the pretending and ego stroking we do for these guys. I've asked Zaria and she views all of it as opportunities to practice techniques she learned in her acting classes.

But tonight, I'm not worried about other hustlers. I zero in on my client. Cammie drapes over me like a well-worn coat as I will the anxiety settling in my stomach to dissolve.

Zay is dressed in typical Zay fashion, lounging back in the massive sectional, surrounded by his friends—those who were at his birthday party and some unfamiliar faces—and other women. I recognized a few from the celebrity events' circuit. The others were either actual girlfriends, newer hustlers, or just groupies.

I don't even have to say anything before Zay spots me, stabbing his blunt out in the damn-near full ashtray. A huge, toothy smile overtakes his face as he stands up, grabbing his half-drank glass. He's probably 6'2" and his big ass stumbles a little on his way to me.

"Gotdamn, baby. You look good as shit."

I knew he'd 'preciate the colors. "Thank you, honey."

Zay snakes his free arm around my waist, roughly pressing my body against his a little. I brace myself with my hands on his shoulders, so we don't fall down.

"Cammie, right? I was wonderin' when you'd show up," Zay says, his lips right on my ear. He smells like some sort of cologne, alcohol, weed, and sweat—a horrid cocktail. When Zay parties, he parties hard.

I smile even though I'm trying not to inhale too much of him. "You remember me, Zay?"

He backs away, his arm still around me. His face twists up. "Hell yeah, I remember ya fine ass." His gaze slides up and down my body.

I laugh a little. "I 'preciate that. Well, it looks like you're celebratin' right."

"Oh yeah, and we just gettin' started. We ain't even *get* to my new shit yet." He tips some of his drink in his mouth.

"I can't wait." I tilt my head, caressing his shirt collar.

Zay leans in closer again, his eyes and voice very low. "You tryna party wit' me later?"

I lower my tone, saying, "Depends on how you wanna party."

"You know what the fuck I'm talm 'bout." His free hand falls lower to grip my ass. "I need ya sexy ass close to me *all* night."

I giggle. "I can do that."

"Good. And how 'bout *when* we party later, we have some fun wit' some company? Some of these other ladies are also clean." He kisses my neck. "You smell good as fuck, baby."

I freeze, my eyes still in their sockets. My heart rate revs up like an old car.

When I agreed to vibe at his birthday party, Miles told me that Zay's friends, and by extension Zay, understood that I play solo should they want sex. No threesomes, no trains, no gangbangs, no girl on girl—none of that. I hope Zay just forgot that part in his cross-faded state. . .

"I 'on't do group stuff, Zay," I say into his ear.

His head snaps back to see my face, his arm loosening around my waist. "Wait, *what?*"

"I don't do it," I say pointedly but still sweet.

Zay smacks his lips and shakes his head. He glances around like he's looking for security to kick me out.

I have to do something quick before he gets belligerent. I need that money. And I want Zay's fat tip. Tim only paid me half up-front so he'll pay me the rest after the night is over.

I lay on Cammie thick: tilting my head, softening my face, batting my mascaraed eyelashes, and wrapping my arms around his waist. "Besides, I wantchu all to myself, honey."

Zay flexes his jaw and looks down at me with hooded eyes, his face relaxing. "A'ight, fine. I 'on't wanna share this good-ass pussy wit' nobody anyway." His free hand squeezes my ass hard as he finishes his drink.

I giggle, but I could exhale. *Crisis averted. Happy client.* "I'mma go get a drink, Zay," I say into his ear. He lets me go so I could prance over to the bar.

Tim

My head has been on a swivel so much today that my neck is starting to ache. I stretch it from side to side and rub the tension building at the nape to ease the pain.

I head over to the nearest bar on the ground floor and order a whiskey sour. Folks working the party get free food and drinks (two max). *Ah, the perks of this job.*

Moments later, the bartender slides my drink to me, and I take a sip, the taste punching me in my salivary glands.

DJ Tone Def begins playing Zay's latest hit "Stick Em" featuring Lil Hibb, that new rapper who was all in Camesha's face at Zay's birthday party. The crowd goes wild, already knowing the lyrics and vibing as the lights flash in sync with the bass.

But man, was it intense with Camesha before I dropped her off at Zay's section. The long gazes, the energy simmering between us. She *had* to feel it like I did, whatever it was. *But because we're both professionals, we pro'ly ain't gon' do shit about it.*

Anyway, I pull my phone out of my pocket to see if I missed anything. I answer a few non-urgent messages from my event collaborators, asking if they need any immediate assistance. And speaking of colleagues, my new one texts me:

Cammie (11:55pm):

> Zay knows I don't do group play, right? Ik he's fucked up rn, but he just asked me about it. I think I got him to agree to just me tho

Shit! I purse my lips and clasp my forehead. I should've asked her what her rules are. It slipped my mind. *Slipped ya mind cuz you got caught up, my guy—Focus, Tim*, I chastise myself.

If Miles negotiated that with Zay's friends and Zay smashed, did he know or understand that that was one of her stipulations? Probably not since he was out of his mind then and he is now.

I frantically respond to Camesha:

Me (11:56pm):

> Im SO sorry! I forgot to ask u bout that. Im comin up

Cammie (11:56pm):

> No, it's ok. Plus, Zay is about to announce his new album rn

I look toward the stage, and sure enough Zay and his crew are huddled up on the side.

DJ Tone Def scratches the turntables to cut the song off. He grabs a mic and screams, "Yoooo whaddup, LA?!"

The crowd echoes his excitement.

"Yo, y'all showed the fuck out for this one. That's good cuz it's time for some," he throws his head back to yell, "neeewwww shiiit!"

The audience goes bananas again. If they've been here since the party started at 8:30pm then they've been waiting to hear Zay's new project for three and a half hours. "Y'all, give it up for my boy, Zay Duuuuuuubb$!" His name reverberates all over Club BLUR.

Zay staggers up the stage, definitely looking faded like a vapor. It's hard not to focus on anything else but him with that loud outfit capturing your attention. DJ Tone Def and Zay dap-hug, before he passes the mic over to Zay. "Los Angeleeesss!"

More screams.

"I just wanna say, thank y'all for comin' out. The love here is unreal. I mean, just look at this fuckin' club!"

Folks clap and hoot.

"Thank you to e'rybody that made this possible. Y'all know who you are. Give it up for 'em." Zay motions around the building and the crowd applauds and hollers.

I cheers to that after the long hell this day has been and sip my drink.

"Look, this my *fourth* album. *And* I just turned 30."

People shout for that.

"Yeah, a nigga gettin' old outchere." Some people laugh. He flashes them a white smile. "Maturin' and shit. But listen, I'm really proud of this new album. So, I hope y'all know that . . . I'm *The One They Lookin' Foooorrrr!*" Zay shouts and the backdrop behind him falls to reveal his beautiful album cover: Zay, wearing one of his many printed silk shirts, sitting in a throne with multicolored flourishes surrounding him. He actually commissioned the renowned Kehinde Wiley to paint it.

The crowd screams as DJ Tone Def starts the first song on the album, "Off The Walls," a bouncy beat with synths and brass hits. When Zay's verse starts, his entourage bombards the stage and vibes out with him. This only eggs the audience on as they jump around and wild out, too.

I text Camesha back:

Me (12:01am):

Im otw

With my drink in hand, I walk around the dance floor, so that people don't accidentally bump into me and spill my glass. I make my rounds, checking on bar and food supplies, eyeing colleagues to make sure they're good. Benny's posted up at a bar, sipping the fourth drink I've seen him with.

I feel my phone buzz in my pocket. *Must be Camesha's reply.* I don't look at it to respond since I'm already climbing up the stairs to Zay's VIP mezzanine. Since Zay and his friends are onstage, only a few women and Camesha remain. She stands up from the sectional and meets me halfway, a little sway in her walk like she's looser with alcohol.

I lean in and say in her ear, "You good?" my hand ghosting the small of her back in case she loses her balance.

"I'm good, Tim. I said I think I've got him over that idea now." She offers me an easy smile.

I nod, flexing my jaw. "I'm *really* sorry again, Cammie. I shoulda asked you 'bout ya rules. I shouldn't've relied on Cross-faded Zay to know and remember 'em." I just *can't* shake the idea that I possibly put her in an uncomfortable position.

Her smile widens easily. "It's okay, Tim. I still think you're a professional."

I scoff, a smile worming onto my face. "Okay, good. Cuz I can't have bad Yelp reviews."

She throws her head back and really laughs—uninhibited, probably from the alcohol. But regardless, her laugh is cute.

Camesha comes down from her fit and says, "And before you ask—no, I'm *not* drunk. I had *one* drink. It was just strong as *fuck*."

I chuckle at all the emphasis she put on certain words. "Aye no judgement here. I had one whiskey sour and I'm *definitely* feelin' that shit." *I'm feelin' you* almost slips out, too, because of that same drink. I glance away from Camesha to refocus since I'm still working.

And like the boisterous disruption they are, Zay and his friends return to the section. I tense at the noise. The other ladies get up to greet them, some of them congratulating Zay on his album.

I return my attention to Camesha who looks calm and collected. An easy smolder brews in her eyes.

She's Cammie again.

"Duty calls," she says, like soft music in the midst of the chaos. So soft that I have to read her plump lips. My pulse quickens and I flex my jaw to calm down.

"Yeah. But lemme know if you need anything else. *Like water*," I tease.

"Shut up, Tim!" Her face breaks the seductive look as she laughs, playfully slapping my arm. I shoot her a "see you later" smile before walking over to Zay who's ordering a drink at the bar.

"Yo, Zay, congrats on the album, man!"

"Timbo Dubb$!" *That's a new one.* He pulls me in for a dap hug, slapping me hard on the back. "'Preciate it."

When he thankfully releases me from his sweaty hold, Zay looks at me with droopy eyes. *Jeez, he's so fucked up right now.*

"You been drinkin' water?"

Zay smacks his teeth, waving me off. "Fuck outta here wit' that, Tim." The bartender slides him his drink. "Soundin' like my damn mama. I'mma grown ass man. Of course I been drinkin' water. I know what I'm doin.'" He takes a sip.

I throw my hands up in surrender. "A'ight, was just checkin' up on you."

We dap up again. It takes everything in me not to glance at Camesha before I head out.

Coming off the steps, I peek over the crowd and notice some commotion going on near the entrance. I can't hear it that well, but as I get closer, I smell *her* before I see her.

GiGi.

A magenta wrap dress that stops right above her knees compliments her body, the skirt flaring out to accommodate her ass. Her toned legs are propped up on baby-blue stilettos. Her usual afro is slicked down into a low ponytail. She accessorizes with hoop earrings and a small tote purse.

"Timmy! Please tell this *gentleman* to let me in," GiGi says, an edge in her sweet voice, pointing to the burly security guard with her long red nails.

"Should I?" the guard asks, looking annoyed.

I'm pro'ly gonna regret this. "Let her in."

A huge grin smears GiGi's face as security steps to the side to let her saunter over to me. She takes her time, knowing she has an audience: me and any other man double-taking in the vicinity, which is a lot. Her presence is just undeniable.

I glance around to break free from her typical song-and-dance. But that's not enough because her short, fine ass stops right up under me and smooths my polo shirt over my chest. "You clean up really nice, Tim baby." Her voice is a warm shiver.

I chance a look at her and find her gazing up at me with those alluring brown eyes of hers underneath faux eyelashes. *I gotta get away but I can't shove her off of me.* That would be unprofessional and cause a scene.

"Timmy," she lets out, her fruity breath blowing up in my face.

"Whassup, Gianni?" I don't look at her, keeping my hands anchored in my pockets, hoping I look more nonchalant and relaxed than tense. Honestly, I shouldn't've had a drink. My mind is a little muddy and one needs to be level-headed when dealing with GiGi Savage.

"You didn't call me. . ." I can hear the pout in her voice, but I refuse to look at her face. "You didn't tell me Zay needed me tonight. I had to fight to get in here. And Tim baby, I'm *way* too pretty to fight."

GiGi's voice is too smoky and sexy for rational thinking. She's making this hard as hell . . . *and my dick hard, if I'm bein' honest. God, I sound pathetic. I might just need to jack off when I get off. Between Camesha* and *GiGi, I am out of it tonight.*

My neck twitches a little when I look at her. "He didn't request you tonight. I'm sorry." *And I didn't tell him you wanted to come either.*

GiGi tilts her head to the side and drops her hands from my shirt. "Don't lie to me, Timmy."

"I'm not lyin', Gianni. I'm sorry."

Something flicks across her face, like a glitch in her crafted façade. Then she takes a step back. "I need to talk to him," she says, a slight stiffness in her voice. She shifts her weight to one leg as both hands now clutch her purse in front of her.

I narrow my gaze at her to see if I can read her, see what her angle is. "No pro'lem. How you wanna do this?"

She looks ready to fuck shit up and I can't have that. Once this album finishes playing after 1am, the party will be winding down and the team and I will have three hours to clean this place up. I can't let GiGi set us back if she came to do damage.

"Baby, you know I can find my way up there without you and make a scene. If you don't want that for ya client, have him meet me somewhere private." She ends that with a smile and a tilt of her head.

I swallow. *This can't be good.* "I can do that. Follow me."

She skitters over to me to grab hold of my bicep before I escort her to the manager's office past the stalled bathrooms and kitchen. After I open the door, GiGi turns to me, reaches up to clasp the back of my head, and pulls me down to press a long kiss to my cheek. "Thank you, baby."

She swishes into the room and plops down in one of the plush, leather armchairs.

I lock my jaw, breathing through my nose as I close the door. I call over a security guard standing near the hallway entrance, tasking him with making sure she doesn't leave that room. After going to the bathroom to check that her lipstick didn't leave a mark on my face, I beeline for Zay's mezzanine so he can talk to GiGi.

4
In the Light

Saturday, September 30

Camesha

I didn't end up sleeping with Zay after his album release party.

We were laid up on the huge sectional in his mezzanine—him yapping in my ear about his album, me bigging his head up—when Tim approached us with a cautious facial expression. Zay and I sat up. Tim informed Zay that someone wanted to speak with him in private. Zay told me he'd be right back and kissed me on the cheek before standing. Tim pursed his lips at me and left with Zay.

But Zay didn't return. And by the time DJ Tone Def finished spinning his album, folks started filing out of Club BLUR, stumbling over one another as security tried to keep order. I texted Tim, asking if I can leave or should I wait for Zay. Instead of responding, he showed up in Zay's section and offered to walk me to my truck.

And outside in the fresh air, we . . . kind of had a moment:

"So, Zay is pro'ly *not gonna be available for the rest of the night. He and his,"* Tim dropped his gaze to search for the right

word, "associate *are still talkin' in the manager's office.*" He *stuffed his hands in his pockets and shrugged.*

I nodded. "I understand." I was relieved to be able to go home. I can't wait to take off these gotdamn shoes, *I thought.* "*Well, thank you for everything tonight, Tim." My voice sounded softer—shy, which I didn't like.*

There was a pause. Tim did that thing again where he clenched his jaw and looked at me with those intense, warm eyes. I tried to steady my breath, the air rolling and rising within my chest.

"*You welcome, Camesha." One side of his mouth curled up into a grin.*

I tucked in my lips and looked away, pushing some hair behind my ear. He'd been able to effortlessly switch between calling my real name and my professional one. I don't know, but something about that kind of . . . turns me on.

"*Oh, and lemme transfer the rest of ya payment right now." I watched him take his phone out of his pocket and type on it before I hear my cell chirp.*

On the inside, I melted. He wanted to show me that he was going to do what he said he was going to do. I've had to chase down handlers and clients to pay me at times.

"*Thank you." I don't know, something told me I can trust that Tim sent me all the money, so I didn't check my phone.*

"*Of course." His gaze softened.*

And then nothing but silence and eye contact. Both of us squirmed under the attention, but we kept looking, eyes mapping one another's faces. Our mouths didn't say anything, so the partygoers noisily leaving the parking lot filled the air.

Our staring contest felt like the one earlier in the night. Where I was trying hard to breathe, shoo the internal butterflies, and to not drop my gaze to look at his mouth. Where Tim's eyes dove into mine and he flexed his jaw. God, I love that.

But then Tim broke the silence by clearing his throat. "I-I should get back inside. Gotta help facilitate *the clean-up," he chuckled, even though it's not funny as he rubbed the back of his neck. I know that pain well.*

Immediately, I felt the overwhelming desire to comfort him. To hold him against my chest and run my fingers through his hair. Give him a massage to loosen his neck and shoulders. He looked so damn exhausted. He worked hard that day.

But I didn't do any of those things. Instead—and I don't know what came over me—I reached up to kiss Tim goodnight on his cheek.

With my heart in my ass now, I quickly retreated, unlocked my Toyota Venza, and got in. My windows are tinted so he couldn't see me looking at him or my red cheeks. Tim offered me a small grin before he backed away, so I could pull out of my spot.

I left the club that night buzzing and dizzy. From Tim's scent to the way he looked at me, to his damn jaws clenching. I was so horny and immediately handled that when I got home while I imagined Tim *handling* me. . . *Ugh, get it together, Eesh!*

I don't know what it was about that night, but something in me shifted about Tim. Maybe it was because he was my handler, and I got to experience him looking out for me personally. There was something about me being one of his responsibilities that felt comforting. Knowing he was there made my usual anxiety at an event like that fall away, like shedding skin. I could comfortably lean into Cammie when I knew Tim was around, looking out for me, and he *knew* Camesha. Or rather, I was allowing him to get to know her.

On top of all that, I felt more attracted to him. And I felt like he was attracted to me. There was too much lingering eye contact for me *not* to believe he was also attracted to me. I've studied men long enough to know.

But then again, I'm also questioning my attraction. Am I only intrigued by Tim because he treats me with respect and kindness? Am I reeling because I'm not used to men behaving like that with me *unless* they want something? Am I only interested in him because he offered care and concern? Do I like Tim for the right reasons? A long time ago, Mama taught me that *"Just because a man is polite doesn't mean he likes you."*

This whole situation with Tim has plagued my mind this past month. Besides him asking me if I got home fine that night, I haven't heard from him. Nor have I seen him at the two other events I worked. I thought about texting him but stopped myself since that felt inappropriate, especially since he has my work phone number, not my personal one. We're not friends, so I wasn't sure if we were cool enough to just text each other. If anything, we're the closest to colleagues. So, I left him alone.

Anyway, it's a lovely Saturday afternoon. It's 80 degrees, the Sun is shining, no clouds. The Sunday forecast says it's finna be mostly cloudy so I decided to get all my usual weekend chores and errands done today, so I can just chill at home tomorrow.

After finishing my weekly grocery shopping and my laundry, I head to my favorite Mexican spot. It's a low-key, family-owned Inglewood staple and I love that it's only a few blocks from my condo.

I pull open the door, a bell sounding above me. I see one of the great aunts wiping the table nearby. "Hola, Señora Luz!"

She looks up at me, grinning wide. "Hola, mami!" Her niece said it was hard for her to pronounce my name.

I return the smile.

There's two parties ahead of me as I join the line. I already know what I want: three beef street tacos. A man enters and stands behind me, murmuring on his phone. The woman before the couple in front of me finishes her order and steps to the side to wait. The front door chimes again. *Hmph, they're quite busy today.*

Out the corner of my eye, I notice a tall man approaching the pickup counter, scrolling on his phone. He's wearing a black baseball cap cocked on his head, an oversized olive-green T-shirt, cargo pants, and black and red Jordan 4s.

My eyes snap back to what's in front of me. My heart jolts, threatening to jump out of my damn chest.

Pedro, one of the nephews, approaches behind the counter and raises an eyebrow at the male customer.

"Pickup for Tim Starks." That warm and familiar voice covers me, goosebumps erupting on my skin underneath my light cardigan. My heart is beating so loud in my eardrum, it sounds like someone's stomping in the room.

Pedro turns around and retrieves Tim's order from the shelves between the kitchen, complete with a Mexican Coke from the nearby fridge. He places the plastic bag on the counter.

"Thank you," Tim says, grasping the plastic bag's handles.

I turn my head to look out the window before Tim sees me.

In my peripheral, I see he's back on his phone, but he glances up to watch where he's going.

And he does a double-take. "Camesha?"

I whirl around to face him, my hair whipping behind me. A slow smile spreads across his face. And it feels like a thousand suns shining down on me.

My voice hitches in my throat. "Tim."

This is my first time seeing him during the day. *Why does he look cuter?!* The Sun reflecting off the tiled floor brightens his handsome face. His diamond earrings and the same chains he wore at Zay's parties sparkle in the light.

He looked good before, but I like this version of him more. In the light.

And without my heels on, I definitely feel much smaller under his gaze. Shit, without my get-up, I kind of feel exposed. I'm fully Camesha now, not Cammie at all. Even though I like being Camesha with Tim, he's seeing me now totally stripped of

Cammie's armor. No makeup or nice clothes—just sweatpants, a grandma cardigan, and old sneakers.

"How you doin'? I feel like I ain't seen you in forever," he chuckles, breaking me out of my thought tornado.

A smile claims my face. "I'm good. And it has been a minute."

"Fa real." He clenches his jaw.

My heart flutters at that, but then something hits me. "Wait, do you live *here*? In Inglewood?"

"Nah. I just really fuck wit' this place. And I like to drive." He flashes me a smile.

I drop my head, stifling a chuckle. "Oh okay." *Kinda relieved.*

"What 'bout you? You live here?"

"Yeah."

He smiles and, before he says something else, Pedro yells, "Next!"

I didn't even realize the couple in front of me had ordered and moved out the way. I step up to the counter.

"Uh, I'll let you do ya thing, Camesha. My Jeep is right there if you wanna stop by." He points to the all-black SUV outside.

I nod as he swaggers out of here, his warm citrusy cologne whooshing past me. Blowing out some air, I snap out of it to order my food.

Tim

I damn-near floated outside, surprised to see Camesha here. And to see her like *that*. Without makeup, she looks younger, especially with the few dark marks I saw. *I wonder how old she is.* But even dressed down, she looks absolutely breathtaking.

The last time I saw her, she kissed my left cheek. I was thankful it wasn't the right one where Gianni laid hers on me before I grabbed Zay for her. I felt Camesha's soft lips on my face the rest of the night, which distracted me from focusing on clean-up. That last interaction replayed in my mind since. There was so much I wanted to say to her then. And it looked like she had much to say, too. But we both remained silent.

Honestly, I'm feeling this girl, and the timing couldn't've been worse.

I shake out of those thoughts and get inside my Grand Cherokee SRT—my dream car. When I started making really good money as a handler, it was my first big-boy purchase before I bought my house.

I sit my food on top of the dashboard to clean up. If she decides to stop by, my shit needs to be right. I don't keep a raggedy ride, but it's not spick-and-span either. It's definitely lived-in with gum wrappers stuffed in the cupholders and crumbs in the seat crevices. The backseat and trunk is full of hella plastic bags, lint rollers, power banks, extension cords, extra clothes and old black sneakers for me, and other things a client might need.

I flick the crumbs onto the floor and shove the wrappers and other trash into a plastic bag, tie a knot, and toss it in the backseat.

And soon, I see her pretty ass walk out the restaurant with a plastic bag and a Jarritos. Before I can think too hard about it, I get out and approach her.

"Hey, Camesha."

She looks up at me, strands of hair lightly blowing in the wind. *Damn, this is an amazin' angle.* I blink and continue, "Did you, uh, walk or drive here?"

"I walked."

"Oh okay." I nod. "So, I 'on't know if this is weird or anything, but if you not busy right now, I'm pretty free the rest of the day if," I clear my throat, "if you wanna catch up or some'. . ."

The seconds in between her answer feel like an eternity as my heart gallops.

She nods with a slight grin on her face. "I'd like that, Tim."

My happy ass smiles all big. "A'ight, cool. Here, lemme get the door for you." I step around her to get to my passenger side. Now that we're in the fresh air and not surrounded by the smell of meat and spices, I catch a whiff of her fragrance—something clean and ambery. At this point, I'm convinced she'd smell good wearing anything. Nothing can make me *not* gravitate toward her.

I open the door and watch her slide inside before I shut it.

I jog to my side and sit down. I retrieve my food from the dashboard and place it on the floor behind me. Camesha's scent fills my SUV. *Not a bad thing at all.* Her food is in her lap, and her seat belt is on. I follow suit before starting the car and backing out my space.

"So, you got a favorite place you like to eat at in the city?" I look at her.

She tilts her head, eyebrows knit together. "Like a restaurant?"

I chuckle, "Nah, like where do you like to eat ya takeout."

"Like *besides* my house?"

"Yeah." Her genuine confusion makes me laugh. I know it's an odd question.

She chortles, "Oh. Not really."

I cruise to the parking lot exit, waiting to merge with traffic. "I feel that. Eatin' food you didn't have to cook *at* ya home is amazin'."

Camesha laughs. I want to keep making her do that.

"You mind if I take us to a spot I like?"

"No." Pause. "I didn't know people had spots they eat their takeout at besides their house."

"Well, I 'on't know 'bout people, but I do," I say lowly before getting the road.

She giggles.

"It's not too far away."

I try to use driving to distract me from feeling nervous that Camesha's here. We're hanging out and I feel like an inexperienced teenager again. Extra cautious, driving slower, looking both ways multiple times. And it doesn't help that I can feel her stealing glances of me as I try not to look at her. I'm sure she thinks I don't notice her looking, but I hope she likes what she sees. A nigga been squeezing in some workouts here and there lately, so maybe she's noticing the gains.

To break the loud silence, I speak up, "So, how's life been treatin' you since I last saw you?"

"Uh, life's been good. Day job has been steady. Had a few vibe modelin' gigs."

"What's ya day job?—If you 'on't mind me askin'." I glance at her, and our eyes briefly connect before I focus back on the road.

She takes a beat. "I'm a waitress and bartender at The Adonir Hotel."

"That in Beverly Hills?"

"Yeah."

"Oh okay. I ain't never been there but I know Keyana swears by their spa."

"Keyana?"

Shit, name droppin' like an amateur. "Oh, um, yeah. Keyana Renay. She's one of my clients."

"Oh my God, that's right!" Camesha snaps her fingers. "My friend was just tellin' me she worked witchu once. She was in one of Keyana's music videos two years ago."

I smile. "Word? What's ya friend's name?"

"ZZ."

I make a right onto the final street. "Sounds familiar." I remember Benny telling me she introduced Camesha to him. "But you gotta picture of her I can see?"

In my peripheral, I see Camesha taking her phone out of her pants pocket and start scrolling. When I'm at a stop sign, she holds her phone up to show me an Instagram post of a beautiful, brown-skinned Black woman, tall and toned in a mint-green bikini, posing by a beach bar. "Oh shit, I remember her."

"You do?" she asks, shocked.

I look at her, noticing her eyebrows mushed together. Camesha's confused face is adorable. "I 'on't remember *everybody* I work wit', but I remember her. Keyana found all the girls on IG and DMed 'em for her video. I was just a floater on set."

"Oh okay. She said you were nice and respectful. . . Very professional."

I crack up and pull off. "That becomin' our thing now? Makin' sure we're both professional?"

"I guess so." She laughs, too.

"*And* you were doin' recon on me?" I joke.

"I just wanted to know if she knew who you were," Camesha says mid-laugh.

"Did you do this before *or* after you took the album release party job?" I lift an eyebrow.

"After . . ?" she says in a small voice.

Cruising down the road, I snap my head to her, finding her looking out the window. "If you ain't like whatcha heard that information wouldn't've done ya any good since ya already agreed to do it," I chuckle.

"Well, I didn't sign a contract," she snickers. "And she had nothin' but good things to say 'bout you anyway." Pause. "Plus, I saw how you moved at Zay's birthday party, so I knew I was in good hands." Her voice got progressively softer, like she didn't want me to make out her words.

I brake at a stop sign again. "Well, then I'm glad I left a good impression on both of you."

Camesha turns her head, a smile hanging in a corner of her mouth before averting her gaze to her lap.

"By the way, we're here." I make a left, crossing the street to enter the garage.

"Ya spot is a parkin' garage?"

"Yeah," I chuckle at her disbelief, rolling my window down to press the button on the metal tower to get a ticket.

"You're gonna *pay* to park so we can eat in the car?"

Ticket in hand, I pull my arm back in the car and roll the window up. "The views are worth it, Camesha." I smirk at her.

Slowly steering my Jeep up the ramps and around corners, we make it to the top. The powder-blue sky and the Los Angeles skyline is perfect. I pull into a parking spot in front of the concrete half wall. My SUV is tall enough to see the beautiful city stretching out before us.

"Wow," she exhales, looking at the vista in awe. Her face softens with wonder.

"*Now* you see why I come up here every blue moon." I roll the windows down a bit and turn the car off. After unbuckling my seat belt, I look behind my seat to get my food while she's staring at the view.

Bag in hand, I turn around and come inches from Camesha's face. Her beauty should be studied. I try to keep my eyes on hers, but mine slip down to her slightly agape mouth.

"My bad," I say barely above a whisper, breaking eye contact. My heart is thrumming so loud in my ears.

"You good." A smile twitches onto her mouth.

I flex my jaw as if that'll get my heart rate back to a normal speed. Back in my seat, I place my food on my lap and uncap my Coke to chug. It's all a distraction.

Camesha

Tim and I must stop having such prolonged eye contact. I don't know how many more close encounters with his face and intense stare I can take before I just react and can't take anything I do back.

And honestly, I'm feeling *very* irresponsible.

I untie my plastic bag and remove my lunch. Easy conversation should help push the tension out of his truck. Clearing my throat, I ask, "So, how did you find this place?"

Tim swallows and puts his Coke back in his cupholder. "A few years ago, I used to have a client from Long Beach, so I was comin' from there cuz he was doin' some promo for his debut album. Then I had to go to another client's concert rehearsal afterward in downtown LA at the arena. But I was *hungrier* than a muhfucka. I hadn't eaten in hours, and I was on my *last* leg, Camesha."

I laugh at him clutching his stomach.

"So, I pulled over and got some food, then drove until I found this place to park and eat. The garage was full, so I had to drive to the top. And the view stole my heart. There's good views of the city everywhere, but there's some' 'bout *this* one. . . Maybe cuz it's unexpected."

I just look at him, my face relaxing at his story. "So, did you discover *my* spot at that time, or have you eaten there before?" I tease him.

His mouth falls open, looking at me amused. "A lil' territorial, aren't we?"

"Lil' bit." I pinch the air to demonstrate. I pick up my guava Jarritos from the cupholder and try to remove the cap.

"Lemme get that for you," Tim says before lifting it from my hands. I watch as he opens it with no problems.

"Thanks." My voice is soft, too, in a way I don't like. I sound like a little girl.

"Of course." He smiles and removes his Styrofoam container from his plastic bag. "How you like livin' in Inglewood? I almost lived there when I first moved to LA."

"Yeah? I like it. Makes me feel like I'm on *Insecure*." I drop my head as my cheeks warm, fighting the cringe.

"That's a good-ass show."

He has good taste, I muse. I open my box, and the smell of tacos fill my nose. Glancing over at Tim, I clamp a hand over my mouth to stop myself from laughing.

"What?" He pauses before biting one of his gorditas.

"Tim. That's a lotta food." A chuckle tumbles out of me.

He looks down at his takeout box as if he didn't know he ordered two gorditas, Spanish rice, *and* refried beans. "Aye, I said I 'on't play 'bout my food. I'm a fat ass on the inside, fa real. I swear I'd be big as shit if I didn't have to run behind these niggas."

I can't stop laughing. But he shrugs and chomps down on his gordita anyway.

Damn, he's got a big mouth. My laughter fades as my eyes zero in on his jaw working his food down to manageable swallows. I don't know what it is about Tim's jaws, but they just do something to me.

"Is it good?" I ask him teasingly.

Tim dramatically closes his eyes and nods. "Hell yeah. But *fa real* fa real, I'm only gonna eat one now and the other will be my dinner tonight."

"Okay," I giggle before biting a taco, lifting my knees so my food doesn't have far to fall if it doesn't make it into my mouth.

We eat in silence for a moment, the only sound in his car is the air conditioning and our chewing.

"Oh, and what's every blue moon for you? For when you come up here?" I sip my soda then take another bite.

Out the corner of my eye, I see Tim wipe his mouth with a napkin and blow out some air. He rests his head back on his chair. "Shit, whenever it's a slower day like today and if I'm in between jobs. Or whenever I just take a day off, which isn't often. But I actually just got back from vacation since awards season is comin' up, and *a lot* of prep goes into that."

That's right. I have to be on the lookout for some client invites. I don't attend events as a client's date, but if they win at the award show, they might want to "celebrate" with me afterwards. And if the job is out of town and I have to take off from the hotel, they have to pay me extra.

"Where'd you go?" I ask.

He tells me he found a small beach town online and rented a little house there for five days. He just slept, relaxed, cooked, and drank wine—even saw some wild horses, too.

"That sounds wonderful," I say.

"It was. Much needed because the next several months are gonna be *fucking* insane." His eyes bulge as he looks out beyond the view.

"What's that like for you?" We both bite our food at the same time.

After Tim swallows, he continues, "Busy as fuck. Gettin' *flewed* out for shit."

I can't help but laugh. *I* get "flewed out," but I know what he means.

"What? I do. Niggas callin' me from New York like, *Yo whaddup, kid, can you get here in two days? I need ya help at this award show.* Shit's crazy." Tim shakes his head.

Covering my mouth, I crack the fuck up like a hyena. He sounded like he was mimicking Rugged Rah, an old school rapper from Brooklyn.

"Lots of last-minute trips, errand runs, the actual award shows, the parties—and *oh my God*, the parties. Pre-show parties, afterparties, private parties. It's an all-hands on deck effort for these artists. Like, no joke, awards season is like years' worth of work crammed into seven months."

My eyes widen at that. My vagina definitely gets a workout during that time, even *with* lube. But I can't imagine the coordinating and remembering every client's unique needs and their individual teams and everything else associated with Tim's job. *And* doing that for seven months on super speed.

"Now, Thanksgiving and Christmas provides a nice lil' buffer to all'at. But then it's back to the grind, startin' wit' New Years."

"Damn. That's wild." I stuff the last bite of my second taco into my mouth.

"It is. And I just heard that Zay's up for an award at the BET Hip Hop Awards. That song wit' *Lil Hibb*," Tim says, a slight teasing edge in his voice.

Do Tim and Lil Hibb have beef? "Well, congrats to Zay. I'm sure he's happy to be nominated wit' everything goin' on. . ."

"Right?! That shit is *crazy*." Tim finishes his gordita.

I hum in agreement.

He side-eyes me. "Wait, you know GiGi?"

I shrug. "I'm *familiar* wit' her. I've run into her at events, and we've talked. She's an OG in the game, but she's intense and a lil' pushy if ya ask me."

"*A lotta* pushy," Tim mumbles like that was an intrusive thought I wasn't supposed to hear. He takes a swig of his soda.

I start on my last taco as Tim rubs his forehead, staring at the view. *Has GiGi* pushed up *on him?* And I mean, I wouldn't blame him if he gave in. She's very sexy. I've seen her move very flirty, and straightforward in an indirect way. Men seem to just be weak to her, and she uses that to advance her career. Smart woman. Everybody's got a hustle.

Tim blows out some air. "I mean, I've worked wit' GiGi a few times before and she's always on some shit, but I just knew she was on some *different* different shit when she showed up at Club BLUR uninvited."

"She wasn't invited?" My head snaps in his direction mid chew.

"Remember when I took Zay away toward the end of the night and I said he wouldn't be needin' you cuz he was talkin' to his *business associate*? That was her."

My face breaks—raised eyebrows, mouth an O shape. "And then the next night, I saw on TMZ that she went live on Instagram and said that she's pregnant and that she's certain it's Zay's baby. But he's denyin' that."

"Yep." Tim tucks in his lips and shakes his head. "After his publicist chewed him out for not givin' her a heads-up on this GiGi drama, Zay asked me if I think he should do a paternity test. I said he should if he claimin' he ain't the father." He unwraps his plastic utensils to eat some of his rice and refried beans.

I'm quiet, reminded of *my* pregnancy scare as I eat my taco. Last year, I was with my NBA client, Asa Guillory, and I couldn't remember if he wore condoms or not. After Raw Math, I usually make sure I watch clients put on condoms, but I couldn't recall those times. I'm on birth control, but I like to still be as safe as possible.

Turns out I was just stressed from all the traveling Asa had me doing since he wanted me in several cities after his playoff games. My period showed up when I returned home.

When I swallow, I clear my throat. "Right. And how many clients do you have to work wit' this awards season?"

Tim scoops more food into his mouth before looking at the ceiling of his car, like he's counting his clients. "I have nine clients right now, and *six* of them are either nominated or have other award show responsibilities. Either way, I got hella work comin' up."

"Sounds like it. So, what do you do durin' the holidays?"

Tim

I get one last serving of my sides before I close my Styrofoam box, place it back in my plastic bag, then return it to the second row floor.

Sitting back down, I look over at Camesha, watching her finish her last taco. Fuck the view, *she's* the view today. I mean, even the way she eats is cute. Real respectful. Leaning over her box. Wiping her mouth after every bite. Meanwhile, my takeout box looks like I murdered the gordita's twin brother and did a poor job of cleaning up his remains. *I hope I didn't look like a starved animal as I scarfed that shit down.* I tried to look like I was raised with manners, but I was hungry!

"Sometimes, I stay in LA for Thanksgiving. Me and my friends will do a potluck. Or I go home. I try to definitely go home every year for Christmas."

"Where's home for you?" Camesha asks.

"San Antonio."

She tips her head up. "That explains the hat."

"Oh yeah, baby, gotta represent." I pull down my brim. "The Spurs is *my* team fa real." I yell at the view of the city, "I still fuck wit' LA though, so no offense, y'all!"

Camesha laughs, covering her mouth as she chews.

"But what 'bout you? Where's home for you? You 'on't give me LA vibes, *which is a good thing*," I whisper the last part.

We both chuckle.

"Columbia, South Carolina."

"*Thought* I heard an accent." I nod, a smile crossing my face.

"You do not. I *don't* have an accent." She rolls her neck, narrowing her eyes at me.

Funny enough, her accent came out stronger, making me laugh. "You definitely do." *It's cute though, Camesha—very cute.*

She sits up, a teasing grin on her face. "Well, *you* don't have a typical Texas accent."

"I can explain that though. I *claim* Texas. I spent my high school years there, but I'm a military brat so I was born in Germany, and I grew up in Tampa, Florida, Fairfield, California, then San Antonio."

"Oh, okay. And what branch of the military? My dad was in the Army."

"Nice. My folks were in the Air Force. . ." My jaw stiffens and I drop my gaze briefly before looking at the city.

I don't want to go there right now. It's been such a nice vibe that I don't wanna bring it down—*No offense, Pops*.

I can feel Camesha looking at me, probably trying to gauge the shift in the truck. To try to salvage this hangout, I clear my throat and look at her. "So, uh, how'd you end up in LA?"

But before she could answer, my phone rings. *Fuck! I knew I was havin' too much time to myself today.* I squeeze my eyes as I fish for my phone in one of my pants pockets. "Sorry," I murmur.

"It's okay." Camesha sits back and sips her Jarritos.

It's Amber Royce's manager. "Whassup?" She's asking me to fill in for Amber's personal assistant, who's out sick today. She needs me to pick up all these goods she ordered so her team can assemble appreciation baskets to gift Amber's label at a big brunch tomorrow. "A'ight. Text me the addresses so I can go get 'em." Then I hang up.

"Duty calls?" Camesha asks before sipping her soda.

I look up at her, her face soft with calmness and understanding. "Indeed it does."

Her mouth perks up into a grin before she collects her bag and soda.

My eyebrows smush together, trying to process her movement. "Wait, where you goin'?"

Camesha's eyes widen in confusion as she says slowly and matter-of-factly, "I'm gettin' out? Gonna order an Uber."

Taken aback, I scoff, "Ala! What? No, no—"

"Sounds like you have to go to a few places." She looks at me over her shoulder, her hand gripping the door handle.

Squeezing my eyes shut, I drop my head and grip my nose, frustrated and turned on at the same time. It's attractive that she wants to be independent, but there's no way in hell I'm letting her do that. "Camesha, I'm takin' you home."

Camesha

The emphatic look on Tim's face—his lips all twisted up, his nose crinkled, his eyebrows wrinkled . . . is kind of hot. Tim is *offended* that I was kicking myself out of his car—out of *his* way so that he can handle his business.

He keeps going as I just watch him. His eyes are open now, but he's not looking at me, just glancing around the car as if in disbelief. He's also not really yelling, but his voice is slightly raised, deeper, assertive. He's telling me how it's going to be and that's it. I mean, my pussy might've quivered just a little at his timbre. Tim Starks is kaleidoscopic.

"—You're just—You're *not* walkin' down six flights of parkin' garage stairs and waitin' for an Uber on the sidewalk. I can take you home and *then* run errands for Amber Royce."

I could take the elevator I spotted, but okay. Yes, sir. I let my hand slip from the car door handle. Tim notices, his face twitching into softness.

Just to mess with him, I mutter, "Fine," with the faintest smirk.

He scoffs and tries to restrain the smile worming across his face. "Camesha. I'm tryna keep my Yelp reviews good, girl. What kinda man would I be, lettin' you do some shit like that?" He sits back and puts on his seat belt before starting his truck.

I mean, it wouldn't've been the first time I figured out a way to get home after hanging out with a man. When I was 21, I met a social media influencer named Wallace on a dating app. For our third date, he took me to my first mansion party. He carried me to the hills in his orange McLaren. The party was fine, but I had to clock in at the coffee shop the next morning. Wallace got way too drunk and couldn't take me home, so he told me to "figure it out." Fucking pissed, I left and walked a mile down a dark canyon road until I had enough cell service to order an Uber home I could barely afford.

"Sorry, Tim. You're a professional *and* a gentleman. I get it now."

We both crack up.

"That's right. And no need to apologize." Tim's laughter falters as his face turns serious. "So, where can I drop you off at? Your place or somewhere else?—Ya know, if you not comfortable wit' me seein' where you live." He glances at me a little while he backs out of the parking space.

I clench my thighs together and click on my seat belt. *Eesh, him bein' a gentleman and bein' polite doesn't mean he likes you. The man was clearly raised right,* I tell myself. "No, it's okay. You can take me home. I'll tell you where to go."

"A'ight."

Then we're off—this time with music. At a stop light, Tim asks if I have any *qualms* against Roy Ayers. I tell him I don't know who that is, and he looks at me like I told him sweet potato pie is nasty. He assures me that the songs are amazing, then he starts an album that matches the vibe of this gorgeous, sunny day.

I try not to stare at Tim, but *Ugh, why does he have to look so good while he's drivin'?* So cool: reclining in his seat, wrist hanging off the wheel, knees bent. It's wild that Tim has this side *and* an awkward side. Both are cute, honestly.

As I glance between him and the passing landscape, I have the strangest urge to lean over his console and suck on his neck right under his ear. I want to smell and taste his cologne at its most potent—*Annnddd I'm feelin' feral. . . Damn, bitch, go take care of that when you get home.*

Soon, we pull up to my condominium. Tim chunks his truck in Park and turns to me. "Home sweet home."

He looks at me again, in the same way he did when we first met. Unhurried. Like a client *isn't* depending on him for something. Like *I'm* important. His eyes bore into mine then they dart across my face. *Did they linger on my lips for a second too long?* The muscles in Tim's jaw go haywire. Before I can stop her, my clit jumps at the sight, and I discreetly squeeze my thighs tighter.

"Thank you for the ride, Tim—And the view. That was amazin'."

"I'm glad you liked it." He smiles, parentheses cupping his mouth.

Before I allow my eyes to look at his full lips, I speak up, "And I had a good time in general." My face is hot, so I hope he can't see me blush. *I feel like a teenage girl again, bein' dropped off by a boy after their first date. Except this was . . . well, I 'on't know. A hangout?* Honestly, I can't really remember the last time I hung out with a man who didn't pay me. Shit, the last time I spent time with a man I liked, period! It was definitely at least three years ago though. Today felt different yet nerve-racking, but in a good way.

"Me too. Wish we coulda done this longer, but," Tim looks at me longingly, "ya know." He shrugs.

I swallow and nod. "Well, lemme get out ya way."

"Camesha, ya not in my way. Honestly." There's no hint of humor and lightheartedness in Tim's voice or face at all.

And that makes my heart surge with good feelings.

I think, *Should I say,* 'We should do this again?' *What's the right move here?* "It was nice catchin' up."

"Same. I enjoyed gettin' to know you a lil' bit better." A smile lifts one side of Tim's mouth. "Oh, and, uh, I 'on't know when I'll have another free moment like this wit' everything comin' up, but," he clenches his jaw and exhales out his nose, "may I have ya personal phone number?"

I relax into the seat, relieved and happy he asked. Smiling, I say, "Yeah. Can I see ya phone?" I hold my hand out so I can enter my information.

Without hesitation, Tim unlocks his phone and gives it to me. Not that I was testing him, but it's telling that he gave me his phone with no protest.

After my personal name and number are programmed in there, I pass his cell back to him. "See ya later, Tim."

A piece of his pink tongue flashes across his full lips—*ah fuck!*—before he flexes his jaws. "See ya, Camesha."

With that and slightly damp panties, I open his car door and get out with my now-empty takeout bag. I resist the urge to glance at him over my shoulder as I throw the bag away. I hear his truck leave when I enter my building. And as I trek up to my condo, I can't help but feel warm and fuzzy on the inside.

5
Catchin' Up, Catchin' Feelings

Friday, April 20

Tim

I t feels good to be back on the ground. Not in the air, not on a mountain, not on an island. But in Los Angeles.

These last six months have been a busy blur. I feel like I've lived a thousand lifetimes. My head spinning, my eyes stinging, my body aching. For some reason, *this* awards season really kicked my ass. I'm grateful to return to a calmer, more normal chaos.

My clients cleaned up at the awards, so I'm proud of them, but fuck! I'm happy that most of the shows are over. From flights to rehearsals, dinners, pre- and after-parties, and interviews—it's been a lot.

It was *especially* a lot before the BET Hip Hop Awards.

Days after Camesha and I hung out in my Jeep, Zay's team and I finally got Gianni to agree to meet with Zay and the team. We wanted to do a non-invasive prenatal paternity test before the awards show taping in a few days. Gianni was adamant that the baby was Zay's, but we needed to be diligent and know for certain so that all the drama surrounding her announcement could die down.

All of us met up again when the results arrived days later since Zay's team rushed them.

Zay was *not* the father of Gianni's baby.

Zay was relieved and happy as hell, jumping around like he won the Super Bowl. He already has two children from his first serious girlfriend who lived back home in Atlanta, and he didn't want more. I hope this whole situation inspired him to be more careful with whom he sleeps with to avoid any more pregnancy scares, but I doubt it.

Gianni looked distraught at the news, her star dimming a bit. She now had to figure out who the father was since she was sure it was Zay who impregnated her one wild night in Miami.

While Zay drank Hennessy to celebrate with his boys, Gianni quietly told me how they met. She was visiting some model friends and they all decided to hit up a club. They were surprised to see Zay perform. He sometimes does that, especially to crowd-test new songs. After the show, he spotted and invited them to his VIP section. Gianni and Zay talked, flirted, and danced before she left her friends to go back to his hotel. That night was a personal interaction, but Zay still gave her a little something-something for her discretion. And he promised that he'd keep her in mind for jobs and more private rendezvouses when they returned to LA.

When the world found out that Zay wasn't the father of Gianni's baby—I think it was the snake-ass test administrator who leaked the news—the Internet dragged her. *Hard.* Calling her all sorts of names and saying her "little idea to come up" didn't work. Gianni is used to all the hate, so she defended herself, getting into ugly back-and-forths in the comment sections on her Instagram and other major gossip pages.

But then, months later, after people low-key forgot about the drama, Gianni went live on IG in a whirlwind of tears.

She miscarried her baby *right* before Christmas.

Let the Internet tell it: she was *never* pregnant and just wanted some clout off Zay's name. If any of those weird niggas did a quick Google search, they'd see that she was already successful without being connected to him. But Zay didn't defend Gianni in the midst of all this, like he should've since they had some kind of relationship. He just thanked his fans for their loyalty and asked them to focus on his deluxe album releasing soon. Not going to lie, the way he handled himself made me slower to answer calls and texts from him and his team.

I spent Christmas with my mom in San Antonio. When I returned to LA for New Years, I had a few things to handle for clients then afterwards, I called Gianni. She had stopped posting on her social media, so I wanted to check up on her. To my surprise, she told me to just come over to her house since she didn't feel like talking on the phone. I wasn't sure if that was a good idea, given her flirting with me in the past. I didn't know what I was walking into and didn't want to get caught up in something, fall under whatever spell she had. But Gianni didn't sound like *GiGi* on the phone, she sounded sincere.

So, the next day, after I finished with a client, I pulled up to her house in West Hollywood:

I knocked on Gianni's huge wooden front door. She lived in a two-story modern home with a hedge surrounding it. I'm sure that extra barrier was useful to prevent paparazzi from having too much unwarranted access.

Gianni opened the door, and I almost didn't recognize her. She was still absolutely gorgeous, but she looked dimmer. Not as lively. Which is understandable considering her current circumstances.

She was dressed the most down I've ever seen her. She wore pink form-fitting joggers and a matching cropped hoodie, a big colorful butterfly tattoo visible along her ribs. She didn't wear makeup and her hair was pulled into a puff on top of her head.

She still smelled good, but it wasn't her usual vanilla and floral scent, it was one of those Sol de Janeiro perfume mists.

"Hi, Tim," she greeted me, the slightest polite smile hanging in the corner of her mouth. Her voice was hoarse, not like smooth sweet syrup.

"Hey, Gianni." I had to get in the habit of calling her by her real name since she asked me to. I didn't want to set her off down a worse road by rejecting her request.

"C'min." She moved to the side to let me into her home.

"Shoes off?" I asked her after she closed the door.

"Doesn't matter." She shrugs.

I didn't know how long I was going to be here, but I didn't want her to think I was planning to only be here a few minutes, so I toed off my gray New Balance 2002Rs. I watched her walk deeper into the house. And I'm still a man, so my eyes dropped down to her round ass sitting up in them tight sweatpants. I blinked and snapped out of it before I followed her.

Her interior was nice, too. Dark textured wallpaper. Wood accents. Clean lines. I spotted a crystal-encrusted bar cart parked halfway between the living room and kitchen decked out with stainless steel appliances. Her cart looked ravaged with half-empty bottles, like she's been drinking.

I entered her living room. Luxury fashion books sat on a gold-trimmed glass coffee table. Her heavy drapes were cracked to allow some natural light, but the main light was her dimmed crystal chandelier. Gianni was curled underneath a sherpa throw on her velvet couch, looking at her flat-screen TV. Some soothing oceanic life show was playing at low volume.

I sat down on the other end of the couch, just watching her not be the same Gianni I've known for the last few years. Granted I didn't really know her, but this was shaking me up, seeing her like this. A shell.

"Gianni, how—," I stopped myself. I didn't know what to say to her that wouldn't sound stupid or painfully conventional. I

felt bad about her situation. I just wanted to see how she was doing. How she's coping. And it didn't look good. I hoped she got some real friends and family to comfort her during this time where it seemed like no one had her back or was defending her. "I ain't gon' lie, I 'on't really know what to say. I just wanted to see how you were doin'. So, thanks for lettin' me come over."

Gianni turned her head to look at me. Emptiness in her eyes. "Well, you see me, Tim." She shrugged.

My throat clenched as I leaned forward, elbows pressing into my thighs. "I'm really sorry" was all I could think to say when I looked back at her.

Gianni's facial features softened. She also looked really young with a bare face, like Camesha did. I saw how round Gianni's cheeks were, the largeness of her brown eyes. How tender she looked. How raw.

Before I could process any of it, she unraveled from her blanket, crawled over to me, and straddled my lap. My hands automatically glued to her midriff, her skin warm. She cupped my face and kissed me, her eyes closing upon contact and so did mine. My heart was stuttering like a nervous wreck. My dick twitched a little at the sudden feeling of Gianni's ass and crotch on top of it, but surprisingly, I didn't get fully hard. Her lips were buttery soft. Her breath was surprisingly neutral since I kind of assumed she'd been drinking. I didn't know what to do but I didn't push her off or kiss her back. She didn't try to stick her tongue in my mouth either; it was just a long smooch.

When Gianni retreated, our lips making a soft smack sound, she just looked at me, her eyes ping-ponging between mine. Her hands still clasped my face, and I kept holding her while my heart was pounding in my chest like I did something wrong. She started breathing heavily through her nose and I just remained quiet. "I-I'm sorry, Tim." She didn't move from my lap.

I flexed my jaw and tried to steady my heart rate. "I-It's okay." Or was it? I didn't know.

Gianni's face fell, a frown overtaking and a slight quiver in her lips before she leaned forward and wrapped her arms around my torso, snuggling her face in my neck.

I still held her. Seemed like she needed to be close, needed intimacy.

She started crying. Not really making much sound, but I felt her tears wet my neck and her grip around me tightened. I hesitantly rubbed her back.

After a few minutes of her releasing whatever she needed to get out, Gianni sat back, wiping her face, but didn't look at me. "Thank you . . ." her long, jeweled nails fingered my gold dog tag, "for comin'. I—" She suddenly looked up at her tall ceiling to dam up more tears. "I think I needed . . . to see *that someone cared 'bout me."*

My heart broke for her, hearing that she was essentially dealing with this ridicule and miscarriage by herself. I wanted to know where her friends from Miami were and where her tribe in LA was. But it sounded like they were nonexistent. And that's fucked up. "Glad you invited me over."

"Really?" she asked, her voice lighter as she side-eyed me before focusing back on my chain.

"Yeah," I chuckled. "Happy I was able to," I paused, watching her play with my necklace again before she innocently flicked her eyes to me like she wanted me to continue talking, "be here for you." I swallowed. God, she's gorgeous, *I thought.*

She smiled at me and looked at my chain again. "You're a good man, Tim. Don't change," she said very softly, almost a whisper tone.

Then she grabbed my face and crashed her lips to mine again. I didn't want to give her the wrong idea, so I didn't kiss her back. But honestly, it was tempting even though it felt wrong for some reason. Gianni started grinding on me slowly and I'm sure she felt my dick hopping for joy a little.

It has been a long minute since I had sex, but some sense crept in before it was too late. I gripped her waist, so she'd stop.

Gianni backed off and said, "Oh."

"Sorry." My jaw stiffened as I tried to keep eye contact, but her being so close and on me was making it hard.

"It's okay." Her lips spread into a smile. "I knew you were attracted to me though." She bit her lip, something playful now in her eyes. There she is, *I thought.*

I chortled. "Of course. Who isn't?"

She shrugged. Then a slow smile wormed its way on her face. "And Timmy, you might've just seen me cry, but I'm still a bad bitch." She rolled her neck and twirled her hand.

I laughed. "You are, Gianni."

"Glad you know." Her eyes dipped down, and she softly said, "You have very soft lips, Tim baby." Her thumb swiped my bottom lip before she dismounted from my lap and headed for her kitchen.

My dick jumped again. "Thanks?" came out raspy so I cleared my throat.

Gianni giggled. "You want somethin' to drink or eat?"

I said yes, and she poured us some prosecco. We chatted on her couch about little things so that we didn't talk about the industry. As if she read my mind, she told me that she was fine financially to take this long of a break. She had enough saved and made smart investments to take care of herself for a while.

Afterwards, Gianni walked me to her front door, hugged my neck, and kissed me on the cheek. That felt innocent as she looked up at me with those doe eyes. She needed a friend and appreciated my visit.

I told Gianni to text or call me anytime. She has reached out a little. I made sure to check on her every once in a while and she obliged me with short updates on her wellbeing, especially her doctor's appointments.

Four months later, Gianni is *still* laying low. I haven't seen or heard of her working other events and shoots.

But anyway, my clients did well at the awards this season. Zay Dubb$ and Lil Hibb won Best Collaboration at the BET Hip Hop Awards for "Stick Em." The Soul Train Awards' Best Dance Performance Award went to Keyana Renay for her music video where she and her niece's dance team did a cute routine mixing hip-hop and ballet. Of course, Rugged Rah and ill Yamz won the Grammy for Best Rap Album and the NAACP Image Award for Outstanding Album. People loved that they're bridging the old school with the new, so those were rightful wins. Amber Royce's biggest hit won Top R&B Song at the Billboard Music Awards. Nobody won anything at the iHeart Radio Awards, but there were lots of nominations. Either way, this awards season is in the books, and I'd say it was a success.

Now that things are settled down, I have time to hang out with my boys today. We've been best friends since we met at California State University in Northridge. Bryan was my freshman roommate, and Jaquade was one of my project partners in an introductory music class. Jaquade would come over to my dorm to work on our project and Bryan would be there. It took a minute, but the two eventually warmed up to one another so we started hanging out together. Those two have a big brother-little brother dynamic even though we're all the same age. Bryan is just more strait-laced and mature while Jaquade has a more do-whatever-I-want life approach with petty, dry humor. Despite their differences, they've really been *there* for me, and I for them. We're all really down for our cause.

I park my Jeep along the curb in front of Jaquade's black and brick mid-century modern house in Brentwood. We love hanging out at his house because it's the biggest out of all of ours and his backyard is low-key on a cliff, boasting an amazing view of the city to the left and the beach to the right.

I grab the brown paper bag of Crown Royal apple whiskey and get out. Locking the whip, I push open the unlocked half-gate and stroll to the front door. Jaquade's front yard isn't as amazing as his backyard, mostly just low-maintenance plants and some grass.

I ring his doorbell and immediately hear Jaquade's Doberman's paws clapping the wood floors. "Mic, act like you got some gotdamn sense!" he yells. Leave it to my homie to name his dog after music equipment that sounds like a person's name. He wanted to mimic having a son one day. Honestly, I can see him being an expectant, yet supportive dad.

Jaquade opens the door, side-stepping his dog. "Whaddup, T?" He has dark brown skin and wears his locs pulled back in a loose ponytail while a black bandana wraps around his forehead. He wears a neat beard and a gray T-shirt and black jeans. If I didn't know he was a hip-hop music producer, I'd think he was in a rock band.

We dap hug, his usual "Karst" by Aesop fragrance surrounding me, and Mic nudges his head to try to separate us.

"Damn, Mic, I can't love up on ya daddy?" I joke.

"Chill, a'ight? He just ain't seen yo' ass in a minute," Jaquade says, smirking.

I walk inside his home and bend down to rub behind Mic's ears.

"C'mon, man. Bryan's already here." Jaquade closes the door behind us.

I smack my teeth. "Dammit, I thought I'd beat him today."

"Nah, that nigga stay punctual," he chuckles.

I scoff, shaking my head.

"Whatchu got?" he asks, grabbing my plastic bag from the liquor store.

"Yo' favorite. Witcho basic ass," I chuckle.

"Man whatever. A nigga may got money now, but this shit is good."

He's not wrong, so I just nod my head.

Jaquade leaves, Mic following him, and makes a right to his kitchen. His house is split into two wings. On the right is his garage, kitchen, and living room, and on the left is where his two bedrooms and third-bedroom-turned-studio is located. In front of the entryway is a wall of windows that display his backyard and the LA skyline. The Sun has sunk behind the skyscrapers, but its remaining orange light mixed with the indigo clouds is a beautiful sight.

I slide open the door to enter the backyard, featuring a stone-paved path and patio, a small in-ground pool, and a patch of grass. I round the corner and see Bryan, reclining at the wrought iron patio table with a beer in one hand while he scrolls his phone with the other. A familiar J Dilla track plays softly from Jaquade's Bluetooth speaker sitting in the middle of the table. A stack of paper plates and several unopened boxes from our favorite Korean fried chicken spot is next to the speaker.

"Whaddup, Bryan!" I greet him.

He looks up and immediately stands, placing his things on the table. Bryan is Black and Mexican with tawny-brown skin, a mustache, and that relaxed California accent. He looks like he might've come straight from work since he's wearing a blue button-down and khakis. He's an urban planner for the city.

"Tim! Bro, it's been a minute." We dap and hug before we sit down. Looks like Jaquade's seat is at the head of the table closest to the door to his kitchen, where I see him moving around, probably making drinks. "When'd you get back in town?"

Immediately after finishing my responsibilities at the Nickelodeon Kid's Choice Awards for G1-Otie, the only Christian hip-hop artist on my roster, I flew down to Antigua for a week.

"'Bout three days ago. Best week of doin' nuttn ever. Definitely a much-needed trip."

Jaquade comes out with two drinks: a straight Crown apple for him and a whiskey sour for me. That's become my go-to since Zay's album release party. Something about the sour makes me ready for anything. Jaquade hands me my drink before sitting down.

Even though it's 4/20 today, we're not smoking. Back in college, Jaquade and I smoked a lot of weed. The habit—or addiction, depending on who you ask—worsened when my pops passed of an aneurysm at 48 years old. That was the beginning of my second spring semester. Losing him made me want to drop out, but Ma strongly encouraged me to stay, and I knew Pops would've wanted me to finish what I started.

But my grades slipped and I started smoking more. After a summer of intense grief counseling, I returned to school that fall and tightened up. And my boys supported me all the way through. Bryan taught me how to study, which improved my grades. And Jaquade even stopped smoking in solidarity. They've never even met my pops but were there regardless like true friends, holding me down.

All in all, Pops would be proud of me for quitting. I remember one of the only times he gave me a long talking-to. I was a freshman, home for winter break, hotboxing in my room. He came home early and got on me about it. His talks were never furious, just military-stern, which made me straighten up.

"Well, it's good to have ya back, bro," Bryan pulls me back to the present. "Look, I was able to catch some of the shows and I'm so happy Rugged Rah and ill Yamz won Best Rap Album. *Black Like We Always Here* will go down in history as one of the best." He sips his beer.

"Yeah, that's a dope project. I'm happy I was able to have been a part of it." Jaquade co-produced some of the tracks, so he won awards and nominations.

"You did ya thing on that, Quade." I dap him up.

"'Preciate it, bruh."

We were able to celebrate at the Grammys' afterparty for a hot minute, but a longer hang was definitely long overdue.

It's quiet for a moment, save for the music, as we sip our drinks and dig into the food. Bryan and I make plates, and Jaquade just grabs a mini wing and fry to eat one by one. Just like old times. A chill vibe.

"I 'on't know how y'all do it." Bryan cringes as he chews.

"Do what?" I chuckle, amused.

"That whiskey." He screws his face up.

"How you drink that carbonated bread water is beyond me, too," I jab.

"Yeah, nigga. That's why yo' ass is gettin' chubby. You 'bout thicker than these bad bitches outchere," Jaquade says with a deadpan face.

I crack up with my head thrown back.

"Whatever. Y'all have no class," Bryan says, rolling his eyes. He doesn't have a real comeback because it's true. My boy been eating and drinking real good. "Beer is great. Plus, this is a local indie brewer. I support small businesses." He motions to the six-pack sitting by his chair.

"That's great. But beer—"

"still tastes like piss," Jaquade finishes my sentence. "And you can drink *that* by yo'self."

We both laugh and dap up as Bryan just stews. It's so fun to joke on him because he gets so worked up about it.

I stuff a few fries with kimchi, scallions, cilantro, and spicy mayo into my mouth. "But what's good wit' y'all niggas? What's been goin' on? Catch me up on shit. Like whassup wit' work, Bryan?"

He shrugs. "I just got assigned to a redevelopment project, so that's excitin'."

"That's whassup, man."

His face brightens up, talking about it—all the planning meetings, collaboration, and the insightful forums they've been having with the surrounding community. I love that he and Jaquade do what they love for a living. While I went to school for music business and working with my clients *is* in that field, *handling* wasn't what I had in mind. I've always wanted to be an A&R at a record label, but I'm not even sure if that's what I want to do anymore. . . I'm starting to feel like I've reached a plateau in the music biz.

I say, "Can't wait to see what y'all do wit' the place, Bryan."

He nods and knocks back some beer.

"What 'bout you, Quade? Whassup?" I look left to my other best friend.

"Not much. I'm havin' some fun here and there." He wiggles his eyebrows and I know he's talking about women. "But I really just been workin', man. Matter fact, Snootie P actually hit me up. Wants to work on a few songs."

"That's whassup, bro." We dap.

P's my low-maintenance client who *only* contacts me for absolute emergencies. She knows that me and Quade are best friends and that I could've introduced her, but I respect her hustle, wanting to get in the room with him on her own. She's definitely a very talented MC and their collaboration will make waves. I can just hear her murdering on Quade-0-8 beats.

"That's great, Quade." Bryan lifts his beer and he and Quade cheers.

"Thanks." Quade turns to me. "T, how was Antigua?"

I tell them about me lounging around my private villa. Languishing in my own small pool and sliver of beach, watching the turquoise ocean lap up on the white sand and retreat. How I slept for most of the day. Ordered full-course meals.

"Damn. The only way that woulda been the *perfect* vacation was if you had a shorty witchu. Cuz I just heard you say you had tons of private places to fuck," Jaquade says before knocking down the rest of his drink.

I laugh and Bryan scoffs like Jaquade has no couth. "That vacation sounds relaxin', Tim."

I nod, my mind drifting to what Jaquade said while they go back and forth like brothers.

I shouldn't go there but I immediately think about Camesha. I can *easily* imagine her in Antigua with me. *I'm sure she looks amazin' in a* swimsuit—*Stop it, Tim!* I tell myself because we're friends—I think? I don't know if we are, but I *know* that I like her. And I sense she likes me. What I felt at Zay's album release party, I felt seven months ago when we ate Mexican takeout in my Jeep. The energy between us crackled like a Rice Crispy Treat. Our eye contact, our conversation—everything made the space feel claustrophobic.

Looking at Camesha, her scent surrounding me, I fought to keep my dick tamed so as to not scare her off in case she caught a glimpse of him twitching in my pants. Regardless, it still felt good to be near her and to get to know her outside of work mode.

But honestly, it's hard as hell to read Camesha. I don't want to make a fool of myself or make her uncomfortable if I tell her I'm interested, especially if we have to work together again. Either way, I might still have to speak up or I'm going to drive myself crazy.

Since that September day, Camesha and I have texted here and there. Mostly check-ins like what we were doing and where I was, and we'd crack jokes:

Camesha (4:09pm):

> Hey Tim. I know you're somewhere moving faster than wifi lol

Me: (9:37pm):

> Lmao fr. Im beat

Or

Camesha (9:23pm):

> At a gig, surrounded by finance bros debating the return of NFTs

Me (11:49pm):

> That's crazy af Want me to send help?

Camesha (11:55pm):

> Im ok—thanks tho

Or

Camesha (12:34pm):

> Hope you remember to eat something green today—and no, green skittles don't count

Me (5:19pm):

> Damn, then what am I gonna do with all this candy I got?

See, a lot of times, she'd text me first then I'd respond hours, sometimes *days*, later. As soon as I'd have a moment to relax and scroll through my personal messages, I'd fall asleep. I felt awful, always starting a long-awaited message with an apology. But she'd told me that my response time was fine, knowing that I was busy and tired. I also really couldn't call her and listen to her voice like I wanted to either since I was never really alone until I made it back home or to my hotel room. But by then, I'd be fucking exhausted and crash. And when I had a rare day-off, all I wanted was silence, relaxation, and sleep. Camesha has been incredibly understanding of all of this though.

"Where'd ya go, Tim? You were out of it just now," Bryan says, calling me back to the now.

"N-Nuttn." I shake my head and stuff some fries into my mouth. But I can feel their skeptical eyes on me.

Jaquade smirks and sips his drink, eyeing me over the rim of his glass. "Guess who I ran into the other day at BestBuy?"

"Who?" I ask, my mouth full.

"Taylor."

My ex-girlfriend. I pause chewing. "Fa real?"

"Yep—" Jaquade starts.

Bryan jumps in, laughing, "Remember you called y'all TNT?"

"Corny ass," Jaquade mutters, shaking his head, as they both cackle like kids.

I laugh, too. It *was* a corny ship name, but it was cute.

Taylor and I've been broken up for about the same amount of time we were together: two years. Two years of working my ass off. Of reflecting. Growing. Taking inventory of my life and how I spend my time. Thinking about who I want to spend my time with.

"But anyway, she saw me and said whassup. Asked 'bout you," Jaquade continues.

I raise my eyebrows.

"Not like *that*. I think she was just tryna be nice since she only knows me cuz of you." He shrugs before sipping his whiskey.

Tension I didn't even realize I was hoarding in my face subsides. *I was 'bout to say. . .* I mean, I can only say nice things about Taylor, but that doesn't mean I want us to get back together. We aren't on the same type of time. And my mom warned me of that when I told her my girlfriend was three years older than me. I thought I knew and had enough experience at 25 to handle a relationship like that.

Boy was I wrong.

I clear my throat. "Okay. She good?"

"Seems like it. . ." Jaquade trails off.

"Good. She deserves to be good." I shrug.

Quade squiggles his eyebrows.

"Knock it off," Bryan groans.

"Nigga, you know I'm fuckin' wit' him. I know Tim don't wanna get back wit' that girl."

Bryan rolls his eyes and looks at me. "Anyway, speakin' of women, you seein' anybody, T?"

I sit up straight, my body growing hot with nerves just thinking about Camesha. "Not really." They're my boys so why not give them some potatoes with their steak. "Buuuttt there is one girl I kinda got my eye on."

"Who is she? She in the industry? I know her?" Jaquade asks, side-eyeing me.

I don't know if Camesha knows Jaquade or not. I wouldn't think so. He typically doesn't go to industry events unless he absolutely *has* to, like if he had to speak or was being recognized for something. And to my knowledge, his "roster" doesn't include women in the biz.

"I 'on't think you know her. She works in hospitality." *Not a lie since she said she works at The Adonir Hotel.* Plus, it's not my place to out her hustle like that since, from the little I know about Camesha, she's very low-key and private.

Jaquade just nods. "So, whassup wit' her?"

"I've known her since August—"

"And you just *now* tellin' us?" Bryan cuts in.

"There was nuttn to tell before. And no joke, the last time I saw her in person was end of September. Before awards season prep. We've just been textin' since."

"So, y'all friends?" Bryan asks, eyebrows wrinkled.

"Sorta." I stare at the view, LA getting darker as the Sun slides out the way.

Jaquade shakes his head, kissing his teeth. "You need to step ya game up, folk, and go after her. If you want her, let her know. Straight up."

He's right. Jaquade is the blunt one in our group. If he wanted a girl, he wasn't afraid to tell her that and tell her *how* he wanted her. He's been in two serious adult relationships and was loyal to the soil, seeing long-term futures with them. Well, until one cheated, and the other didn't believe they could make long distance work when she accepted a promotion on the East Coast.

Jaquade gets up to bring Mic outside. We take turns playing catch with him, vibing to the music, and talking shit.

But I think about how I'd approach Camesha in the midst of it. I can't just keep staring at her and saying nothing. It's time to come correct.

Sunday, April 22

Camesha

After using the bathroom, I wash my hands and look at myself in the mirror. I have to give it to him: Asa has good taste in lingerie. This lavender one he bought me is so pretty.

I fluff my usual twist-out in the mirror. I still look presentable, able to walk out of this hotel looking un-fucked. I know some girls who *like* people to peep that they just had sex. My goal with this hustle was to not look like I just had my back blown out. And with some of my clients, that's easy to do since they don't have the length, girth, stamina, or experience to do so. I can easily exit an establishment without much primping on my end with some of them.

But not with Asa Guillory. Some primping is required.

I flick the light switch off in the bathroom and open the door. I see Asa still lying on top of the bedcovers, breathing steadily. Butt-naked, still-hard dick in hand, tattooed arm bent behind his head. He's looking at me, eyes half-lidded while a lazy smile stretches his large lips.

He's the client I thought impregnated me last year. That would've been a horrible wrench in my "plan," but I can't lie, our baby would be cute. Asa is a good-looking specimen.

His skin's the color of milk chocolate and it's just as smooth with tattoos covering his arms and pecs. He sports a sponged temp fade and he's growing a beard. He's a 6'5" shooting guard and small forward for the Los Angeles Breakers. A talented player, charitable, and handsome, he's one of the NBA's superstars.

At some events, friendlier hustlers have told me that they were plotting on Asa. I didn't tell them that he's my client and that he *only* sees me. He's shown me his social media DMs: women throwing themselves at him, auditioning to be a hot fuck, his woman, or to have his baby. Asa peeps the tomfoolery and doesn't give any of those women attention. He shared that his parents told him that as his star was rising in college, don't get caught up in all the new "opportunities his status offers him," but to *always* stay focused on his career and give back.

And when he wasn't doing any of that, he called me.

I lean against the bathroom doorframe. Crossing my arms over my chest and smirking, I feel playful. "Whatchu lookin' at me like that for?"

"*You* know why," he says, his voice a low gravel as he bites his bottom lip.

Asa, Ross, and now Eliot are the only clients out of my current seven total with whom I actually cum. I usually suck Asa's dick after he eats my pussy because he does it so well, so eagerly with his skilled, long tongue and fingers. I just want to return the favor before he fucks me good. Plus, the euphoric, pained face he makes when he busts on my chest *always* makes me feel accomplished.

He sits up and scoots to the edge of the bed, his dick still at attention. "C'mere."

Before I can skitter out of his reach, Asa stretches out his long arm and gets ahold of me, gently yanking me to sit on his right thigh. I giggle, noticing his manhood touching my leg like it's the most normal thing in the world. I look down at his bent head as his lips and beard lazily graze my arm before he pecks up to my shoulder.

The scruff from his fledgling beard tickles me, making me giggle. Asa's fingers tilt my head so he could kiss my neck and along my jaw. My eyes fall close, relishing in the feeling of his pillowy-soft lips. His touch is always so gentle, yet hungry. Even after we have sex, he's insatiable, always wanting more. And sometimes I'll give in, and he'll pay me extra, but others, I tell him to save his money.

Before I get too lost in the feeling, I turn my face before Asa kisses me on the lips. He always thinks he's slick. "Aht, aht, aht."

He sucks his teeth before kissing behind my ear. "C'mon, lemme taste you."

"You already did," I drawl, a smirk on my face.

He comes up for air and looks me in the eye, his eyes half-closed, appearing in bliss. "Then taste yo'self. You taste so good." I can smell myself on his breath: sweet and slightly tangy. He licks his thick lips to entice me.

I mean, Asa's got a nice set, but I don't budge. I don't and will *never* kiss clients on the lips. For some reason, the idea of letting a client press his lips to mine, exploring my mouth with his feels . . . too personal, too intimate. Being face to face, nose to nose, lips and tongues intertwined might feel too much like the real thing for me, and *not* a fantasy I'm fulfilling for them.

Satisfy the client, but don't get caught up—that's the game for me.

"I'm sure I do. But you know my rules, Asa," I croak out.

"I know. And you smell so good," he murmurs into my skin before nibbling and sucking it.

I wear the same fragrance every time Asa summons me, the same one I wore when we first met at The Adonir a year and a half ago: Montale's "Chocolate Greedy." He came in for a day spa treatment at the hotel.

"Thank you, honey," I let out, almost moaning.

That makes Asa stop and lift his head. "Don't moan like that, Cammie. Don't be all soft and sweet on me when you *know* I can be soft and sweet on you."

Not this again, I think, my eyes slightly rolling before I can stop them. Sometimes I forget *this* part when I'm with Asa.

He kisses his teeth. "Why you roll yo' eyes?" His arms loosen, allowing me to get off his thigh.

I pluck the matching silk robe he bought me off the bench at the foot of the bed, wrapping myself in it. "Because you know what this is, Asa." It comes out as an exasperated sigh, which isn't what I wanted. I try to always keep my tone flirty and sultry with clients, but damn, Asa is starting to get on my nerves.

"Yeah, but I want more. I wantchu all to myself."

"So, you wanna make me ya own private trick?" I joke so I'd keep my cool. I know what he's really asking me though.

"No, Cammie. I want you to be my woman," Asa enunciates with a serious facial expression, leaning forward to grab my hand. He finally said the words he's been skating around all basketball season.

He doesn't even know my real name, yet he wants me to be his.

Asa is such a good catch. He can literally have any woman he wants *without* paying for it. So, it's beyond me why he wants to pursue a romantic relationship with me. Guess it's true: people always want what they can't have. Desire is stronger when it's forbidden.

I drag my hand from his large grasp, trying to make eye contact, but the genuinely sincere look on his face isn't making it easy. "Asa, I . . ."

"As much as I love sexin' you in these hotel rooms, I also wanna take you on dates, Cammie. I wanna show you off." His eyes drag over my body before returning to mine. "I wanna know all about you. I wanna be witchu, knowin' you *my* woman and no one else's. I want *you*, Cammie."

I drop my head, eyeing my French tip toes.

No lie, a part of me melts at that. I can definitely see him being a great boyfriend or husband . . . just not to me.

Then the other part of me has to stifle a chuckle. Only one other client tried to take me off the hustle, but that was so I *could* be his personal trick whenever he wanted. He promised to pay my bills and give me an allowance as long as I "kept that pussy warm, tight, and wet for him"—his corny words, not mine. I cut him off after that proposal. For some girls, like Zaria, *that's* a dream: to be a kept woman, but not me. This hustle isn't my stopping point.

Asa is something else. I knew he was possessive, cuddling and kissing on me after a session. And while that *feels* good in the moment, I don't allow myself to see him another way. He's a client. And he will always be one even when he isn't anymore. He can't ever *actually* be my man. And I can only be his woman for the time he pays me.

I glance up at Asa, finding him looking at me intently. I go over to him, and he wraps his sinewy arms around me, his huge hands cupping my back and ass. He's just slightly under my eyeline as I stand in front of him. I lift my hand to caress his beard, the black hair soft as my juices moistened it a few minutes ago. "That's sweet, Asa—"

Before I can finish my thought, he eagerly kisses the inside of my palm. He looks so at ease right here, so at peace and satisfied.

But he's really not, and that's precisely the problem. He wants more. And that's what I don't have, can, nor want to give him.

"—but I just can't. You're *only* ever gonna be my client." I drop my hand from his beard.

Asa tries not to let his face morph with disappointment. He clenches his jaw, but it doesn't do it for me like Tim's. "A'ight. Then I'm not ya client anymore." Tenacious. He shrugs like it's that simple.

"Asa—"

"Just tell me what I gotta do to have you, Cammie." He sounds exasperated as his arms relax around me. He's pleading and it makes me sad. He doesn't have to do this. There are so many other women who want what he wants. It's just not going to be me, his escort.

"There's nothin' you can do. I'm sorry."

Asa drops his arms, and I step back, assessing him. His dick is soft now, probably as a result of my rejection. He doesn't look at me as he stands up to his full height, but I eyeball him. I don't believe he'd hurt me, but you never know. One guy gripped my arm too tight and that was the last time I ever saw him. Men can have fragile egos, especially if they're rich, powerful, and aren't used to hearing "no."

Asa approaches me with a slightly pouting face. And to my surprise, he bends down to press a kiss to the side of my forehead. "I'll get out ya space," he mumbles. He bought this hotel suite for us after winning a playoff game at the arena. He came here immediately, skipping the celebration with his team at a penthouse nightclub.

Asa passes me so that he can use the bathroom. When the door shuts, my shoulders fall as a heavy breath escapes me. I rub my temples and collect my clothes from around the room to get dressed to leave.

I might've just lost a client, but it'll be okay. I'm just $50,000 away from my goal.

Thursday, April 26

I'm heading back to Los Angeles. I slip my sneakers back on and collect my champagne-colored carry-on from the bin after passing through the security checkpoint at Orlando International Airport.

Eliot asked if I could keep him company after his speaking obligations at a three-day tech conference in Orlando. I just stayed in the hotel he put me up at—ordering food, watching TV, swimming at the pool, and sleeping like a newborn.

When he came to my room, he divulged *way* too much. He told me that his stay-at-home wife, Tess, would usually join him on trips like that, but their second youngest child, Chandler, is sick and their babysitter was on vacation, so she stayed home.

I notice when Eliot is nervous or if it's too quiet, he starts yapping. Too much. Needing to fill silence with explanations or small talk. That's when I mount him or demand him to eat me out. He likes it when I'm assertive, and him making me cum keeps me levelheaded to deal with him.

Eliot offered to have a driver take me to and from the airport, but I declined, reminding him to leave as little a trail as possible so that his wife didn't find out about our arrangement. He said, "You're right. Thank you." Eliot is so new to this life, that it's a *tinge* cute that he's naïve, but I don't want any drama with his wife. I don't care how chill he says she is.

It happened once and that was enough: a client's wife called from his phone to confront me. Needless to say, I dropped that man from my roster like leftovers past their prime—ain't worth the risk.

So, I Ubered to the hotel and to the airport.

The weather here is nice, sunny and blue, so the plane should have no delays. I buy a water bottle before locating my gate. My gate is sparse, only a handful of people who showed up early like me. I plop down in a chair parallel to the massive windows. I retrieve my charger from the carry-on to juice up my phone with one of the outlets between my seat and the other next to me.

I scroll through the Google Alerts on my famous clients. I like to keep up with them in case it's useful in the light conversation we have. You know, big their heads up if it's something worth praising. And they might tip me if I stroke their ego enough. Plus, it comes in handy to see who I need to cut off.

Speaking of, I cut off Zay Dubb$. I didn't like the way he carried himself when he learned he wasn't the father of GiGi Savage's baby. He didn't defend her, letting his fans talk crazy to and about her online when I'm sure he knew her enough to shut that shit down. I felt bad for GiGi, so I hope she had some support in her corner.

But no lie, I will miss Zay's jaw-dropping tips. I texted him that I was done then blocked his number, but he had Tim reach out on his behalf and I still declined his many enticing offers.

The only awards season request I had came from Ashton Weeks, lead singer/rapper of the country-rock band The Crossroaders. He flew me out to Nashville since they were nominated for a Country Music Award. They didn't win in their category, so instead of celebration, he paid me so that he could cry with his head in my lap while I ran my fingers through his curly hair. Then to make himself feel better, he sloppily sucked on my titties and toes. Poor baby was going through it. Ashton didn't give me foot fetish vibes, but he's very layered, able to be rough then gentle, cynical then sentimental. Guess that's why he's a good musician.

But back to Tim. I'm a little ashamed to admit it, but I'm *aching* to see him again. To feel his warm energy. To stare into his brown eyes. To hear his voice. To watch his jaw clench.

We've only texted over the last six-almost-seven months. Some award show duties were in LA, so he was around but was just very busy or tired. So, I didn't ask if he was free to hang out again.

When Tim had time and energy to respond, they were welcomed distractions. Tim texted how he talked sometimes, so his messages often made me embarrassingly laugh out loud at The Adonir Hotel's restaurant and lounge while I waited for customers.

I kept replaying our takeout hang over and over again. And how Tim made me wet just from the way he kept looking at me so intently. I just feel like he wanted me and had he made a move I probably would've hesitated off instinct, but I would've given him the green light right there in his truck.

I shake my head to get my mind out of the gutter and chug some water. *Yeah, quench that thirst, girl.*

My phone rings. It's one of my best friends, Nikki. I answer it and hold my phone to my ear.

"Hey, girl." She sounds in good spirits. It's three o'clock here, so it's around lunchtime in LA.

"Hey, Nik. Whassup?"

"Just eatin' my lunch, chil'. I wanted to check up on you. See if you were on schedule to get home."

I hear a dragging, scratchy sound on her end. Chuckling, I imagine her filing her nails while lounging back at her desk, half-eaten sushi in front of her, while her favorite gossip YouTube show plays lowly on the flat-screen in her office.

I smirk. "I'm waitin' at my gate now. You missed me?"

"Yeah, girl. And that old bitch gettin' on my nerves." She updates me on her beef with her co-worker, explaining that she filed an HR complaint to see if that'll fix the problem. The shit sounds straight out of a movie.

"Anyway," Nikki exhales, "nuff of that old bitch. I also wanted to see if you wanna go to Bassment 323 wit' me and Trina next Friday night."

"Oh."

Bassment 323 is a club in a . . . well, basement of a hardware store off Melrose Avenue. It's definitely giving speakeasy vibes with its unmarked door. Only LA natives and long-term transplants hang out there. I've seen a few celebrities stop by for uninterrupted fun. No one really bothers them and if they do, it's all love and peace. But my friends and I will typically go to Bassment 323 after work on Tuesday or Wednesday during happy hour, *not* on a prime night like Friday and Saturday. I'd imagine it'd be harder to get into the club since they only let a certain amount in there at a time to keep it intimate.

Plus, I've only hung out with Nikki's friend Trina two other times. She seems nice, but I try to keep my circle *really* close knit, so close that it's really a triangle.

"C'mon, girl. You've been busy wit' these niggas, but I wanna see my bitch. Now, I can't pay you, but I *can* buy you a drink. Plus, I *know* that pussy needs a break anyway."

Her crazy ass makes me laugh, causing a few strangers to glance my way before returning to their loved ones or their devices. "You're a trip."

She chuckles, "I'm serious. It'll be a nice, chill night, Camesha."

I remove the phone from my ear to quickly look at my calendar to see if I'm available. No gigs. "Let's do it."

Nikki squeals in my ear. "Yaaasss, *that's* my girl. And I'm serious 'bout that drink, but only one, bitch."

I laugh. "Of course. Don't wanna run ya pockets."

"Yeah, cuz I ain't one of ya tricks. My money ain't *that* long."
Nikki works in marketing at a talent agency, so while her money
ain't that long, it's enough to keep her comfortable and afford
her expensive nightlife budget.

"So, we gettin' a table?"

"Yeah. One of Trina's patients rolled over her foot wit' their
wheelchair, so we *definitely* sittin'."

"Oh my God. She okay? She can go out?"

"Yeah, she's fine. This night was her idea. I asked her if I can
invite you. I knew Lu was gon' go to bed early before her big
open house the next day." Our other bestie is a real estate agent
with some celebrity clients.

"Okay, well as long as we have a table, I think that'll be nice."
A smile touches my lips. It's been a minute since I've had a night
out when I'm not working the room or a client.

"Cool, lemme make this reservation. Text me when you
land."

"I'll text you *both* in the group chat."

Nikki scoffs and says lowly into the phone, "Girl, quit playin',
ya know I'm ya favorite."

I roll my eyes, chuckling. "I love both of y'all *equally*."

Nikki always talking about a beef with that old lady at her
job, meanwhile she's been having a one-sided beef with Oluchi
to claim the "bestest best friend spot." There's no hierarchy. I'm
eternally grateful to have finally found people I can trust and
depend on out here. Those first years in Los Angeles were rough
as hell because I lacked that. But Nikki and Oluchi's authenticity
broke through my many walls. They earned my trust and now I
can't imagine life without them.

"All right," Nikki fake whines. "Love you. See ya soon."

"Love you, too."

We hang up and I relax into my seat. Then I see the plane
taxiing into my gate, making me sigh in relief.

6

God Really Loves Me

Friday, May 4

Tim

Bassment 323 is live as hell tonight. I usually come here with Bryan and our friend Moe, but tonight I just wanted to go out alone. Plus, this club attracts many other solo partyers, so it's not that weird I'm by myself.

It's Freestyle Friday, so the visiting DJ has been spinning and scratching the fuck out of these songs. I mean, everything from electronica-house to dry-humping R&B. Now, he transitions from "Back To Life" by Soul II Soul to "Just Fine" by Mary J. Blige. The folks occupying the small dance floor go dumb. One group even starts doing a line dance I've never seen before. I'm leaning back on the counter opposite the bar, just bobbing my head to the song, screwing my face up as I try to follow their moves. Yellow and purple lights dart around in sync with the beat.

Tonight, I've just done this: vibed and watched on the sidelines.

Bassment 323 is such an intimate and immersive experience, which is why I like coming here. It's unpretentious, just a place for LA to let their hair down, chill, drink, and dance. The music feels omnipresent here, courtesy of their amazing surround sound system. I can feel it thumping in my chest, leaving my body cloaked in warmth.

I turn around and grasp my whiskey and rum cocktail to take a sip. But none falls into my mouth. I've been here for two hours and have sipped two of those. Cupping the empty glass, I head for the bar across the room, shimmying through the crowd.

Bassment 323 looks like an unfinished rectangular basement. Exposed reddish-gray bricks and ductwork. Concrete walls and floor.

The layout is brilliantly simple. The DJ booth is to my left against the wall. The bar is to the DJ's left. Six groups of black leather couches and coffee tables with Edison bulb lamps are set up near the hallway to the bathrooms, small-plates kitchen, and the vestibule. Eclectic art hangs on the walls, too—some abstract, some mixed materials.

At the bar, I stand at the end closest to the DJ booth. The music is almost making my skin vibrate. I set my glass down and wait to flag down the bartender since he's with a customer on the other end. I quickly check my phone for the time, seeing it's now after midnight.

On the other side of the bar, the silhouette of a woman sidles up. I can't really see her since the only light in this area comes from the blue-backlit bottle shelves. Everywhere else is dim and briefly lit by the darting lights. She looks down at her phone and I squint to get a better look at her. And when she glances around, I damn-near freeze, breath stilling in my body.

Camesha.

Damn. After seven months of not seeing her in person, this feels like the first time all over again. She's gorgeous and glowing in this dark room. Gold highlight touches her cheeks and . . . *her nose? Oh my God, that's cute as shit.* Medium-sized gold hoops and a dainty necklace compliment her makeup. Her long hair is in a low ponytail with a few curls dangling down the sides of her pretty face. And she appears to be wearing a dark-colored long tube top.

As my eyes zoom in to slowly study her frame, my jaw tightens. My pulse quickens, threatening to leap out of my neck as my chest thumps—not from the music, but my rising anxiety. I start hyperventilating through my nose, but the air in here is stuffy.

I have to talk to her.

I dig through my jeans pocket—and thank God I brought my mints with me. I pop one into each side of my mouth before heading over there, gently nudging folks out the way.

The bartender arrives and takes her order. Camesha's attention returns to her phone as I step up next to her.

Before the bartender can leave, I say, "Yo, man, can ya get me a water?" and slide my empty glass to him.

"Sure thing," he says with a grin and turns to get to work.

Camesha must've not heard me as she's still scrolling her phone. I lean in a little, keeping a respectful distance. "I hope ya ordered some water wit' all those drinks, Camesha."

She snaps her head in my direction with a slight scowl on her face. Like a "Who the fuck is talkin' to me? And how do they know my name?"-type of face. I watch as she slowly recognizes me, her face relaxing. To my surprise, she jumps me into a hug, throwing her arms around my neck. "Oh my God—Tim!"

Chuckling, I catch her, my arms circling her midriffed waist. *God, her skin is so soft.* My eyes slowly close as I get deliciously lost in the "Good Girl" fragrance emanating from her warm neck. I try not to be a creep and inhale her, but my nose has a mind of its own.

Then suddenly, Camesha low-key pushes me off of her. *Shit, did I make her uncomfortable?* I wonder. She avoids eye contact a little as she tries to move her tendrils behind her ear, but they bounce back in place. *Why is she so cute?* Just as I'm about to apologize, she speaks up, "Sorry. I didn't mean to crowd ya personal space like that."

"Nah, it's cool. I-I was actually gonna ask if I can give you a hug." I lock my jaw as if I can take back what I already admitted.

"Oh. . . Y-Yeah, you can hug me." She finally looks up at me, all bashful, her eyes encapsulated in a smoky color and winged eyeliner. Camesha's painfully cute and fine as hell.

"Cool." I clear my throat. "I can't believe you're here."

She grins. "I can't believe *you're* here. I've never seen you here before."

A smile curls on my face. "Oh, I be here, girl."

She giggles, tilting her head.

"I usually come Friday or Saturday nights."

"Oh, okay. I come wit' my friends on Tuesday or Wednesday happy hour."

"Here you go." The bartender calls out, sliding water to me and setting two cocktails on top of tiny white napkins.

Camesha and I both say "thank you" at the same time and laugh like kids. Dude smiles and slides to the left to help other folks.

"So, happy hour, huh?" I lean on the bar, watching Camesha over the rim of my glass as I sip. The music fades into the background and all I see and hear is her. I peep her two-toned lip gloss, flared pants, and heels to complete her outfit. She's looking so good tonight that I have to restrain myself from biting my bottom lip.

"Yeah. . ." She looks at a loss for words, like I am. Her features soften as she watches me watch her.

I set my drink down, just shaking my head to hide my twitching neck and taut jaw. "I ain't even gon' hold you, Camesha. . ." I lose my train of thought as I try to maintain eye contact and not scan her body again. "You look absolutely *amazin'*. Like, ya hair, ya makeup, just everything—," I word vomit, but it's the truth.

Camesha

Tim squeezes his eyes shut like he didn't mean to say *all* of that, like the alcohol aided his boldness.

Under his penetrating gaze, I feel hot. In every sense of the word. Then again, I am wearing black at a club, so that could be it.

I feel like a nerdy teenage girl, blushing at one of the popular boys telling me I'm cute.

Tim is looking *so* good tonight that I have to cross my legs to discreetly clench my thighs to keep my clit from jumping. He's sporting a white tank top underneath an open boxy black denim shirt and jeans set with white stitching. His same two chains sit on his chest. Something about seeing some of his chest with those necklaces against it do something to me. His curls look juicy, and his facial hair is neat. *Ugh, his lips look more kissable than ever—Down, girl, down.* A quick glance and I see he's rocking the classic "Chicago" Air Jordan 1s.

And when I surprised my damn self by hugging him earlier? Oh my God . . . he smelled like another one of my favorite masculine fragrances: Dior's "Sauvage." Oluchi says that the scent is very basic now, having "lost its edge," but I don't care, the shit smells good.

I snap out of it to respond to his compliments. "Thank you, Tim. You look," *Keep it cute, keep it classy, Eesh,* "great. And it actually looks like we're sorta matchin' a bit."

He stands up to his full height to dramatically scan himself and me head to toe. "Oh, shit, we are!"

I chuckle.

"Not you tryna copy my swag, girl. *I* rock all black when I step out." He smirks, pointing at himself.

I playfully roll my eyes and push him in the arm before I can stop myself. *Anything to touch him, huh?* "What-ever."

Tim's face morphs into something more serious. "Aye, and I know I've said this a thousand times, but I *really* am sorry for not hittin' you back in a timely manner these last few months."

It's cute that he's this worked up about it. My head tilts as I say, "It's okay, Tim. I understand. *Really*. You were busy. No need to keep apologizin'."

A grin touches his lips. "Okay."

I return the smile. And then I remember something: "Oh shit! Lemme get these drinks over to my friends."

"Oh, you not here alone?"

"No. Are you?"

"Yeah. . . I do that sometimes." Tim shrugs.

"That's cool." I wish *I* could do that, but I don't want to be bothered—swatting men away or rejecting their unsolicited drinks.

"Glad you think so. My boy Jaquade thinks that's weird," he chortles.

I laugh, shaking my head. "I'll be right back."

"Fa sho. And uh, you, uh," Tim's face twists up as he points behind him, "you wanna dance?"

My heart flutters at his invitation. I shouldn't be feeling this giddy on the inside, but despite myself, excitement gets the best of me, tugging my lips into a wide smile. "I'd love to."

His lazy, heated gaze slowly slides over different parts of my face. Then Tim does the thing I love. He *clenches* his jaw and licks his lips. *Okay, he* must *be doin' it on purpose now.* "A'ight, cool."

I shoot him one last grin before collecting the cocktails and leaving. As I leave the bar, I hear Tim gulp his water and it makes me smirk, thinking back to when he told me to hydrate after I had a strong cocktail at Zay Dubb$'s album release party.

"Whatchu all smiley for?" Nikki asks.

I must've floated here because I don't remember my short walk. *Be careful, Eesh—gettin' gone off this man over nothin',* my conscience says.

"Nothin'." I shake my head to be present here and sit the drinks down on our coffee table.

I don't want to tell Nikki about Tim yet. I want to keep this to myself for right now because I don't want her to get excited if our connection is a fluke. But my *heart* is telling me that's not the case. That there's been something brewing between us since we met at Zay's birthday party. And I intend on finding out more, maybe even call it out to see if Tim is feeling what I'm feeling. Dancing with him should help.

"Took you forever to get the drinks. Is the bartender on some bullshit? Wait 'til I tell Cassidy 'bout this."

"No, girl, there was a slight . . . wait." I smirk at her mention of Cassidy. "Please, don't tell ya boo 'bout the bartender."

"He is *not* my boo." She rolls her eyes as she flips her goddess braids over her shoulder and leans forward to sip her margarita.

Cassidy handles reservations and events here. I saw the way he looked at Nikki tonight when he checked on us. I'm sure he moved Heaven and Earth to get us this section when she called the club with little notice. He must have a soft spot for her, but she's too stubborn to admit it because I *know* she peeped.

"And thank you for the drink," Nikki rushes out as she side-eyes me.

She's bold like only she knows how to be in a red lip, satin camisole underneath a leather biker jacket, wide-leg pants, and spiky stilettos.

"Yeah, thanks, Camesha," Trina says, taking her second tequila soda of the night.

"Y'all welcome."

We've been taking turns buying drinks for each other all night. As promised, Nikki bought me one drink, a rosemary lime rum punch. We've picked at some small plates throughout the night since we didn't go out to dinner beforehand. We've chatted, danced, and sang and rapped when the DJ played "our shit." Some men have approached our section, asking us to dance and the girls obliged. I didn't.

Until now.

Like Nikki said, tonight has been a nice break. And now I want to continue it with Tim. I *have* to.

"I'll be right back." Before they can say anything, I head in the direction of the bathroom and when I'm too far away in the dark, I change directions and beeline for the bar.

Tim is lounging back against the bar, holding his water as he watches the crowd dance languidly to a funky house song. He looks really relaxed. And I wonder how many drinks he's had tonight.

"Hey," I say.

"Hey." Tim knocks the rest of his water back and flexes his jaw again. I have to glance away, or I'd melt into a puddle, like the one beginning to squish in my panties right now. "C'mon." He stands up straight and gently grabs my hand to lead me to a spot on the dance floor.

This whole thing's giving me déjà vu. Tim's warm hand—not clammy this time. This angle of his back and shoulders in front of me. Us weaving through a crowd. He's bobbing his head to the current song, but I'm so distracted, I can't even hear it.

Then what feels like lightning bolts strike my stomach. Tim slows down and turns to face me, dropping my hand in the process. I'm nervous as fuck right now. *What kinda dancin' was he talkin' about? Does he want me to twerk on him?*

So many other questions fly in my head, but when the DJ starts "squabble up" by Kendrick Lamar, the club erupts and more people flood the space, pressing Tim and I closer together.

He catches me as I stumble in my heels. I look up at him, my eyes slightly dropping to his mouth.

My breath hitches, but I mouth "I'm okay" and he smiles. Tim starts two-stepping with hand gestures as he raps along with Kendrick. I laugh as he makes funny faces at me. He's doing his thing, which makes me feel comfortable to do mine. My eyes fall closed as I just let the music guide me, letting loose like I'm at home.

Somehow, I end up with my back to Tim as he raps other songs in my ear, making me giggle when he changes the lyrics to say something funny. Then the next thing I know, one of my favorite Afrobeat songs comes on: "Drogba (Joanna)" by Afro B—another thing Oluchi, a Nigerian-American, clowns me for being basic. The whole club screams. Green and red lights flash around the room.

My hips have a mind of their own as they start swaying. Tim catches the rhythm and dances *with* me. With his warm body against mine, I feel every shift of his movement and when he lightly cups my exposed waist with both hands, electricity shocks through me like a man has never touched me there. Well, not a man I *like* in a long time. Tim's touch leaves me tingling, wanting more.

Throwing caution to the wind, I throw my ass back on Tim with the music and he catches it. Not really dry humping me, but enough to show me he's got some mobility in his hips—a pleasant surprise. *Okay, sir!*

I glance over my shoulder, finding Tim's heavy-lidded eyes and his bottom lip between his teeth. He registers me looking and licks his lip before lazily smiling at me. *Did he do that to tease me?* My heart skips a beat at the sight. *Oof, if I didn't have a drop of self-control right now, I'd pull his head down and kiss him.*

Then the DJ slows down the vibe with "Hrs & Hrs" by Muni Long. *Ugh, I love this song, too.* Red lights in sync with the beat shoot across the dance floor. I'm so loose and relaxed—the music is a sedative. My eyes closed, my head lolls back onto Tim's chest as I slowly roll and grind my body on him.

He follows my lead, keeping his body glued to mine. I can feel him watching me, but I keep my eyes closed as I let my body do its thing in response to this song. One of Tim's hands wrap around my waist, pulling me closer to him.

Muni sings about getting devoured, instantly making my walls clench at the thought of *Tim* devouring me. His face dips down even more because I can feel his nose rapidly pulling in and pushing out air on my exposed neck and shoulder. Goosebumps explode on my skin. The smell of Tim and "Sauvage" overpower all of my senses.

I get hot in the best way because we're so close. This feels intimate. Like we *aren't* dancing. The crowd melts away and it feels like it's just me and Tim on the floor.

I feel reckless as I grind my ass into his crotch a little more deliberately. I almost jump when I feel his erection through his jeans, but it makes me smirk. *Uh oh, he might be packin' a lil' some'-some'.* Any common sense or hesitations crumble away, if only for the night. *Thank you, alcohol.*

The air feels different now. Thicker. Hotter. Claustrophobic like it was in his Jeep all those months ago. We're so close but not close enough. Not in the way I'd want.

And I want *him*. Which feels weird to admit.

We haven't seen each other in person in so long and when we do, we grind in a small basement club. This whole thing is surreal, yet feels effortless, like we've danced together before. Like we *are* together.

The DJ transitions to a song I don't know and it's as if a haze lifted. My surroundings merge back into focus, and I feel my armpits prickle with sweat. My heart is beatboxing in my chest so hard. From dancing so intimately with Tim to the hot air, I feel like I might pass out.

I unravel from Tim's arms and his overwhelming presence to stagger my way to the bar. My legs feel like jelly after all that dancing in heels like I was Megan Thee Stallion. Upon arrival, I wave the bartender over and ask for water.

Before I know it, I'm gulping water and Tim is leaning on the bar next to me. "You wanna get outta here?"

Mid-swallow, I almost choke. My body stills and goosebumps reemerge. *Is he askin' what I* think *he's askin'?*

"We can go to Canter's Deli and get some bigger plates. I 'on't know 'bout you, but I'm *starvin'*," he chuckles.

My breathing returns to normal. *Of course. Food.* I face him. "Yeah, I'm kinda hungry, too."

He smiles. "A'ight, cool. I'mma use the bathroom, then we can go?"

"Yeah. Lemme tell my friends."

"Bet."

I watch Tim leave, a slightly loose swagger in his gait. Again, unhurried and present.

Honestly, I'm excited. I don't know what's going to happen next, but I'm trying not to think too far ahead and just enjoy this moment by spicy moment.

Tim

I hang out in the vestibule, waiting for Camesha to wrap up with her friends. I'm trying so hard not to jump for joy that I'm pacing like an addict. If the security guard wasn't standing outside, I'm sure he'd tell my ass to calm down.

And man, that moment on the dance floor was *everything*. The way it felt like it was just us out there, I saw and felt no one but Camesha. The way her body moved against mine. Her fat ass grinding on me. Her "Good Girl" and hair products filling my nose. Her exposed neck and shoulder looking lickable. She looked and felt so good that I had to restrain myself from kissing her. Even my damn mouth was salivating, and I bit my bottom lip to keep everything at bay. This woman was turning me on so hard that my dick kept poking her while she grinded on me. I'd be embarrassed as fuck if it wasn't a normal response. Shit, a part of me thinks she danced on me like that *knowing* I'd get hard.

But anyway, the sound of clicking heels makes me look up, seeing Camesha approach with her purse in hand.

I clear my throat. "Ready?"

She nods.

Without thinking, I gently grab her hand and open the door for her to walk out first.

The guard bids us a safe trip home as we walk up the ramp to get to the parking lot.

Bassment 323 is located underneath a hardware store, so the parking lot is spacious. It's in the 60s outside and cloudless. The coolness helps further sober me up, airing out my tipsy haze.

A slight breeze makes me glance at Camesha. She doesn't have a jacket on, and her shoulders are hiked up to her ears. I already know the answer, but I ask her with a chuckle, "You cold?"

"No," she answers through gritted teeth as she shivers.

I scoff, laughing. "Camesha, if you cold, just say that. Hol' on." I let go of her hand and stop walking to remove my denim shirt and drape it over her shoulders.

"But aren't *you* gonna be cold?" she asks, looking all adorable under my shirt.

"I'll be a'ight. You look like you need it more than me. Besides, I think I have another shirt in my car."

Camesha pulls my shirt tighter around her, looking cozy and warm. "Thank you, Tim. I knew I shoulda brought a jacket."

"Of course. C'mon." I gently guide her by the small of her back toward my Jeep. I open the passenger door for her, and before she gets in, she turns around, peering up at me curiously. "What?"

Camesha rubs her glossed lips together. My jaws twitch at that. "Tim, do you . . . open doors for every woman?"

My heart rate revs up as my body gets hot. "Uh, no, not all the time."

"Why not?" she asks softly, her eyes darting across my face. I notice a slight rapid rise and fall of her chest but avert my gaze so I'm not staring at her breasts.

"It doesn't always cross my mind—I mean, I also don't floss every night. I *brush*, but I be forgettin' to floss," I sneak in a joke to deflect.

She giggles but keeps going, "So why does openin' doors cross ya mind wit' me?"

I just look at her, the *real* reason clogged in my throat. She stares back at me, waiting.

Then a clanking metal sound makes me whip my head around and I see a group of homeless men pushing their mobile homes, cussing up a storm. "C'mon." I just about shove Camesha in the car and she lets me. I circle to my side and get in, locking the doors. A puff of air escapes my mouth. *Saved by the grocery cart bell.*

The real reason is that I like Camesha. Simple as that. I like to think of myself as a gentleman, but I also just want to make her feel special. I hope my actions have shown her that I like her but tonight might be the night I do like Jaquade and just come out with it.

I start my Jeep and turn on the heat. Camesha's quiet as I rifle through my backseat for an extra shirt.

"You 'on't have an extra shirt?" she asks a moment later.

"Nah. I think I wore 'em all and they're in my dirty hamper." I turn around and put my seat belt on.

I look at her and see a concerned expression on her face. "Do you want ya shirt back?"

"Are you warm?" I offer her a lopsided smile.

"Not yeeettt," she sings.

I chuckle, "Then keep it." I pull off toward Canter's Deli.

Camesha

My panties are wet. From Tim's smile, to him making me blush, to the shape of his pecs and arms in this tank top... I'm surprised he doesn't have any visible tattoos.

Tim's not super muscular, but he's lean and toned. The muscles in his arms flex and ripple as he turns the wheel. I have to look out the window as my heart flutters. His shirt smells so good, but I don't want to be weird and sniff it. I feel hot in his truck... And it's not the heat blowing from his AC.

I noticed he didn't really answer my question about him opening doors for me. I try not to get too ahead of myself and think too much into it. But damn, maybe he doesn't like me like that. I was hoping his answer would reveal something I can hold onto. So that our moment on the dance floor didn't just *feel* like we have a connection, but that it *confirmed* it.

Anyway, the soft sounds of Tim's music—a Maxwell song about getting to know a woman—plays in the background. I take a glimpse of him, seeing him bob his head. He catches me and cracks a smile.

I smile and turn my head, my cheeks betraying me with blush blooming under my skin.

Soon, Tim's turning into the Canter's Deli parking lot where there are a few cars. As soon as he throws his truck in Park, Tim's out to open my door. I can't help but smile at his chivalry.

I grew up with a daddy who opened doors for my mama, me, and my sister. He wanted us to know how real men treat women. Too bad I've gotten so *unused* to that treatment since I moved to Los Angeles. But Tim's changing that.

"Thank you," I say as I get out the car, holding my purse.

Tim grins. "Of course."

"The professional and the gentleman strikes again," I mutter.

He throws his head back and cracks up, the sound and sight of his joy making me warm despite the cool air. I like that I'm able to make him laugh like he makes me laugh.

"Yooo, that'd be a fire LinkedIn banner." Tim lightly grabs my hand.

Other times, he asks if something is okay, but when it comes to holding my hand or when his hands found my waist on the dance floor, he doesn't ask. Almost as if he wants to make sure I'm with him, that I'm within reach in case shit goes down.

Or at least, that's what I'm telling myself as we stroll on the sidewalk.

"Oh, here! I 'on't think I'mma need this in here." I take off his shirt and hand it to him.

He arches an eyebrow. "You sure? I'm good."

"I'm pretty sure you need to wear a shirt inside."

He shrugs. "A'ight. I get it. You 'on't want me lookin' like a *ruffian in this fine establishment*," he says with a faux white woman accent, making me cackle.

Tim slips on his shirt then opens the door for me. I throw a "Thank you" over my shoulder. And next thing I know, a host sits us in a red half-circle booth. I've only eaten here once, on a first date with an LA native who was showing me around when I first moved here.

Tim and I are sitting in the back, slightly secluded from other people. We can see the entire restaurant in front of us—Well, *I* can't since Tim is sitting in that seat. *Awww, does he wanna keep an eye on the front door for safety reasons?* I shake my head to snap out of that thought and focus on the large menu.

An older white woman with a top bun and a pen behind her ear comes over. "Hi folks. Can I start you off wit' somethin' to drink?"

Tim and I both say water, and she grins, saying she'll return soon for our order.

"Glad to see you stayin' hydrated," Tim jokes.

I roll my eyes, fighting a laugh. "Stop! I was *not* drunk at Zay's party."

He smiles all big. *God, he's so cute.* "I know, I'm fuckin' witchu. I was feelin' my whiskey sour that night. I think that club just makes strong-ass drinks."

I nod before we both peruse the menu. "Whatchu feelin'?"

"Uh, I'm thinkin' The Sunrise, a classic bacon egg and cheese. You worked up my appetite, tryna keep up witchu on the dance floor, girl."

My cheeks warm at him mentioning our dance. A giggle tumbles out of me. "Well, you knew *every* word to every song."

He shrugs, smiling. "I love music."

My eyes roam his face. He *looks* refreshed at one-something in the morning. His skin is clear, no bags under his eyes. "How are you doin', Tim?" *Don't make it sound grave, girl.* "Like, after award season and all."

He blows out some air. "I'm good, Camesha. Thank you for askin'." He nods and grits his teeth. "I was gettin' sick of a few clients, but I survived, and they all did pretty well out there."

I chuckle.

"How are you?"

Just then the AC makes a shiver rip through me. "I guess I'm cold," I laugh.

Without saying anything, Tim slides closer to me. "Maybe body heat will help."

Something warm blooms in my chest being this close to him again. I just look at Tim as he stretches his arm across the back of the booth. Instinctively, I scoot closer to him, and I *do* feel warmer.

"You need my shirt again? Or you good?" he asks, just loud enough for me to hear him inches apart.

I nod as the waitress returns. Tim orders The Sunrise with potatoes and I'm having two fried eggs, toast, and a fruit cup. She collects our menus before leaving.

"How you been, Camesha? I can't believe it's been, like, *seven* months," he exhales, his breath smelling minty, making me wonder if he threw in a mint when I went to the bathroom where I also had one. I appreciate a man who likes having fresh breath.

"Me neither. Yet it feels like we were *just* in ya Jeep eatin' takeout from *my* favorite Mexican spot," I joke.

A smile stretches across his face. "You *claimin'* that muhfucka. I really can't like 'em, huh?"

My eyes twitch to his slightly agape lips. *Just* for a second. "Nah, you can like 'em, too." My voice is too soft. Too shy. I'm *not* shy. But I am around Tim. He just disarms me.

"Camesha," Tim says before licking his lips. He sits up in his chair, his eyes swimming in mine. "The reason I make sure to open your doors is because I *like* you."

I must've not heard him right. I *must've* because it's not computing in my brain. I start hyperventilating, shallow breaths rolling too high in my chest. My heart skips several beats. My stomach cramps up. And it's not because I'm physically hungry.

Tim's eyes rapidly ping-pong between mine. The muscles in his jaw flex like crazy. *A nervous tic?* I surmise.

"I like you, too," I exhale, a weight fleeing from me.

A ghost of a smile hangs in the corner of his mouth. "Really?"

I nod ever so slightly.

Something shifts in Tim's gaze as he slowly looks down at my lips then back up to my eyes. "Might be a lil' too soon, but," his jaws tighten again, "may I kiss you?"

A little too eagerly, sounding like a sex-starved widow, I breathe out, "Please do." My inner self rolls her eyes at the desperation in my voice. I haven't kissed a man in *years*, and I'm almost scared I don't know how.

But the worry dissipates as Tim leans down. Both of our eyes fall close as our lips meet. *Oh my God, his are so soft.*

At first, it's a long smooch. But then I open my mouth, letting him know to keep going.

Tim follows suit, our lips folding into one another. I can't help it—my hands cradle his face, feeling the jaws I've ogled for too long. My heart has skipped so many beats, I'm afraid I might have a heart attack.

His hand that rested along the top of the booth falls behind me and firmly pulls me closer to him by my left hip. His other hand cups the back of my neck as he introduces his big tongue into my mouth. *Fuuuccckkk, I knew his mouth was big!* A moan escapes me during our exploration. This feels so fucking good.

Tim lets go of my neck and grips my left thigh. Like he'd try to pick me up to straddle him in this booth.

And crazy part is, I would let him.

Tim

Gotdamn! I'm happy as hell Camesha said she likes me back. I had a feeling, but to hear her say *it* makes me feel like Zay at his parties: high as fuck. I thought we'd share a nice little peck, but *she* wanted more, and more I *definitely* wanted to give her. I've been desiring this woman since I first saw her. And that hasn't eased up as I got to know more about her these last several months.

Feels good to know that Camesha desires me, too.

I palm her thick-ass thigh, really wanting her on top of me. If we get kicked out of Canter's Deli because we're making out, fine by me. I want her bad like a fat kid wants cake.

Camesha's soft lips feel heavenly. Her acrylic nails clutching my face adds another sensation. Her scent this close and personal? *Fuuuccckkk.* My dick jumps and thank God there's a table in front of us, so people can't see just how good she's making me feel. I'm breathing hard as hell through my nose to keep my groans at bay though the pleasure of this kiss and the pain of my stiffening dick is making that challenging.

I hear somebody clearing their throat and placing plates on our table.

I will myself to pull back from Camesha's grasp and her lips. I look up, seeing our waitress. "Thanks," I rasp, my voice now gone.

Before leaving, she gives a fake smile like she wishes we'd stop. *I bet if she kissed Camesha she'd understand.*

I return my attention to Camesha. Her face softer, her eyes low, her pretty lips swollen. She's a gotdamn dream.

"Sorry," she giggles a whisper, the pads of her thumbs swiping my lips. "Got my lip gloss all over you."

I scoff, fighting back the desire to suck her thumbs. *Shit, I've got it bad for this girl.* "It's a'ight. How I look though?"

"Wit' lip gloss on?" she giggles again. Smiling, I nod and she says, "O-kay. . ." Her eyebrows knit in confusion.

"Damn. I was hopin' to hear fine or sexy or some'."

"You're a goofball." We laugh.

There's nothing but eye contact for a moment. I clear my throat to admit lowly, "I've been wantin' to kiss you for a while."

"Me too." Camesha grins, looking so adorable as her nose blows out some air, making a tendril dance. "You think that lady is gonna kick us out?" she chuckles, looking a tad worried.

I chortle, shaking my head. "Nah. I'm sure they get plenty of people comin' in here late at night who be makin' out." I push her plate in front of her.

Then, surprisingly, we both silently bow our heads and say grace.

"You say grace, too?" I ask, taking a bite out of my sandwich. *Oh yeah, that hits the spot.*

"Yeah." She chuckles. "I grew up Baptist. Some habits don't break. I still pray, but not often. . . *And I 'on't read my Bible as much anymore*," she mumbles the last part softly before she cuts and slips some fried egg into her mouth.

"Why not?" I ask mid-chew.

Out the corner of my eye, I see her snap her head to me. "Uh, my hustle, Tim," she says that in a *'duh'* tone, like it's an obvious reason. "I feel weird readin' it, knowin' how I make most of my money."

I scoff, feeling sad that she's judging herself like this. "Camesha, I think it's great that you revere the Word like that, but don't keep yo'self from God. He cares about ya *heart*. And from what I know and seen so far, you got a good heart. And like you said, it's a hustle—a job. He knows that." I bite more of my sandwich, but I notice she's not eating.

"Really?" She looks incredulous, her face twisting up in confusion.

I set my sandwich down on my plate and wipe grease off my fingers with a napkin before turning toward her. "Yeah. And He knows *why* you're doin' it."

"Right. Do *you* care?"

"About ya job? Not really. I *met* you while you were workin'." I chuckle like it's no big deal—It is, but it isn't—I mean, we're not together yet. And I know she's not going to do it forever. Not going to lie and say her escorting hasn't crossed my mind or given me some pause as I caught feelings for her. Because it has. But that pause is as big as a breath before a "yes." Nothing's stopped my mind, heart, and body from wanting to know Camesha.

She tilts her head and pulls her eyebrows together. "Wait, so when we first met, you knew what my role was the whole time?"

A smile overtakes my face. "When I walked up to the buffet table, I ain't know fa sho, but I had an idea. You were too cool and collected to be a guest, so I figured you were definitely one of the vibe models a handler hired. But then when you ran ya game on me, *that* told me," I lower my voice, "the other role you play."

"I was *not* runnin' game." She playfully pushes me, laughing. "I got into character cuz I thought you were a guest."

We laugh. As we calm down, Camesha's face settles into a serious look. "But thanks for sayin' that, Tim—about God. I've never looked at it like that."

A smile touches my lips, and I want to touch my lips to hers again. *But not wit' bacon on ya breath, my guy.* "You're welcome, Camesha."

She grins and leans forward to kiss my cheek.

We continue eating, trading stories about our times at Bassment 323.

It's after 3am by the time we leave Canter's Deli. With my jazz soul playlist serenading us, I drive to her condominium in Inglewood. I unbuckle my seat belt and almost get out to open Camesha's door, but she grips my arm.

"Wait," she says all low.

I whip my head at her, my eyes roaming her face to see if something's wrong. Camesha's not looking in my eyes though. She's looking down at my mouth. *Oh.*

And the next thing I know, her fingers grasp my shirt, pulling me forward over the console. *Oh shit.* Our lips meet and this kiss is hungry, like we both ain't had our late-night breakfast not too long ago. I can taste the sweet fruit she ate as our tongues mingle. Her fingers graze my jawline and slightly tug at my chin hair, making a groan leap out of me. It doesn't hurt, it's just unexpected. And it turns me all the way on as my dick stiffens a little. *Oh shit!*

Camesha pulls back, a dopey smile on her face. I too feel happy drunk, and we've both sobered up from drinking at this point.

"*Damn*," I let out in a whisper.

"Sorry," she laughs, covering her face.

"Nah, don't apologize. Th-That was . . . That was amazin'. *Anytime*, you want a kiss, you get one." I lick my lips, just looking at hers.

She titters. "I will keep that in mind."

"Please do." I hop out the SUV and open her door, helping her onto the sidewalk.

"Thank you, Tim. 'Night—"

"Don't say that yet. I'm walkin' you to ya door," I chuckle, pointing at her building's entrance.

She side-eyes me. "You 'on't have to do that, Tim."

"I know that, Camesha. It's late and dark. I wanna make sure you get in ya place good. Is that okay witchu?" I step closer.

She just stares into my eyes and nods.

"A'ight then." I grab her hand and let her lead the way to her condo. I couldn't stop staring at her ass in these pants and resisted grabbing a handful. I know we just made out—twice—but I didn't want to start touching on her either. Baby steps.

We take her stairs up to the second floor and walk down the hall until we stop on the left. Condo 2N.

Camesha lets go of my hand as she turns around to face me, her back to her door. "I had a lotta fun tonight, Tim. It was great seein' you again." She looks shy, finding the carpet more interesting than my face as she sways her purse in front of her.

I tilt my head to force her to look at me. "It was *lovely* seein' you again, gorgeous."

She grins wide and blushes, making me feel warm inside.

"So, are you . . . are you, uh, doin' anything later today?"

She stares off into space, thinking. "I 'on't think so."

I nod. "Cool. Would you maybe . . . wanna spend more time wit' me?" The high-pitched nervous lilt in my voice makes me want to kick myself as my heart slams against my chest.

"I'd love to." Camesha's voice is raspy now like I've worn her out talking all night. Or she pulled one of her Cammie moves on me. Either way, I love the way she said that, all sultry and shit.

I bite my bottom lip. "A'ight, how 'bout we check in 'round noon? Cuz I 'on't know 'bout you, but I'm not tryna get up before then."

She giggles. "Same."

"I'll call you then." I step closer to her, my hands sliding to her waist to pull her toward me. She immediately cups my face as I kiss her like she kissed me in the car.

As I retreat, her eyes slowly open as she looks up at me under her mascaraed eyelashes.

"Goodnight, Camesha—Or good mornin'. I think either works."

She giggles again, "It does. See ya, Tim."

I back away, watching her unlock her door. She waves at me before closing it and I leave. I march my happy ass back to my Jeep with a goofy-ass smile on my face.

Not only did I have a good night out, but I told Camesha I liked her. She said she liked me. And I didn't get one kiss, but *three*! God really loves me.

7
The Heat Is On

Camesha

The day Tim took me home after Canter's Deli, he called me that afternoon, saying he could get us a table at his favorite brunch place. I was down, way too giddy to hang out with him. It's quite attractive that he's well-connected.

As I got dressed for brunch, Nikki FaceTimed me since I didn't text her when I got home. Whenever we go out and don't leave together—typically, she's the one who leaves with someone—we agreed to call or text to let the other know we were good. I felt bad that I didn't do that since as soon as I got in, I crashed on top of my covers. In the group chat, Nikki complained about this, but on the phone, she let my offense slide and side-eyed me, wondering if I didn't call her because I got "free peen" from the guy I left with. All I could do was laugh at my girl.

I still wanted to keep this thing with Tim to myself. At least for now, until I see if it goes anywhere. And I'm not even sure I can handle that right now, but he damn sure got me intrigued.

When a knock sounded at my door, I knew it was Tim. I hurried Nikki off the phone and hung up. I was nervous and excited, my heart doing a flipping, galloping thing. I opened the door and Tim and I hugged in the hallway like we didn't just see each other hours before.

I was too happy to ride in his truck again. Of course, the view was immaculate. It reminded me of those pictures I saw on Pinterest: a woman's hand cupping the back of her man's head while he drove. Tim isn't my man, but Lord *knows* I wanted to recreate those photos—he looked so good. He peeped me looking at him and cracked a joke, which lessened the thickening tension between us.

Watching Tim drive with the same ease and swag he had back in September was a panty-wetter. Squirming so much in my seat, I realized since being near him that I was in definite need of a good orgasm. I mean, I cum when I'm with Asa, Ross, and when Eliot eats me out, but it's not the same because I know they're my clients. The last time a man who *wasn't* paying me made me cum for real was at least three years ago.

After brunch, Tim and I got real touristy and spent the majority of the day at the Getty Museum. The last time I was there was on a date with the same guy who took me to Canter's Deli. I barely remember his name, but I remembered the views at the Getty were amazing. So, I was excited to see that again, but with Tim.

We took our time, going from building to building, viewing the art and joking around. Or rather, Tim was joking and making me laugh, pretending to be a snooty art critic. We ate a snack there and chilled on the grass, him tickling me as I lounged back in his arms. That felt too natural, just lying like that as I ran a hand along his leg and felt his nose brushing my hair.

Then that evening, we were going to go out for dinner at a low-key Chinese spot, but one of Tim's clients called him with an emergency. I was a little sad that our time was cut short. He apologized and made sure to give me a fulfilling see-ya-later kiss before he dropped me off at home.

I didn't realize how kiss-starved I was until Tim and I kissed the first time. And because that kiss was so amazing, I've craved his lips. His kisses are so full and unrushed. I like that he takes his time with me. If we weren't careful, I was finna become addicted.

At The Adonir Hotel that week, I was beaming a little easier, the smile coming on more naturally, less of a put-on and more genuine. I was even making small talk and joking with customers. Some of my co-workers even noticed, cracking jokes that it *must've* been a man. I waved them off, not wanting to share any of my business.

But they were absolutely right.

Tim texted me throughout that week, too, slipping in unexpected jokes. The text exchanges were very easygoing and nice reprieves from the repetitive monotony of my waitressing and bartending shifts.

At night, if we were both free, we'd call each other—sometimes on FaceTime, others just a phone call. I enjoyed hearing his voice in my ear, the timbre of it warming my body and leaving goosebumps.

None of my escorting clients have requested me. I'm super relieved because I feel like being with them after my time with Tim would feel weird. I'm feeling too good as Camesha that I'm not sure if I'd be able to keep up Cammie's façade while with them.

It's been a very good week. And now I'm home after getting waxed. I have a standing appointment every three weeks with my wax lady, and she always gets me right in her private suite. I like her because she's efficient and doesn't pry, keeping the conversation professional and surface-level. I don't know too much about her and vice versa. Just how I like it.

I connect my phone to my Bluetooth speaker. I play my "Liked" songs on shuffle and "Meditation" by GoldLink, Jazmine Sullivan, and KAYTRANADA starts. I wiggle my hips in circles as I wash my hands and start pulling out ingredients to meal prep for the following week. I usually do this on Saturday or Sunday, but I have a vibe modeling gig tomorrow night, and I'm obligated to stay the whole time.

Besides, me and Tim might hang out on Sunday. . . He said he looks free right now. I can't lie and say I'm not excited to see him in person again. It's wild, but I already miss him.

Even though Tim said what he said about my hustle and God, I'm unsure about dating him—if that's even what we're doing—*while* escorting. He *said* he doesn't care, but he's still a man. If we were to date officially, I'm sure at some point he'd get territorial and would want me to stop. And he's not wrong to want that.

Honestly, I'd probably stop on my own. I couldn't fuck other men and have sex with *my* man at the same time.

But I store that necessary conversation in the back of my brain for a later time.

As I finish washing my vegetables for the week, my music is interrupted by an incoming phone call. I dry my hands on the dish towel then go to my phone on the opposite counter.

I squeal when I see it's my younger sister Simonique. I always seem to miss her calls, and we end up having to schedule another time, but it's nice to just pick up the phone.

"Heeeyyy, Nique!" I answer on speaker phone.

"Eesh!" her raspy voice comes through clearly. "It's been a minute, bitch. A very *long* minute."

I laugh. My God in Heaven, she and Nikki are so similar. "It has. And I'm sorry."

"It's okay. . ." I can almost hear her side-eyeing me, making me chuckle. "Whatchu doin'?"

I grab my chef knife from the block, a cutting board, and now dry bell peppers to start chopping. "Just meal preppin.'"

She kisses her teeth, going on and on about the food not being fresh. And I tell her how it works, knowing her ass is pre-judging the process.

"If you say so." I can imagine her rolling her eyes and I laugh. "Anyway, lemme see you. I ain't seent you in a minute."

I chortle as I drop my knife and change the call to FaceTime. I prop the phone up on my backsplash so she can see me as I keep cutting. "There."

Her phone looks set up on her bedroom windowsill. Simonique and I have the same bronze-brown complexion and she's two inches shorter than me. Our hair is the same texture, except she wears hers short and curly or in protective styles. She's also thicker than me.

It grossed me out when the senior boys in my class would ask to hook them up with my 14-year-old sister! If I could fight them and not get my ass whooped in the process I would've beat the dicks off of them. But instead, I just cussed them out. I tried to protect her from all of that, but her body got her more attention than all of us would've liked. She learned to navigate it though, knowing how to spot the dusties and who deserves her time. I'm proud of her for not letting all that attention get to her and for staying focused on school.

Today, her hair is in long twists with tiny gold jewelry embedded in them. She's chilling in her childhood bedroom, lounging with the Sun in her face, wearing a purple Clemson T-shirt and her cursive nameplate necklace.

She just moved back home and, next week, she's graduating from Clemson University with a Marketing degree and a Brand Communications minor. I am definitely flying back home to see her walk across that stage.

"Ooo, the titties sittin' *perty*." She tilts her head, making a lewd face.

I chuckle, glancing down at my racerback tank and biker shorts. Leave it to Simonique to hype me up unprompted. She's four years younger, but sometimes under her gaze, *I* feel like the roles are reversed. She always makes me blush.

"Quit blushin' like you 'on't know the bad bitch you are. My sis is pressure."

I poke my lips out and snap my fingers before I continue slicing the peppers. "Period."

"Pooh." She beams, showing off her slight gap and dimples.

My parents have a gap, too. That gene skipped me because my teeth go on without a pause. I remember feeling so insecure about it as a kid, wanting "to be a part of the family." Mama would humor and comfort me, while Daddy would just laugh. That phase of my life makes me crack up now at the ridiculousness of it, but back then I was tore up about that.

"I see you reppin' ya school and ya twists look new. You ready to graduate?"

"Oh, I had to hit up Lanelle cuz I was lookin' *to'up*. And hell yes—I am ready, baby." She throws her arms up like *hallelujah*.

I laugh, setting the sliced peppers aside to prep the broccoli for my stir fry.

"*Your* parents, Clifton and LaWanda, are stressin' me the fuck out." Her hands steeple her head.

"I love how you disown them when they gettin' on ya nerves," I crack up.

"I mean, I love 'em, but *damn*! Daddy keep askin' me 'bout that job I thought I had lined up. I 'on't have the guts to tell him that they *went in another direction*." She rolls her eyes, putting air quotes around it. "Mama stay *inquirin'* 'bout my living situation with Destiny in the fall. It's drivin' me insane. Meanwhile, Montrell is fuckin' up, too. This nigga gave the owner of a local brewery the wrong quote for a pop-up event we're plannin' for 'em in a couple months." She clutches her forehead like it's bound to explode. My poor baby.

"Oh my God. Bless his heart," I titter.

Montrell is Simonique's partner in her event planning business. She planned a few Clemson University activities, and they were so popular that people asked her to throw events around the city, too. Then word spread back home in Columbia.

Honestly, I think Montrell is messing up because he's trying too hard to impress her. I've only been around him once, but from that and the stories Simonique shares, it sounds like he has a crush on her. But from the way she's going off, she's not ready to hear that.

"I'm 'bout to *bless* him wit' an ass whoopin' if he keep fuckin' up like this." I laugh as she keeps going. "Might have to cut him out the business soon."

"Easy, tiger. Don't cut up just yet. Let's just get through graduation first, and then you can address everything else after that."

She nods repeatedly. "You right, you right. I can't go to jail these next few days."

"*Ever* in life, the fuck?" We both laugh. "By the way, where are *our* parents?"

"Daddy's cuttin' Ms. Irma's grass and Mama is out wit' her friends."

"Busy bees. I'll have to give 'em a call soon."

Daddy texts me every blue moon, but when I call him, he typically answers. Mama calls me at the weirdest times, and we have to reschedule. I think she sometimes forgets about the time difference. Either way, she sends me Bible scriptures and words of encouragement almost every morning and checks on me throughout the week. She sends different scriptures to Simonique. Mama says they're just based on what the Lord places on her heart to send to her babies.

My heart always swells with appreciation for her messages, for still thinking about me even though I'm so far away and rarely visit. It helps me feel like I'm still at home, connected. *Damn you shame!*

The sound of my knife cutting through the broccoli and hitting the board is the only noise for a moment.

"Eesh, I absolutely *love* your place," Simonique gushes, propping her head on her hand.

I glance back at my living room like I didn't know it was behind me. "Thanks, boo." I love my place, too. Nique always compliments my décor. . .

"Sooo," my sister interrupts my thoughts. I look at her, seeing her wiggle her eyebrows. "When can I visit you in Los Angeles?"

I knew it was coming. Simonique has never been out here, and she's been asking to come since I moved. The first few years, I was living with roommates and didn't think having my younger sister share a room with me and a bathroom with three other women would be ideal. And of course, these last three years, I've been hustling. But now with my own condo, I think I feel comfortable inviting her to LA.

"Earth to Eesh," she repeatedly sings in an alien voice to snap me out of my head.

I laugh and shoo her away to make her stop. "Uh, you can come over sometime this summer."

"Really?" She sits up in her bed, her face lighting up, and it's not from the sunlight. "I thought I'd have to convince you some more."

I laugh and scoop my chopped broccoli into a glass bowl. "You're graduatin' next week, and I feel like this is a good time."

I open my spinach bag to cut those up, too.

Glancing up at the phone, I find Simonique looking at me funny—head turned to the side, and her eyebrows and lips are squiggly lines. "Eesh, that was, like, too easy—Not that I 'on't appreciate it. Don't wantchu rescindin' the invitation, sis. I'm just sayin', I used to have to make my argument." She drops her voice. "So, who is he?"

I throw my head back and laugh. "Whatchu talm 'bout?"

"Don't be coy wit' me, bitch. Who is he? I know it *has* to be a man. You got a boyfriend?"

Something jolts my heart. Tim is my . . . friend? But not really because if I had guy friends, I definitely wouldn't be making out with them. *I guess I'd have to add that to things we need to talk about, too.* "No, I don't."

Simonique deadpans me. "Camesha that wasn't convincin'."

I kiss my teeth, trying to focus on folding and chopping my spinach. "We're friends. I *do* like him though. And he likes me," my voice gets quieter.

"So, what y'all doin'—wastin' each other's time?" she chuckles. "Is this some Hollywood shit? Why 'on't y'all just date?" Simonique makes a confused face like it's that simple. It would be in Columbia, but not here.

I just laugh. It'd be hard to explain my situation with Tim without the full truth.

I have never told Simonique and my parents that I vibe model and escort. They just know that I work at a "fancy hotel in Beverly Hills," as Mama puts it. I send them money in small amounts, never large sums. I don't need them wondering how I'm making so much on a waitress and bartender salary, even with good tips.

The money I send my parents is to help them pay bills, mostly the mortgage on my childhood home. They always say they don't need help, but it doesn't take long for me to convince them to accept it since I know they're ready to start taking road trips. They've never come to LA either; they hate flying.

Honestly, transferring money to them is the least I can do since I don't talk to or visit them much. I also occasionally send Simonique a little something for her school supplies or just because. She never asks for it, but she always responds, "Thank you, big sis." But I don't do it for the praise.

I also anonymously donate 20% of my hustle money to several organizations every quarter: support funds for sex workers, women's shelters, girls' mentorship programs, and even the clinic where I get my STD tests. It's not generosity. It's guilt, clinging to me like a fussy toddler on a plane—loud, annoying, hard to shake. It's me trying to make the money mean something more than what I did to get it.

All of this doesn't necessarily make me feel better about hustling. It just feels *slightly* redemptive or at least balances the scales. I like knowing that the money's helping people. Pries it out of shame's greedy, sticky fingers.

While I still figure out what other big thing to do with the money once I reach $500,000, I just want to feel like I'm using my earnings correctly.

But I'm sure if I did tell Simonique about my hustle, she would be understanding. Daddy would quickly hop on a plane and snatch my ass back to South Carolina, saying I don't need to do that to make money. He might be right, but I wasn't enjoying my stagnant predicament nor income when the opportunity arose. Mama would *try* to understand, but in the end, I think she'd be sad for me. I don't want pity. I chose this life. And I don't want to explain myself and experience their reactions, albeit probably loving and concerned ones.

I blink back to the present and speak up, "Just know that he's cool. I'll let ya know if anything progresses."

Simonique doesn't look convinced, but her side-eye lets up. "Okaayyyy."

I salvage the conversation and steer the focus back to her—her job hunting since the other one fell through, her moving in with her friend Destiny, her navigating the situation with Montrell. By the time we end the call, I've prepped all my produce and started my brown rice in my rice cooker.

It's 9pm and I'm chilling on my couch, my limbs and blanket all tangled up as I watch a rerun of *Sister, Sister*. My work phone dings next to me, and I pick it up. Might be my handler for tomorrow's event, Chey. I'm filling a party for an actor's foundation's casino-themed fundraiser. She said my role is to make men "feel lucky" as they play. That actor is not a client of mine in any way, but I've worked with Chey before.

But it's not Chey, it's Asa:

Fish (9:23pm):

> Hey Cammie. Can we meet tonight? If u got time.

My eyebrows smush together. Curiosity's got my attention, but I couldn't help but think about the last time we saw each other and how hurt he was after I rejected him when he asked me out. I don't want to deal with that again. I don't want to see Asa sad.

Gray bubbles pop up, indicating he's typing.

Fish (9:25pm):

> I really just wanna talk. Not on no bullshit.

I sigh because I don't know if I really believe him. *He only wants to talk?* Only a few times has a client paid me so they can talk.

Fish (9:26pm):

I'll ofc pay you extra for this late request.

I blow air out my nose as I type my response:

Me (9:26pm):

Send me your recent STD test results.

He immediately sends me an attachment of his results. Clean. Then I share mine.

Me (9:28pm):

Get a room and tell me when to meet you.

Fish (9:28pm):

Ok. Will text you when the room's booked.

I "like" his message and sip my vodka soda before I stand to change my clothes.

My Uber driver pulls up in front of a Marriott hotel downtown. If a client lives in Los Angeles, I always make sure we never meet at their home. And we never meet at the same hotel several times in a row. Space them out and be low-key, under the radar.

"Thank you," I say to my driver as I get out. I shut his door and hear the sedan peel away behind me.

Pushing my middle-parted hair over my shoulder, I strut into the hotel lobby, my red bottom heels clicking on the marble floor. Asa said he just wants to talk, but *if* he changes his mind—which I hope he doesn't—I'm wearing the blush-pink lingerie set he bought me underneath a multicolored cropped jacket and skinny jeans.

Asa said he's already in the room, so I beeline for the elevators. Up to the 11th floor and down the hall, I knock on his door. Within seconds, he opens, his towering body filling the doorframe. He grins, but he also looks tired. I checked my Google Alerts on the way here, learning the Breakers had a home playoff game tonight. Even though they lost, he did pretty well.

Dressed comfortably in a gray Nike tech sweatsuit, he steps to the side letting me in. Once the door is closed, I face Asa and he bends down to wrap me in his long arms, the scent of his eucalyptus mint body wash enveloping me. I reluctantly give him a one-arm hug as I hold my purse in the other hand.

I'm surprised he wanted to hug me after last time, but I'm thinking Asa has a thing for touch.

"How you doin', Cammie?" he asks into my hair before kissing the top of my head.

We separate and I look up at him. "I'm fine. You wanted to see me. . ." I can't pick up on Asa's vibe right now, which makes it hard to be Cammie.

He passes me to drop down into the armchair in the corner. "I did."

I follow him deeper into the room. He usually books a hotel suite, but this is a standard guestroom with a bed, table, and chair. *Okay, so maybe he* doesn't *want sex.*

Sitting on the edge of the bed, I set my purse down next to me. "Well, ya seein' me. How do I look?" I tilt my head, a sultry grin on my face as I cross my legs.

Asa slumps further into his chair, spreading his huge thighs. *No print. Hmph.* He bites his big bottom lip. "Fine as hell. Like always."

A faux laugh drips from my lips. "Thank you." I pause, watching him just sit there ogling me. "I didn't see the game, but I heard you did well. 34 points, 5 assists. That's impressive."

Asa blushes, dropping his gaze. It always seems to catch him off guard when I give him a compliment, so I like dishing them out and watching his big ass squirm. I know it's only because he's humble, always attributing his talent to God and his hard work. "Thank you. I 'preciate that, Cammie," he says, fighting a chuckle.

I smile, trying to read Asa's face. He's not looking at me as he toys with his bottom lip. My mind spins, debating on whether I need to turn Cammie up a notch. *Does he want me to seduce him?* "What's goin' on, Asa?"

He clenches his jaw, still eyeing the fuck out of the carpet. "Do you, uh," he clears his throat, "you know GiGi Savage?"

My head snaps back. *Camesha, be Cammie*, I coach myself as I slip back into persona.

I never discuss women in the industry with clients—Well, I don't know if GiGi is escorting, too, but rumors have always circulated.

Asa lifts his eyes to mine, a soft sincerity on his face. "You know her?"

I'm not sure where this is going, but I'm trying to go along for the ride. "I know *of* her. I see her at events and in music videos and commercials."

He drops his gaze again, appearing in thought as he nods his head.

"Why you askin' me 'bout GiGi?"

Asa rubs his neck like he's got an ache, but a very small smile lifts his mouth. "I met her at the grocery store the other day. Both of us were dressed down and in partial disguise. She asked me to get some' for her on the top shelf."

I *really* look at Asa as he talks. His face doesn't light up, but he looks less tired than he did when he opened the door, like talking about GiGi gets him excited? *Oh*. He looks . . . fond of her as his smile spreads wider.

"The grocery store, huh?" I ask teasingly.

"Yeah. She recognized me. Told me her cousin was a big fan, so we took a selfie so she could show it to her."

His nonexistent eye contact is aggravating and kind of making me uncomfortable.

Asa continues, "I invited her and her cousin to today's home game."

I hum to coax him to go on, so he can get to the point of him bringing up his first interaction with GiGi.

I 'on't wanna give Asa the wrong idea, but maybe gettin' closer will hurry this meetin' up? I stand and sashay to sit on his lap. *Now* he looks up at me as he accommodates my new seating arrangement, setting his feet out and spreading his thighs as wide as they can go in the chair so my legs can be in the middle of his. I lean against him and rest my left arm along the backrest, crossing my right leg over the left.

Asa's massive hands cup my back and right thigh. I focus on playing with the string of his hoodie as he continues, glancing from my fingers to my face. "She and her cousin came tonight. One of my teammates saw her and told me who she is and 'bout all'is drama she been in last year. Tellin' me that's why her social media is inactive. You know I 'on't be on social media like that, but I just let him talk." He pauses and I look up at him, my fingers stop. "I 'on't know, Cammie, am I crazy to be kinda interested in GiGi?"

I stare at him, seeing he's serious. A grin worms onto my face. "Do you have a crush, Asa?" I tease him, running my left hand up the back of his head, feeling the sponged hair of his temp fade.

He drops my gaze, his neck twitching a little at my touch and I stop. Asa kisses his teeth before talking, "Nah—I mean," he huffs, "I 'on't know. Just seems like there's more to her when we met. She felt guarded, but . . . open at the same time."

Seeing and hearing Asa sound a little infatuated with GiGi makes my heart flutter. He really sounds sincerely interested in her.

And that makes me finally realize that this might be our last session. Him asking to just talk, him booking a regular room—it all makes sense now.

Asa sounds like he's ready for more. He really wants to date someone instead of just paying to fuck and cuddle. I can understand it gets old. I've only had one client outright cut ties with me. When he got divorced—because of his "free affairs," is how he put it—he couldn't afford to pay me anymore. I usually cut off clients or they just stop contacting me.

"I mean, if you're interested in her, go for it," my voice is softer, higher than I'd like. I think a little bit of Camesha found her way in there.

Asa looks at me. Desire darkens his half-lidded eyes as he licks his lips. His gaze briefly drops to my mouth. I resist the urge to roll my eyes at that, not wanting to have to dodge his kisses again.

"Fa real?" he asks all low.

The character must still be played for the night. I slip into my Cammie register, saying, "If she's whatchu want."

Then Asa leans in, his right hand tilting my head up to access my neck. He latches his big lips to my skin. I *am* wearing his favorite scent, so I'm not surprised he's found his home there. My hand that rested along his chair is now clinging to his hood. I try to control my breathing as he makes out with my neck. "You remember when you told me you thought I knocked you up?" his voice rumbles against my skin before he licks me.

My eyebrows mash together as I wonder why he's bringing that up in this position. I murmur, "Yeah. Why?"

"If you were pregnant, ya know I woulda taken care of you and our baby, right?" His warm breath on my wet skin makes me moan involuntarily before he goes back in.

"Of course. You're a good man, Asa," I croak out.

I believe that. If I were pregnant, I have no doubt that Asa would've believed it was his child, and he wouldn't't've hesitated to take care of everything.

"Thank you," he groans, sounding pleased and pained.

His lips and teeth nibble my neck a little, making me suck in a tight breath. "Why you ask me that?" I ask around the pleasure of his mouth on my skin. I mean, the man has skills.

Asa lets my face go and comes up for air. He gazes deeply into my eyes. "Because I wantchu to know I'm fa real, Cammie."

I take note of his "fa real" face. The way his eyes squint. The way one side of his mouth scowls, almost as if he's in disbelief that I asked the question.

"And this is our last time."

I thought so. Before I can say anything, he lifts me. I immediately clutch his shoulders even though I know he wouldn't drop me. Asa lays me on the bed, hovering and eyeing me like he's going to destroy me.

Not going to lie, I'm turned on. But it's not him though. I wish it's Tim in this position—*Down, bitch. You've only hung out wit' the man twice.*

I blink back to Cammie, wiping on a smirk as I match Asa's smoldering gaze. "Is that right?"

"Yeah. I want some' real, Cammie. I want love. I know that you can't or won't lemme experience that witchu." He stands up straight to reach behind him to pull his hoodie off, revealing his tattooed body.

I play along. Biting my bottom lip, I run a hand up his abs.

He bites his lip, too, bending down and grabbing my hand to kiss my palm. Then he surprises me by putting my index finger in his mouth to suck it. Watching Asa as he watches me watch him, makes me, again, wish it's Tim doing it. My lips fall open a little, a breath escaping me as my pussy throbs and gushes at the fantasy.

Asa pulls my finger out of his mouth and whispers, "I need to taste you one last time."

My breath hitches in my throat, but I salvage the little bit of Cammie left and say, "Sounds good to me."

He chuckles lowly and unzips my jeans before dragging them down my smooth legs.

Asa gobbles me up, sucking and licking me like I'm his last meal. I'm happy he's realized his limits with this arrangement, and he wants to move forward with his life. He wants a woman of his own and if that could be GiGi, I wish them nothing but the best.

I'd say this is definitely a joyous farewell as I cum twice and hard on Asa's handsome face. He enjoys the fuck out of it, dragging his hand down his face to collect all my juices so that he can lick it off. That shit is hot as fuck.

But again, I don't see Asa. I imagine it's Tim. *Shit! I sound like a thirsty bitch. I need to handle this when I get home.*

I leave that hotel a few thousand dollars richer, satisfied, and more excited to see Tim on Sunday.

Saturday, May 12

Tim

It's one of those chill days at home. They come every blue moon, so any chance I can just relax, I take it.

I *would* hit up Camesha, but she told me she had a vibe modeling gig last night and would be sleeping a lot today since she had to stay until the event ended at four in the fucking morning! Meaning she made those niggas feel lucky for seven hours. That's *insane*, so I hope she was handsomely compensated. And knowing how she moves, I'm sure she was.

Right now, I'm just lying back on the chaise of my brown leather sectional in my living room. A "Speakeasy" candle from Harlem Candle Co. is burning. The Sun is shining through my cracked open blinds. I'm sipping a rum and coke. The TV is off, and instead I'm spinning a vinyl record: The Isley Brothers's *The Heat Is On*. It's a vibe if I do say so myself.

And as I listen to the music, I feel the familiar, yet long-lost urge crest in me to write.

It's a damn shame that I haven't written poetry in several *years*, having been so busy with work, but I used to write all the time. When my ninth grade English teacher taught a unit on it, I became *hooked*. I admired how poets say so much with so little. Telling their truth in a way that felt universal? I wanted to mimic that.

As a military brat and an only child, I found that after moving around so much and not having close friends, writing poetry helped me sort through my emotions when talking to someone felt insufficient or didn't fully convey exactly what I was going through.

For the first few years after my pops passed, I tightly clung to poetry. I filled countless notebooks with unsaid questions and feelings in line and meter. Mostly sadness and rage, not much else in between. Me and God weren't good back then—well, *I* wasn't messing with Him like that. I couldn't understand *why* He took Pops away from me and Ma.

Honestly, I still don't understand, but I've come to accept that I can't know everything and that things have their time. And I guess, Pops' job on Earth was done.

So, I get up to rummage through my bedroom's nightstand drawer for my notepad and pen. Once I have it, I sit back down on the chaise and free-write a list. My poetic muscles haven't been used in a while—not saying they've atrophied but just jotting something down might warm me up.

After a few minutes, I kiss my teeth, *cringing* at what I've written. *"Skin like bronze, statue-esque body". . . Yep, rusty like a muhfucka.* I toss the pad and pen to the side.

In need of a distraction, I pause the album and call my mom. On the first ring, she picks up.

"Ma Dukes, whaddup!" I howl obnoxiously, knowing how she'd respond.

"Timothy, why are you so loud?" she chastises. I can just hear her twisting up her face.

Reaction achieved. I crack the fuck up. "You know I only do it to get on ya nerves."

She scoffs. "And *you* know I'm old and on veteran benefits. Don't make my hearin' worse, boy."

I chuckle, "You not even old, but you right, my bad."

"Thank you." She takes a deep breath before asking, "Anyway, how are ya, baby?"

I adjust in my seat, bending a leg on the couch. "Good. Sleepin' better."

"Glad to hear. You too young to be havin' sleep problems."

"Well, these clients ain't no joke, Ma," I chortle, scratching the back of my head.

"You gotta take care of ya'self, baby. I'm happy you were able to go on vacation to unwind. Things are back to normal now?" I hear what sounds like her opening a plastic bag—maybe chips.

"Yeah, most award shows are over. But the BET Awards are comin' up so a few of my clients are nominated and set to perform. We preppin' for that."

She blows out some air. "You know I can't keep up wit' all these award shows, so I only caught the NAACP Awards and the Grammys. I liked that Keyana Renay music video. Very cute. Glad they won."

"Yeah, Key and the girls did their thing."

"Mmm-hmmm," she hums and starts crunching on her chips.

"Ma, I hope them chips ain't the only thing you ate today."

"Boy please, I had breakfast. This is my afternoon snack."

I peep the time on my phone. It's two here, so it's four in San Antonio. "Okay. Did you have lunch, too?"

When she doesn't answer me right away, I know what that means. And it ain't because she's chewing her food.

"*Ma*." I clasp my forehead.

"*Timothy*. I'm fine. I wasn't hungry at lunch. This is just enough to curb my lil' bit of hunger pangs right now." My mother served in the Air Force for over 30 years, so she had to maintain her weight to meet fitness requirements. And now that she retired three years ago, some of those habits remain. But she's going about it in an unhealthy way. I ain't the healthiest or most in-shape nigga, but I know not eating for hours on end isn't good for you.

"Okay, okay." I twiddle with the tag of my 8-ball throw pillow.

She sighs. "I'm tryin', baby. I'm listenin' to my body, so I only eat when I'm hungry. I meal prep, too, so I always have food around."

"Okay, Ma. You know I just worry cuz I love you."

"I know. I love you, too, Timmy," she says, all chipper.

That makes me laugh.

"So, what else been goin' on, Mr. Hollywood? You datin' anybody? Cuz you sound more relaxed, lighter, and I *know* it wasn't just vacation," she teases.

Oftentimes, I wish my mom bought an iPhone already so we could FaceTime, but right now, I'm thankful she can't see me. My cheeks are blushing like crazy, thinking about Camesha. Our dance, our kisses, our all-day hang, texting and calling all week.

"Maaa," I whine a little, squirming in my seat.

"Don't *Ma* me. Answer the question."

I tilt my body from side to side. "I'm kinda seein' someone."

"What's that mean?"

To play with her, I mutter, "She's cool."

"Boy, I ain't ask if she was *cool*. I wanna know who she is—Wait, is she a celebrity? Is *that* why you can't tell me?" It sounds like she just sat up in her seat abruptly.

I laugh, "Calm down, woman. And no, she's not."

She exhales a deep breath. "Oh okay. Is it new?"

"Yeah, so new that I haven't even really asked her on a date yet," I chuckle.

"Okay, well if she's gotchu like this now and y'all ain't went out yet, I'd say she sounds special already. And you really like her."

Bracing my jaw, I nod in agreement. "Yeah, I'm interested in her, fa sho." I pull my chin hair, having a flashback to when Camesha kissed me in my Jeep last Saturday. Clearing my throat, I say, "But Ma, what's been goin' on witchu?"

"I see you tryna change the subject—you not slick, Timothy." But she obliges my question and updates me on everything from the soap operas that she's now able to watch, to her part-time job at a popular winery, and her book club drama.

I know that part of why Ma has all these activities is so she's not in the house by herself since Pops is gone. Sometimes, I worry if she's lonely and unhappy. She assures me that she's fine and has friends, that she doesn't need me to move back home to be near her. She doesn't want me to put my life on hold for her and miss out on chasing my dreams. But still, she was with Pops for most of her life and now she's had to continue life without him for nine years. I can't imagine the void she feels.

But I'm happy that she seems to enjoy her normal life after retirement.

8
Not Just Takeout

Sunday, May 13

Tim

It's a beautiful day. Since it looks like I'm free today, Camesha and I are seizing the moment and linking up.

I'm working up the nerve to ask her out officially. And not going to lie, I'm a tad—no, *really*—nervous. We've talked and hung out a few times now, but ain't *nothing* like a proper date. I want to do stuff right with her. And I ain't felt that in a while.

I turn into Camesha's condominium parking lot and find a space in front of the same entrance I've dropped her off at. After parking, I pick up my phone from the cupholder and go to her contact, which I've already favorited. *Down bad like a muhfucka.* So that I *"don't have to walk up and down the steps"* she told me to call her when I arrive so she can meet me outside.

Scoffing, I call her, and on the second ring, she answers, "Hey, Tim!"

"Hey, I'm outside. You real wild for not lettin' me come up there."

She giggles, "No, I'm not. Relax. I'm on my way down now."

Chuckling, I say, "A'ight," and we hang up.

I turn my Jeep off and hop out to wait for her on the curb. Just as I lean back on the front of my whip, my phone chimes.

Gianni (1:18pm):

> All good. Thanks for asking, Tim.

Hmph, no callin' me Timmy or Tim baby?—Not that I want her to call me those things, but she usually does. I texted her a couple days ago to check on her since I haven't heard from her in weeks. I don't want to pry.

Me (1:20pm):

> Glad to hear, Gianni

She immediately "likes" my message, making me smile. If she's really good, then that's all I can hope for.

But then Amber Royce's manager's name pops up. *What now?!*

Camesha

As per usual, my mother texted me a Bible verse early this morning. It's still ringing in my head:

Mama (5:08am):

> Good morning, baby! Happy Sunday

> I don't know what you're facing but I felt led to send you this. Whatever it is, God got you
> Joshua 1:9 (NIV): "Have I not commanded you? Be strong and courageous. Do not be afraid; do not be

discouraged, for the Lord your God will be with you wherever you go."

I "loved" her message and thanked her for sending it. She has no idea how much the verse resonates with me. I definitely need all the courage I can muster to have this serious talk with Tim about my hustle. I don't know what we are, but whatever we're doing, I want to allow us an opportunity to really clear the air about *that* part of my life. Especially since we met while I was working.

But I *don't* want that conversation to start because Tim spots the hickey Asa's big lips left on my neck Thursday night. That's why I wanted Tim to wait for me downstairs: I needed enough time to cover the hickey with makeup.

I fluff my twist-out one more time, slip my purse onto my shoulder, and head out of my condo. It's 76 degrees today so I opted for a cropped *Living Single* graphic tee, denim shorts, and some cute slides. I don't know what else we're doing besides eating lunch this afternoon, but I don't care. I just want to be comfortable and ready for anything.

Coming off the last step, I see Tim and I slow down to scan him. High-top Converse, denim cutoffs, a vintage Fubu tee, and his usual jewelry. A black LA baseball cap is cocked on his head like he just threw it on before he left his house.

I've kind of missed Tim. He looks so sexy, leaning back on the hood of his truck. I watch the muscles in his arms flex as he talks on the phone, glancing off to the side. By the look of his knitted eyebrows and the serious tone of his voice, it's most likely a client.

As I get closer to him, he double-takes my way. "A'ight, add that to my calendar. Bye," Tim hurries whoever off the phone before sliding it in his shorts pocket. He unabashedly takes me in. "Hey. . ."

Cat got his tongue? Good. And more can get on that ton—"Hey," I push out. I stroll right up to Tim, and he stands up from the truck.

"Camesha, I 'preciate you lookin' out for my 28-year-old knees, but when will you understand that I'm a gentleman, girl? I coulda easily came and gotchu."

I just giggle like a little girl.

Tim comes forward, his light, woody fragrance surrounding me. "And not you copyin' my swag, girl."

I playfully slap his arm. "Shut up! You don't own the graphic tee look." I mean, I may or may not have tried to dress like him. . .

"It's cool though. You look good," he says.

I glance away to hide my blushing. "You do, too," I whisper, again, too shyly. Tim disarms me.

His warm hands pull me closer to him, causing a pleasant shiver to shoot up my spine. I may have worn a crop top for this exact reason, too.

My hands run up his arms to cup his face. As our faces near, our eyes close and Tim clenches his jaw underneath my fingers, sending a shock to my heart. This kiss is like the other ones: slow, passionate, and fluid. Our lips and tongues involved, making my heart skip too many beats. My arms eventually wrap around his neck. He leans forward, making my back arch, his hands slide down to the small of my back, pressing me against his body. *Ugh, I wish he'd just grab my ass already, but he might be tryna stay respectful.*

When we come up for air after giving my neighbors a free show, we rest our foreheads against one another's. I haven't made out in public like that since I was a teenager kissing my first boyfriend. It's the same thrill, but better and sexier.

"Would it be too soon to say I've missed you?" Tim says lowly.

I smirk, my voice all shy, "No, cuz I've missed you, too."

He smiles, showing his teeth. "That's whassup."

I step back, cracking up. Leave it to Tim to make me laugh unexpectedly.

"C'mon. I'm hungry." He grabs my hand and opens the passenger door. Tim ensures I'm inside before circling to his side.

I turn around in my seat, seeing the bags of Earle's on the decluttered floor of Tim's Jeep. I haven't eaten Earle's beef jumbo dog and banana pudding in a while. It can't top my mama's banana pudding but it's a slice of home I appreciate.

"Thank you for gettin' that, Tim." I try to hide the giddiness in my voice, but I'm too excited for this food.

Tim puts his seat belt on and says, "No pro'lem. Been a minute since I ate there, too."

I watch him swipe on his phone until he presses his "Sunny Songs" playlist on Spotify. Amerie's "Why Don't We Fall in Love" plays at low volume as Tim starts his ignition. It's a nice vibe.

He backs out of the parking space and steers out of the lot.

Moments later, I ask Tim about his day.

"Chill. Cooked breakfast and watched a sermon. The pastor preached about steppin' out of ya comfort zone wit' God. Don't be afraid but instead know that God is witchu in uncomfortable places. And there you may find good things to grow you and bless you. If I'm rememberin' correctly, the verses were Joshua 1:1-11."

I gasp. "Oh my God. That's wild. My mama texted me Joshua 1:9 this mornin'."

He stops at a light before snapping his head to look at me. "You serious?"

I just nod, smiling all goofy and wide.

And at the same time, we mutter, "The Lord works in mysterious ways."

"You owe me a Coke!" Tim rushes out, making me laugh. "But that's cool we both received that."

Is this some sorta sign, God? What does this—

"So, how ya week been, C?" Tim breaks me out of my thoughts before I start going down a rabbit hole.

"C? What, Camesha too hard for you to pronounce?" I tease.

Immediately, Tim snaps his head at me again, but this time looking apologetic. "Oh no, I-I—"

Chuckling, I touch his forearm resting on the console to stop his cute stuttering. "Tim, I'm joking."

He looks at me again. "Oh." Then an easy smile smooths onto his face before the light turns green and he pulls off.

"My parents can be really indecisive and that's evident in my name and my sister's."

"Whatchu mean?"

"Camesha was the result of my mom wantin' to name me Aisha and my dad likin' Cameron. Then my sister's name is Simonique. Simone and Monique." I pause for dramatic effect.

"Simonique," he repeats. "Aye, at least you ain't gon' meet anybody else wit' those names."

"True."

"And it sounds like ya parents know how to collaborate."

"They do. They're . . . a good team." A small smile claims my face as I remember watching my parents' marriage in action. When they disagreed, it was just that—no arguing or fighting. I mean, maybe they *did* argue, but never in front of us. They always spoke sweetly to each other and laughed often. Mama even confided in me that sometimes Daddy wasn't really *that* funny, but she knows he loves her laugh.

"That's awesome," Tim says, taking me out of my trip down memory lane. "But fa real, you 'on't mind my lil' nickname?"

Hearing the genuine concern in Tim's voice, I swivel my head to look at him. He must feel my eyes as he glances my way before he makes a turn. "I don't mind, Tim. I just now have a lotta nicknames."

"Same. Shit, Zay called me *Timbo Dubb$* at his album release party. He was faded as a muhfucka when he said it, but I was still briefly afraid that he just inducted me into the Dubb$ Fam cult or some'."

I crack up, thinking about Zay's imprint label and how newly signed artists have Dubb$ in their stage names.

We talk about our weeks and soon, Tim turns into the parking garage with his favorite view of Los Angeles.

"I just can't wrap my head 'round us last bein' here seven months ago. That's just insane," I remark.

"Fa real. Feels like a long and short time ago."

I unbuckle my seat belt and retrieve our food from the back as he parks at the top. Now with the windows cracked and the truck parked, I hand Tim his bag and watch him unpack his two Jamaican beef patties and fries. We both have water bottles.

Throughout our lunch, we just make small talk, sometimes singing along to the songs on his playlist. After we finished eating, we laugh watching one another pop in a mint, commenting on how neither of us can stand the taste of lingering food in our mouths.

That banana puddin' hit the spot, I muse as I toss its empty container into my bag.

After I put that on the floor, Tim speaks up, "So, Simonique should be graduatin' soon, right?"

My chest warms at him remembering that. No joke, I might've texted him that during those seven months. "Next week, actually. I 'on't know if I told you, but I'm flyin' home for her commencement."

"Congratulations to her."

"I'll be sure to tell her. I'm very proud of her." I look out the corner of my eye, seeing Tim smiling all wide. "She just moved back home but she and her friend will be movin' into an apartment at the end of the summer."

Tim nods, taking a sip of his water as he looks at the view.

"And speakin' of summer, she's visitin' me 'round July Fourth."

"Dope. She been out here before?" He puts his bottle back in his cupholder.

"Nope, it'll be her first time. She's been askin' to come since I moved out here *years* ago, but I finally feel comfortable havin' her here. I'm a lil' more stable and my place is big enough."

"Sooo, am I gonna be able to meet her?" Tim asks, squiggling his eyebrows.

My breath catches in my throat. "You-You wanna meet my sister?" *Cut the stutterin', girl!*

Tim's face morphs into a serious expression. "I mean, on ya time, of course. Whenever you're ready."

My gaze drops to my lap as something swells in the pit of my stomach. Nerves, warmth, happiness. It's overwhelming, but the thought of Tim meeting Simonique actually doesn't sound that bad. *But are we movin' too fast? What exactly is our situation?*

Tim pauses "Spotless Mind" by Jhené Aiko. His voice comes out soft but firm, "Camesha, I wanna take you out."

My eyes snap back to his, my brows furrowing as my heart rate picks up speed. "We're already out. . ." I force a chuckle out of me.

"Ya know what I mean—a *real* date." He chuckles, too. "I wantchu to know I take you seriously, Camesha."

I dive deep into Tim's eyes. Nothing but warmth and sincerity. A slow smile breaks my neutral face. "I know you take me seriously, Tim. But yes, I'd *love* to go on a *real* date with you."

Tim beams at me before dropping his head as if in relief. "Cool. I gotta plan some'. Ya know, cuz takeout in my car ain't the *only* thing I do."

I laugh. "We hung out all day last Saturday and that was really fun. You asked me out then."

"Yeah, but I ain't *ask*-ask you out, ya know? Did *you* feel like that was a date?"

Would I be down bad if I felt like I was already wit' my man then? Yes, bitch, my inner voice says.

I look at Tim and decide to be really honest. "I just enjoy spendin' time witchu, Tim. Doesn't matter where we go or what we do," my voice weakens as my heart flutters and butterflies storm my stomach.

Tim smiles softly and leans forward. "Me, too, Camesha." Then he kisses me chastely on the lips. Our first peck.

I miss his mouth already, but we have some things to discuss. "So, how would we, um," I swallow nervously to coat my drying throat, "navigate datin' in this industry? How would that look?"

Tim squints his eyes, searching my face. "However we want it to look. I mean," his tongue pokes the inside of his mouth, "what are you *really* askin' me, Camesha?"

I avert my gaze to my lap, fidgeting with my gold bracelets. Here it goes. "I 'on't know, wit' me bein' a vibe model *and an escort,*" I whisper the last part then huff out a breath, "I just . . . I 'on't want people in my business. That's why I try to move very low-key. And I 'on't want people lookin' at *you* funny cuz ya datin' me. I 'on't wanna negatively affect ya career."

Tim

Hearing Camesha express her worries about us dating makes me sad. She moves so unbothered and poised as Cammie that I guess I didn't think that that was part of her persona.

I lift her chin with a curled index finger so she can look me in the eyes and see how serious I am. "First of all, *please* don't worry 'bout me. I'll be fine. Hella people *look* in this city, but a lot of 'em ain't brave enough to step to you either. They might say wild shit to other people or online, but not to ya face. And if they do, I can handle that. Plus, if my clients and other folks

I work wit' feelin' froggy? They *all* got secrets I could air out in this bitch if we bein' honest. They better find some' safe to do."

She sucks in a breath then tucks in her lips.

I let go of her chin to grab her hands sitting in her lap. "Secondly, we can move however you wanna move. Whatever makes you comfortable. If somebody say some' crazy 'bout or to you, trust, they can come see me."

Her lips try to hold it in, but a laugh tumbles out of her.

"I'm serious, Camesha," I chortle, "I might be a jokey-ass nigga sometimes, but I 'on't play 'bout the people I care about."

"I'm-I'm sorry for laughin'. I believe you." A smile touches her face, then it falls as she looks down again. "And Tim?"

"Whassup?" I ask, my thumb rubbing her knuckles. This is the shyest I've seen her, and I'm getting concerned.

"You're *really* okay wit' me escortin'?"

I pause for a second to swallow as my throat instantly dries up. "I said I was," I nervously chuckle.

Camesha looks at me, and she pushes some hair behind her ear. "I know you did, but," she blows out some air, "I 'on't know, you 'on't ask me much about it. I know you *know* about it, but I just," pause, "I just wantchu to be honest wit' me. *Really* honest 'bout how you feel." Her eyes search deep into mine and I hold my jaw rigid at this impending conversation. "I promise, nothin' you say will hurt my feelings."

I let go of her hands to pull at my chin hair. "I mean, I ain't gon' lie, when we first met, I ain't *want* you to sleep wit' Zay. I didn't know you that well then, but after our short conversations, you captivated me, and I guess I was feelin' a tad territorial." I chuckle, scratching the back of my head. That sounds so silly now that I said it out loud, so I don't dare look at her even though I feel her eyes on me.

"But knowin' how you move witcha selection process and ya rules, I see you're a careful professional." I glance at her out the corner of my eye, seeing her drop her head to stifle a giggle.

"And I know you're doin' it to meet a goal." She told me that over text a while back. "I respect ya hustle. I mean, we all got one."

Camesha nods, and a subtle red blooms underneath her cheeks.

I smirk and clear my throat. "Now bein' really, really honest," I raise my arms in surrender, "if you my lady and we get down like that, I'd wantchu to *only* sleep wit' me. I 'on' t wanna share."

She nods, a grin twitching on her lips.

"But I 'on't wanna diminish ya efforts either just to soothe my ego and make myself feel good. To me, that doesn't sound fair to you and whatchu *been* had goin' on *way* before we met." I sit back in my seat and exhale a deep breath, relief settling on me.

"I," I lock my jaw, trying to keep the word inside, but fuck it, "I *trust* you, Camesha." *Is that too soon to say?*

She looks at me, her eyes welling with tears as she takes quickened breaths. But I wish I could peek into that pretty head of hers and see what she's really thinking.

"Camesha, I 'on't wantchu doubtin' my feelings for you cuz of this. I *really* like you and I wanna keep gettin' to know you." A very pedestrian answer, but straightforward and honest, nonetheless.

She squeezes her eyes shut and her hands cover her face.

Did I say some' wrong? I 'on't wanna make her cry. "You okay?"

"Can I have a hug?" she speaks into her hands, her voice muffled.

"Of course." I quickly get out the car and circle to her side.

Upon opening her door, she throws her arms around my neck, tucking her face there.

"You okay, Camesha?" I ask, rubbing circles into her back. She smells like sweet spring.

She surprises the hell out of me when she backs out of the hug and pulls me in for a kiss. It's so passionate that my hat falls off and hits the ground, but I don't care. I hold her closer to me, getting so into it that it takes me a moment to realize she retreated—my eyes still closed and everything. She giggles and pecks my lips before I open my eyes.

Camesha's still holding my face when she says, "Thank you for tellin' me all'at, Tim. I really like you and wanna keep gettin' to know you as well."

One side of my mouth curls up. "Can't keep stealin' my lines, girl."

She drops her hands as she cracks up. "It's how I feel," she whines.

I just smirk at her cute ass.

She grins. "But fa real, it's helpful to know where you really stand."

"Thank you for askin' and pullin' all'at outta me. Honestly, I ain't wantchu to think or feel like I was knockin' ya grind. I respect you. Straight up."

Camesha's facial features soften. "I 'preciate that, Tim. Really." Then she screws up her lips and side-eyes me. "And I figured, since you're a man, that if we were to get together, you wouldn't want me doin' it anyway, regardless of whatchu said in Canter's Deli."

We both laugh.

"I mean, I was honest then. I just *omitted* a few things. Timin' didn't feel right to me."

"Fair nuff." She wraps her arms around my neck again and I slip my arms around her waist. "Sorry 'bout ya hat," she whispers.

I smirk, glancing at the ground. "Fuck that hat."

She cracks up. "So, when is our date?" She cheeses, and I'm happy she seems excited.

"Well, you goin' back home this comin' week for Simonique's graduation, so when do you return?"

"Saturday afternoon."

I nod. "A'ight, so let's say that followin' Friday or Saturday night for our first real date—*if* you're free." I wiggle my eyebrows.

"I am." Her eyes quickly drop down to my mouth as she bites her plump bottom lip.

"Good," I whisper, and we make out again.

I feel all good and warm and fuzzy on the inside as my mind spins with ideas for our first date. I want to make it unforgettable.

9
No Rush

Friday, May 25

Camesha

I've been thinking about my "real" date with Tim nonstop for almost two weeks. He hasn't told me anything about what we're doing, except to—in his exact words—"wear some' that looks like you're goin' to a gala at a fancy nightclub." I immediately racked my brain, thinking about where we could be going and what I already have in my closet. But nothing was giving the vibe he mentioned so I ordered something from my favorite Black-owned boutique in LA.

Simonique's graduation was amazing. When they called her name and she strutted across that stage in gold heels, like the educated queen she is, my parents and I and a few other family members stood, cheering for her like we ain't got Southern manners. She beamed and waved at us as she collected the faux diploma and posed for a quick photo.

That entire moment caused excitement to swell inside of me, for her and myself. Since I'm only a few thousand dollars away from making $500,000 hustling, the idea of using the money to go to college appeared like a good omen. Not sure what I'd major in yet, but I could work part time at The Adonir Hotel to attend classes—But I don't know, just a thought.

In the parking lot of the Clemson University's Littlejohn Coliseum, we had a mini Russell family reunion. Everyone hugged and kissed Simonique, telling her how proud of her we were. She accepted all the praise and thanked us for our support.

Since her graduation was in the afternoon, we had dinner at Ruth's Chris in Columbia. The next evening, our family gathered at our house for a backyard cookout to further celebrate Simonique. My daddy and some uncles threw down on the grill, while my mama and aunts came through with the sides and desserts.

I ain't seen some extended family in years since they're spread out across South Carolina and the South, but it was nice. Although I left home because I didn't know where my life was going after high school, I also left the warm, comforting nest. But sometimes staying in one's comfort zone can stunt growth. Not sure if I've truly grown much since leaving, but my bank accounts have.

Nique, some cousins, and I blasted music from a speaker, cutting up on the grass:

Tired from dancing to Jagged Edge and Nelly's "Where the Party At," I staggered to the patio underneath the awning where a few empty plastic picnic chairs were.

I pulled my personal phone from my jeans back pocket before plopping down to relax a bit. I told my clients and handlers I'd be busy for a week, so I left my work phone at my condo. Also, I've been thinking a lot about what Tim said about my hustle, so I'm considering my next moves. I like him a lot and I want to see where our connection grows.

Scrolling through my notifications, I saw a text from Tim, smiling before opening it:

Tim (6:37pm):

> Hope u having a good time. Tell Simonique I said
> congrats.

And he included a selfie of him doing a military salute with a goofy smile on his face. I giggled at that.

"He's silly, but cute," Simonique said, coming up behind me before sitting in the chair next to me.

I jumped a little at her sudden presence, dropping my phone in my lap. But it was too late. She had already seen Tim's picture. My spatial awareness is usually top notch, but I got caught slipping.

Nique must've came from the other side of the patio where the cooler was because she had a Lime-A-Rita in her hand. She leaned in and said all low, "Is that ol' boy? The friend who you like, and you think like you but both of y'all are in the business of wastin' time? And don't lie, bitch."

I did *think about lying, but what was the point now?* "Yeeesss. . ." *I let out, trying to avoid eye contact as I smooth down my low ponytail.*

Her face lit up. "Ooo okay. Lemme see his pic again."

I relent and show her my screen.

"You told him 'bout me? Awww." *She side-eyed me and pouted her bottom lip.* "And *he spelled my name right? Bonus points."* Then she squinted, "And Tim? *He 'on't look that old to be havin' that old-ass name." She laughs.*

"Shut up! It's a classic name." *I playfully slapped her arm and sat back in my seat.* "His full name is Timothy."

"Harold is a classic name, too—and classic is code for old but go off—don't mean I wanna moan Harold!"

I crack the fuck up at her shenanigans.

"But at least Tim is cute."

True, *I think as she nods and sips her drink.*

"You tell Mama and Daddy 'bout him yet?"

"Nah, I'll tell 'em when there's more to tell. We're actually goin' on our first date next week." I couldn't fight a smile from smearing on my face if I tried.

Simonique beams. "Ooo yay! And please tell me how it goes."

"I will."

So, I have to update my sister and my friends on the date. And right now, they are asking me a million questions about it as I get my pedicure done.

I'm talking to them with my Air Buds in on group FaceTime as my tech gets my toes right. To match the vibe Tim told me to dress for, I had an idea: long, almond-shaped manicure with 3D gold squiggles and tiny jewels, then just gold gel for my pedicure.

The day before, I gave myself Fulani braids with a curly braid-out at the back of my head. Simply, I wanted to go all out and see Tim's mouth hit the floor when he picks me up.

"I'm excited, y'all, but I'm a lil' nervous," I admit to my friends, clenching my teeth.

Earlier, when I texted them that I had a real date coming up, I came clean and said it's with the guy I left Bassment 323 with. Nikki replied with a gazillion emojis, saying she "FUCKING KNEW IT." Oluchi just sent a simple excited text. She's the chillest person out of the group, and oftentimes, the more reasonable one. She's also the oldest at 30 years old.

"Why?" Lu asks, her oval face wrinkling. She's a few shades lighter than me and Nikki with long, silk-pressed hair. She's a real estate agent who helped me find my first apartment for when I moved out of the place I shared with roommates I met online.

"It's been a long time." *Three* plus years to be exact since I've been on a date.

When I started hustling, I stopped dating. It would've been too difficult to date a man I was actually interested in *and* try to be Cammie for clients. I have to act in my role, but that'd be *too* much acting. I'm not trying to get my big break like Zaria.

"Yeah, but from what you've told us 'bout Tim, he makes you feel comfortable, so it sounds like you really don't have anything to worry about. Just be ya'self."

I take a deep breath. "You're right, Lu."

"You a bad bitch, Camesha. Remember that," Nikki chimes in, pointing a finger at the camera.

I giggle. "Thanks, girl."

"Always. Send us some pics of ya 'fit and from the date. If you can get him in some, please do. I wanna see how he matches ya fly."

I sent them the same selfie Simonique saw, and they agreed with her: Tim is silly, but cute. I could only laugh, but they're right.

"I will."

My nail tech taps my leg, letting me know she's done. I look down at my toes and squeal. *They look so pretty! And suckable*—I mean, *not* that I necessarily plan on sleeping with Tim tonight, but if the feeling sways that way, I'm not going to stop it. I'm going to be looking edible and smelling delicious, and I'm sure he's going to as well.

"A'ight, y'all, I'm all done here. I'll talk to y'all soon."

"Pictures, bitch!" Nikki reminds me before hanging up.

Lu rolls her eyes at Nikki's dramatics and says, "Have a good time, Camesha," before leaving the call, too.

Now, I have five hours to get ready before Tim picks me up for our 7pm dinner reservation at God-knows-where.

Tim

My heart is galloping like it's competing in the Kentucky Derby. I feel like I might have a heart attack at its current rate. I usually listen to music while I drive, but not now. I need to focus.

At this point, I've picked up Camesha from her crib several times, but knowing I'm going over there to pick her up for our first *real* date has made me anxious all day. . . Well, and the fact that I have a surprise for her and I'm not sure how she's going to react to it. I don't know if this move is doing too much, but it's how I feel and I want her to know that.

I crank up the AC so I'm not sweating and stink. I carefully thought out a look to complement her because I just know she's going to pop out looking fine as hell, so I felt I had to come correct. A fresh shape-up. A printed sage-green and rust-orange Cuban shirt underneath a brown suit, shiny loafers, my usual jewelry, and a new fragrance I picked up just for tonight.

I turn into Camesha's lot and park my ride. In the visor mirror, I check myself out one more time. *Lookin' good, Starks, lookin' good.* As I walk in and climb the steps to her condo, I take dramatic-ass, deep breaths to calm down.

At her door, I knock and stuff my hands in my pockets. After waiting for five seconds, I start pacing and my heart rate picks up.

Then the door opens. My jaw drops. And my eyes drag all over Camesha's body.

"Damn, baby," the words fall from my lips before I can catch them. I bite down hard as if that can keep more words from flowing out.

She tilts her head, a teasing smirk on her face. "*Baby*, huh?"

"I'm sorry—I mean, unless you okay wit' that," I try to recover the vibe.

"Sounds good to me," she says softly, batting her mascaraed eyelashes.

I huff out a breath, relieved. Her hair is half cornrows, half curls and some tendrils dribble down the sides of her face. Her cheekbones are gold, her eyes are captured in a smoky color, and brown gloss accentuates her perfect lips. All her jewelry is gold: small hoop earrings, dainty chain, and thin rings. And then this rust-orange silk dress—*my God*. It flows over her hourglass figure, the mid-thigh length exposing her smooth, shimmery legs in these metallic heels.

"You like?" Camesha asks coyly, low-key posing with her legs crossed, clutch in hand.

My mouth opens to answer, but none come out. I just shake my head, astounded, as I walk toward her. I grab her hand and hold it up. "I love ya nails, too. Twirl for me."

She obliges.

"Oh my God—*and* you backless? You tryna gimme a heart attack, girl?"

Camesha laughs sweetly. "Maybe a lil'." She pinches the air with her index finger and thumb. "Ya jaw's on the floor so that's close enough." She steps closer to stroke my chin hair.

I bite my lip at her touch, getting a whiff of her fragrance. She smells like an orange creamsicle. *And I wanna eat her up*, I think impulsively. My mouth waters as my hands find her waist.

Her hand presses into my chest. "Aht, aht, aht. I 'on't wanna ruin my gloss just yet."

I smack my teeth. "A'ight, well can I at least get a hug? You smell so damn good."

She smiles and wraps her arms around my neck. With my hands on her warm back, I nuzzle my face into her neck, pressing kisses there. She giggles, probably from my facial hair tickling her.

We back out of the hug, and Camesha scans *me* up and down all syrupy-slow. "You look," she pauses to find the right words, "*foine*."

Under her unabashed gaze, I feel shy, blushing like I ain't never gotten a compliment before. I chuckle like a light-skin nigga. "Thank you. Just tryna make sure I look like I belong next to you when we out." I shrug and she grins. "And I love that we matchin' a lil' wit' the orange."

She steps forward again and wraps her arms around my neck, my hands immediately gluing to her waist. "Where're you takin' me, handsome?"

"Nice try, C." I tap her nose and unravel myself from her arms while she sighs. "C'mon, let's go 'fore we miss our reservation." I offer her my bent arm for her to hold as we walk down to my Jeep.

Camesha

Warm feelings flooded my system when I saw Tim's speechless reaction to my outfit. Mission accomplished: his jaw dropped big time.

But I was *not* prepared for him looking as good as he wants to look tonight. His usual diamond studs and gold chains along with his brown suit complement his skin so well, especially in golden hour. I want to kiss him and get lost in his mouth, but I'm serious about that lip gloss. I tried a new technique I watched on YouTube, so I'd rather fuck it up in a make-out session at least after dinner.

But, oh my God, Tim smells so fucking delicious, something spicy and warm. With other guys I've dated, I was never clingy, but if Tim keeps coming around smelling this good, I might want to live in his skin—move in and everything.

He cranks up his truck, and I stop him before he goes to play something on his Spotify. "Lemme deejay tonight since you planned the date."

He raises an eyebrow at me. "You sure, C? I 'on't mind you just sittin' there, lookin' all pretty, my passenger princess."

I blush and grin at that. "Thank you. But I think I got some' that'll fit this vibe. Just *don't* kick me off the AUX if you 'on't like it."

"I would never. I'm a gentleman, remember?" He smirks.

I giggle and he backs out of the parking spot, heading to the road as I nervously swipe to my Spotify. I might've spent hours last night crafting a playlist.

When the beginning notes of "Nothing Even Matters" by Lauryn Hill and D'Angelo plays, I anxiously glance at Tim as he drives.

A wide smile breaks out, telling me he recognizes the song. "Yo, this is perfect."

I grin, too, slightly shimmy-dancing in my seat.

For most of the drive, we listen to the music, sometimes singing or rapping along. As we enter downtown Los Angeles, the setting Sun plays peek-a-boo behind the skyscrapers.

I pause "Be My Summer" by Snoh Aalegra when I notice Tim joining a line at a high-rise building. "Is this valet?"

He briefly glances my way. "Yeah. I figured you'd be wearin' heels, so I picked a spot wit' valet."

My heart flutters at that. "Tim," I whimper, "that's very considerate."

He looks at me and offers a crooked smile that could wet my panties if I don't hold it together. "Of course."

He says it like it was a no-brainer. Once we're at the front of the line, Tim parks his truck and gets out to open my door. I admire the huge glass building as he speaks to the employees before handing over his car key, slipping his lanyard in a pocket.

Hand in hand, we walk up the few concrete steps and into the revolving door. The building boasts a massive entryway: marble floors and walls, a huge chandelier, sunlight pouring through all the glass. This is *really* nice. I don't dare ask Tim where we are because he'd just give me a knowing smirk.

We follow an older couple in front of us into an elevator. The man presses the button to the 15th floor while Tim and I claim a corner. He's standing behind me, his hand comfortably resting on my hip as I lean back into him, his body heat and scent a nice cocoon. This feels like we do this all the time, like this *isn't* our first "real" date. The comfort with him is unreal. Our interactions make me feel like I'm floating—dreaming even, but I'm not. This is real life. *Tim* is real—At least, I pray he is, that my gut is right about him.

The elevator doors open, and we all turn to the left and come up on an entryway decked out in a modern Art-Deco style. Brown glass, gold light fixtures over the host station, dark marble archway into the restaurant. I read the glowing cursive sign: The Lenox Room.

I grip Tim's arm as I ogle the entrance. "Oh my God, we're havin' dinner *here*?"

I feel his eyes looking at me. "Yeah. I guess you're excited since you're cuttin' off the circulation in my arm."

"Sorry." I loosen my grip, patting his arm.

I've heard hustlers at events talk about this restaurant, from working a dinner to going on dates with their clients here. I've aways been curious about this place and now to be here is surreal.

A pretty hostess, wearing a white dress shirt under a black double-breasted vest and navy-blue tie, returns after seating the first couple. I see Tim briefly speak to her before she beckons us to follow her inside.

Now, *my* mouth hits the floor. To the left, golden sunrays seep through the floor-to-ceiling windows. Downtown LA is glittering. An island bar with velvet highchairs and orange backlight is in front of the windows, occupied by a few folks and a showman bartender.

Up ahead are some glass double doors to a terrace with lounge seating. And to the right of those doors is a hallway to the private dining rooms and the restrooms, the hostess explains.

To the far right, opposite the bar, is the stage where a jazz quartet is playing in front of drawn navy-blue curtains. Fanning out from the stage in a tiered semi-circle are the tables: velvet half-circle booths and free-standing tables all outfitted with cream tablecloths and little faux candles.

Art-Deco-style sunburst and peacock-printed wallpaper in navy blue and brown with gold foil. Paintings and black-and-white photographs of Black people—one I recognize as Langston Hughes—hang on the walls. Dimmed warm lighting. Orange and brown glass everywhere.

The hostess takes us to a booth on the far wall. She places the cream-colored menus with gold letters on the table. Tim motions for me get in first before him.

Tim

This date has barely begun, and I think I've outdone myself.

The Lenox Room first opened in New York City seven years ago, paying homage to the Harlem Renaissance. Given the success there, they brought it to Los Angeles three years ago. Ever since then and hearing clients rave about this place, it's been on my bucket list. Now felt like the perfect time to experience it and the perfect place to take Camesha for our first real date.

I grab her hand and kiss the back of it. "You're dazzlin', Camesha." As corny as it is to say, it's true. She's glowing, every part of her catching the little bit of light in here. She's an ethereal dream.

"Thank you. And Tim?" Camesha says. She's smiling, looking like she might cry and mess up her makeup. She's gazing at me like she could kiss me and hurt me at the same time.

Intrigued, I smirk, stretching my arm along the booth wall. "Whassup, C?"

"This feels like too much. Like, this is *really* nice." She gestures her hand around the room.

"Never that." I lean down and kiss her shoulder.

She lifts my head and just barely pecks my lips, not to mess up her gloss. "Thank you."

With my eyes half-lidded, I grin, ready to devour her mouth—*fuck that gloss*—but a server walks up. "Hi, I'm Kelby and I'll be takin' care of you all tonight." She goes on, asking if we've "joined them for an experience before," and we say no. She excitedly welcomes us and recommends a few menu items before leaving so we can peruse the Harlem Renaissance-inspired menu.

"Everything sounds so good," Camesha muses as her eyes dart across the page.

We discuss the appetizers and decide to share the Smoked Oxtail Croquettes.

"I've heard so many good things 'bout this place. The ambiance is amazin' and I'm excited to try the food," Camesha says.

"Same. Since Rugged Rah lives in New York, he was tellin' me 'bout that location. But then I remembered that Keyana knows the chef here, so I asked her to help me make a reservation on such short notice."

"If the food is hittin', be sure to thank her for me." Camesha comes forward to kiss my cheek, quickly swiping her gloss off my face afterwards.

"So, you can kiss me, but I can't kiss you? Unfair." I shake my head as she covers her face, laughing.

Kelby reappears. "Hi folks, have you decided on what to start out with?"

I inform Kelby that I'd like the Brownstone Old Fashioned and that we want to share the croquettes. Camesha orders the Savoy Honey Sour, a bourbon sour with Harlem-harvested honey.

After Kelby leaves, Camesha and I bask in the music a little, being whisked away to Brazil as the jazz band plays a Bossa Nova number. The sound is at the perfect volume for conversation.

"So, Camesha. Tell me: how'd you end up in LA? What gotchu where you are now?" I set my bent elbow on the table and rest my head on my fist.

She tears away from the quartet and giggles. "Just startin' wit' questions, huh?"

"Yeah, since this our first date and all," I say impishly, wiggling my eyebrows.

She grins, but then it fades a little as she begins nervously playing with her hair. Hesitantly, she launches into her story.

After graduating high school, she wasn't sure what to major in at college, what she's passionate about. So, she decided to work at a local coffee shop so she can reflect on a career path. Her first boyfriend, Travis, said her idea to move to LA to figure herself out was "dumb," that she could do that at community college like him.

Her idea wasn't dumb. It just wasn't practical. But some dreams aren't practical, and this city is filled with impractical—and sometimes—*delusional* dreamers. I don't think Camesha was delusional though.

At 19 years old, she packed up her used car with all her savings and drove to LA to see if she can make something shake.

I learned that she's *always* been a hustler. For the first few months, while she worked at coffee shops, she lived out of her car and cheap motels before she saved up enough money to move in with three roommates she found online. But for years, she made coffees and modeled for indie brands before ZZ introduced her to vibe modeling and escorting.

At some point during Camesha's story, Kelby brings our cocktails and asks for our entrée orders.

After listening to Camesha and hearing the shaky vulnerability in her voice, I can only look at her with admiration. She was brave to move out here with no real plan. I know a lot of people do it, but they're hungry for other things like fame or screen dreams. Camesha was unsure of her purpose and gifts, so, starved of many nontraditional opportunities back home in South Carolina, she sought a change of scenery to discover it.

"Ya know, ya life could be a movie?" I say, stroking my chin hair.

She shakes her head bashfully.

"Fa real, there's some' there. That's an inspirin' story, Camesha." I sip my drink, the black walnut bitters and smoked maple syrup is a delicious addition to this classic cocktail.

She shrugs. "I might know someone who could act in it."

"See, you already gotcho lead. I'm sure I can ask around and get y'all in a room wit' a writer and a producer."

She just laughs, waving me off, even though I'm serious.

Movement to my right snatches my attention away from her. Some patrons stand near their seats and start slow dancing. I now realize that the quartet transitioned into a slower song, the saxophonist blowing soft, fluttery notes. It's really smooth.

I look back at Camesha, smirking. "You wanna dance?"

A sexy smile curves her glossed lips as she breathes out a "Yes."

Camesha

Tim gets out of the booth and gently pulls me to my feet. His right hand is warm on my waist while his left holds my hand. We start slow dancing to the music.

Being this close to him, I get dizzy as his scent captures me in a bubble. Telling him part of my story felt nice though.

But I'm thankful when he talks low, lifting me from my trance. "So, how was ya sister's graduation?"

I tell him all about Simonique's commencement, my family wilding out at the ceremony, our private dinner, the family cookout. Nique peeping his photo. . .

Tim laughs a little. "So, I passed Simonique's looks test, huh? But not without bein' called *silly?*"

I laugh because it does sound bad. "Yeah, but you passed though. . ."

Tim just looks at me with a peaceful and content expression, his face open and soft. "I'm glad. And I'm glad you were able to go and celebrate her witcha family. Sounds like you really needed to be home."

"I'm glad I went home, too." I visit home for Christmas and sometimes Thanksgiving if I can take off from the hotel, but this trip felt much more necessary. A nice, welcomed reset to think about what's next, what I want . . . who I want?

A slight smile touches my face. I lean toward his shoulder, careful not to get my makeup on his brown suit.

Tim kisses my temple.

The band transitions to a more piano-heavy song now. I take in a deep breath and say, "And ya know what, seein' Simonique graduate," my voice sounds scratchy, so I clear my throat, "has me thinkin' 'bout possibly applyin' to schools this fall. . ."

Tim backs away to look at me, his eyes sparkling as a smile lifts his mouth. "Fa real?"

"Yeeessss," I sound unsure. "I'm just—"

"That's *awesome*, Camesha."

I blush, dropping my head a little. "Thanks, Tim." I look up at him again, finding his gaze unwavering. "But I *am* a lil' nervous."

His eyebrows meet. "'Bout what?"

My heart is pounding against my chest like crazy as I trip on the words, trying to force them out. "A-About leavin' the hustle. N-Not knowin' who I am or what else I can do w-without it. It's been a part of my life for so long—I-I 'on't know. . ." I huff out.

This is the first time I've admitted that out loud. I think that's why I've never really tried to sit down and think about what else I'd do for myself with all that gotdamn hustle money. I don't think I really *believed* I could actually amass all that. I just felt like I should shoot for the stars in LA. That I did, getting so good, yet annoyed at being Cammie that sometimes it was hard to just be Camesha. Or sometimes I didn't even *want* to be Camesha. After all, *she* didn't make almost half a million dollars in three years by attending parties and fucking rich men.

Tim places both my arms around his neck then pulls me closer to him by my waist. I can't help but look at him now, a concerned look marring his face. "Camesha, I need you to hear me," he says low, yet emphatically.

I try to drop my head to escape his intense gaze, but he says, "I need you to look at me when I say this, too, baby." I peer up at him, and he continues, "You are *so* much more than what you do or *have* done. You're not just a hustler. You're *not* just Cammie. You are you. Camesha. And that's enough. That's *always* been enough."

My chest tightens. My eyes sting, threatening to cry at his affirmation. But I keep looking at him.

Tim clears his throat. "I mean, I'm sure you know that, but I just wanted to remind you," he says softly, eyes flicking across my face. "The unknown is scary, but you've already done it before by movin' out here. That's some brave and powerful shit, C." He lets out a chuckle, like he's impressed with me.

I blush, and he continues, "And as cliché as it is, it's true: you can do *whatever* you want." His face softens a little. "And the fact that you're even thinkin' about the possibilities like school? Maybe it's a sign, an invitation to figure out whatchu wanna be and whatchu want now—I mean, not that you not doin' that already, I'm just sayin', sounds like that's what's on ya mind."

I let Tim's words sink into my skin then settle into the pit of my stomach. My fingers rub the close-cut hairs of his fade at the nape of his neck. He slightly shivers and clenches his jaw at my touch, making me grin. "Thank you for sayin' that. I think you're right."

Tim's lips lift into a slight grin. "I'm here. I support you."

I grin, too. "Thanks," I say, my voice too quiet.

Tim dips his head to kiss my cheek before straightening back up, his eyebrows meeting again. "Wait, so if you thinkin' 'bout not hustlin', does that mean you hit ya goal? I know you said you had a lil' bit left."

I melt on the inside at him being concerned about that. "I *haven't*, but it's gonna be okay."

He starts to nod and stops himself, frowning. "Wait, are you doin' this cuz of what I said a few weeks ago?" He glances around mouthing cuss words and kissing his teeth. "Camesha, that's *my* pro'lem, not yours." Tim is just so cute when he's worked up.

Despite trying to stay serious, I can't keep it together and I laugh. Tim's surprised at this, too, judging from the confused and shocked look on his face.

"No, baby, it's for me." A smile softly touches my lips. "I've made more than enough and wit' the money I have, I got options. Whether it's school, even if I still 'on't know what I'd like to major in *like I didn't know eight years ago*," I whisper the last part, "or some' else. I think I just need time to figure some things out." This comes out more resolute, more solid. No real plan yet, but the possibility of one.

My eyes dart across his face, his features relaxing.

"Okay. Well, ya know, I'm here if you need or want some help. I gotchu." Tim offers me a warm smile.

A painful jolt strikes my stomach at that. Maybe it's because I'm on a date, but those words remind me of Eric, a 32-year-old man I dated when I was 22. He seemed mature and reliable. Always told me he "got me," always paid for our dates. He even sent me some money a few times to cover my part of the rent at my shared apartment. But over time, this nigga felt like I owed him sex because he "helped" me out so much. That's when I stopped answering his calls and texts. He didn't do those things for me because he was kind, he just wanted to keep me in his back pocket.

But man, I want to believe that Tim genuinely means it when he says "I gotchu." One part of me does, and the other is still proceeding with caution. It's just, like Eric, some people don't always help out of the goodness of their heart. But so far, all I've seen from Tim is goodness. *Maybe he's* too *good to be real?* I wonder. Even though our trajectory seems to be trending positively, I still want to be sensible and not get too caught up even though it *feels* right.

Besides, transitioning out of the hustle life and into college or whatever is something I need to figure out on my own anyway.

I blink and smile at Tim before speaking again, "Thank you for sayin' how you really felt about my hustlin' cuz I 'on't know if I would've considered quittin' right now had you not said that. So, in a way, while I might not do it *for* you, it's partly *because* of you." I playfully poke him in the chest.

I hear commotion behind us. We separate as we watch Kelby set our two plates down on the table. Tim's Blackened Duck Breast with Hennessy Glaze over creamy stone-ground grits and sauteed collard greens. My Honey-Lacquered Salmon with bourbon butter, black-eyed pea succotash, and charred okra. Everything looks and smells great.

"I hope you enjoy," Kelby breaks the silence with a warm smile.

"Thank you," Tim and I say simultaneously.

"You owe me a Coke—and a real kiss, Camesha," Tim points at me.

I laugh as I slip inside the booth, and he follows. I take my phone out my purse and snap a photo of the food to share with my friends. "Can you take a selfie wit' me?"

Without protesting, Tim leans in, one arm stretched out behind me along the backrest while his other hand grabs my phone to hold it out for our selfie. *Excuse me. Just took the lead.* I snap my thighs together as the pulse between my legs quicken at Tim's assertive move.

He takes pictures of us posing: us smiling, him kissing me on the temple, us holding up silly hand signs.

We look damn good together.

After our little photo shoot is over, Tim grabs my hand and bows his head. *Oh.* I follow suit as he leads us in grace.

He says, "Amen," and we lift our heads and open our eyes. "Hope you ain't mind that. Figured we can say grace together."

I feel warm on the inside . . . or rather hot. *That* was very hot. "Not at all," I say too softly.

He quirks up a grin as we begin to eat, moans and groans floating up from our table at the food. Everything's so juicy, tender, well-seasoned, and pairs well with our cocktails.

"Definitely thank Keyana for me. This food is *it*."

His mouth full, Tim laughs, nodding his head in agreement.

With more jovial jazz music now playing in the background, Tim and I transition from the heaviness of me leaving the hustle to us trading wild stories from our respective sides of the industry.

As we finish our meal, popping mints into our mouths, the jazz quartet stops playing and patrons clap tastefully but enthusiastically. Tim and I join them.

A male employee dressed in a uniform—black double-breasted vest over a white dress shirt with a *gold* tie—walks up from backstage to the mic in front of the quartet. "Give it up for the smooth sounds of the Pacific Blue Notes!"

I lean toward Tim to tell him that they play at The Adonir Hotel, and he says they're dope.

"We're really proud to showcase fantastic local jazz talent here at The Lenox Room." More applause. "And now onto the next portion of our evening's entertainment." The man steps back to pull a paper out of his vest pocket.

I feel Tim lean in. "I'mma use the bathroom." He kisses my temple.

I nod, watching him slide out of the booth and toward the back hallway.

"Poetry Open Mic! Folks, we have a fantastic lineup so please warm this stage up for our poets!" The crowd applauds and so do I.

I sit up, feeling a tad giddy at the idea of hearing poetry. I don't engage with poetry often, and I'm not going to lie, I may not *always* understand it, but it *sounds* pretty... *I wonder if Tim knew they'd be doin' this tonight.* This is a nice addition to our already amazing date.

Tim

I ain't *really* have to use the bathroom. However, I do need time to calm down.

The restroom's interior design matches the restaurant, but it's brighter in here. I can hear the host talking about the Open Mic before he introduces the first poet.

I look in the mirror, my eyes going crazy. My chest is tight. Feels like Mike Tyson's mouth got my motherfucking lungs in a vise grip. I suck in a few deep breaths to loosen up.

Once I look like I'm not about to throw up all that delicious food, I step out the bathroom. I round corners until I'm backstage, checking in again with an employee.

I hope Camesha likes what I wrote since it's about her.

When Keyana helped me make a reservation, I learned that The Lenox Room was hosting their monthly Poetry Open Mic tonight, so I asked the manager if I could join. They had a few more spots available for the hour-long event, so he added me. They said the order would be random so either join the lineup backstage or be prepared to leave my table at any time. I want this to be a surprise—a pleasant, well-received one—so, I decided I was going to hang out in the back. Plus, while Camesha was busy ogling the restaurant's entrance when we arrived, I informed the hostess that I'm here to perform at the Open Mic and she marked my attendance before leading us to our table.

A small group of us open mic'ers are huddling behind the stage. We exchange pleasantries and nervous smiles. Some explain they've done this here a few times, others are professional working poets with some stage fright. *I* feel like the odd one out, having not written nor done spoken word in so long, but I'm not here to impress these people. I'm here to express to Camesha how I feel about her. *I hope this isn't too much and doesn't scare her off.*

Then, I hear it, "Please, welcome to the stage: Tim Starks!"

Here goes nuttn, I think. I vacuum in a few deep breaths as I hustle up the steps and emerge from behind the curtains. I dap up the host as he passes me, whispering an upbeat "Good luck" in my ear.

A few feet from the mic, I swallow hard, my mind debating on whether I look at Camesha or not. I can't *really* see her from up here with the stage lights in my face, but I know where our

booth is. I wish I knew what she's thinking, to gauge if this is still
a good idea.

Taking in a massive breath, I step up to the microphone.
"How y'all doin' tonight?" I force a smile to see if that helps calm
me down.

It doesn't.

A few patrons respond brightly. I could see silhouettes
of waitstaff milling around, hearing them softly interact with
customers.

"Good, good." Another deep breath. "Honestly, I ain't done
this in a while, so *please* bear wit' me." I look toward our table,
imagining Camesha being open-minded to this gesture. This
corny shit could blow up in my face, but I *have* to let her know
how I feel about her . . . about an us.

"I've, uh, recently been inspired. This is entitled 'No Rush.' I
hope *you* enjoy," I say, hoping Camesha caught that I'm talking
to her.

I step back from the mic, rolling my shoulders back and
closing my eyes, quickly scrolling through the poem in my mind.
I pray my anxiety doesn't make me forget it, even with two
weeks of practice under my belt. I only have five minutes up
here, but I take my time getting ready, slowing my heart rate,
calming my nerves.

At the mic, I open my eyes, staring in her direction and pour
my heart out onstage:

"I've been in my game for almost seven years—done seen a
lotta pretty faces.

But upon seein' yours for the first time, I think my heart got
to racin'.

"I swear it's easy and hard witchu.
Ain't gon' lie, sometimes it's really hard to read you.
But if I'm sensin' correctly, you really feelin' me, too. . .

"Damn, I ain't really talk to you in seven months.
But when we reconnected, we made 'bout seven jumps,
humps—dancin' witchu was magical.

"I 'on't wanna move too fast,
but every moment feels built to last.
Time bends different when I'm witchu.
And when I'm not, is it weird if I already miss you?
Witchu I ain't tryna rush.
I ain't think at my big age, I'd ever have a crush.

"I ain't felt this way 'bout someone in a long time.
I 'on't wanna mess this up. I wanna long, long mine
this connection that we're buildin' and see where it goes.
Drive it 'til the wheels fall off, see where the wind blows.

"If there's a chance at an us, I wanna gamble it.
Cuz either way, you the prize, baby,
and I *know* I can handle it.

"I'll take whatever you willin' to gimme.
I 'on't wanna waste ya time.
Again, I *don't* wanna rush you.
But you *gotta* know . . . I wanna make you mine."

Camesha

After his last line, Tim squints his eyes. I don't know if he can
see me from the stage, but my eyes threaten to cry and fuck
up my makeup. He winks at me very subtly and turns to leave
backstage. The host passes him then says his name into the mic,
calling the audience to give it up for him. We've been snapping,
but they applaud.

I . . . I don't know how to react. I'm feeling all over the place in the best way. I'm overwhelmed, shocked, flattered. . . *Hot. Wet.* Butterflies crowd the insides of my body.

I understand every part of Tim's poem: he likes me *a lot* and wants to see where this goes. *Same, Tim, same.*

He said that two weeks ago but hearing it in this fashion is something else. He just bared his soul in front of all these strangers.

If he doesn't try to get some, I'm definitely *offerin' him some pussy*, I think. I don't know if that makes me a down bad hussy, but I don't care.

I black out during the next poet's turn, luxuriating in the warm feelings Tim induced. Out the corner of my eye, I see him slide in next to me. Before he's in his seat good, I throw my arms around his neck. The hug is short-lived because I *need* to kiss him now. My hands cup his jaws, and I kiss him with abandon. He matches my energy, and we make out, both of us moaning and groaning since we haven't kissed each other in over two weeks. I don't give a fuck about my lip gloss now as I taste him, remnants of his mint and cocktail.

When our lips and tongues untwine with a slight smack, he exhales, "Damn. I'm gon' have to write more poems for you then, huh?"

I laugh, blushing. "That wouldn't be a bad idea." With the pads of my thumbs, I rub my gloss off and around his lips, giggling at the mess we've made. Smirking, his fingers lightly swipe around my lip line.

Staring into his half-closed eyes, my chest heaving, I breathe out, "Tim . . . that was beautiful. That was the *sweetest* thing anybody has ever done for me."

His lips curl up into a slight smile. "I'm glad you liked it, baby. I meant every word."

"I *loved* it." I caress his cheek and peck his lips.

Tim smiles. "Camesha?"

"Yeah?"

"Will you be my lady?"

My brown cheeks are probably beet-red right now. It's so cute of him to formally ask me, although, I'm taken aback because he already expressed that he wanted me in his poem. And in my mind, whether it's immature or presumptuous, he'd already been my man. He just ain't know it yet.

But then again, maybe it's too soon. It is our first date—No, don't overthink this. You want him. He wants you. I get out of my head to respond with an "Of course."

A lopsided grin overtakes his face. "Bet." And he kisses me again.

"That was an amazing poem, Tim," Kelby whisper-yells, interrupting us.

I add, "Yeah, *Himothy.*"

Tim tickles my sides before looking at our server with a wide smile. "'Preciate it, Kelby."

"Of course. Can I interest you all in any dessert?"

He diverts his gaze to me. "You want some', beautiful?"

"That Sweet Potato Bread Pudding with Praline Sauce sounded good."

Without hesitating, he tells Kelby, "We'll have that."

"Great choice." She smiles again and jets off.

With my back against Tim's chest and his arms around my waist, we cuddle as we enjoy the rest of the Open Mic. At some point, Kelby brings our dessert with vanilla ice cream and two spoons. Not thinking too much about it, I scoop some bread pudding and ice cream and turn a little to hold it up to Tim's mouth. In awe, I watch over my shoulder as his lips capture the morsel, his tongue licking the corners of his mouth for any leftovers. His jaws going as he chews and swallows. Me loving that might be a lil' creepy, but it never gets old.

After the Open Mic, the host announces that the Pacific Blue Notes will return in 10 minutes. Tim pays the bill, and we decide to continue the night lounging on The Lenox Room's rooftop terrace. I offer to get us more drinks, and we both opt for espresso martinis.

With downtown now awash in silver light instead of gold, we sit comfy on a couch. Drinks in hand, we're sitting perpendicularly—my crossed legs thrown over Tim's bent ones. I prop my elbow on the couch to support my head and Tim's arm is stretched along the backrest.

"I almost called Kelby over so she can have one of the male employees go check on you in the bathroom before I saw you get on that stage. You were gone way too long."

He chuckles at that. "It was all part of the surprise."

"And it was a *really* good one, Tim." I beam.

He grins shyly.

"So, you handle rappers, *and* you can also spit like 'em, too? If not better? Why didn't you tell me you write poetry?" I side-eye him.

He throws his head back, laughing. "No joke, I ain't write in years. Until I met *you*." He rubs my shin and I Kegel to keep my pussy from twitching. *Settle down, bitch.*

I swallow before saying, "That's amazin' then. You just started writin' again and it sounds that good? I mean, I'm not a poetry expert, but judgin' from that applause, other people liked whatchu had to say as well."

"That's nice and all, but I was more concerned 'bout what *you* thought." With his hand still on my leg, Tim leans forward and presses a long kiss to my lips. Before I could grab his chin hair and deepen the kiss, he retreats. "Besides I wasn't sure if that'd even go over well witchu. I knew it was extra as fuck and corny as shit, but hey, I might just be that type of nigga." He shrugs exaggeratedly. "Or, at least witchu I am."

I blush. "I like Extra and Corny Tim," my voice drops to a shy level.

He looks at me, smirking.

Clearing my throat, I keep going, "But not gon' lie, ya line: 'Cuz either way, you the prize, baby, and I *know* I can handle it' especially gave me butterflies. Very smooth, sir."

Now, *he* blushes and cheeses big as hell. "Thank you. I 'preciate that, Camesha." He lifts his glass so we can cheers before we set them down on the brown glass coffee table nearby.

"So, now that I know you got poetic skills, you mean to tell me you really *didn't* have a lil' roster out here?" I tease, referencing a text conversation we had a while ago.

While vibing and escorting, it always amazed me how the most assholey of guys have a gaggle of women, but it almost feels unfair when good men like Tim don't. But honestly, that's okay because it makes me like Tim even more. It's consistent with what I've seen of him so far: he's not a douchebag.

Tim cracks up. "I really didn't. Why 'on't you believe me?"

"I mean, you're clearly a gentleman," he laughs at that word, and I continue, "considerate, sweet, romantic, *and* got the gift of gab? The math ain't mathin', Tim."

We laugh.

"I *promise* you, I ain't have a roster, Camesha. I was never that guy—never smooth wit' women. I was mostly workin' anyway, too busy to try to date anyone. I mean, I hooked up wit' a few women, but my last relationship was two years ago."

"How long did it last?"

"Almost two years."

I tilt my head, taking a beat. "If you 'on't mind me askin', why'd y'all break up?"

"She's three years older than me and was more established in her career, so she was ready for things that I wasn't ready for yet. Like movin' in together, pets, marriage, kids. I told her I wasn't in that headspace yet—wasn't lookin' to settle down like that." He looks out at the skyscrapers and clenches his jaw.

Listening to him, I admire his profile: the close fade leading up to the curls on top of his head, the slope of his button nose, the pout of his full lips.

"I've *always* wanted those things, but now, I'm ready for 'em. I'm in a much better spot financially and mentally, too." Tim takes a deep breath, and his jaw tightens before he continues, "Ya know, like wit' my pops passin' and all."

I lift my hand to caress the back of his head. Back in February, somehow parents came up in a text conversation, and Tim told me about his father passing from an aneurysm when he was a sophomore in college. I wanted to call him right then and there, but he had to go since an award show was starting. We eventually talked about it more another time.

"Plus, I wasn't always present wit' her. I let work have too much of my attention a lotta the time. I was too available for clients."

That makes my eyebrows raise. Because so far, Tim's been *very* present with me. I've never felt like his attention was elsewhere anytime we were around each other. Lingering eye contact. Winding conversations. Hell, even his damn poem is called "No Rush". . . I guess he learned to be present after his last relationship.

He briefly drops his gaze before clearing his throat. "I ain't gon' lie, it hurt for a minute—her breakin' up wit' me. But now, I'm older, wiser, more settled. I've even started blockin' time off on my calendar for myself and for the people I care 'out. Like you." He winks at me.

Heat rushes my cheeks and butterflies flood my stomach. I fight to maintain eye contact.

"I'm serious, Camesha." He smiles crooked, the hand along the couch lifts to caress my cheek.

I lean into his warm palm, goosebumps erupting on my skin. "I know." That's scary—the intensity of his feelings and mine. My skeptical side wants to believe that Tim's just *saying* that, that his pretty words—from the poem to his admission now—isn't true. But my gut is telling me that from the way he's looking at me and his demeanor, Tim is genuine.

His grin widens. "You've got my whole attention, Camesha."

A slow smile smooths onto his handsome face.

And just like that, my panties are wet again. *Bitch, these shits are ruined*, my inner self says.

Tim

I'm feeling good as hell right now. My poem didn't suck. Camesha *loved* it. We made it official. Life is pretty swell if I do say so myself.

Now, we're riding in my Jeep with the windows cracked and Camesha's playlist at a great volume.

"Ain't gon' lie, C, you did yo' thing wit' this music," I say over Sade's "Kiss of Life," glancing over at Camesha as we cruise down I-10.

"Awww, that means a lot comin' from you." She stuns the fuck out of me when she grabs my hand that's resting on the console to hold it in her lap. My heart quickens as I swallow hard at the softness of her thighs in her slightly hiked-up dress and how close my hand is to her crotch. I mean, I can feel the heat radiating from it.

Shit, shit, shit! I hold my jaw rigid to relax.

By 11pm, I'm turning into her building's parking lot. I think at this point she's in the habit of me opening her door as she doesn't make a move to get out of the car. Once she's out, she grabs my hand and leads the way up to her place. That's sexy as hell.

"You lookin' at my ass, sir?" Camesha teases.

"Yes ma'am," I admit, chuckling and shaking my head.

She cracks up. "At least you're honest."

"Aye, I'm just admirin' God's creation." Her ass looks amazing swishing in this silk dress.

Camesha laughs as we make it to her door. I watch her dig into her clutch for her keys.

"Now *this* was a date," I remark.

She spins around to look up at me, shaking some curly hair off her shoulders. "It was *really* nice, Tim. I had a great time. And," she pretends to think, her finger near her mouth, "I'mma need that poem framed."

I laugh. "I can definitely do that for you." I step forward, slipping my arms around her waist as she holds my biceps.

Before I can lean down for a goodnight kiss, Camesha speaks up barely above a whisper, "You wanna come inside?"

Breath catches in my throat. We haven't been inside each other's cribs yet. I've dropped her off at hers and she's never been to my house. I mean, this feels like the natural next step—you know, now that Camesha's *my lady* and all. Still doesn't mean I'm not a little nervous. It's a level she's granting me access to, and I take that seriously. "Y-Yeah," I say hoarsely before clearing my throat.

A slight smile touches her lips before she turns out of my arms and unlocks her door. She walks through first, holding it open for me as she flips on her lights.

Camesha's place is exactly how I imagined it—*not* that I've been imagining it like I've been dying to come inside.

It's just her. Luxurious, yet low-key. On the other side of her condo is an open door to a dark room, which I'm assuming is her bedroom. To my left is the kitchen and two small doors, while to my right is her living room.

One of her taupe couches is overflowing with a plush blanket. The TV remote, coasters, and a half-burned lavender vanilla candle rest on a ribbed wooden coffee table. A flat-screen sits on a matching storage console.

As I explore a bit, Camesha scurries around behind me. Next to her small dining table is a bookcase with some books, a Bluetooth speaker, and framed photos of her family. A good-looking bunch with gapped smiles, except Camesha doesn't have one. Her window is covered with a drawn curtain.

I make my way to her kitchen. A little window with blinds hovers above her sink and cream-colored countertops. Only a bowl of fruit occupies the space. If she has small kitchen gadgets, she must store them in the cabinets. The appliances I can see appear stainless steel.

"So, this is me," Camesha breaks the silence.

"It is." My gaze glides to her standing in the kitchen and she shrugs with a cute grin on her face. "I dig it. You do interior design or some' on the side? Cuz this looks straight outta magazine."

She claps a hand over her mouth as her eyes get big as saucers. "That's crazy you say that cuz. . ," she trails off.

I smile. "Cuz what?"

She blinks and shakes her head. "Nothin'. Thank you for sayin' that, Tim." She clears her throat. "I know we've been drinkin' all night, but do you want anything else?" She changes the subject, pointing behind her where her fridge is standing to the right of that little window.

"Water, thanks. But what were you 'bout to say, Camesha?"

She looks down at the floor. "It's silly. Seriously, it's nothin'."

"You sure? Whassup?" My eyebrows pull together as I watch her, staying on the other side of the counter.

Camesha looks at the ceiling, chuckling and sighing. "Goin' to school is a *new* idea of what I can do wit' the hustle money. But sometimes I *dream* about bein' an interior designer," she says flippantly, like it's impossible, like her dream is childish. "But I 'on't know. Just cuz my friends, my sister, and now *you* agree wit' me that my place is nice doesn't mean anything. Not sayin' I 'on't appreciate the compliments though." A grin twitches onto her lips before she deeply inhales. "At this point in my life, I want security and stability. *Something* tangible, practical. I know you said I can do anything I want and that's true, but the hotel is *real*. I'm doin' it now and I got a lotta experience in it. Shit, I'd count vibe modelin' and escortin' as experience by the way I had to cater to some of those niggas. I just *don't* wanna keep chasin' shit—"

She stops rambling when her gaze lands on me, realizing that I'm now standing in front of her.

"Sorry," Camesha mutters, avoiding eye contact. She's breathing through her nose, her chest rising and falling rapidly.

"Ain't nuttn to be sorry 'bout." I clench my jaw to brace myself for what I'm about to say. "And ain't nuttn wrong wit' dreamin'. Ain't nuttn wrong wit' pursuin' those dreams." I chuckle, eyeing her fidgeting. "And you ain't wrong to wanna advance in ya current career, either." I clear my throat and lift her chin, so that she'd look at me. "But I'm *not* gon' let you downplay ya desires, Camesha. Ya dream of wantin' to be an interior designer is valid and very possible. *If* that's whatchu wanna do."

Her eyes appear more round as she looks at me with soft intent.

A grin tugs on my lips. "Shit, I actually know an interior designer. So, say the word and I can introduce you to her."

Instantly, her eyes widen and brighten. "Really?" And just as quickly they shrink and dim, making me frown a little.

"Yeah, Camesha," I chortle. "Whatever it is, I'll support you." Shrugging, I offer her a small smile. "Just, ya know, positive self-talk, baby." To end on a lighter note, I softly peck her lips before backing out of her personal space.

Camesha just looks at me before clearing her throat and rubbing her lips together. She opens her fridge, which is neat and organized. "I, uh, have some infused water if that's okay?"

Smirking, I say, "Yeah, that's cool."

I hope Camesha heard what I said a moment ago. I understand having to let things marinate. My pops was the king at telling me shit that had me staring at the ceiling as I laid in bed.

Camesha pulls out a pitcher of water. "I just made this last night. It has lemon slices, cinnamon, and raw honey."

I hum at the recipe as she moves to get a glass from a cabinet. Unashamed, I watch the slight rise of her dress as she reaches for the cup. The thing isn't on a high shelf, otherwise I would've helped her, but damn, I'm enjoying the view of her pretty brown legs and the way her ass pokes out—

I snap out of it, clearing my throat. "This drink sounds like it'll clean me out."

"It's a detox *and* cozy drink," she titters, sliding the glass to me.

I can feel Camesha's eyes on me as I gulp, quenching more thirst than I thought I had. When I set the cup down, I exhale, "*Ahhh*. That's good, C."

A smile spreads on her face. She drinks some, too.

She keeps our car vibe going by turning her playlist on the Bluetooth speaker. With our water, we migrate to the couch in front of the TV, and I remove my blazer. She asks me about my poem and tells me which other lines were her favorites. I'm flattered that she remembers and wants to discuss them like we're at a writer's talk. I can tell she's genuinely interested in my explanations. . . But I can also tell, she's trying to keep the attention on me and not her. Maybe it's a leftover reaction from her being vulnerable with me a few minutes ago.

I don't want to press her about anything, so, I ask about her family. She indulges me with hilarious stories about Simonique. I hope Camesha allows me to meet her when she visits this summer.

And then there's a slight lull in conversation. "Rain" by SWV fades in, the lush and dreamy song shifting the energy in

Camesha's living room. Like shy teenagers who don't know what to do next, we giggle when our gazes briefly meet and set our now empty glasses on the coasters.

Nodding to the beat, I say, "This song is sexy," before mouthing the lyrics to her. I can't do it justice like Coko though.

Camesha giggles, then a *look* settles on her face. Her chin down, her eyes darken and narrow at me.

"You're sexy," I breathe out, damn-near drooling on myself. I lock my jaw and try to keep eye contact, so she doesn't see me mentally kicking myself for not thinking. I'm not smooth at all.

"You think so?" she asks, her voice like dripping honey. And I got a sweet tooth.

I lean toward her alluring presence. "Yeah. And I *love* this hairstyle on you." My curled index finger ghosts down a curly strand along the side of her face.

She smirks. "Thank you."

As my face gets closer to hers, my eyes drop repeatedly to her delicious round lips. Looks like she might've re-glossed them when we separated to use the restrooms before we left the restaurant.

We're so close now, her fragrance has me in an embrace.

Camesha bites her bottom lip and captures my face as we kiss. *God, I love when she takes control like that.* Maybe I'm feeling emboldened, or my cocktails are still in my system, but I cup her waist and lift her onto my lap. Her dress hikes up, her legs straddle me, my hands cradle her exposed back. My head's hitting the back of her couch as we make out, our lips and tongues in a familiar dance.

Then . . . Camesha starts grinding on me. Very. Slowly. Enough for me to not notice if my senses aren't as alert as they are right now being in her condo.

Camesha surprises me again when her lips wrap around my tongue and she sucks on it, moaning. My heart violently jolts and skips several beats. A loud moan escapes my mouth as I grip her waist a little too tight and hold her down on my lap to stop her slow wining. It all feels so torturously good. My dick is jumping for joy.

She retreats a few breaths away, her hands dropping to my shoulders.

"I'm sorry, I'm sorry," I exhale out of breath like I just ran a marathon.

"Did I do some' wrong?" she asks, concerned.

"No, no, not at all, Camesha." I swallow to calm myself down. "Honestly, ya doin' *everything* right, baby."

Her face softens just a bit, a little grin appearing.

"It's just . . . it's been a minute for me. And I 'on't think I'm ready or can handle it right now. That's all."

I haven't had sex in over a year. Since Taylor broke up with me, I had a few one-night stands and while the sex was fine—meaning, I came—it all confirmed to me that I am *definitely* a relationship guy. I love getting to know and being with one woman.

"Oh." Camesha's gaze drops.

Shit! I hope she's not mad at me. The music transitions to an R&B song I've never heard before.

Unsure what to do, I lift her chin. "Trust me, I definitely *want* you, Camesha. I would love to take you down right now."

She averts her gaze momentarily, giggling.

Okay, that's a good sign. "I just don't wanna rush into sex either—if that's okay witchu."

She nods before her face morphs into worry. "You think we're rushin'?"

I shake my head quickly. "Not necessarily. I just wanna take my time witchu. Like I said in ya poem, I 'on't wanna rush what we got goin' on."

Camesha's face relaxes a little as she plays with the collar of my camp shirt. "*My* poem, huh?"

I lean forward, saying it pointedly, "Yeah, *your* poem." I tickle her waist, and her head falls on my shoulder as she laughs.

As her laughter dies down, I whisper into her ear, "Again, I'm sorry."

Her head pops up and she looks me dead in the eyes. Seems like she's about to say something, but I interrupt her, "I wanna make sure you know that I'm *not* rejectin' you—I mean, I *kinda* am right now, but overall, I'm not." I squeeze my eyes shut so that I'd stop yapping. "Sorry."

"It's okay, Tim," she snickers.

I crack open my eyes.

"Besides, I can *feel* that ya not rejectin' me." She smirks, subtly dropping her gaze to my lap, referencing my erection.

I can't help but chuckle at that even though I'm blushing. It's a natural reaction, so I try to shake off the embarrassment. *Hell, what straight man* wouldn't *get hard wit' Camesha grindin' on 'em and suckin' their tongue?*

"I mean, believe me, it's takin' *everything* in me to exercise every bit of self-control that I have." Pause. "We had such an amazin' night, so I just hope I didn't ruin the mood."

"You didn't, Tim. If anything, you *enhanced* the mood. . ." It sounds like it could be a question as she sort of looks off.

My eyes enlarge as I smile. "Really?"

Camesha pokes her lips out and nods. "I like that you wanna wait. *I can't lie, it makes me wantchu even more,*" she says the last part all low, bashfully.

"Word?" A lopsided smile worms onto my face.

"Yeah. But I like kissin' you, too, so it's cool." She lifts her eyes to mine. "Ya know you were my first kiss in three years?"

I think back to the rules of her escorting. And no kissing was a rule. "You didn't date while hustlin'?"

"I stopped datin'. I ain't think I can do both. And now that I'm witchu," Camesha locks her arms around my neck and my hands glue to her back, "I *definitely* don't wanna do both—but again, it's not only for you, it's for me, too."

"Good." I lean forward and peck her lips. "I'd feel terrible if you stopped hustlin' just to appease me. I wouldn't wantchu to resent me or nuttn down the road."

She just softly gazes at me before she leans in. We continue kissing, but she doesn't suck my tongue again and I'm glad because I'm not sure I'd be able to keep it strictly at first base after that.

When we come up for air, we rest our foreheads on one another's.

"Cherish the Day" by Sade is playing now. The perfect way to end the night.

I take a glimpse at the time on her TV set top box and see it's after midnight. I might say, "Fuck self-control" the longer I stay here, especially wrapped up in her arms and her sweet perfume. "I should pro'ly get goin'," I whisper.

Her eyes just swim in mine before she responds with a slight nod.

We get up. She pauses her music, and I slip on my blazer. After exchanging promises to talk and see one another soon, we hug and share a peck before I leave. In the hallway, I face a wall to command my dick to soften up so I can leave Camesha's building without a third leg.

10
Time to Move On

Wednesday, May 30

Camesha

T im texted me the morning after our first date:

Tim (10:17am):

> Good morning, gorgeous. I know u said I didnt, but I feel bad for turning the mood last night. I hope ur not mad at me for wanting to wait a lil.

I chuckled. His feeling bad about this reminded me of how he kept apologizing for not responding quickly to my texts during award season. I immediately called him to ease his worries and tell him that I meant what I said last night, reassuring him that he didn't ruin the mood.

And I did mean what I said about him wanting to wait actually makes me want him more.

After he left my condo, I used my favorite vibrator in the shower. And while lying in the bed. Obviously, it doesn't compare to the real thing, but it helped relieve some built-up tension from our date. Thoughts of Tim, his lips, his hands, his erection—had me *all* hot and bothered, and I just knew that if I didn't take care of myself that night, I wasn't going to get much sleep trying to ignore it.

I mean, Tim's poem *alone* had me unraveling. While we made out and he sat me on his lap, my dress hiked up, I could feel his dick bricking up through the seat of my soaked panties. My overwhelming desire took over, and I started grinding on him a little and sucking his big tongue.

I was turned all the way on. And Tim clearly liked it from his erection and his moan.

When he stopped me and explained that he wasn't ready, all I could do was respect that. But he made it clear: he wants me as much as I want him. So, when the time comes, I just know that sex with Tim Starks is going to be amazing. And damn, it's been a long time since I've had sex with someone I actually liked.

Besides that, I still can't believe I fucking spilled all that shit about interior design to Tim like I was a kid who finally got some attention. It was as if Tim broke the dam and the words poured out of the deep crevices of my mind. I felt raw and exposed like a gutted fish when I realized what I just did.

But Tim didn't look at me weird. Instead, he listened. Then this man, whom I'm still getting to know, offered to introduce me to an actual interior designer he knows. *Of course, he knows one. Tim knows people all over the city—hell, pro'ly across the country.* But *if* I meet this person, what would I even say to her? Gush about décor like a teenage girl? And will she *really* share her tricks of the trade with me—a nobody—so that *I* can come up in her field? What'd be in it for her? If it's one thing I've learned since living in Los Angeles, it's that everyone has an angle, an endgame. And they may not always make you privy to it, but trust, you are a pawn, a step to help them get to the next level. And I already feel bad enough sleeping with men for money. Money that I *still don't* have a real plan for, mind you!

Still, something in me *wants* to trust Tim. My gut says he's good. He makes me want to feel okay letting him help me. It doesn't feel like he's trying to swoop in and save me like Captain Save-a-Hoe. I didn't move to the other side of the country to have a man do everything for me. I moved here to figure out what I *want* to do—hell, what I *can* do that feels fulfilling.

But shame still calls my name. I have a supportive family, but sometimes, I feel like I failed them. That's partly why I don't talk to or visit them much: I don't want to one day see the deep pity on their faces. The eldest daughter who hasn't really done anything with her life. Meanwhile the youngest daughter is killing it—has a bachelor's degree, a thriving business, *and* full-time dream job prospects! And I'm not even jealous of Simonique—I'm extremely proud of her. It's just that it sometimes feels like I should've figured this life shit out before her. That I should've led by a good example *because* I'm the oldest.

Plus, I don't want my family encouraging me to move back home because it's hard out here. *Life* is hard.

My parents worked their asses off to provide my sister and I with so many opportunities. Simonique took those lemons and made bomb-ass lemonade. I came all the way out here and ended up hustling. Sure, I have a fat savings account, a thick investment portfolio, a nice condo, and a new-ish car, but compared to Nique's path, I feel like I let my lemons rot.

I tell myself that my seven years in LA weren't wasted, but too often, I let the harsh reality in front of me keep me from dreaming. I stopped imagining more for myself.

Honestly, I'm just fucking exhausted. I'm tired of hustling, tired of being afraid. I do want security and stability. But Tim reminded me that it's still okay to want more. And with him around, I don't know whether to lean into my dreams . . . or brace myself for disappointment when reality kicks in again.

But I haven't been able to see Tim in person since then, but we text throughout the day and call at night. And afterwards, if our virtual interactions stay with me too long, leaving me craving him, I take care of myself in *that* department.

When the release subsides, I'm reminded that there's work to do. Because I don't have a manager nor an agency, I realized that leaving the hustle *is* truly up to me.

Over the last few days, I just kept going back and forth with myself on if that's *actually* what I want to do. I mean, in over three years, I've made about $470,000 vibe modeling and escorting. . . It boggles my mind how much money I've earned doing this. And I'm just $30,000 away from reaching my goal.

If I'm being honest, I *could* wait for a desperate client like Ashton Weeks to hit me up. I could come up with some story, so that he'd pay me a little more. Or hell, I could unblock Zay and let him come back so I can earn a huge tip—*No, no, no, Camesha*, my inner self chastises.

She's right. I should stop. I've proven to myself that I can do hard things and survive it. But I don't want to do that anymore. I want to actually enjoy my life and thrive.

Plus, I really want Tim. And he wants me. I don't want that money more than I want a man to want the real me. Even if I haven't shared all of me yet, like what happened with Raw Math.
. .

Anyway, I asked Oluchi to help me write a professional "resignation" text. So, in between shifts at The Adonir Hotel, I've been texting handlers and clients that I'm done vibe modeling and escorting. The handlers couldn't really say much since I'm independent. They took my decision well, wishing me "good luck on my future endeavors." Benny Munz even threw in a little paragraph, saying he was happy to have been the first handler to work with me.

My work phone has been lighting up with client text messages and phone calls, even though I told them to *never* call me.

R2:

> Thanks for letting me know. Take care.

Ross Reynolds was the only one to respond to my message almost immediately. Always prompt and straightforward, necessary traits as an in-demand forensic accountant. He was my only client that didn't require fluff from me. In and out. Nice and easy.

7D:

> fuck! cammie i wanted to see you tomorrow

> one more time. please? ill pay you extra

> cmon, im going through it rn

Ashton Weeks is an emotional man, and a beggar, and can be dramatic at times. His responses didn't surprise me. But I held my ground:

Me:

> I'm done.

He's called me a few times now, so I had to block him. Later, comedian Edgar Clinton replied:

EC:

A'ight, love. It was fun while it lasted. If you free and need a laugh, come by the Comedy Store tonight at 9pm. You can just tell em you're my special guest so you can come in for free. Would love to see your pretty face in the crowd. You could still be my good luck charm.

One thing Edgar will always do is promote his shit, whether it's a new set, sketch, or special. I respect his hustle just like he always respected mine. He does a slower, storytelling type of comedy like Ali Siddiq and Dave Chappelle—captivating and funny as hell.

Me:

You don't need me for luck. Break a leg.

All he did was "love" my message.

I had merit leave, so I took off from the hotel today. This afternoon, I'm at a Mediterranean restaurant in Santa Monica, sitting at an outdoor table, waiting for Zaria to arrive. With a view of the beach to my right and a cocktail and a small dish of Castelvetrano olives in front of me, I swipe on my work phone to delete my Google Alerts. I get to my last one: Eliot Novak, thinking about these last couple of days.

He was taking my resignation from the hustle harder than Ashton—which I didn't think was possible—anxiously texting and calling me like crazy. For two days, he asked me if my leaving was because of something *he* did, which made me laugh. *No, white man it's not you* this *time.* He asked what he could do so that I stayed around—even going as far as offering me three times my fee that I almost choked on my spit when I saw the figure. Not going to lie, I did think about taking him up on that, but I held firm on my stance:

Me:

> I'm just done. It has nothing to do with you. Don't make this difficult.

The gray bubble popped up and disappeared a few times, telling me that Eliot's contemplating his message.

Starr:

> Okay, Cammie. I'm sorry. Thank you for everything.

I was happy that he didn't put up a fight anymore.

I didn't need to text Asa since we had our last session a few weeks ago and he told me that *he* was done.

Honestly, I'm considering blocking all of these contacts and getting rid of this phone. I already threw out all my gifts and lingerie that clients bought me. I just think that if I'm truly going to move on from this life, I want to *completely* cut it off. I want to slice the heads off the hydra and cauterize the stumps, so they don't grow back. I want no remnants of the hustle or surprise pop-ups.

I'm meeting Zaria to tell her that I'm done. I owe that to her since she introduced me to this life.

I've never been to her place, and she's never been to mine. Even though she likes to say we're friends, we've really kept our relationship mostly professional. In many ways, she was my mentor and I her protégé. And now I have to tell her it's time for me to move on.

It might be time for me to move on *from this lunch cuz she's almost 20 minutes late. I know for a fact that if I was Marlon Reed, her ass would be on time*, I ponder.

My work phone chirps with a notification, the banner briefly showing it's a text from the last of my escorting clients to respond to my resignation message. Luxury car dealership owner, Greer Weston.

W$:

oh aight

I roll my eyes at that. He's 45 years old but sometimes he acts 15. Very immature. I'm relieved that I don't have to deal with his ass anymore.

Glancing up, I see Zaria. She's wearing a reddish-orange midi dress and strappy heels, a lime-green purse dangling from her elbow. She removes her oversized sunglasses and pushes them into her passion twists.

"Hey, girl! You look cute! I love that color on you," she says, sitting across from me.

I glance down at my outfit like I don't know what I'm wearing: a blue ombre mesh maxi dress and brown sandals.

"Thank you. Red's ya color."

"Isn't it? Thanks."

I chuckle. "And would it kill you to get *anywhere* on time?" I playfully side-eye her, but she knows I'm serious. This has been something we've talked about before when it came to our meetings.

"Bitch, I *have* to make an entrance. You know that 'bout me."

I just roll my eyes and shake it off with a laugh.

Zaria picks up her menu and leans back in her chair. "Anyway, to what do I owe this lunch? You almost *never* invite me out and I have to track you down and drag *you* somewhere." *Not true, but true.* "And does this mean this is *your* treat?" She peeks over the menu, wiggling her threaded eyebrows.

I fight the urge to roll my eyes and instead just scoff a chuckle. "That wasn't my plan."

She eyeballs me briefly before speaking, "Okay, I'll pay for me then." She shoos it off like she's doing me a favor. "And I already know what I want. You ready?"

I nod and she shoots her arm up to get our waiter's attention. He takes our order and when her glass of sweet red wine returns, I launch into why I invited her out.

I tell her how I met someone. That I'm still figuring out what to do with the hustle money. How my sister's graduation got me thinking about going to college. That I told my former handlers and clients I'm done.

In typical Zaria fashion, she interrupted me a few times with reactions and questions that I later answered in the rest of my spiel.

Our entrees arrive when I finish talking. I said a lot more than I thought I would, but I figured I could be honest with her.

But Zaria's just sitting there looking . . . kind of sad? Her lips are poked out, and her eyes are vibrating with oncoming tears. "Awww, I'm gonna miss you, girl."

"Really?" That just slips out.

"Yeah, of course." She tilts her head up and, with a bent index finger, pats at her eyeline. "I 'on't have friends in this game, so it was nice havin' someone who can relate to all'is."

I nod because she's right. Many women in the field aren't friendly, always thinking you're trying to reel in their big fish.

Swallowing hard, I reply, "As much as you grate on my *last* nerve," she perks up a smile, "I liked knowin' I had you in my corner." I pause to glance down and clenched my teeth. "You're a good mentor, Zaria."

I look back up to find her staring at me, both hands damming tears. "Awww, bitch, I could kiss you."

Shaking my head, I laugh.

"But fa real, that's very sweet, Camesha. Thank you." She holds her wineglass up and we cheers.

This might be the first time I've seen Zaria like this. . . Just truly sincere. *Unless she's actin' right now, and if so, she's really good.*

"And honestly, all'at is great. I'm so proud of you. You're very smart so I know you'd kill it in school—whatever you decide to study. And whoever this mystery man is, y'all must be serious, or y'all are *becoming* serious if he's offerin' to help you explore interior design. And you *know* I'm a sucker for love." She pretends to swoon, shimmying in her chair.

"I know."

We share a laugh.

"I like him and we both wanna see where our relationship goes. Ya know I haven't dated in over three years, so I'm a lil' nervous but also excited about him—about us." I can't stop the blush from overtaking my cheeks.

Zaria looks dreamy-eyed as she leans forward, propping her elbow on the table and her face in her hand. "Awww, that sounds nice. I hope he's everything you want and need."

A small grin twitches on my lips at that. Honestly, I think Tim could be. And that's scary—how good he is. I know he's not perfect, but I'm trying to convince myself that I deserve a good person. I know I definitely *want* him, but do I *deserve* him? Can I handle him? Can I fully trust him? After everything I've been through, I don't know, but I so badly want to. And I so badly want my gut to be right about Tim.

I just hope I can really show up the way I need to. Not even just for Tim, but for me.

"But anyway, I wanted to bring you out so I can tell you all'at. I thought I owed you this much since you introduced me to everything."

"My Padawan has graduated to Jedi Knight. I'm a proud Master." Zaria finally lets her tears fall now.

I crack up at her allowing herself to cry at *that*, which in turn makes her laugh.

Once we finish howling and we start eating our food, I say, "Speakin' of guys, how's Marlon?"

I knew that'd get Zaria talking. She updates me on her quest to gain Marlon's love. All the signals she's throwing him, all the hints, all the moves she's putting on him in the bedroom—shit she *only* does with him. I want to tell her that she can't fuck her way to his heart, so that he can look at her differently, but she doesn't allow me a space to jump in. Besides, I'm sure she already knows that anyway. She's just so dickmatized and "in love" that she's blind to the errors of her thinking and ways. Mama always said *never* to let a man have control over you in any way. And it looks like Zaria is gone.

I guess it counts, too, in my case since Tim is *all* that I've been thinking about lately. *Just be careful, Eesh.*

Tim

Everyone is quiet on the set of Keyana Renay's music video for her song "Bedroom Eyes." Her music producer sampled a deep-cut 80s R&B song as the foundation for the slow drums and sultry piano. It's probably one of her sexiest songs, and one she pulls off without using cuss words. So, I was surprised that when she dropped her third album *Velvet Season* recently, this song didn't get as much love. But this video should do the trick.

The set is made to look like a hotel room. The warm lighting the crew set up makes Keyana's brown skin glitter. Wearing a three-piece lingerie set, she's rolling around and twirling on the bed flourishing with white linens. She's actually singing, *not* lip-syncing, while the instrumental plays in the background. She's staring very intimately into the camera like it's the lover she's referencing in the song. To my knowledge, she's not dating anyone at the moment; this song is aspirational.

The entire crew's eyes are glued to her. Well, not mine. I'm looking at her new social media manager's phone as she whispers and swipes through a slide deck of her ideas for Keyana's music video promo. Key just hired this girl, so she really wants to impress her.

"I mean, I ain't know expert—I just post casually, but ya ideas seem solid. Looks like you clearly know her audience, so I think all'at could work."

She grins hard. "Thank you so much, Tim."

"No pro'lem." I shoot her a smile.

The veteran director yells "Cut" and the set buzzes with activity. Keyana's team robes her and touches up her makeup while her manager talks to her about something.

We have two more scenes to do then we're done. I weave through the crowd, making way toward the craft services table. It's basically ravaged since we've been here for four hours today, but I want to nibble on something to hold me over.

As I'm making a meager plate of some cheese, pepperoni, and brownie bites, I feel a presence approach me. One has to always be alert at this job.

"Yo, Tim," I recognize the gravelly voice as another handler named Vaughn.

I spin to face him. "Whaddup?"

He's a little taller than me with dark skin, a pudge protruding out of a gray T-shirt, and it looks like he's past his expiration date to rock wolfed 360 waves. "You worked wit' a vibe model named Cammie, right? She was at Zay's album release party?"

I resist the urge to slit my eyes, wondering where he's going with this. He worked the party, too, helping set up the stage since he was a production assistant before he became a handler. "Yeah. Why?"

"Man, she bad as hell. Like *really* bad." Vaughn furrows his eyebrows and rubs a hand down his "waves."

I lock my jaw to stay cool. While Camesha and I aren't *hiding* our relationship, I also haven't told anyone except my friends and my mom. She doesn't want industry folks in her business, especially since she's now quit hustling. I'm respecting that, but a nigga coming up to me talking about how bad as hell my lady is without knowing she *my* lady now is crazy work.

Popping a brownie in my mouth to stifle my real feelings, I say, "A'ight. And?" I want him to hurry up with whatever he wants to say. I want to eat my food in peace.

"Look, I gotta new client interested in doin' some *content*. So, do ya know if Cammie is interested in," Vaughn glances around and leans in, his breath smelling like straight up garbage, "doin' a lil' *camera* work?"

My body ignites with anger at his question. My throat starts to close up. My heart is revving up and thumping in my ear. *Did this nigga just ask me what I think he asked me?*

Vaughn leans in closer to whisper, his foul-ass breath stinging my eyes. "My guy wants a specific look for a few videos, and I thought of her. I heard she escorts, so maybe she'd be down to fuck on camera." He shrugs like he asked me if Camesha would be down to help him move a fucking couch, like his question is normal. And maybe some vibe models and escorts *do* make porn on the side, but hearing this proposition with Camesha in mind has my blood hot.

I bare down on my teeth so hard that I'm sure they'd shatter if I don't relax. "First off, fall back, bruh. I can't get sick. I gotta work the BET Awards in a few weeks."

He smacks his teeth as he backs up. "Nigga, I ain't sick."

"Whatever." I roll my shoulders back. "And second of all, I 'on't think she's interested."

"How ya know? Can ya ask her?—Better yet, send me her contact info." Vaughn presumptuously pulls his phone from his jeans pocket.

I glance away to calm down, silently praying that *someone* interrupts us. His eager-ass face is annoying the fuck out of me as he opens up a "New Contact" page on his phone. "I told you: she ain't interested."

"Nah, you said you 'on't *think* she's interested."

I squeeze my eyes closed and grip the bridge of my nose. "Vaughn."

"A'ight, fine. Just thought I'd ask. Sound like you know her pretty well and shit, so I guess I'll take ya word for it." I look up at him, seeing his arms raised in surrender. "But if ya know anybody else wit' a similar look and vibe, send 'em my way. My client would like to start filmin' in a couple weeks," he says, walking backwards like we're not on a crowded set.

I watch him turn and leave before pulling my phone out. Still buzzing, I go to text Camesha:

Me (3:23pm):

Hey baby. U good? Just thinkin bout u

Slipping my phone back in my pocket, I start eating my snack. I need something to distract me, so I don't ruminate on Vaughn's audacity to ask me something like that about my lady. I know he doesn't know she's my lady, and I know he's just trying to handle stuff for his client, but still. I don't fucking like that.

Out the corner of my eye, I spot Keyana guzzling water near the drinks station.

I walk toward her. "Yo, Key!"

She twirls around, her voluminous curls flipping behind her. She drops the bottle from her lips and says, "Hey, Tim!"

"This video is lookin' legit. I think this gon' really get folks' attention."

"Yeah, I was a lil' butt-hurt it didn't make a big splash, but hopefully the visuals help."

"I think they will. *Especially* after whatcho social media manager showed me." I smirk, shooting her a knowing sidelong glance.

"Really?" Her face brightens. "I knew I hired her for a reason. I'm excited to see what she came up wit'."

I nod. "Oh, and thank you again for helpin' me make reservations at The Lenox Room. My date and I had a good time. She told me to tell you the food was *it.* That's an exact quote." I can't help but cheese all dumb just thinking about Camesha and our amazing official first date.

Keyana gushes. "Awww, I'm so happy y'all enjoyed ya'selves. Now when can I meet this woman or at least know her name? Is this new?" She wiggles her eyebrows.

Before I can answer, the director calls everyone back for the next scene and I'm super thankful.

"I'm happy for you, Tim." She downs more water.

"'Preciate it, Key."

She throws a wink over her shoulder as she struts over to set.

My phone vibrates and I open it to see the text:

Camesha (3:25pm):

Yeah, I'm good. Are you?

Me (3:25pm):

I am now

Me (3:26pm):

Emoji just for good measure. I don't want her to worry.

Camesha (3:27pm):

> Good lol.

Me (3:27pm):

> Lets get dinner on Sat. I need to see u in person.

Camesha (3:28pm):

> Ooo, okay. Can't wait to see you

A soft smile touches my face, and I try to stop myself from blushing. I feel better knowing she's good. Even if Vaughn asked me that wild-ass, disrespectful-ass question.

Saturday, June 2

Camesha

Tim and I are having dinner at an Italian restaurant on Melrose. It's dim with only a little lamp illuminating our square table in a corner of the dining room. The atmosphere hums with a Frank Sinatra song and conversation. I wish we were able to snag a booth so I could sit closer to him, but there were none available when we got here an hour ago.

We've decided to share food tonight, twirling pasta on our forks and feeding one another. We've even swapped sips of our cocktails.

I *still* can't get over how good Tim looks when he eats, his jaws flexing as he chews and the way he closes his eyes and moans a little as he savors his food. *I wonder what he looks like when he's eatin' pussy. I have a feelin' his big-back ass knows what he's doin' down there*—I shake my head and clamp my thighs shut to keep the flood at bay.

We've finished most of our food and we're now waiting for the server to return so that we can order dessert. I'm sipping my white wine, listening to Tim's story about his client Kush Li who, a few years ago, had a breakdown at a fan experience because he couldn't blaze up. Tim had to calm him down.

". . . and then on top of that, the muhfucka had me sort through the jellybeans cuz he *only* wanted the purple ones." Tim clutches his forehead. "I said, 'I know *you* fuckin' lyin.'"

I crack up as he concludes his story, "So now, he 'on't call me as much anymore cuz I told his ass that he *most likely* smokes too much weed if he couldn't function without it for a few hours." Tim shrugs his shoulders.

I shake my head, cheesing like crazy.

"I'mma use the bathroom. Be right back, gorgeous." He leans forward to kiss my cheek before he scoots his chair back and leaves.

I let out a breath before I take a sip of my drink.

Then, I feel a towering presence approaching behind me, interrupting my comfortable little bubble. "Well, well, well. Cammie."

My stomach drops at that oily-slick voice. I turn to my right to see Greer Weston. He's skinny, wearing a slim-fit burgundy suit. When my gaze drags up to his face, his obnoxiously colored-in chin strap beard and smirk make me itch. He kind of reminds me of Jafar from *Aladdin* with that facial hair and thin mouth. Besides Asa, Greer also tried to kiss me several times, so I put him on probation until he understood that my rule had no exceptions. Even him wanting to pay me extra wouldn't change that. Unlike Asa's, Greer's lips do *not* look kissable.

He removes his oversized sunglasses and perches them into his permed curly quiff—Well, I don't know if it's actually a perm, but I'm almost certain this man uses S-Curl regularly. "I didn't expect to see *you* here. You look. . ." he openly scans me from my nude-colored heels up to my side-parted curls, "*ravishing as always.*"

Who the fuck still says that? I'm trying so hard to look unaffected and keep my eyes from rolling. "Greer," I sigh, attempting to keep my disdain for his public confrontation in check. I was hoping my text messages would avoid this. At one point, I thought about just ghosting everybody, but Oluchi reminded me that a heads-up was considerate and professional.

"I've been tryna reach you, girl." He motions toward me, and I can smell his usual cologne—something sweet and strong, clinging to the air like his ego. I never liked how it smelled, but he swore he was the shit when he wore it.

"I told you: I'm done."

"Done? You 'on't look *done* to me. You look like you're doin' public appearances now. And who is that guy?" He jabs a thumb toward the restrooms, referring to Tim. "I 'on't recognize him. Is he one of those nepo babies or young start-up founders? You had to drop me and however many other clients you had to move onto bigger fish, huh?" He grins wider. "I mean, baby, if it was 'bout money, you *know* I'm good for it." He makes a show of digging into his blazer's inside breast pocket and pulling out a wad of cash in a clip.

I almost laugh since I know that that's most likely not *his* money.

"May I help you wit' some'?" Tim's voice—but deeper, sterner—cuts through as he appears next to Greer.

Tim is a couple inches taller than Greer, but he still squares his shoulders and narrows his eyes at him. With his jaw set and his eyebrows pulled together, Tim's face is challenging yet calm.

Seeing him stand his ground makes me sit up at attention with desire.

Greer eyes him up and down. "Oh," then he snaps his gaze to me with a wide smile smearing his face, "This isn't a client, is it?"

I just deadpan him, tired and done with his games.

"Aye man, I'd 'preciate it if you left us alone," Tim speaks again.

I glance around to see if I can find anything to use as ammo to make Greer flee from our table. I don't see his wife, the 30-something former Miss Thailand, around. I only know of her because I was channel surfing one day and came across *The Hillside Wives* reality show where I saw her friend, who's a cast member, invite her and Greer to a party.

A few people are glancing our way, noticing a scene brewing.

"This is your *man*, isn't it?" Greer chortles, finding this whole situation funny. "Does he know 'bout me?" he whispers like this is scandalous, like he was my sneaky link or something.

Joke's on you, asshole. Tim already knew 'bout my escortin'.

I can't help but roll my eyes now. Slowly, I stand up, slipping my chain strap purse onto my shoulder and wiping on a sweet smile. I step close to Greer so he can hear me at my normal speaking volume. "I 'on't know why this is funny, Greer. Because it's nothin' for me to go to the news, tell them who I *was* to you, and *show them records* that you used your *dealership's* money to pay me." I tilt my head and narrow my eyes.

Greer *barely* cares about his marriage—clearly—but he cares immensely about his dealership, or at least its image. During our sessions, when he wasn't trying to run lame game as if he wasn't paying me, he almost exclusively confided in me about his concerns regarding his business. For a year, it's barely made enough money to cover its expenses. Greer told me he's paid his employees—the man at least sounds like a good boss—but *he* took a huge pay cut, so he's mostly surviving off of his meager stock dividends, unbeknownst to his wife. And I saw his dire situation in action when he stopped paying me from his personal account and instead used his business one. I knew I shouldn't've accepted the money, but it cleared . . . and I wanted to reach my goal. *Ugh, priorities.*

Slowly, the dumb smug look on Greer's face disappears and is replaced by quiet, seething worry. I can see the rapid undulation of his chest as he licks his lips, careful not to touch his dyed facial hair. "Y-You 'on't know whatchu talkin' 'bout," he croaks out without his signature unearned cockiness.

"I know plenty. So, unless you want the world to know that ya business isn't doin' too hot, walk away and leave me—leave *us*," I motion to Tim, "the hell alone." My voice is even, but on the inside, I'm all over the place, pissed at his unmitigated audacity.

Greer doesn't make a move and instead glances from me to Tim, who arches an eyebrow at him. *Oh my God, Tim, stop makin' me wet.*

"Door's that way, bruh." Tim tips his head to the left.

My clit jumps at his quip.

Out the corner of my eye, I notice what looks like a manager walking over. "Is everything okay, folks?"

"Yeah, our friend was just leavin'," Tim says, grinning.

Greer's neck twitches as he clears his throat and adjusts his blazer. He chuckles, wiping on a smile before he faces the manager. "That's right." His attention returns to me and Tim, saying, "Was good seein' y'all." He leaves and the manager follows behind him.

My heart is pounding in my chest at the sight of Greer exiting the restaurant and walking down the sidewalk through the window. Tim steps toward me, wraps an arm around my waist, and says into my ear, "You okay?"

Nodding, I close my eyes and blow air out my nostrils.

"Let's get outta here." Tim steps back and gently grabs my hand to take me to the waiter's station so he can pay.

Minutes later, we're driving down the road with no music playing. Tim *always* has music playing when he drives. *Uh oh.*

A few blocks down, we hit a stoplight. I can feel Tim glancing at me. And I can sense he has questions but isn't sure what to ask or how.

So, I take in a deep breath for four seconds, bracing myself to talk about what just happened. Tim came face to face with a side of my hustle he's never seen before. Sure, he coordinated my sleeping with Zay the first night we met, but that was *his* client. Tonight was different.

I turn in my seat to look at him, his face neutral as he focuses on the road. "I used to be Greer's escort."

The light turns green, and Tim slowly pulls off. He opens his mouth, but before he can say anything, I keep going, "And I *will* return the business money he used to pay me. I know I shouldn't've accepted it in the first place, but I did." Breath hitches in my throat. "I-I'm sorry 'bout all'is Tim."

"Camesha, you 'on't have to apologize," he says gently, glancing at me. "I just hate that you had to deal wit' all'at. Ya tryna move on and muhfuckas like him are tryna pull you back, keep you boxed in the way that they've experienced you in the past and not let you grow into ya future."

Okay bars! A smile twitches onto my face before I realize something he said. "What do you mean 'muhfuckas like him'? Who else is tryna pull me back into that life?"

Tim tightens his jaw and shifts in his seat a little. "Nuttn."

"Tim . . ," I let out, my voice soft yet firm.

He relaxes his jaw and meets my gaze briefly. "I 'on't know if you know the handler Vaughn Terrell, but on Wednesday at Keyana Renay 's video shoot, he asked me," Tim licks his lips and deeply exhales, "if you'd be interested in doin' some *camera work.*"

I sit back in my seat and look at the street. I'm not surprised. At all.

I've been asked that plenty of times, and once by a literal porn producer at a party in the Valley. But never has a handler offered the job before. All I can muster in response is, "Oh."

"Yeah. . . I wanted to tell him to go fuck himself." I turn my head in time to see Tim flare his nostrils.

I can't lie, it's a huge turn-on, seeing Tim get upset on my behalf. In no way do I want him to fight anyone for me, but from Greer to this, *now* I could see him willing to go there if the situation called for it.

I try to keep the amusement out of my voice when I say, "It's okay, Tim. He doesn't know I'm not in the industry anymore. I'm sure one of the other handlers I worked wit' will tell him soon."

"Hope so," he mutters, turning onto La Brea Avenue.

"I just stopped hustlin', so this is all still new." A heavy breath escapes me.

Shockwaves of anxiety still reverberate through my body as a result of Greer confronting me in public. That was another rule of mine regarding escorting: besides me not doing public appearances, I also said we will *never* acknowledge or speak to one another outside of our hotel rooms.

"I know. And you ain't gotta do this alone, Camesha. I'm here. I gotchu." Tim surprises me when he reaches across the console to hold my hand in my lap.

That same phrase pangs my heart again, sending that thing fluttering like a bird. I don't know when I'll ever get used to hearing them come out of Tim's mouth.

I surprise myself when my other hand wraps around his bare forearm. I give his hand and arm a squeeze. "Thank you."

"Of course." His thumb brushes over my knuckles as he glances at me, grinning.

Something warm swells in my heart, then flows down to my stomach, making me suck it in. I'm so hyper aware of Tim's hand in my lap, so close to my cooch that I have to calm my thudding heart rate.

Moments later, Tim stops at a stoplight, and I see we're close to my place. I don't think myself out of it, I just act.

Before he can even register me letting go of his hand and forearm, I'm out of my seat belt and leaning over the console, my hand grazing Tim's jawline as I press my lips to his right ear.

He sucks in a breath at the contact, the action and sound only making me wetter. I glance down to see if he has an erection in the faint orange streetlight pouring into the truck. His dick is poking through his slacks a little bit.

Smirking, I bite my bottom lip. "It was so sexy how you stepped to Greer in there, baby," I murmur. My eyes fall closed as I take Tim's earlobe into my mouth. I nibble on his flesh as my tongue traces his stud earring.

His hands grip the leather steering wheel hard. Is it wrong for me to tease him? Maybe. I know he wants to wait—and I do respect that. I just want to show him I appreciate him for having my back. And I'm sure both of us didn't know that that would turn me on.

Tim lets out a strained chuckle, and I can feel him clenching his jaw hard. *Fuuuck. . .* "Of course." His voice is gritty, barely above a whisper. So sexy.

I feel very irresponsible, like I could lick his face or something. So, I muster the strength to let him go and retreat back to my chair before the light turns green. Slipping my seat belt back on, Tim exhales, and I smirk knowingly.

"You tryna make me crash, girl?" he chortles, pulling off at the green light.

"Of course not," I say playfully. "Besides you were at a stoplight."

A quick glance and I see Tim shaking his head, fingers still gripping the wheel. "You stay yo' fine ass on that side of the car, C. I'm tryna get you home safe."

I giggle. "Yes, sir." I melt into the seat. *I know patience is a virtue, but damn.*

11
Lovely Days

Wednesday, June 27

Tim

T he BET Awards was a success this past weekend. I was pulled in so many directions that night that I felt like a marionette. Since I was handling for many clients, I stayed on my phone, keeping two portable chargers in my jacket pockets. Everyone's teams and I coordinated smoothly, ensuring our artists were on schedule and comfortable, and even quickly diffused situations before they got out of hand.

All of my clients, except for Kush Li and Amber Royce, are Black, so many of them attended, performed, or were nominated for something.

Rugged Rah and ill Yamz performed songs from *Black Like We Always Here* and they won the Best Group award. Keyana and Zay both performed, but they didn't win anything in their categories. G1-Otie and his song with this famous choir won the Dr. Bobby Jones Best Gospel/Inspirational Award.

Yamz hosted an afterparty at his new mansion and it was insane. I met motherfucking Terrence White, an R&B legend who's been in the biz almost 30 years but still cranking out hits like he just came out. Rah and Otie introduced me to him, and his smooth ass complimented my work ethic. He even offered me a job on his upcoming tour. . . But honestly, all that went in one ear and out the other. People like to talk all day long in this city. I've gotten so many "job offers" over the years that they don't even faze me.

But now all of *that* is done—thank God!

Today is Camesha's birthday. She's 27 on the 27th, so I planned something for her. I combed through my memory and our text messages for some low-key ideas that would also make her feel special. She's told me that I don't have to go all out, that she just enjoys spending time with me. While I love and understand that, as *my* lady, I want to show her a memorable time, *especially* for her birthday.

I found a text conversation we had months ago where we were talking about our favorite foods, so instead of taking her out to a fancy dinner this evening, I took off work today to try cooking some of her favorites. Camesha told me that she doesn't work on her birthday, so I told her I had a surprise for her and to wear something cute and comfortable. I sent a driver, Marvin, to pick her up at 5pm. I needed them to be in some rush hour traffic so I could watch a YouTube video on how to set up the picnic as nicely as possible.

I discovered this grassy spot overlooking the beach a couple of weeks ago on my way home after Keyana sang at a private celebrity wedding. At 6pm, golden hour has just begun in beautiful Los Angeles. The orange Sun is starting to dip below the horizon, painting the partly cloudy sky gorgeous warm colors. There's a nice salty breeze wafting from the Pacific Ocean, too.

I pace, keeping an eye on the picnic set-up to busy myself. I brought a blanket from home to set on the grass, and I found small wooden crates from a photo shoot nobody ended up needing in my trunk. The crates will serve as our table and will keep the blanket from blowing away. I arranged pillows for us to sit on and sprinkled rose petals for the romance. Then I set down a water-filled vase and an ice-bucket of semi-sweet white wine. And of course, I grabbed my Bluetooth speaker to play a specially curated playlist for her birthday. The vibe is set.

My heart is racing so fast, I can feel my pulse leaping in my neck. I suck in and blow out some air to calm down, but that's not helping. A pinch winds at the nape of my neck so I roll my shoulders to alleviate the tension. Sweat prickles my armpits and I pray that it's not visible through my shirt. I want to look nice, not nervous, even though I am.

We've been an official couple for about a month now, but it feels like I've been with Camesha longer. This is the first birthday we're celebrating together, so this whole thing feels like a big deal.

Even though my phone's volume is all the way up and I'll be able to hear it when I get a text, I pull it out anyway to see if Marvin sent me an update. I asked him, when he's safely able to do so, to text me along the way so I know how close they are. Just as I start typing a message, a black Mercedes sedan crests the winding dirt road. I see Marvin's weathered face through the windshield, grinning at me.

My heart rate picks up speed. *Showtime.*

As Marvin slows to a stop, I deeply inhale and exhale, letting the air relax my shoulders. I go to open the door where I see Camesha's silhouette through the tinted window, and I'm immediately hit with her scent: her hair products and today's fragrance, which smells familiar.

She looks up at me through her mascaraed eyelashes, and a slow smile spreads open her signature glossed lips. Her fluffy curly hair is in its usual middle-parted style. Her face is devoid of any makeup—but maybe it's that natural look. Either way, I can't help but smile at her as I offer my hand to help her out of the car.

Camesha grabs it, letting me pull her to her feet. "Hi," she says, her voice melodious in the breeze.

"Hey, birthday girl."

I guide her to the side so I can shut the car door. I notice that Marvin rolled his window down. "Yo, Marvin, 'preciate you for her gettin' her here safely, man."

"Of course, Tim. You young folks have a good time," he says before rolling up his window and whipping the car around.

I turn my attention to Camesha, holding her hand out to twirl her. "And as always, you look absolutely gorgeous." She's wearing some sort of red strapless bandana top with a beige flared-out skirt. And from the brief glance over and down her shoulder, her ass is sitting too nice in this material. Brown sandals show off her marigold toenails. A matching mini purse hangs off her shoulder.

"Thank you, Tim." She blushes. "You look really handsome. I *really* like this combination on you." She eyes my mandarin collar chambray shirt, olive green chinos, and neutral-toned Nike Waffle Debuts.

"Thanks. Thought I'd try some' different for you."

Hand in hand, I walk us around my Jeep to reveal the picnic with our amazing view. "Happy birthday, Camesha." Just then, "Lovely Day" by Bill Withers plays softly through my speaker. *Perfect.*

She gasps loudly, her hands flying to cup her nose and mouth. "Oh my God! Tim . . . baby," she whimpers like she's about to cry.

A pleasant shiver ripples through me at the sound of her voice easing out that word. I can't lie, I feel good as hell, knowing I've done my job today in thoroughly surprising her and making her feel special. "So, I take it you like it?" I chuckle even though I know the answer.

She nods as she pads over and squats down to inspect the details of the set-up.

I take this as my opportunity to retrieve the stacked warmer containers of our dinner and her bouquet of black baccara roses.

At the sound of me shutting my car door, she swivels around and drops her hands. "Tim. . ."

A big smile smooths across my face, knowing I *really* got her now. "Our dinner for the night: some of ya favorite foods. Blackened salmon in a creamy Cajun sauce, sauteed garlic kale, honey butter cornbread, *and* banana puddin'. Now, *I* didn't make the banana puddin' since you said Earle's was the closest to ya mama's. But I made everything else, so I hope I did 'em justice." I set the food on the blanket and give her the bouquet. "I never asked you which flowers you like, but these reminded me of you." *Cuz they're sexy as hell.*

Camesha ogles them and takes a whiff. "They're so pretty."

"Not as pretty as you," just falls out naturally. I'm not even embarrassed anymore by the corny shit that pops in my head. I just say how I feel, and she seems to appreciate this side of me.

"Thank you." She bends to place the flowers in the vase on the blanket. Standing up straight again, she glances around at the picnic, the view, the Sun, the ocean. "Tim, I 'on't know—"

Chortling, I say, "Stop. When will you turn 27 on the 27th again? Never."

She giggles. "I really 'preciate all'is."

"Ya welcome."

A look I've come to recognize settles onto her face. "C'mere," comes out all low, but I don't have to hear her to know what time it is.

My giddy ass bites my lip as I step closer. As my hands magnetize to her midriff, hers find my jaws like they always do, bringing my face down to hers. I love that she's not afraid to show me she wants me. We peck a few times before it turns into a full-on make-out session. I grip her waist and pull her closer as she resorts to wrapping her arms around my neck.

I'm tempted to slide my hands lower, but I'm afraid if I touch her ass, I'd lose all self-control. We're still waiting—and man have we been close a few times! But honestly, the sexual tension is building nicely, so right now, getting lost in her mouth is satisfying enough.

I squeeze her waist to stop after a few moments. With our foreheads touching, I say, "Are you wearin' that fragrance you wore to The Lenox Room?"

Her head snaps back in surprise. "Yeah, you can tell?"

"Of course. You got my nose wide open, C. In more ways than one," I chuckle, nuzzling my face into her neck to smell and kiss her.

She giggles, probably because my facial hair is tickling her.

Unashamed, I take one last whiff before retreating. "Wear whatever that is more often, and if you run out, lemme know. I'll keep you stocked wit' it."

She laughs.

"C'mon, let's eat, birthday girl." I help her lower onto a pillow before I sit down, too. Grabbing her hands, I say, "Can I say grace?" She nods and we both close our eyes before I pray. When I open mine, I find Camesha smirking at me. "What?"

A grin tugs on her lips. "I love that you do that."

I smile, trying my hardest to hide the blood rushing to my cheeks. I unstack the warmer containers then remove the lids, steam rising to reveal the meal I cooked.

"Tim, this looks *amazing*."

"Looks can be deceivin', C. I mean, *I* think it tastes good." I touch my chest. "But I'mma let you be the real judge since these ya favorites." I free a fork from its plastic prison, chuckling, "Pardon the cheap silverware."

She laughs. "I'd honestly do the same thing. One less thing to wash."

"I love that you get it."

I scoop up some salmon then hold it up to Camesha's mouth. She makes intense eye contact with me as she tastes the food. My heart skips a few beats, watching her plump lips wrap around the fork before I slide it out.

She averts her gaze while slowly chewing. "Ooo, that's *really* good, baby," she moans.

I don't even realize my shoulders are up to my ears until I drop them. "Oh, thank God." I clear my throat. "I know you favor semi-sweet white wine, so would you like some, madam?" I ask in my best snooty gentleman accent, gesturing to the wine chilling in the ice bucket.

"I would, kind sir," Camesha plays along, making me break character and laugh. I love that she can be just as goofy as me sometimes.

I uncork the wine and pour us plastic glasses before I hold up mine for a toast. "Happy 27th birthday, Camesha."

She lifts her glass and smiles all big. "Thank you, Tim."

We clink glasses and seal it with a kiss before we dig in.

"Damn, I got me an ol' lady fa real now."

She deadpans me and slaps my arm. "Shut up! *You're* older than me."

"True but you gettin' up there, woman."

"Sir, you'll be 29 in August. *You're* gettin' up there."

"Touché," I say nodding.

We trade stories about our days as we eat. She pampered herself at a fancy spa and answered birthday texts and calls from family in South Carolina. Her friends blew up their group chat and told her to prepare to "get fucked up for her 27th" when they take her out Friday night.

Camesha says, "Tim, you really did ya big one wit' this food. I feel very special. This is so thoughtful. Thank you."

She makes me blush at her over-thanking me. "You're more than welcome, baby."

A small grin quirks her lips. She clears her throat before speaking again, "So I have some news. . ."

I glance up from my food to find her looking at me, squiggling her eyebrows. "Whassup, C?"

Camesha

I set my fork down, my stomach fluttering. Tim gives me his full attention like I'm about to drop life-changing news. And, honestly, maybe I am.

I blow out some air before I start, "So, before I left work yesterday, my manager, Klay, told me," I pause because I'm still trying to wrap my head around it, "that there's an openin' for the assistant service manager position at The Adonir Hotel's sister property, The Aubade in Laurel Canyon. He highly recommended me for the job." That still feels unreal in my mouth, but I can't help but cheese like a fool, excitement rising in me like a geyser.

Tim's eyes widen and his mouth forms an O shape. "Yooo! Camesha, that's big!" He leans forward to peck my lips. "So, what happens next?"

"I told him that I was interested. He said I 'on't even have to apply. The Aubade is interested in me, and they'll reach out very soon to set up an interview." I suck in another breath. "It'd be a step up—managin' servers, handlin' VIP guests, more pay." I happy-shimmy on my pillow.

"Ala! That's awesome. I'm excited for you." Tim just grins at me all warm.

"Same," I let out though it comes out quieter than I mean it to.

I collect some kale with my fork, needing something to do with my hands to distract myself.

If I get this job at The Aubade it will be a new chapter—a *clean* one. I may not have to worry about running into old clients. I could go back to using my real name at work. I could feel like I earned being somewhere again. No more shame gnawing at me like it's been for the last three plus years.

Just the fact that Klay clocked my work ethic, how I handle customers, and believes in me enough to recommend me for the job means a lot to me. I appreciate him so much for that and will be getting him *something* to show him.

And I don't know, maybe what Klay sees in me can translate to interior design somehow? But *this* opportunity is here, more concrete.

I shake my hair off my shoulder and look at Tim again. "It was definitely a nice birthday gift—Not as nice as *this* one though." I motion to his entire gesture.

He smiles, creasing the skin by his eyes.

I return the smile before looking at the amazing view, the orange sunlight making everything feel possible.

If I get this manager job, the pay won't even *touch* what I made hustling. But honestly, that's okay! That's why I saved and invested most of that money.

All of this—dare I say—*feels* right? It'd be a promotion. I'd be moving in a good direction. Opening up a door to another level in the hospitality industry.

It feels like coming up on purpose.

And maybe it is. Who knows, if I decide to go to college, maybe hospitality management could be my major since I already have some experience.

"Maybe givin' up the hustle wasn't a bad idea after all. . ." I think out loud.

"I 'on't think it was a bad idea." Tim clears his throat and shrugs. "And who knows, maybe interior design ain't *just* some dream or some wild thought you had either." He leans in to gently squeeze my thigh. "Maybe all'is—the hotel, the hustle, how you put ya condo together—it's been you practicin' all along, baby. You know how to take care of people and make 'em feel comfortable. Ya stylish as hell. You can set a vibe. Ya girls see it. Ya manager sees it. I see it. And prayerfully, The Aubade will, too."

His hand moves to hold mine, warm and steady. "Sometimes God gives us the ingredients. We just have to cook. Maybe this promotion is another ingredient so that you can finally cook what you were made to all along." Tim screws his face up. "I hope that made sense."

A small grin twitches onto my face. *Mmm-mmm-mmm, this man. Why does he have to be so good wit' words?* I think. Even though the air is warm, I shiver, soaking in what Tim just said—no, *preached*. I feel both tethered to the ground and able to float at the same time. My heart rate slowly picks up speed as my body gets warmer. Maybe it's comforting confirmation that I'm for sure on the right path.

Without thinking too hard, I scoot over to Tim so I can straddle his lap, wrapping my arms around his neck. He accommodates my new seat and leans back with his hands propped up behind him.

"Let ya'self cook, C." One side of his mouth curls into a smile.

I drop my head as a giggle tumbles out of me at his corny ass. Leaning in, I cup his face and press a long kiss to his lips. "Tim, I-I," I bite my bottom lip to stop stuttering, "I 'on't really know what to say except *thank you*. I feel like I needed to hear that."

"Anytime, gorgeous." He kisses my cheek. "And remember, I know an interior designer. She's real chill. I can introduce y'all if you'd like to talk to her. Just think about it."

There's that offer again. My eyes dart all over his face as I just nod. "I will. And what're you doin' July Fourth?"

"Jaquade usually hosts a cookout, but I ain't heard anything about it yet. So, I guess nuttn right now." A mischievous smile worms its way onto his face. "Why? You wanna celebrate the birth of this country witcha boy?"

I scoff, cracking up. "My sister's comin' next week—"

"That's right." He briefly squeezes his eyes shut. "I promise I ain't forget."

"She and my friends wanna meet you."

Tim tucks in his chin, his eyes focusing on me. "Fa real?"

I nod. "Yep. So, I figured I could introduce my friends to Simonique and you to the girls" I drop my hands to his shirt, running a finger along the white thread of his chest pocket. "Do you wanna meet 'em, Tim?"

He sits up and takes my hands in his. "Camesha."

I look up at him.

"I would *love* to meet 'em," Tim says with a bright smile.

A mix of anxiety and joy swirl in me so intensely that I wrap my arms tightly around his neck in a hug.

He hugs me back. "Should I bring anything to ya shindig?" he asks in a voice to make it sound like I'm squeezing him.

I laugh, letting him go. "Just bring ya'self. I got everything else. After all, you did enough today. You really put ya foot in this food."

"Thank you. And well, ya know, I do got big feet," he whispers, easing out the words with a cool smile before biting his bottom lip.

Is he . . . Is he referrin' to his dick size, too? Why'd he say it like that? my horny ass thinks, making me suddenly realize something: I'm in a skirt, sitting on Tim's lap. A few layers away from his dick again. He's not hard underneath me this time, but *I'm* getting really excited. Hell, his affirmation earlier got my panties damp. I shift in his lap when I finally feel how squishy-wet my panties are. *Shit, I hope I 'on't leave a stain on his pants!—Or maybe you do wanna leave a stain—Shut up, bitch!* I war with myself.

Blinking, I climb off Tim as some sense kicks in. A glance down and I don't see a wet stain. *Thank God!* He stands and helps me up.

"I got one more thing for ya birthday evening, Ms. Russell." He turns and goes to his car. "Turn around, no peekin'."

Giddy, I follow his direction, spinning around to face the beach.

A moment later, Tim says, "A'ight, you can turn around now."

I do and see that he's holding a large light wood picture frame.

He flips it around and I gasp. The title "No Rush" is above two columns of words. The poem he performed on our first date.

"I *hope* you ain't think I forgot 'bout ya request to have *your* poem framed." He hands it to me.

I skim over the words I heard a month ago, words from Tim's heart that he voiced onstage in front of all those strangers. My eyes start to brim with tears, and I look up at the sky to not to get any on the poem.

He takes the frame and lays it on a clear spot on the large blanket. He steps closer and I hug his torso, his arms going around my neck.

"One of the best birthdays ever," I mumble into his shirt.

Tim pulls back, and swipes some of my tears away before he bends down to kiss me.

Saturday, June 30

Tim

"I really 'preciate you comin' through for me, man," my client Snootie P says, her hands in praying formation. She's 5'2" with a quiet presence. Until she spits on the mic. I've seen her destroy careers in cyphers with both women *and* men. P's a real-deal MC.

"No pro'lem." We dap up and I whisper in her ear, "Ya know you one of my favorite clients, right?"

We back out and she laughs.

"I'm serious, P!"

She just waves me off, ever so humble. Her manager comes over to whisk her away and I head out the door.

Since she's one of my low-maintenance clients, this task was definitely an emergency. Her team hit me up to retrieve an extra outfit from her house in Leimert Park since she changed her mind about the one her stylist put together for her appearance on the popular YouTube show, AUX + SOUL with Kia B and C-Note. This is a big deal because this afternoon's recording would be her first talk show interview and performance in her three-year career.

In my Jeep, I pull out my phone, seeing it's 30 minutes before showtime. I block out the rest of my calendar before a client hits me up about something. Then I call Camesha.

The phone rings twice before she picks up. "Hey, baby."

Her upbeat voice makes me smile. "'Sup? You busy?"

"Nah. Just cleaned my bathroom and now I'm meal preppin' for the week."

I nod like she can see me. "Cool. I just finished wit' a client. You, uh, you mind if I slide through for a minute? I can be useful in the kitchen. Ya know my cookin' skills are solid."

We both chuckle.

"Yeah, c'mon," she says.

"Bet. I'mma go home and shower real quick before I come over. Want or need me to pick up some'?"

There's a pause on the other line, probably because she's thinking. "I'm good."

"A'ight. See ya soon."

Two hours later, I'm parking my whip next to Camesha's Venza. I forgot that the salesperson at the high-end wine shop sold me on *two* bottles of semi-sweet white wine for her birthday, so I bring the second one upstairs with me.

I can hear some music through her door. Thank God she's at the end of the hall, otherwise, I'm sure her neighbors would have a cow. I knock and seconds later, I hear the music's volume fade to a lower level before the locks disengage and the door opens. Camesha's comfortable in some black biker shorts and a red T-shirt with a Bit-O-Honey candy graphic on it. Her curly hair is middle-parted and she's barefoot, her pretty marigold toes on display.

"Tim, I said you didn't have to bring anything." She looks at me fake-disappointed.

"I forgot I had it. It's white wiiine," I sing, holding the brown paper bag out to her.

Grinning, she rolls her eyes and takes it before heading toward her fridge. My eyes zero in on her ass in them shorts. I clench my jaw and avert my gaze. *Jesus be a fence. Maybe comin' over here was the wrong move?..*

I walk in and close her door, recognizing the trap soul artist Rayo Cruz serenading in English and Spanish in the background.

This is my first time inside Camesha's condo since our first date. We've tried to go out at least once a week and sometimes that didn't require me picking her up at her place. Like meeting up for lunch because I just so happened to be in Beverly Hills for a client.

As I toe my sneakers off, I notice Camesha hung up her framed poem by the front door above one of her couches. Somewhere visible where guests will easily be able to see it.

Pride and something softer swells in my heart. "I see you hung up ya poem."

Beaming, she says over her shoulder, "Oh, yeah. I really love it, Tim. Thank you again."

"Of course." I stroll over to the island, trying to keep my eyes on her back and not her butt.

"So, how ya girls treat you yesterday? Y'all ain't get too fucked-up, right?" I smirk.

"Do I *look* fucked-up?" She turns around, an eyebrow arched.

I playfully inspect her up and down. "Nooo. . . But you might be a pro drinker or some'."

She laughs. "Definitely not. We had a good time wit' an *appropriate* amount of alcohol."

I nod. "That's good. So," I clap, "whatchu in here makin', Chef Girl-ardee?"

She throws her head back and howls. "That's a good one," she says, pointing a finger at me.

"I aim to please," just comes out.

We hold eye contact a little longer, a sizzle crackling in the air. Or maybe it's whatever she's cooking in that skillet.

Camesha blinks. "Um, I'm just makin' my first lunch option for the week: shrimp fajitas. I already prepped mini frittata muffins and overnight oats for breakfast."

We chat about how she meal preps since my ass could definitely try to plan my meals better. Mostly surviving off protein bars, Mio-ed water, craft service tables, and takeout ain't it for the long haul.

"I wanted to use the rest of my shrimp and make Cajun shrimp and quinoa. Ya Cajun salmon inspired me." She flashes me a smile and I swear a literal spark shines off her teeth.

"I'm glad. I actually just finished those leftovers yesterday."

She pouts. "I wish I coulda had some more."

"A nigga had to eat, C." I clutch my stomach, making her laugh. "But I promise to cook for you more often."

"I'd love that, Tim." She nods. "And you can help me right now. Can you chop that spinach?" She points at the plastic bag near a cutting board on her island.

I chuckle at her bossing me around. "Yes ma'am." I wash my hands at the sink before getting a Cutco knife from the wood block.

Camesha stirs the fajita mixture a little, making sure they're coated in her sauce before pushing them into the three glass meal prep containers sitting on her island.

Then a quiet synth note and vocal run flowing through her speaker causes Camesha to flip out. "Oh, *this* is my song!" She places the now-empty skillet and spatula on her stove to go to her speaker. She starts the song over and turns up the music. Now I recognize the bop as "Swing My Way" by K.P. & Envyi.

I put the knife down on the cutting board as a smile overtakes my face, watching Camesha passionately lip-synch Envyi's famous run as she saunters back to the kitchen. And when the beat kicks in, she starts dancing, bouncing her shoulders and wiggling her hips. She surprises me even more when she starts rapping K.P.'s verse with hand motions and facial expressions. All I can do is laugh at her goofiness as she confidently raps to me. It's sexy as hell.

Once the second verse comes, I join in on the shenanigans and do the running man dance that went viral when the world rediscovered the gem "My Boo" by Ghost Town DJs years ago. Camesha breaks character and staggers around the kitchen, cracking up at my moves.

We keep dancing and goofing off, but then in the middle of K.P.'s third verse, Camesha slowly saunters toward me, switching her hips hard. She raps aloud, talking about getting a tenderoni.

I stop dancing, just focused on her, distracted by the shift in the air. She doesn't rap the rest of the verse, gazing up into my eyes with *that* look: head tilted, eyes narrowed, chin tucked, half of her bottom lip between her teeth.

My jaw clenches as I search her face for a sign that she's for real. I can't really tell but fuck it. I swallow hard and slowly approach her. My hands land on her waist as I crash my lips onto hers. She cradles my face as we start making out, both of our mouths opening to invite one another's tongues.

But it's not enough. None of it is.

So, I don't think, I just act. I let my hands slide down her back and palm her round ass. My dick jumps a little in my shorts as I feel how soft it is in this material.

Camesha

A moan leaps out of me as Tim's big hands squeeze my ass repeatedly.

"Fuck," he exhales against my mouth.

As we kiss, he slaps and massages my booty, making me yelp and my pussy spasm. *Shit feels so damn good.* "Swing My Way" soon transitions into Teedra Moses's "Be Your Girl" as Tim bends down to hook his hands underneath my knees before lifting me in the air.

Our lips disconnect and our foreheads touch as we deeply inhale hot, charged air. My arms try to wrap around his broad shoulders as he sits me on the island. Both of our eyes are half-closed as we stare at each other.

Tim nudges his head forward to kiss my neck, my hands clasping his head to keep him on my spot. "I wantchu," he breathes into my skin.

A record scratches in my mind. I snap my head back, my eyes flashing open. "What?"

His eyes open just a tad more as he stares at me, looking *hungry*. His full lips are slightly swollen, his chest softly rising and falling. "I want you, Camesha," Tim reiterates at the same volume as before.

My heart jolts at that. "Are you sure?" I hold his face out, searching his eyes.

"Yeah." A smile lifts one side of his mouth, revealing his teeth. Then it disappears, concern marring his features. "Wait, do *you* not want me? Did I misread this?—"

Tim tries to step back, and I slide my arms around his neck, locking him in. "I want you, Tim."

A smile slowly replaces his frown. "Okay." He leans forward and we lip lock again. Tim picks me up off the island, my legs automatically wrapping around his waist, my ass sitting in his palms.

"Room's right there," I mumble against his mouth, pointing to the door next to my fridge.

With Teedra's song still playing in my living area, Tim takes wide strides to my queen-sized bed. He lays me down on it, his body covering mine as we keep kissing. My bedside lamp is on, and the window's blinds are slightly cracked, allowing some evening sunlight to seep through.

I run my hands up his back covered in his plain black T-shirt. "Shirt off," I let out breathily, hating how desperate I sound.

He wants to have sex with me. I want to have sex with him. We've been waiting and desiring this, so I shouldn't feel ashamed.

"Yes, ma'am," Tim chuckles lowly. He stands to his full height.

With quickened breaths, I wait in anticipation.

And when he yanks his top off from the neck hole, his body is like I imagined it. Tim's lean with no tattoos. All broad chest and slim waist. A happy trail disappears into his shorts. Biting my bottom lip, I sit up a bit and rest back on my elbows to run a hand up his flat stomach. I chuckle since I know his ass eats a lot and works out sparingly. *No fair—his genes just blessed him wit' a flat tummy while I gotta work for mine.*

"Whatchu laughin' at, C?" he asks with a lopsided grin.

"Nothin'," I giggle, shaking my head.

He leers at me as he lifts my T-shirt over my head, throwing it somewhere. I pull my bra straps down, unsnap it from the back, and shrug it off, flinging it to the other side of the bed.

Tim's eyes drop to my breasts, and he licks his lips. "May I?"

"Please," just comes out and if I wasn't so horny right now my inner self would chastise me.

Tim leans down and his mouth latches onto my right breast. I throw my head back onto the bed, reveling in the feeling of him sucking and licking my nipple. His hands grope both breasts, his fingers tweaking the left one. My panties and my biker shorts are soaked.

Tim's mouth migrates to my other breast, showing her some love, too.

"Can I taste you?"

His voice is so light and breathy that I almost didn't hear him. *But we love consent.* I lift my head to look at Tim, his kind eyes awaiting my answer. I nod my head feverishly as my pussy leaks with anticipation.

"I need to hear you, baby." He smirks and bites his bottom lip.

"Yes, Tim, please," I barely get out in an exhale.

His eyes seem to darken as he slowly treks his way down my stomach, leaving a trail of wet kisses. When he gets to my biker shorts, his fingers curl into the waistband and he pulls down both my shorts and panties.

I spread my legs for him, wincing when I feel Tim's hot breath hitting my wet center. He deeply inhales and exhales. "Fuck, you smell good, Camesha."

He runs a long finger along my slit before easing it in and out of me, my wetness making noise. My walls clench around his finger and I gasp at how good it feels.

"You ready for me, baby?" Tim breathes out.

Impatient and whimpering, I lift my hips toward his face.

Chuckling lowly, Tim removes his finger and his big tongue takes a slow lick of me down there. He groans, sounding pleased before he goes to town and that makes me wetter.

"Shit, Tim!" My hands find his curly hair, holding him there as he devours me. Involuntarily, my legs try to close around his head. But he holds my legs apart and his forearms press the inside of my knees back as his fingers, one still wet with my essence, grope my breasts. *Good thing I stretch when I work out.*

"Lemme eat, baby," he murmurs before going back in, his big tongue curling into my folds.

I knew his big-back ass was an eater, I think.

But when Tim wraps his full lips around my clit, I almost lose it. He sucks it and slowly pulls away until I hear a *pop*.

"Shit!" I hiss. My legs try to snap shut again, but Tim's grip is relentless.

"Unh, unh, don't run. I ain't done," he mumbles before sucking my clit a few times.

And moments later, my eyes roll into the back of my head, my orgasm surging through me until I stiffen. Tim grumbles something against my crying pussy as he groans and licks up all my juices.

I imagine I'm on a beach paradise as I come down from the high. I'm so boneless and satisfied, a warmth settling over me, that I just lay there and enjoy the feeling of Tim's mouth hungrily cleaning me up.

"You sweet as hell, Camesha."

Once feeling returns to my body, I sit up on the bed, pulling Tim's face to mine. I lick and suck his tongue to taste myself. Asa always tried to convince me to kiss him for this exact reason. *He was right though—I* do *taste good.* Tim's body collapses on top of mine as he groans in pleasure.

We disconnect for air, happy-drunk smiles smearing our faces. I caress his handsome face then drag my hand down to pull his chin hairs, which are now moist with my essence.

"You tryna fuck me up, huh?" he asks.

"Maybe." I smirk and bite my bottom lip.

Tim stands up and I watch him rummage through his shorts pockets until he retrieves his wallet. Impatience and frustration skew his facial features as he rifles through it.

"I have some in my nightstand drawer." I point to the nightstand where my lamp is, closest to my bathroom. I might've bought some condoms recently just in case. . .

Since I'm looking at the ceiling, Tim leaves my view for a moment to follow my directions. I listen closely to the music in the room, recognizing "Permission" by Ro James. I smirk at how fitting my shuffled "Liked" songs have been today. Tim's not the only one who knows how to set the vibe.

He returns with a lopsided smile. "Sorry for the commercial break."

I softly laugh, sitting up on my elbows. I watch him push his shorts and boxer briefs down.

Tim's dick springs to life and my mouth waters. He's a pretty brown color like the rest of him with trimmed pubic hair. Cut, thick, and the perfect length. *I knew he was packin' some' serious.* I can feel him watch me as he sheathes himself with a condom. I look up at him, finding his hazy gaze.

"This okay?" He slowly strokes himself with a goofy smile smearing his face.

"*More* than okay, baby."

Tim leans over the bed, his arms supporting him and caging me in. His damn chains dangling in my face do something to me. Impatiently, I pull his face down to kiss him as my legs spread to accommodate his body.

Tim

I back out of our kiss to position my dick at Camesha's entrance and rub the head against her smooth folds. The contact makes me shudder at how wet she is. She moans and I have to snap my mouth shut, otherwise, I would drool all over her pretty face.

I bend down to bury my face into her neck before I slowly guide myself inside of her tight pussy. *Fuck! It's been a long-ass time.* She tasted so good and now she feels too good, gripping the fuck out of me. If *I* don't get a grip, I'm going to cum way too fast.

She gasps and cups the back of my head. Her lips suck on my earlobe as I ground myself in her, getting adjusted. I bite my bottom lip to stifle the hiss wanting to escape my mouth. I slowly start moving inside Camesha, using the R&B song playing in the background to help me find a rhythm. *She got this music too right today.*

I back up to look at her face. "You good, C?" I breathe out.

Her eyes are closed as she nods.

"Look at me, baby."

Her doe eyes flash open, looking cute as hell.

I stop moving. "Tell me whatchu want. I need to hear you, Camesha."

"Okay, Tim," she exhales.

I bend down to kiss her nose before tucking my face back in her neck. My hips start slowly thrusting again as she wraps her legs tighter around my waist.

"Deeper," Camesha whimpers in my ear.

I do what she says while licking and nibbling her warm neck. She smells and tastes like a praline.

"Right there, Tim," Camesha moans repeatedly.

Her acrylic nails scratch up my back, an encouraging sensation. I keep going, adjusting my tempo and stroke when she instructs me to. I can feel her walls closing in around me as she meets my thrusts.

And in probably a few embarrassing minutes, I croak, "I think I'm close, baby," feeling the familiar, yet long-lost tingle coil in my body.

Camesha holds my face at arm's length. Turned on and confused, my eyebrows scrunch up, trying to read her.

"I wanna ride you," she says barely loud enough for me to hear her over my breathing and the music.

I'm still inside her, but she's definitely in control now. Careful not to cum yet, I pull out and fall on my back next to her. With a determined look in her eyes, she gets up, and I hold up my dick, ready for her to mount me. She slides down on it and slowly starts wining her hips, a hand planted on my chest for support.

Her curly hair flowing down her arched back, her boobs bouncing, her face morphing with pleasure—What a view. I mutter cuss words as I grip her hips, just holding on for the ride. Camesha increases her pace a little, her moans mingling well with the music. I reach one hand up to tweak a nipple and the other rubs her clit as she bounces faster on me.

"Shiiittt," she sings, exasperated.

"Cum for me, baby," I sigh, all strangled.

Then the delicious feeling reemerges. My heart rate speeds up, my abdomen tightens, my balls contract—"Fuuuck!" I let out a long groan as I nut into the condom. And Camesha's right there with me, her second wind gushing down my shaft.

She dismounts and collapses on top of me. My hand wraps around her waist as we both try to catch our breaths. I'm sure we both look like seals washed up on the beach, sweating and breathing hard as shit.

"I can help you clean up all'is," I say around my heaving breaths, breaking our tired silence.

Camesha doesn't respond right away, making me look down at her. "Thank you." She kisses my jaw.

But then a familiar song fades in. *I recognize that piano.* "Bedroom Eyes" by Keyana Renay.

I close my eyes, chuckling as I drag my other hand down my face. "Yo, this is weird, C. *Thank God* I ain't hear no clients' songs while we were doin' it."

Camesha's head pops up. "But I *really* like this song, Tim," she says amusedly.

I open my eyes, finding her pouting. "It's a good song, but I 'on't wanna hear Keyana's voice while we like this. Can we *please* change it?"

"Fine," she huffs out.

We had sex on top of her comforter, so she just slides off of me and the bed. I sit up to slap her fat ass, making that thing jiggle. She giggles as she heads for the living room.

Then, I hear nothing.

"You ain't have to turn off the music completely," I chortle.

She appears in the doorway and shrugs. "I'mma use the bathroom real quick." She leaves for her half bath near the front door.

I take that as my cue to get up and do the same. Her en-suite bathroom has a reed diffuser, making it smell like a five-star resort in here. An insane lineup of hygiene and skincare products are organized on her counter. I slip off the condom, wrap it in toilet paper, throw it away, and pee before washing my hands.

When I return to her bedroom, Camesha's waltzing in, cellphone in hand. "I'm cold."

We pull back her ecru comforter and champagne-colored sheets as the decorative pillows tumble to the carpet. She puts her phone on the nightstand before we slide into bed, feeling warm immediately.

Her sheets smell like her. *Shit, I can still* taste *her. I ain't mad at any of it.*

Camesha curls into me, her head and hand on my chest with her leg thrown over my now soft dick. Instead of wrapping my arm around her waist, I rub on her booty.

"Woo! I finally get booty rubs now," she sighs all low.

I crack up. "You been waitin' for 'em or some'?"

"Yesss! I almost didn't think you liked me that much since you never touched my ass until today."

I laugh again. "I didn't wanna just be touchin' on you like that. I was tryna be respectful. Plus, I knew that if I *did* touch ya ass, we'd probably end up here, and I didn't wanna do that too fast."

Her fingers trace circles on my chest. "Fair nuff. So, why *are* we here? What made you ready at this moment?"

I take a deep breath. "You."

Her head pops up as she looks at me with a smirk.

"You gave me that *look*, and I was like, 'Fuck it.' I want her and she lookin' like she want me." I return the smirk.

"What *look*? I 'on't have a look," Camesha laughs.

"*You* know that sexy look you do." I demonstrate, making her howl.

She lays her head back down.

"But fa real, it was *that* and I was just ready. I feel like we're connectin' really well. The mood and the moment felt right today—It wasn't my plan to come over here for this though."

"I know cuz you didn't have a condom," she mutters.

I chuckle, slapping her ass and making her giggle. "I just genuinely wanted to see you." With my other hand, I gently grab her chin and bring her face toward mine to peck her lips.

Camesha lays back down. "Well, I'm glad you came over. The moment felt right for me, too." Her fingers move to my sternum. "This was great, too cuz I got some dick for my birthday," she murmurs.

I howl laughing, loving this more silly and funny side of her. I think she's just feeling more comfortable around me, so I intend to keep nurturing this growing trust. I want her to keep revealing parts of herself to me, and vice versa. Hell, when she rambled about her dream of being an interior designer, I knew that was her heart talking even if she looked mortified that she said all that. And if she trusts me enough to let that slip, I need to make her feel safer to just be open with me.

Camesha laughs, too, and a beat later, her fingers ghost over my clavicle. "A tattoo right here would be so sexy on you."

An amused smile worms onto my face. "Is that right? You like clavicle tatts?"

She titters, "Not really. I just think it'd look good on you. I'm actually surprised you *don't* have tattoos."

"Well, you 'on't have any." I tickle her side, her laugh filling my ears. "They're cool, but I could never commit to some' on my skin forever. But I can commit to *you*." I kiss the top of her hair.

She looks up at me, giggling, "I like that." Camesha tucks in her lips before speaking again, "And I gotta question."

"Whassup?" I gaze down at her.

"Do you and Lil Hibb have, like . . . beef?"

My eyebrows knit together as I jog my memory. "Oh, the rapper that Zay won the BET Hip Hop Award wit'?"

"Yeah."

"Nah, I ain't got no beef wit' him. Why you ask me that?" I chortle.

Her fingers rub my chest again. "Because you were actin' so weird whenever his name came up at Zay's parties when we first met."

I think back on that and laugh. "Oh," pause, "that's cuz I liked you. I *didn't* like him all up in yo' face at Zay's birthday. So, I ain't wanna talk about that nigga."

I glance down, finding Camesha peering up at me, smirking. "I thought so. I just wanted to confirm."

"Oh yeah?" I tickle her again.

Camesha giggles as I move to get on top of her. Like second nature, she immediately wraps her legs around my waist and my dick hops, tapping her plump lower lips.

I kiss her and she smiles, fingers pulling at my chin hair.

"You hungry, handsome?" she asks.

The first thing that pops in my head is "For you." But I *am* hungry for some actual food. "Yeah." I roll off of her and lay back down.

"Whatchu want?" Camesha sits up to reach over me to get her phone from the nightstand. With her head resting in her hand as her bent elbow pierces the pillow, she starts scrolling on her cell.

I copy her position. "Whatchu doin'?"

"Pullin' up Uber Eats," she says matter-of-factly.

"Nah. You ain't gotta do all'at. You got any lunch meat and some bread? I can just make a quick sandwich. Or I can go home," I joke, jabbing a thumb over my shoulder.

Camesha looks up at me and pushes my hand down. Softly, she says, "Stop. You're not goin' home, Tim."

My jaw tenses, hearing her say it like that. She basically told me to stay. I like that.

She clears her throat. "And don't piss me off—I'm gonna pretend you didn't just say you can make a sandwich," she scoffs, going back to scrolling.

"I'm fa real, C," I chortle, "You ain't gotta order nuttn."

She stops scrolling again to deadpan me. "I want to. Let me do this for you, Tim."

I swim in her eyes, finding sincerity. "What did I do to deserve this? A nigga put it down and now you 'bout to feed me?" I reach out to rub on her hip underneath the covers.

She tries to fight it, but a wide smile spreads her lips apart. "It was that dick and that mouth," she mutters.

"I'm sorry, whatcha say?" I heard her loud and clear, but I just wanted the ego boost again.

"I said, you know whatchu doin', Tim," she reluctantly says, her cheeks reddening.

I smile big as hell. "Yeah, girl. I just ain't done it in a while," I chuckle. "I'll let my lady order some' for me. But I'm gettin' the food when it arrives."

We decide to order Fat Sal's Banh Mi-Ki and some fries. When the driver arrives, I put my clothes on to meet him outside. Camesha and I eat our dinner, drinking the wine I brought, as we watch something on TV. Then I have her for dessert.

12
Blow This Up

Wednesday, July 4

Camesha

It's been two days since Tim and I had sex for the first time. I can't stop thinking about it.

The need in his eyes and the soft assuredness in his voice when he told me he wanted me and looked *ready* to have me. How hungry he moved yet took his time. How he listened to what I wanted. How he *savored* me. *God, Tim ate me out so good.* I don't know how long a "minute" was for him since his last time, but I couldn't even tell. Sex with Tim Starks was everything I imagined and more.

But right now, I have to put our time together on the backburner. I took off work this week so I could hang out with Simonique while she was here. I already knew it was finna be a time when I picked her up Monday afternoon:

I waited for Nique in my Venza with the radio on low. She's texted me since she landed here 45 minutes ago, updating me on where she was. I told her that LAX is huge, so I knew she was lost.

My phone chimed and I opened it up, seeing a text from Tim. I smiled without even seeing the message yet.

Tim (1:47pm):

Simonique with you yet? ⊠

Me (1:47pm):

Not yet.

Tim (1:48pm):

Yall have a good time!

Me (1:48pm):

We will! See you Wednesday! And don't bring anything, Tim.⊠

Tim (1:49pm):

⊠aight fine

A tap on my window jolted me out of my texting conversation. I dropped my phone into my cupholder before scrambling out of my truck. "Nique!" I squealed, grabbing my younger sister into a hug.

"Eesh!" She hugged me back and we were all dramatic, rocking side to side.

Last time I saw her in person was in May for her graduation. But this is her first time here—in the city I've called home for the last eight years.

We separated and she held my hands out, eyeing my chill airport outfit. "You look so *good!"*

I blushed. "Girl, you look *good! I love ya nails. And did Lanelle do this?" I ran my fingers down her goddess braids.*

"You know she did." Simonique playfully slapped my arm. "Girl, you weren't lyin'—that airport is huge*! Why the fuck they design it like that?"*

I cackled, moving to get her burnt orange suitcase. "I 'on't know, but you made it."

Simonique and I load her suitcase and her matching carry-on into my trunk before getting inside.

"This truck is so cute, pooh!"

"Thanks," I giggled.

I pulled away from the curb, and I asked her about the flight since I knew she had only been on a plane two other times in her life. That was her longest flight so far and in typical Simonique fashion, she spins the story into something straight out of a comedy, cracking on the terrible snacks and the annoying passengers.

Cruising down the highway back to my condo, she ran down all the things she wanted to do while she was here this week. I thought of and planned a few things myself, but I should've known her ass was going to have an agenda, too. In hindsight, we definitely should've planned her trip together.

After she gushed about my condo, she unpacked her suitcase, transforming my living room into her bedroom. I said we could share my bed, but she said she "ain't want to sleep in the same bed I fuck in." I mean, up until Saturday, there ain't been no fucking there in years! But fair, *I thought.*

"So, how is Tim? Is he ready to meet us?"

I told Simonique that I was inviting my friends to my July Fourth gathering, too. I've shared stories about all of them to each other, so they're all excited to meet. I'm definitely anxious and eager to see how Nique and Nikki will fare together since they're so similar to me.

"He is ready. I was happy when he said he didn't have any plans that day." She was quiet and I glanced at her briefly. "What?"

"Biiitch, I can't wait *to meet him! Ya know you're blushin' right now, just talkin' 'bout him? And you ain't even say some*

cute shit. He must *be special cuz I ain't never. . ." she just trailed off, making me laugh.*

I shooed her before I got ready for our first activity: a hookah lounge off Sunset Boulevard where she heard some of her favorite artists hung out. I don't smoke, but apparently, Nique does, but I obliged the wild goose chase to spot celebrities on a Monday night.

We ended up not spotting anyone, but Simonique had a fun time and that made me happy.

Maybe it was all the secondhand smoke we inhaled, because when we got back to my condo, I was feeling really bold and truthful.

Nique took her heels off and laid back on her couch-bed while I slumped in the other couch.

"Nique. . ."

"Yeah?"

"I gotta tell you some." My throat got dry, making it hard to breathe. I sat up.

She must've felt the shift in the room because she sat up, too, her eyebrows smashed together.

I swallowed hard so I could talk. "I used to vibe model and escort for three years. I just stopped doin' it."

Her face didn't register what I just said. "What?"

I repeat myself slowly . . . and slowly, I watch her realize what I just told her.

"Wait—escort? You used to fuck men for money?" Confusion marred her features.

I gave her a pass for the harshness in her word choice since we're both a little high, but I still wasn't expecting that bite. "Not all men, Nique. I had standards, rules, a system. But yes." A pang of embarrassment and shame struck me as I tried to defend my old hustle to my younger sister.

She nodded her head repeatedly. "Okaaayyy. . . And what's vibe modelin'?"

"Club promoters, handlers, and celebrities hire young, attractive women to attend events and fill venue sections. Or to just entertain the men comin'. They'd even take videos or pictures for social media of me and the other models havin' a good time. All of it was to give folks FOMO and make people come out. And sometimes, men would proposition me, and they'd become an escortin' client," I rambled. It felt weird explaining all of this to her so openly and honestly, spilling a part of myself I kept zipped up from my family.

Simonique cupped her chin quizzically, making me chuckle inappropriately. "Why are you laughin'?" she giggled with a scowl, like she was mad I broke our serious streak.

"I'm sorry. You just look like a cute version of that Thinker *statue." I coughed to stop laughing. "And ya know I laugh when I'm under the influence."*

She snickered, the mood lifting. Just a smidge. "So, you made a lotta money then, huh? All'at money you sent to Mama and Daddy and me? That wasn't *just ya hotel job income?"*

I shook my head.

She nodded and exhaled a long breath. "Ain't gon' lie, Eesh . . . I'm a lil' mad that you didn't tell me this sooner. I thought we tell each other everything."

I dropped my head briefly, shame's cold air making me shiver. "I know. I just didn't know what to say and I didn't wanna risk Mama and Daddy findin' out."

"Now you know *I wouldn't've told 'em if you told me it was a secret." She tilted her head, deadpanning me.*

I frowned. "I know. But you were also still so young when I started and you were startin' school, so I didn't wanna tell you and add to ya plate. I didn't wantchu to worry 'bout me."

She pursed her lips and sighed. "I guess I can understand that." Then Simonique clasped her hands in front of her lips. "Eesh, I have to ask. . ."

I looked her in the eyes, trying to anticipate what she's about to say.

"Did you want to do it?"

I winced a little at her insinuation. I know for a fact that some women didn't want to do it, and I shudder at the thought, my heart aching for them. That's why I donate to those sex worker support funds. But I did choose to escort.

"Yes, I wanted to do it." I swallowed and watched Simonique sigh in relief, her tense shoulders dropping.

I told her how I got into the hustle as she hung onto my every word, soaking in all of my rambling. The seemingly endless coffee shop jobs. Zaria mentoring and training me. I detailed my rules and boundaries, my Cammie persona, my dissociating when I was with clients. I told her that when I stopped hustling, I was $30,000 away from making $500,000 in three years. Her mouth dropped open.

I even told her about the new job opportunity at The Aubade and how I'm thinking about applying to college.

But I didn't tell her about what happened with Raw Math. I wasn't that high.

When I finished yapping, Simonique stood up and sat down next to me on the couch. I immediately wrapped my arms around her and simultaneously let go of all that which I'd been holding in. All the heavy shame and guilt that's been eating away at me for three years.

She lightly stroked my hair as my face rested on her boobs, her fragrance most intense and soothing there.

I let her go and her thumbs swiped my face, careful not to poke me in the eye with her stiletto nails. I didn't even know I was crying.

"I actually met Tim while I was workin' a party."

Nique's eyes got big. "Really?"

"Yeah. I even tried to hit on him, thinkin' he was tryna spit game by talkin' 'bout appetizers." I rolled my eyes then palmed

my face, embarrassed at the memory that felt like a lifetime ago already.

My sister and I laughed.

"He knew my job there but still treated me like I was just a guest." A grin touched my face.

"Awww, that's sweet." She poked her lips out. "Pooh, ya blushin' again."

I stifle a chuckle.

"Thank you for tellin' me all'at, Camesha. I wish I had known earlier but I get you wantin' to keep that to ya'self. I'm happy ya figurin' out what's next for you though. And I'm glad you have Tim and ya friends to support you out here."

"Yeah, they're . . ." I thought of a good word, but the first one that pops up fit, "great."

"Like Tony the Tiger?" Simonique smirked, making me crack up.

"Yeah."

A smile smooths onto her face. "I can't wait to meet 'em."

It was an intense day for Simonique: traveling across the country, unpacking, partying at a hookah lounge, and learning that her older sister used to vibe model and escort for over three years. But overall, she was understanding and supportive of me. We talked all night and fell asleep in each other's arms.

Then yesterday, we went on a celebrity homes tour and ate at Roscoe's Chicken & Waffles. That inspired us to start binging *Insecure* from the beginning last night.

Today is the Fourth of July. Not going to lie, I've been running *ragged*, trying to get things ready for this gathering. Simonique and I cooked all day and now that it's almost 3:30pm, my friends should be on the way since I said the party starts at four. I told Tim that we're starting at five so, that way, all the girls can get acquainted first and hopefully help calm my frayed nerves.

I reserved one of my complex's courtyards so we can set up outside since Simonique took over my living room and it would've been a crime to be inside when it's such a gorgeous day.

Nique and I position all the warming containers, drinks, Styrofoam plates, plastic utensils, and napkins on my island so they're easy to grab and take outside when my friends get here.

She pauses her "Ratchet Hoes" playlist on my Bluetooth speaker. "You okay, sis?" she asks with an arched eyebrow. She's cute in a white graphic muscle shirt, blue denim shorts, white sandals, and gold jewelry.

"Yeah, I'm fine," I say passively.

She side-eyes me. "Eesh, ya nervous."

The coil that's been residing in my back today tightens. I huff out a breath, dropping my shoulders. "Okay, I am."

She laughs and hugs me. I wrap my arms around her, nestling into her scent. I can't pinpoint the smell so it must be like a pheromone type of thing.

There's a knock at my door, and the coil intensifies. I retreat from my sister and shuffle to the door. *Lord, please let Tim be on time or late today.*

I look through the peephole. And I let out a breath. *Thank God.*

I open the door for Nikki and Oluchi.

Nikki says, "Were you in the bathroom or some'? Not very hostess-like of you to make us wait out here so long." She dramatically rolls her neck, her auburn faux locs falling in her face.

I see she's holding a bottle-shaped brown paper bag. I really didn't want anyone to worry about bringing anything, but Nikki *begged* me to allow her to bring her "famous" rum punch.

Lu just rolls her eyes and playfully slaps Nikki's arm. "Hey, Camesha," she says, walking toward me with open arms.

She's slaying an olive-green linen co-ord and her hair falls in voluptuous curls as oversized sunglasses sit in it.

"Hey, Lu." In her arms, I mean mug Nikki for being so damn dramatic. She sticks her tongue out and when I let go of Lu, I hug my other bestie.

"Y'all, this is my sister Simonique. Nique, these are my friends, Nikki and Oluchi." I close my door and turn around.

"Hey, y'all!" Simonique beams and waves at them.

Nikki sets her punch on the island. "Hey, boo! I heard you were an Aries like me, so I think we gon' be on the same wavelength." They are outfit-wise, except Nikki's boldly wearing a white tube top *and* white shorts and white sneakers.

"Ooo, okay. Ya know, I've always wanted an Aries sister," Nique says, pointing at her.

"And our nicknames are similar, too? I think this was in the stars, girl!" Nikki says and they cackle like long-lost hyena sisters.

"It's nice to meet you, Simonique," Lu simply says with a wave.

"You as well," Nique matches her energy.

Okay, so far so good. I take a deep inhale as my sister plays her music.

They all start chatting, asking Simonique how she's liking Los Angeles so far. Of course, her and Nikki are discussing *more* things she needs to do while she's here, adding to our already full itinerary.

We take trips carrying everything we need to the courtyard to set up.

As the clock nears five, I feel the urge to text Tim to see if he's close. But one glare from Simonique tells me to calm the hell down and relax. *He'll get here, Eesh. And him meetin' the girls will go well*, I coach myself.

Tim

I know Camesha told me not to bring anything, but can she argue with me when I show up with margarita mix and tequila? Women *love* margaritas.

I park my Jeep and grab the bag from the passenger's side before hopping out. I check myself out in my window, making sure I'm straight. Rocking my same jewelry, I'm wearing a simple sky-blue tee, black Nike shorts, my Waffle Debuts, and a black LA Dodgers trucker hat. Keeping it relatively simple for that first impression.

A few hours ago, Camesha texted me that she reserved Courtyard 2, so I just follow the path around her building until I see the sign a few yards away.

I see Camesha's worried eyes darting around, but when she spots me before her girls do, a smile breaks her face.

She leaves her people who're chilling and talking while music plays. As Camesha gets closer, I just stop mid-stride and admire her. She's wearing an orange tiered dress that skims her curves and stops just before her knees. Her hair is half-up, half-down and her edges are laid, so I can see more of her gorgeous face.

"You look good as hell, girl," I let out.

"Thank you, baby." She gets on her tippy-toes in her white sandals and pulls my face down to kiss me on the lips.

"Um, excuse me, Ms. Russell, please bring Mr. Starks over this way," one of her girls wearing all white interrupts.

We separate and Camesha stifles a laugh. "C'mon—," she stops herself, pointing to the bag in my hand and pouts, "Tim, you said you wouldn't bring anything."

"It's for margaritas!" I hold it up in surrender.

She shakes her head, trying to fight the smile from spreading on her face. "You're hardheaded."

I lean in and kiss her cheek. "Only for you, baby."

She catches my quip and playfully slaps my arm before leaving.

I follow behind her to their cookout set-up. But from the looks of it, either the nearby grill hasn't been used—which would be blasphemous—or they just cleaned that motherfucker before I got here.

"Y'all, this is Tim. Tim, this is my sister, Simonique," Camesha gestures to her and I immediately remember her gapped smile and dimples from the pictures in C's condo. "And these two are my best friends, Nikki and Oluchi." She points to them.

"Nice to meet y'all," I say, making sure I look them all in the eye.

All at once, they return greetings. And Simonique throws in there, "You're cuter in person."

Caught off guard, I choke on a laugh. "Thank you." I clear my throat. "And, uh, I brought some margarita mix and tequila if y'all wanna make drinks." I hold up the bag.

Simonique and Nikki mirror impressed facial expressions and "Ooo" in response.

"Oh, you *really* want us to like you, huh?" Nikki takes the bag and removes the bottles. Looks like I might've picked brands that are up to her standards by the way she's eyeing them and nodding. "And this outfit is cute and all. I peep the hoochie daddy shorts," we all laugh, having not heard that reference in a while, "but I hope you not a hat-fish. . ." She squints at me, making the girls laugh and Camesha sigh at her antics.

Takes me a second to know what she means, but then I chuckle and lift my hat. "Nah, I got hair."

She nods, before returning her attention to the alcohol. "But I have to say, it's *especially* nice to meet you cuz you gave my girl some good dick."

Shocked, Simonique and Oluchi's eyes get as big as saucers, and everybody audibly gasps. My breath catches in my throat at Nikki's bold words as I bring my fist to my mouth. I look at Camesha, seeing her mouth is an O shape as she shoots eye-daggers at Nikki.

But I can't lie, a warm sense of pride settles on me. *Camesha talked 'bout our first time wit' her friends?* And *she gave me a glowin' review?* That makes a nigga feel hella good.

Nikki looks up from the bottles, unbothered and unashamed. "What? She needed it. She's less uptight now. I been could tell her ass was in need of a good orgasm. So, thank you, Tim." She shoots me a lopsided smile.

I grin, fighting a blush, unsure what to say.

Camesha lightly slaps her friend on the arm, but Nikki just playfully dismisses her. "Oh my God, Nikki. And because of ya loud ass, my whole complex pro'ly heard you."

"So? It's a good thing, girl. Good dick is a blessin'. *And* from a good man, too? Chil'!" She throws a hand up like it's a hallelujah moment.

Simonique reaches over the table to high-five her. Oluchi just looks tickled, shaking her head. Camesha grips the bridge of her nose and walks over to me, apologizing in a low voice.

"All good, C. I'm happy it was worth callin' home about," I say so only she can hear me. A grin worms onto her face as I bend down to kiss her blushing cheek.

"A'ight, nuff of that cute shit. Let's eat and get down to business," Nikki interrupts.

"You said you *wouldn't* grill him. He doesn't need to be grilled," Camesha huffs. *It's cute that she's lookin' out for me.*

"And I won't. I just have a few questions for Mr. Tim."

Camesha sighs and rolls her eyes.

"That's cool, Nikki. And speakin' 'bout grillin' . . . whassup wit' *this* grill?" I ask, pointing at the unused-looking thing.

"Whatchu mean? It works." Camesha shrugs.

"Okay, good. But it *looks* like y'all ain't use it."

"Oh, that's cuz I bought barbecue," Camesha says matter-of-factly.

My eyes widen at that. I might've just suffered a mini heart attack, too. "You *bought* it? Baby, I coulda grilled for us."

Simonique chimes in, "A man."

I chortle as Nikki snaps her fingers in agreement.

"I didn't wantchu to worry 'bout it. I just wanted everybody to meet, and we have a good, *chill*," she emphasizes the word, snapping her gaze to Nikki, "time."

"Amen to that," Oluchi lets out.

"A'ight." I just shrug.

Nikki's the first one to start making her plate. Two out of the four wooden tables in the courtyard display the impressive spread. Barbecue ribs, grilled chicken, hot dogs and buns, baked beans, potato salad, garden salad, watermelon slices, a variety of chips and dips, rum punch, my margarita mix and tequila, and a cooler full of water bottles and wine coolers. I'm definitely taking leftovers.

As I make my margarita, Camesha tells me that she and Simonique made everything else. I just nod, impressed.

Once I sit down, I silently say grace. Before I can even take a bite of anything, Nikki starts bombarding me with questions: what I do for work, who I work with, where I went to school, what my taste in music is like—shit, *even* asked about my credit score.

Camesha low-key chokes on her hotdog to chastise her friend. My dick twitched a little at the sight, but I snap out of it and be a good boyfriend by lightly patting her back and making sure she's okay.

Nikki's very straightforward. I can tell she's always going to keep it real and not sugarcoat anything. She reminds me of Jaquade in that way.

She even asks me how I felt about Camesha vibe modeling and escorting the first time we met, and I tell the girls what I told Camesha back then. They just kind of glance at one another and nod like I passed a test. No lie, I exhale in relief before asking the ladies stuff to get to know them.

At one point, there's a lull in conversation, so I say, "So, Simonique how you likin' LA so far? What y'all been doin'?"

Her face lights up, telling us about the adventures she and Camesha have been on. Since I've lived here for so long now, I sometimes forget how magical the city is. How much of an extraordinary time you can have when you really take it in, especially for the first time. I can't help but beam, happy that she's loving it here.

"That's awesome. I'm really glad you're enjoyin' ya'self." I take a sip of my margarita. "So, Camesha told me you're a big Keyana Renay fan. . ." I trail off purposefully.

Simonique tucks in her chin and stares at me with wide eyes. "Yeah. . ."

I crack a smile, feeling Camesha's eyes as she sits next to me. "She's actually one of my clients and she has an intimate show Friday night. I have extra tickets and backstage access if you wanna come and meet her." Then I look at Camesha, Nikki, and Oluchi. "This goes for all y'all."

They all stretch their necks back in surprise.

"Oh my God, really? You good in my book, Tim." Simonique reaches over to high-five me. "I would *looove* to go and meet her." She shimmies in her seat, bursting with excitement. . . But then her face falls. "Wait, but I leave on Friday."

Shit, I forgot 'bout that! My jaw stiffens and without thinking too hard on it, I blurt out, "No pro'lem, we can change ya flight. I gotchu."

"Really?" Her eyes focus on me, vibrating with tears.

"*Really*, Tim?" Camesha asks, forcing me to look at her.

"Y'all let that man do a nice thing for Simonique," Nikki encourages with a wide grin on her face. "And I wanna go, too."

"That's very sweet of you, Tim. And I would definitely like a ticket to the show," Oluchi adds softly.

"Great. Then consider it handled," I respond to them, but I'm looking at Camesha with a slight smirk on my face.

She tilts her head, her eyes boring deeper into mine.

Camesha

Is he bluffin'? I can't tell. He's smirkin'. Is he bein' serious right now? I think he's serious. My body is unsure, too, as my breath quickens.

Tim breaks our eye contact when Simonique says, "Thank you so much, Tim! I really 'preciate this."

"Ya welcome," he says with an eye-creasing smile. He looks genuinely happy to do this for her and my friends.

A pang jolts me in the heart, leaving me stunned. Underneath the table, Tim slides his hand onto my thigh, lightly squeezing it. It's like he knows my nerves are raging at the idea of him paying for my sister's airfare and he wanted to calm me down. *Have we entered that stage where he can read me that well now?*

The idea of that makes my anxiety ramp up as my throat goes dry. He finds my hand and interlocks our fingers. I'm sure I'll hear a lecture from him about why I should let him do nice things for me and, by extension, my sister and my friends. But that's the thing I'm seeing and learning about Tim: he's just kind, sweet, and thoughtful like that. Honestly, it doesn't feel real sometimes.

Everyone continues to talk, making extra plates and drinks throughout the evening. I'm chiming in but I'm not really *here*, my mind flooded with so many thoughts. Before it gets too dark and it's hard to see, I get up to start cleaning, urging everybody to stay seated and continue enjoying themselves. I go to the first table with food and supplies on it to throw and pack stuff away.

Besides right now, this gathering unraveled my anxiety about everybody meeting for the first time. Simonique and Nikki are connecting—almost *too* well. Nikki did too much with the questions and her antics, but Tim handled himself like a pro, taking it all in stride with an amused look on his face. He even asked them questions and made them laugh. This whole evening, it felt like we've all gotten together before.

Tim seems to fit into my life—into all of my worlds. And that's scary.

I hear somebody approaching behind me, making me roll my eyes. Whirling around, I see it's Nikki.

She's nursing her second red Solo cup with her rum punch. She already finished a margarita, too. "Need any help?" she asks coolly, slightly slurring her words, and wiggling her eyebrows. But I can tell Nikki's here with an agenda.

"Nah, I'm just gettin' everything ready so it's easy to bring back upstairs," I say, my voice upbeat. I'm trying to throw her off my scent, from sensing the uneasiness twisting my stomach. I don't think I'm going to throw up, but if I have to, we have a lot of trash bags here. I pivot to stack the remaining plates.

Nikki doesn't leave—no, instead she circles me and sits on the brick knee wall surrounding the courtyard. "Mmm-hmmm. Looks like you're stallin, movin' 'round to stay busy. Ya just gon' play maid while ya man's over there charmin' the squad?"

I just ignore her and keep moving.

"You got ya'self a good one, Camesha." Her voice is softer, making me look at her. "I'm *really* happy for you."

I grin but it slightly falters. Her words hit me hard, shocking my heart like a defibrillator. I break eye contact, busying my hands again.

"What is it, Camesha?"

Fuck, her half-drunk ass noticed! "Nothin'." I shake my head. "C'mon now, don't lie to me. Spill."

I smack my teeth and sit next to her. "He's-He's good to me," my voice is quieter than I'd like.

I chance a look at Nikki . . . and she's just staring at me like I'm stupid. "Yeeesss," she nods slowly, "That's a great thing."

"I 'on't know. It just feels—"

She rolls her eyes, scoffing, "Don't start this shit, girl. You deserve good things. You deserve a good man."

I open my mouth to speak several times, but no words come out for a moment. "It's just so wild and scary. I met him hustlin' and he liked me regardless—"

"That's great, too. You deserve someone who sees all of you and wants you."

"It's just he's so good, like almost *too* good and—"

"Lemme cut you off again, friend, cuz I know whatchu doin'." Nikki points a finger at me. "Don't get in ya head 'bout this and ruin it. You like him, he likes you. Nuff said. Period." She makes a *done* motion with her hand. "Don't push him away because you're scared. Don't question who he is 'til you have an actual reason to do so.

"That man over there really likes and cares 'bout you. And him hookin' ya sister up wit' a concert ticket to see one of her favorite artists *and* he gon' pay for her flight?" Her eyes enlarge. "That's chef's kiss." Nikki pauses. "That's a *man*, sis. And he's *yours*."

I drop my head, blushing at that. *Tim is my man.*

"I like him," she shrugs, "if that means anything to you. Which it should since I'm one of ya best friends." I giggle as she stands and pulls me to my feet to hug me. "Don't blow this up, bitch."

Rolling my eyes, I snicker. "I'll try not to."

"Don't try, just don't do it. I'm rootin' for you." She points at me.

"You gotta funny way of showin' it," I mumble.

"I can only be me, girl." She shrugs again, ambling back to the group.

I let Nikki's whole spiel roll around in my head as I return to cleaning and packing up.

Tim

I can't believe I've spent over three hours here, having a good time with Camesha, her sister, and her friends. It's a vibe and I can see my homies blending with her group well. Simonique and Nikki are similar, making me howl with laughter at their stories. Nikki feels like a bolder, wilder female-version of Jaquade, and I can see Oluchi getting along with Bryan since she's so chill and poised, just enjoying the craziness on the sidelines.

Nikki returns to the group, leaving Camesha alone to finish cleaning up. My baby has an unreadable look on her face, like she's deep in thought. I excuse myself from the table as Simonique starts sharing a story about one of her sneaky links.

"Camesha," I say firmly to stop her from moving around.

She looks up at me, her eyes bulging a little like I startled her.

My eyebrows meet, concern creeping in. "You okay?"

She wipes on a smile, but I see past it. Her eyes tell a different story, one I intend to figure out soon if she'd let me. "Yeah." Before I can say anything, she speaks up again, "You havin' a good time?"

"Fa sho. You and Simonique *threw down* in the kitchen."

She grins, blushing.

"I mean, I wish you woulda lemme help. I *am* from Texas, so I know my way 'round a grill. I been grillin' since I was 14, girl."

She laughs as I step closer, my hands settling around her waist. "I just wanted you to relax and meet them. *That* was enough work for the day," she says.

"Y'all, I hear some cracklin'. I think the fireworks are startin'!" Simonique yells across the courtyard.

I grab Camesha's hand and damn-near drag her to the group.

I love firework displays. They always bring me back to when I was a kid in all the many bases I've lived. Up until I was eight years old, my pops would sit me up on his shoulders to watch them. Being surrounded by other Air Force servicemembers and their families, watching the displays always made me feel very patriotic. And very close to Pops. He was a man of few words, but a display of colorful explosives in the air always got him excited, ooo'ing and ahhh'ing like a kid.

The first firework shoots into the sky, cracking, and bursting with color. I shift Camesha in front of me and wrap my arms around her. She's a little stiff and I try not to think too much about it as I watch the show.

But after a few moments, I decide that maybe she needs some space. Maybe I'm doing too much PDA, even though she kissed me as soon as I got here. I loosen my arms and step back a little, but she leans back into me and pulls my arms tighter around her. A smile breaks my face and blood shoots up my neck.

I just tuck my face near her temple and look at her while Simonique's videotaping the fireworks and Nikki and Oluchi are staring up in awe.

"Uh, sir, ya know the fireworks are up there, right?" Camesha turns her head a little to glance at me out the corner of her eye, pointing at the sky.

"Yeah, they cool and all, but the way you explode wit' me is even better, baby," I whisper against her temple before kissing it.

I bite my bottom lip when Camesha stiffens in my arms. "Oh my God, Tiiim-uh," she whines softly.

A chuckle tumbles out of me as my fingers tilt her chin up for a kiss. Her left hand cups the back of my neck as she slips in some tongue.

"The cute shit is killin' me! Stoooppp!" Nikki whines.

"Leave 'em alone, Nik," Oluchi says, sounding jokingly exhausted of Nikki's shenanigans.

Laughing, Camesha and I both drop our hands and stop kissing. My arms tighten around her as we finish watching the fireworks.

13
Positions and Options

Tuesday, July 24

Camesha

We all went to Keyana Renay's show on Friday, July 6. Tim was working the small club but made sure to check on us several times in VIP. Keyana's celebrity friends and their entourages were there, so Simonique introduced herself, gushing about their art and even plugging her event planning business. I've always admired her boldness and business savvy and definitely channeled her energy when I was Cammie.

Keyana wore a maroon velvet minidress while her live band and DJ were behind her onstage. At the beginning of the show, she shared that she chose to perform at an intimate venue to hear the crowd's verbal feedback and to see their facial reactions to the music. She wanted to test a few songs that she was thinking of putting on her third album *Velvet Season*'s deluxe version. That's why staff took their phones when they entered—she didn't want anything leaked. I already enjoyed the project, so I was excited for this sneak peek.

Simonique's ass was definitely verbal as fuck when Keyana asked how the crowd liked a track in between songs. Nikki and Oluchi vibed out, enjoying the atmosphere and the music. I think Keyana should definitely add the songs "Bare Sugar" and "Heels On, Lights Off." The last one is *especially* sexy and if she wasn't Tim's client, I'd love to fuck him in my heels while that song plays in the background, but he wouldn't allow that.

When the show was over, Tim ushered us backstage. Keyana's face brightened when she met us. Shit, she even called Simonique by name before she spoke. Tim must've told her about Nique, which made my heart swell. My sister almost fainted—I'm sure of it—her mouth an O shape as she just stared in shock. *When Nique goes back home, I'll definitely show Tim how much I 'preciate him for puttin' all'is together for us,* I thought.

And I did. Put his ass right to sleep.

Keyana enthusiastically welcomed pictures and Simonique snapped several selfies of them, their arms wrapped around one another like longtime friends. Tim even took a few group photos of me, my sister, and my friends with Keyana.

But what surprised me was that while we were hanging out backstage, nibbling on hors d'oeuvres and nursing cocktails, Keyana sidled up to me at the bar, her creamy floral scent preceding her:

"Sooo, how'd ya like The Lenox Room?" she asked, her eyebrows wiggling as she took a sip of her rosé champagne.

Immediately, my face grew hot. Tim told me that she helped him reserve a table, but how did she know who I was?

Then fear and stress crept up my neck. Did Tim *not* honor my request to keep our relationship private for right now? *I wondered.*

Keyana must've recognized the distress marring my face and my quickened breaths, holding her hand out and shaking it. "Tim didn't tell me anything. I," she glanced down briefly, "I can just tell, ya know? By the way y'all are interactin'." She giggled like she was in on a secret. And she kind of was.

So, not only is Keyana Renay beautiful and a talented singer and dancer, but apparently, she also has the observation skills of a hawk because Tim and I were barely *interacting that night since he was working. We didn't really talk much, we kept our hands to ourselves, except when his hand gently grazed my back to let me know he was around, and we* might've *made subtle eye contact across the room. We've honed our secret language. But I guess Keyana did, too.*

Her keen observation made me blush as I avoided eye contact and took a sip of my cocktail, the Velvet 75, Keyana's twist on the French one.

"Camesha," she said, my name sounding foreign coming out of her mouth, "I get it, and I respect y'all wantin' to keep y'all's relationship private. Hell, I do the same thing when I really like someone now."

A little calm blanketed me, but then something else entered my mind: Does she know I use to vibe model and escort? Like, does she have *that* ability to know what I used to do?

I chanced a look at Keyana, finding a soft smile on her face. I just offered her a small grin before sipping my drink.

"Tim's a good man. I only work wit' him if I need one handler for a job. He's always reliable and gets shit done fast." She winks. "You really got a good one, girl."

My cheeks betrayed me as I blushed. Feeling relaxed and warm, I reply, "Yeah, I do. . ." *We both turned around and leaned back on the bar, looking out at the backstage greenroom. "Thank you for helpin' him set up the reservation. The place was gorgeous on the inside and the food was the bomb."*

"I'm glad you enjoyed it." She smiled wide, sipping her drink.

"I definitely did. And his poem?—Oh my God! Did you know he'd do spoken word?"

Keyana sat her flute down on the bar. "*Nooo. . . Tim performed?*"

I nodded, feeling gushy on the inside at the memory. "*He did. He wrote it for me. He basically got onstage and told me how he felt 'bout me, then he asked me to be his lady when he got back to our booth. I was* so *in shock.*" Who am I, spillin' all'is to a stranger?—Well, Keyana Renay, but still. *I guess talking about Tim has come easy.* He's *made that easy.*

She just looked at me, grinning. "*Wow. And it was good? I ain't know Tim wrote poetry.*"

"*It was* very *good. I asked him to frame it for me. It's hangin' up in my condo now.*"

She nodded her head, looking impressed. "*Lemme find out Tim be writin' songs, too. Might need him to co-write some new shit wit' me. . .*"

My eyes bulged, I was so excited. "*Really?*"

She shrugged her shoulders before taking a sip. "*I already trust him to get things done, so if he can write well, too, I'm definitely interested to see what he got.*"

I can see Tim writing songs. I hoped Keyana really offered him that job because I'm sure he can handle that, too.

We ended up changing subjects, and I told her which songs I felt should be on her deluxe album. She listened intently, like she was really considering my opinion. Keyana seemed to really value her fans—or as she kept correcting me, supporters.

Movement caught my attention, and I glanced away from Keyana as she gave me insider information on her promotional plan for the deluxe. I saw Tim across the room, moving shit around and instructing the breakdown crew. He wore a khaki set with a yellow trucker cap, so he was easy to spot. He looked in his element, a serious expression on his face—creased eyebrows and his tongue poking the inside of his mouth.

He must've felt my gaze because when he lifted his eyes, they immediately glued to mine. A small smirk wiped on his face before he subtly winked at me. My breathing hitched a little at that, and I forgot where I was.

Until Keyana said, "Y'all cute as shit."

I blushed before I could stop myself. She's right.

My friends had fun at the show, too. They liked Keyana like me, but we weren't superfans like Simonique. Backstage, Nikki flirted and took so many pictures with celebrities, while Lu milled about, chatting to a few other handlers. It dawned on me that several of the people here were her real estate clients, so she wasn't starstruck.

Simonique definitely got her Los Angeles experience, and I was happy she was able to do and see what she wanted while she was here. She's already been texting and calling me, asking when she can come back.

Anyway, now, I'm the assistant service manager at The Aubade retreat in Laurel Canyon!

They moved fast after the Fourth: set up an interview, offered me the position a day later, and I just started two weeks ago. My old co-workers at The Adonir Hotel sent me off to my new job with a self-care kit, which was very sweet of them.

I've done one-on-one training, shadowed other managers, and now, The Aubade has let me off the leash to work solo. I'm still getting used to telling people what to do and them asking me questions. Dealing with customers as a manager feels different, too. I'm figuring out how best to quell a dissatisfied customer and ease their worries, so that they don't leave a bad review online.

But it's all good. I'm still learning, growing, or "being stretched," as Mama says. I told my parents I was nervous to be starting this job, and Mama texted me this scripture: "For God has not given us a spirit of fear and timidity, but of power, love, and self-discipline" (2 Timothy 1:7). I've been meditating on that these last few weeks to encourage myself since I'm out of my comfort zone. It's been something I can lean on. Besides *my* Timothy.

Anytime I've expressed doubt or fear of not doing a good job in my new role, Tim's been speaking life into me. Reminding me that I'm there because many people felt that I could do it. Reminding me that I can only do my best. He said that even though I got the ingredients, no one's expecting me to "know all the different ways to finesse 'em yet." I adore his cooking metaphor, and it helps that it also makes me laugh anytime he says it, cheering me up.

My new manager, Nile, has checked up on me often to see how I'm adjusting. As the general manager of the restaurant at The Aubade, he works daily in the middle of open hours. Those are very long days, which makes me wonder if he's married or has children. If he does, his spouse must be very understanding and supportive of his career. I just hope he's making his time-off count because burnout is real.

I appreciate Nile's check-ins, but it's also nerve-racking, knowing I'm being watched—though *not* scrutinized. He's been very helpful and encouraging. I still don't want to mess up though. If this assistant manager position is really a glimpse into the kinds of opportunities that could open up for me because I left the hustle, then I *really* want to do well. *Maybe hospitality is the lane I focus on fa real. Or maybe, I take Tim up on his offer and meet his interior designer friend. . .* I often ponder.

Right now, since it's a little slow before the dinner rush, I'm reviewing the reservations list to figure out where to seat people tomorrow at the manager's station.

"Camesha, may I talk to you for a sec?" Nile's hoarse voice cuts through my concentration. Something tells me that his voice isn't naturally hoarse, but after years of talking a lot in this industry, his voice gave out. *Damn, will my voice do that, too?*

I lift my head from my tablet, seeing Nile, a thin, 50-something-year old white man with a slight pudge.

"Just wanted to check in. Come to my office when you have a chance." He offers a pursed smile before leaving.

I save my seating arrangements and close out of the reservations list on the tablet. Weaving through the back hallway of the restaurant, I arrive at his office, his door open as I find him seated behind his desk.

When I come in, he stands to close the door. "Please, have a seat."

I drop down into one of the plush armchairs facing his desk. He's been working at The Aubade since it opened nine years ago, and his office demonstrates that. The Aubade and California memorabilia, knickknacks, and photos occupy his walls, desk, and shelves. I also notice a framed picture of him with a male partner and two grade-school aged children posing in front of what looks like a ride at an amusement park.

Nile sits at his desk, now blocking my view of his family photo. "I saw you lookin' at tomorrow night's reservations. That's smart—gettin' a head start on that rather than tryna figure that out when customers start comin' in." He nods and pokes his lips out like I impress him. "Wednesdays are one of our busiest nights."

I smile wide, feeling proud of myself. Honestly, I was doing it because I was anxious and not sure what else to do since we were slow, but I'll take the compliment that I was being proactive. "Thank you."

"Thank *you*, Camesha." He pauses. "I just wanted to say that I think you're doin' an excellent job. I know that goin' from a non-managerial role to a managerial one can be a little dauntin', but you're handlin' it very well."

I grin trying to hold back happy tears and not mess up my makeup. I've been very emotional since I started this job.

"From Klay recommendin' you, tellin' me you've never got any customer complaints, to your references from your previous employers? . . I think I definitely chose the right person for this job." He shrugs like he didn't just make my day.

The tears well up and I drop my head to pat my eyeline, warmth ballooning in my stomach at his glowing performance review. "Thank you, Nile. I really appreciate you sayin' all of that. Honestly, I was very nervous about this job, but I'm also just so excited and grateful for the opportunity."

He nods repeatedly, a slow smile working its way across his thin lips. "Well, like I said, you're doin' a great job. Just remember, if you need any support or have any questions, *please*, come talk to me. I'd be more than happy to help."

"I definitely will."

He purses his lips and glances at his computer. "Well, it looks like your shift is almost over, so I'll let you go."

I stand up.

"Just . . . keep it up, Camesha."

"I will. Thank you, Nile." I turn and head out.

To text Tim, I pull out my phone from the back pocket of my slim-fit black trousers.

Me (4:57pm):

> I'm on my way⊠.

Tim (4:58pm):

> Can't wait to see you⊠

Tim texted me on my lunch break, telling me he blocked off the rest of his day and asked if I'd like come over to his house for dinner.

Since I now work nine to five, Tim has come to my place more, sometimes late at night after a job, even crashing overnight, or he'd pick me up and drive us around and we vibe to his music, eat takeout, and talk. I've now become a person who has their own list of favorite places to eat takeout outside their house, too.

I'm so excited for dinner since this is my first time at Tim's house. He lives in Culver City, which isn't too far from Beverly Hills, but still, the traffic and I could fight.

It takes me 35 minutes to drive the five miles from The Adonir Hotel to Tim's picturesque street, looking so out of place. It looks and feels like I'm not even in Los Angeles anymore. Trees, sidewalks, and cute homes in various styles line the road.

Then my GPS says I've arrived, and I pull into Tim's driveway. His blacked-out Jeep is parked closest to the one-car garage positioned off to the side and behind the house. The one-story home is periwinkle with black shutters and a black door. Bushes sit underneath the windows. His lawn is cut and edged, making me wonder if he does it himself. . . *I can just see him now—shirtless and sweatin', takin' care of his yard*, I daydream.

Nerves gather in my stomach at the thought that I'm about to enter his world. Ain't nothing like inviting people to your home—your sanctuary. I was nervous to invite him inside mine after our first date, but he's proven himself trustworthy in my space. *Tim has handled me wit' care so far and I hope he continues to*, I tell my anxiety.

I cut off the engine and as I'm collecting my purse from the passenger seat, a tap on my window scares the shit out of me. I snap my head in that direction, finding Tim wearing a black tank top and a huge smile. He can't see me through my tinted windows, otherwise, he would've seen me jump.

"C, unlock the door," he chuckles.

I do and he opens it. Upon seeing my startled facial expression, he laughs louder. "Damn, did I scare you, baby? I ain't mean to." He leans down into the truck to engulf me in a hug, the smell of his fragrance and smoke greeting me, too.

I don't hug him, wanting to play mad a little longer since he scared me.

He backs away, noticing my narrowed eyes. "See, what had happened was," he makes me crack my façade with laughter, "I thought about callin' out ya name from the stoop, but that was givin' ghetto, so I thought the gentlemanly thing to do is to get my lady from her car."

I laugh, a smile branding my face until my cheeks hurt. He holds his hand out to help me out my Venza.

Now on my feet, Tim eyes me up and down. "You gotta be . . . the finest manager I done ever seen in my life."

I throw my head back, cracking up. My uniform is not sexy: just a magenta-colored bow-tie blouse, black slacks, and short black heels, complete with a gold nametag.

But there's no humor on Tim's face. He's not trying to flatter me. He *actually* finds me fine in this outfit.

I glance away, his attention feeling too heavy on me. But then Nikki's sentiments from the July Fourth cookout ring in my head: *You like him. He likes you. You deserve this. You deserve him. Don't overthink this.*

"Thank you, Tim," I say softly. My gaze drops down, seeing he's wearing sweat shorts, socks, and slides like somebody's grilling-ass uncle.

He pecks my lips before retrieving my purse from the passenger seat, which makes me blush.

I close my door and lock the truck. "So, what's for dinner?" I ask, following Tim up his walkway.

"It was just too nice *not* to be outside grillin', so I grilled some pork chops."

"Ooo."

"Yeah, it's *thee best* way to eat pork chops—Well, accept smothered pork chops. But I 'on't cook that cuz my mom makes it way better than me."

He opens the front door to his house, and I can immediately smell the grilled meat.

"I found this bourbon peach seasonin' blend the other day and," he does a chef's kiss, "it's that *gorl*—or whatever women be sayin' nowadays." Tim closes the door behind me as I laugh at his silliness.

"You came at the perfect time—I just finished makin' the salad." He places my purse on the wooden entryway table in front of the door, a gold freestanding coat rack nearby.

I happy-shimmy. "I'm so hungry, I could almost taste the air, Tim."

He beams at me. "A'ight, but before we eat, lemme give you the grand tour, Ms. Future Interior Designer." He winks at me and grabs my hand.

My cheeks flush at that. *He can really see that in my future?*

"Get comfortable, baby." He points to my heels, and I toe them off quickly.

The open living space—his living area, kitchen, and dining table—has matte gray walls, gold light fixtures, and dark wooden floors. I notice underneath my now bare feet is a runner rug and along the walls of the entry are photos of him and his family.

"Oh yeah, those my folks," Tim says.

"You were such a cute kid," I coo, looking at a photo of baby Tim on his dad's shoulders, mid-clap with a toothless grin. His mom stood next to them, looking up at her son. Tim definitely resembles both of his parents.

"I'm *still* cute, girl." He bumps me with his hip.

I turn to him. "No, baby, you're sexy."

His eyes widen like he doesn't know that already. "You think I'm sexy?"

"Very," I drop my voice and pull his face down for a wet kiss. I break it before he gets too happy, his hands finding my waist, seconds away from gripping my ass. *Maybe after dinner, Tim, cuz right now I'm hungry as hell!*

He clears his throat, "That picture in particular was taken on the Air Force base in Germany where I was born."

I nod and he continues talking, explaining a few other pictures. Since we reconnected in person, Tim has shared more and more about that terrible time in his life—him heavily mourning and grieving his dad's death. My heart goes out to him because I can't imagine losing my daddy, but I love the way Tim honors his. I never press him about any of that, he's just comfortable enough to share with me. . .

Tim directs my attention to the living room behind us. A brown leather sectional with a chaise lounge faces the wall where a TV sits on a long storage cabinet. A funky red accent chair is perpendicular to the couch and faces the two three-paned front windows. A unique coffee table of sorts sits in the middle of the room.

Tim talks about his sizable vinyl collection that's lined up in the open shelving of his storage cabinet as I eye his record player and the Bluetooth speaker behind it.

"This is where the magic just happened," Tim says, gaining my attention to look at his kitchen. Brown wooden cabinetry, black appliances, an island with red bar stools, a dark countertop housing a pan of pork chops, a salad, and something that smells like—

"Did you make mac n cheese?" I swirl around to look at Tim, my ponytail slapping me in the face.

"Maybe. . ." He squiggles his eyebrows.

A huge smile captures my face.

"We gon' eat soon. Tour's not over yet." Tim leads me to his primary suite.

A low platform king-sized bed with gray and black bedding—*typical man colors*—and two nightstands is on the opposite side of the room. Sunlight pours in from three single-paned windows. A TV is hung up above his dresser and a chair with a lamp over it is in the corner.

I laugh as we walk further into his room. I turn around and see that the wall the TV is hung up on is black and has geometric wood paneling. "Oh, this is so cool."

"Yeah, Jaquade referred me to the guy who did his bedroom."

I nod, satisfied with Tim and his friend's taste in interior design. I pop my head into the bathroom, noticing the periwinkle walls and faux baby succulents. Then we move to his walk-in closet next door. "This is where all the graphic tees, sneakers, and hats live," I proclaim dramatically, eyeing the hung-up clothes and shoeboxes neatly lining the floor and shelves.

He just laughs before grabbing my hand to guide me out his suite and to the sliding door near his square-shaped dining table.

Since I'm barefoot, I stay inside while Tim gestures around his porch, which houses a grill and a few lawn chairs. He has a nice plot of land with cut grass back here, too.

"See, that's what a *used* grill looks and smells like, C." He points at it. "Thought y'all was tryna fool me at that cookout," he jokes, referencing July Fourth.

I playfully slap his arm. "Shut up!"

He cackles like a kid who thinks he's clever. "I'm thinkin' 'bout gettin' an above-ground pool and hangin' some string lights or some'. Make it real vibey outchere, na'mean?" He's rubbing his hands like Birdman, making me giggle. "Whatchu think? I need a professional's opinion."

I giggle, blushing hard. "Those are good ideas, Tim."

Tim just nods, a grin curving onto his face. "Thanks. Let's eat."

We wash our hands at the kitchen sink as he takes out plates. He points to the other side of the house, telling me that that's where his laundry and guest bedroom and bathroom are located. He said they're fairly undecorated since he barely has guests. Except that one time he let his client Aye Bandz crash here to sober up after a club performance a couple years ago.

"You have a really lovely home, Tim. I'm pleasantly surprised by how well-decorated it is. You made it sound like you didn't do much wit' it cuz you barely be at home, but it's nice."

"Well, the design would be *off the charts* if I spent more time here. But I 'preciate the compliment, since you got good taste and all."

My brown cheeks betray me again with the blushing shit.

He goes to his Bluetooth speaker and next thing I know, I hear "Tuesday" by ILOVEMAKONNEN featuring Drake. I haven't heard this song in *years*. I look at Tim, seeing him mouth the hook, headbanging like we're at a concert. "This is what this feels like right now—us havin' a dinner party on a Tuesday night!" he yells over the music.

"Party? It's just us."

He comes over to me, his hands finding my waist. "Girl, *every* day witchu is a party."

I can't be serious with Tim when he hits me with those corny lines. We both crumble and cackle before he finishes making our plates.

I ask him to pile on more of that delicious-looking mac n cheese. He pours himself some whiskey from his decanter and without me asking, Tim pours me some semi-sweet white wine. The thoughtfulness has my kitty purring.

He stops the music when we sit down at his dining table with our plates and drinks. I'm thankful that he wanted to eat indoors since I didn't see a table outside.

Tim says grace, as per usual, and we dig in. I moan at the taste of the juicy pork chop.

"That shit is *it*, huh?" Tim jokes, referencing me saying that about the food at The Lenox Room.

I giggle, covering my mouth as I nod. I fork some mac n cheese into my mouth. "Tim. . ." I point at the food, "*this* is very good."

He grins so hard, lifting his cheeks. "Glad you like it."

Some moments go by of us just eating and humming at the taste. I ask Tim about his day, and he tells me he worked with two clients: helped one make an emergency social media video statement to quiet a possible ghostwriting allegation scandal, and another with a last-minute show rehearsal.

He flips the question back to me, and I tell him about work and Nile's positive performance review.

Tim drops his fork on his plate and just beams at me. "I love that he's noticin' you killin' it. That's whassup, Camesha."

"Yeah, it definitely made my day," I say bashfully with a huge smile on my face, glancing at my half-eaten plate.

"As it should. Soak in every compliment and question every critique."

I nod, agreeing with the sentiment, but then my neck snaps back when I realize, "Okay bars."

He laughs and waves me off like he didn't just drop a gem. I get lost in his jaw as he goes to town on his pork chop.

Until Tim asks me, "What's an experience you had in LA that you'll never forget?"

That question makes me freeze. Then I grab my wineglass and take a hefty gulp to calm down my revving heart rate.

I have a lot of unforgettable experiences, but one *always* lingers in my mind like humidity. The one I never told anybody. My chest tightens just thinking about that night.

Back then, Dorell "Raw Math" Mathis didn't have a gazillion allegations glued to his name like he does now. He wasn't in the news for all the horrific shit women have said he's done to them. He was in the news for his legacy in hip-hop, earning music legend awards, mentoring young rappers signed to his imprint label.

Throughout my life, I had heard a few of Raw Math's songs. Knew he was important in the industry. I left that night knowing something else.

Back then, I was still learning the ins and outs of the hustle. Zaria and Benny Munz were still heavily mentoring me. I was still shaping Cammie, still getting used to her.

A handler I don't work with anymore hired me to vibe model at Yung Grizzle's party where he was celebrating his recent album going platinum. It was hosted at his label's entertainment venue in their office building.

It wasn't until Raw Math got onstage to say a few remarks about Grizzle that I realized this was his label.

At that time, I thought Raw Math was handsome. A dark suit stretched across his muscly body, complimenting his toffee-brown skin. His bald head and diamond studs gleamed under the lights as giant sunglasses blocked his eyes. His close beard was perfectly neat.

Not too long after the toast and the party resumed, I saw him approaching me. I was standing off to the side, sipping a cocktail and taking a break from entertaining Yung Grizzle and his homies in their section. Some people stopped Raw Math to dap-hug him and chat. He obliged them but didn't break his stride.

I couldn't tell at the time that he was drunk and high. He moved slowly, but with swagger. Now I can say he resembled a big cat.

Once he got within a few feet, I could smell his cologne. Spice, smoke, musk. I'm thankful I haven't smelled that scent on anyone after that night. A smile stretched his lips open to expose his veneers.

He asked me if I was enjoying the party. I said yes. He complimented my platinum sequined minidress. Raw Math made sure to tell me that if it hadn't been him who signed and developed Yung Grizzle, his album wouldn't've gone platinum. I wanted to roll my eyes at that.

Then he asked me how much to celebrate upstairs. Since I knew he was the man in charge, I threw out a ridiculous number.

He didn't even flinch. Only smiled slowly.

After I told him my rules and he agreed, Raw Math escorted me upstairs to his huge, sleek office. The glass wall overlooked the party below. He lazily mentioned that we could see them, but no one *could see us.* That should've been my first red flag. But I stayed. In hindsight, I also wondered if the room was soundproof.

I watched him saunter over to his safe, his massive body shielding it as he punched in the code. After digging through it, he returned to me and handed me wads of cash. I kept my eyes from enlarging even though I was holding the most amount of money I've ever seen in my life at the time. I didn't bother counting it—I saw the hundred-dollar bills.

When I turned to stuff the cash in my clutch, I felt him come up behind me. Raw Math radiated so much heat. His hands clutched my waist as his lips attacked my neck. That close, his breath smelled a tinge like liquor and something else.

He pulled up the back of my dress.

I reminded him, "No anal."

Raw Math chuckled. "I 'ont wantcho ass, baby girl." Then he bent me over his desk. My eyes flashed open when I felt him enter me raw. I opened my mouth to tell him that he needs to stop and put on a condom. But no words came out. I was frozen, my brain stalled.

My body knew then and there, but it took me years to realize that Raw Math violated me that night.

I didn't think I had to tell him to wear a condom. I just assumed he would because every client before him always wore one. *At the time, I thought it was common sense that when you have sex with someone you barely know, you protect yourself and them.*

Raw Math was the first and only person to do that. So, after that night, I made a new rule: every client must wear a condom every single time.

I was thankful he wasn't that big as he drove into me, but he was panting like he was going hard and he wasn't. I blinked back into character, whimpering for him to cum on my back when he announced he was close. At that point, I really disassociated and shifted into survival mode.

Thankfully, Raw Math followed my direction and came on me. When he turned me around, I saw his dick bobbing out the fly of his trousers. He placed his large hands on my shoulders and tried to push me down to my knees. Fear jolted through me as I resisted and croaked out, "I-I 'on't wanna do that." Before we went upstairs, I told him that giving a client head was always at my discretion.

With his sunglasses on, it was hard to read his facial expression. I waited for his response, my heart thudding in my ears. But he just kind of smirked and chuckled lowly.

He lifted me onto the desk and went down on me terribly. When he got his fill, he stood up too fast, his big ass swaying. With his jaw slack, Raw Math slurred, "C'mon now, baby girl. I just ate yo' pussy. You gon' *suck my dick." He said it like he deserved head just because he ate me out, like me reminding him of my boundary meant that I really wanted him to persuade me to let him be the exception.*

His hands started reaching for my head.

That *snapped my mind back to the room. I just reacted.*

My heart hammering against my chest—I don't think I 've ever been so scared in my life—I grabbed my clutch and pushed his chest as hard as I could so that I could slide off the desk. He stumbled backwards and fell in one of his office chairs.

With my dress all in disarray and stickiness in between my thighs and on my back, I fled his office and scrambled down a side staircase.

It wasn't until I made it outside that I breathed. I took so many deep breaths that I got lightheaded.

Now, every time Raw Math's face flashes on the news or I hear his name, my chest tightens, my stomach turns, my skin erupts with goosebumps.

I got away, but that could've gone *so* much worse. That "what if?" keeps me up some nights. And so does the thought that maybe I should've taken more precautions, that I could've done something different to avoid being in that situation at all.

But I don't want to tell Tim all of that right now. He just cooked this amazing meal, and we were having such a good time. I don't want to sour the mood.

I feel Tim's hand cover mine, all warm and steady, bringing me back to the present. I have half a mind to jump, but his touch is so gentle. My attention snaps to his eyes.

He says,
"You fascinate me through and through,
Like a secret only meant for two.
I wanna learn you line by line,
trace ya thoughts and call 'em mine.
Not to *own*, but just to know,
to let this thing take time to grow.

"No need to rush, no need to chase,
I'll meet you atcho perfect pace.
And if there's a chance at an us,
I'll hold my cards, I'll earn ya trust.
Because some' in me—quiet, but true—
says I've been waitin' a long-ass time to meet you."

I blink, warmth settling on me. "Was that . . . Was that another poem?"

A sheepish grin claims Tim's face as he laces our fingers together. "Yeah. You like it?"

"I *love* it, Tim." I blush. "That was beautiful."

He smiles, lifting my hand to kiss the back of it, but then his face falls. "And I'm serious 'bout what I said, Camesha. You went somewhere just now, and I 'on't know why, but you 'on't have to tell me if you 'on't want to. Go at ya own pace. Only share whatchu *want* me to know right now."

I drop my gaze, squirming a little in my seat. All of his words settle in my stomach like his food has.

Tim is so comfortable openly sharing hard details about his life that sometimes I feel bad for not sharing some of mine.

But something like that? Yeah, I'll wait.

I do appreciate Tim not rushing me though. That seems to be our type of time. He always seems to know when to affirm and reassure me.

I curl my index finger to beckon him to me. He grins and we share a sweet kiss.

When we sit back in our chairs, I share a lighter unforgettable experience: when Nikki, Lu, and I went out for the first time. A guy started flirting with Lu, but then he said something misogynistic. Nikki crashed out behind her, and we got kicked out of the club. On top of that, her car got towed so we Ubered all over the city, trying to find the impound lot.

Tim laughs throughout my story and asks some follow-up questions. I'm just happy the heavy mood lifted, and we were back to having fun. I know that if we keep dating, I will eventually have to tell him what Raw Math did, but right now, I'm not ready.

I ask Tim about his handler origin story.

After graduating college, he and one of his best friends, Bryan, moved into an apartment together since their other bestie, Jaquade, was living with other aspiring music producers so that "iron sharpens iron."

Tim studied music business in college so that he could be an A&R one day. So, while working at a streetwear store after college, he interned at a record label to get closer to his dream. He says it wasn't glamorous work, but it got him visibility, and he learned a lot by simply being around the biz and its people. Toward the end of his six-month internship, Tim assisted at a photo shoot for the rapper, Ezzy J. He noticed Tim's quickness and problem-solving skills and decided to hire Tim as his personal assistant when his internship was over.

After Ezzy died in a car accident a year later, Tim's phone rang off the hook with people wanting him to work his magic for them.

"That was my rough entry into the world of celebrity handlin'," he says all dramatically, making me giggle. "After Ezzy passed, my first huge client was Raw Math."

I almost fucking choke on a piece of my pork chop, but I catch myself. My heart jolts.

"He always dropped so many gems on me. And he even paid me my biggest checks at the time."

Then Tim's jaw tightens, and he glances away as he stabs some mac n cheese. "But as soon as that first sexual assault allegation came out two years ago, I immediately quit workin' wit' his ass. I 'on't fuck wit' that." He shakes his head indignantly, like that's a hill he'd gladly die on.

Tim scoffs. "It's fucked-up how you can be 'round somebody for three years and really don't know 'em. How you really don't know what they're capable of." He shakes his head. "I hope they quit playin' and lock his ass up for all'at shit."

I just stare a hole into Tim's cheek as he keeps eating. Then I snap out of it and clear my throat. "Yeah, same."

After he finishes chewing, he says, "But yeah, so that's my story. Almost seven years in the game."

Then the realization hits me squarely in the chest: we're both hustlers. Warmth spreads throughout my body.

Tim

"Handlin' wasn't my goal, but it got me into the industry. But I ain't even gon' hold you, Camesha," I raise my eyebrows and scratch the back of my head, "I 'on't know if I even *wanna* work at a record label anymore," I voice the idea that's been bouncing in the back of my mind for almost a year now.

She frowns. "Awww. Really?"

I nod, running a hand over my curls. "Yeah. I mean, I been inspired to write lately," I leer at her, making her blush, "so I *might* wanna take poetry more seriously. Maybe go to grad school or, at the very least, take some writin' workshops."

She smiles big, her eyebrows quirking up.

"Or," my voice drops a little, grasping her attention, "go on tour wit' Terrence White as his executive assistant. . ."

Her eyes bug out and she repeats what I said but as a question.

Terrence White has maintained relevance without a hitch for 30+ years. He's adapted his sound with the times, adding more and more fans to his base. And he actually wants *me* to work on his tour.

"Tim, that's amazin'!"

I smile at her excitement. Clearing my throat, I reply, "It is, but," I lick my lips, "the tour starts in the fall. Terrence is friends wit' Rugged Rah and G1-Otie, so he's heard good things 'bout me as a handler. He approached me 'bout the job at Yamz's BET Awards afterparty but I ain't think he was serious. Then he recently called me 'bout it—musta got my number from one of the guys—so I'd have to let him know some' soon." I grit my teeth.

Camesha's shoulders sag. "And how long is the tour?"

"Like, six months and it's a *global* tour. Terrence said it might be his last one for a while—or forever—But *don't* tell anybody I said that," I try at a joke to lighten the tension.

Camesha's mouth twitches up, but she doesn't laugh as if this ordeal is taking away her sense of humor. I mean, granted my joke might've been said at the wrong time, but I want to see her smile since we were having fun before I dropped this on her.

Her eyes dart around her plate like her brain is thinking in overdrive. To calm her and ease her nerves, I cover her hand with mine again. "I 'on't wantchu to get too worked up 'bout this. Hell, I 'on't even know if I *want* the job or not."

She swiftly shakes her head. "Well, don't *not* take it cuz I feel some type of way. Tim, if you want the job, take it."

I scoff a laugh. She sounds just like me when she had me share my honest feelings about her hustle. "So, you *do* feel some type of way 'bout all'is?" I say, smiling and playfully wiggling my eyebrows.

Camesha drops her head, fighting a smile. "Of course I do, Tim." She sighs heavily.

My eyebrows knit together. "What?"

"I 'on't know, can we survive another several months of not seein' each other fa real?—Not to be dramatic cuz I'm sure we *can*, but . . . I 'on't wantchu to be gone that long," her voice is small, almost shy.

A smile tugs at my lips as warmth fills my stomach.

This tour job sounds like a great opportunity, but it's coming *way* too early in our relationship. Although we were only casually texting then, we didn't see each other for seven months. And *now*, Camesha's my lady. I've enjoyed spending time with her, making her laugh, holding and kissing her.

"Same," I say. "I mean, sure, it'd be a much more consistent check, and he'd pay me *very* well." She deadpans me and I chortle, reaching up to cup her face. "But I 'on't wanna be away from you either."

Her facial expression softens as she leans into my palm.

"Honestly, I might be leanin' toward tellin' Terrence no. . ." I trail off to gauge her reaction.

"Are you *sure*, Tim?"

My thumb swipes her cheek. "Baby, I've been thinkin' 'bout this a lot since he called me a few days ago." I clench my jaw. "I wanted to know ya thoughts on this cuz you're important to me, Camesha. And I value your opinion."

She smiles, blushing.

"Plus, some' else came up."

She sighs like she can't take all this news, making me laugh.

"Keyana hit me up, askin' 'bout my poetry. She learned I write and said she could use a fresh voice in her songwritin' sessions. . ." I narrow my eyes at my lady. "I ain't tell her I write poetry, so it musta been *you* who told her, C. I saw y'all chattin' at her show a few weeks ago."

Camesha purses her lips with an amused look on her face, suddenly finding the ceiling more interesting than me. "I mean, she asked me 'bout The Lenox Room, and I was honest."

I chuckle. "My poem was that good, huh?"

"Baby, if it was trash, I wouldn't've asked you to frame it for me so that I can hang it up in my condo."

I laugh. "Damn, not even to support ya man?"

She snickers, shaking her head. "Nooo? . . Sorry."

I smack my teeth, chortling. "So, you think I could really work wit' Keyana in that way?"

Camesha stands up from her seat and straddles my lap as I scoot my chair back to accommodate her. Her arms circle my neck as mine settle around her waist. I love when she gets bold like this.

"I think so. Is songwritin' some' you'd be interested in?"

I look off to the side of her as if it has the answers. "Maybe. Honestly it never crossed my mind 'til now. But I'd be willin' to try it out. I trust Keyana would be a nurturin' mentor." *Yooo, am I really considerin' this shit?*

"I think so, too," she says, caressing the back of my head. "I'm glad you have options."

"I'm happy you got options, too. Whether it's continuin' to move up in hospitality or goin' back to school or pursuin' interior design—or hell, all of it, I'm here for you, Camesha. Whatever you wanna do." I lean forward to peck her lips a few times.

Sitting back, I notice *that* look on her face. We meet each other halfway for a passionate kiss, slow and hungry, like we both didn't just eat dinner.

I hoist her up as I get out of my seat, her ass in my hands.

"We're not done eatin'," Camesha whimpers, holding onto my shoulders.

"I know. I want my dessert now if that's a'ight witchu," I say, eyeing her slightly agape mouth.

She surprises the fuck out of me when she murmurs, "I have no qualms wit' that."

A smile slowly creeps onto my face before a chuckle tumbles out. And I carry her off to my bedroom.

14
Birthday Boy

Friday, August 3

Tim

I am 29 years old today. Got . . . damn! *One* more year before the big 3-0. While that's a huge birthday in and of itself, I definitely woke up this morning with a heavy need to reflect, like being 29 requires it. I have a feeling this will be a transitional year with lots of changes on the horizon. I mean, just from considering a different professional path to my relationship with Camesha, things will be different. Shit, come February, it will mark 10 years since Pops's passing. It's wild to think that he's been gone *that* fucking long! That Ma, who was with him for most of her life, hasn't had him for a decade. I'd definitely have to go home to support her around the anniversary.

Per Camesha's loving encouragement and many reminders, I blocked off my entire day on my calendar. I'm thankful because, a few times before, I've forgotten to take off on my birthday and found myself doing shit for *other* people. Those years, I didn't plan ahead so my day just snuck up on me. This go-around, I took off with enough time to inform my clients. Some of them know my birthday, and typically only contact me for emergencies, but still. Camesha wanted to make sure I didn't work so that I'd properly celebrate.

And that I did: slept, relaxed, watched movies, and I called Ma—*three* times with no answer. I texted her, asking if everything's okay, but my texts weren't going through! I tried not to freak out but now is when I wish I had some of her new friends' phone numbers to see if they've heard from her. *Maybe she's gonna wait to call me later today. . .*

The guys and I have been wanting to check out a spot in Hollywood called Linden. It's Black-owned and has an intimate dining room, the perfect place to celebrate my 29th born day. And the perfect place to introduce my lady to my best friends, and vice versa.

Bryan's punctual ass beat me to the restaurant. I don't know how he got here early in the middle of rush hour when his office is in downtown LA.

He stands to greet me, already holding his hand out. "Happy birthday, my guy!"

A huge smile spreads across my face. "Thank you." We dap-hug and I sit down on the bench in front of the windows across from him.

A server comes over, asking if we want to start with something to drink. Bryan orders the 805 beer, and I ask for the Cherry St. cocktail, then we start chopping it up about our days. He updates me on the revitalization project he's working on, which sounds exciting.

The door opening to the restaurant captures my attention. It's Jaquade.

But *not* Jaquade. He doesn't look like himself. Bryan and I stand to greet the last member of our trio.

"'Sup wit' y'all niggas?" We all dap before he plops down into the seat next to Bryan. I love that they just knew that the seat next to me is reserved for Camesha.

"Happy G day, T!" Jaquade says.

"'Preciate it, bruh." My eyes trail over his outfit, shocked that he's not wearing all dark colors, but instead is rocking a green polo and brown pleated pants. "*And* you dressed up for me, my nigga? I feel special." I fake-gasp and place a hand over my heart.

Quade smacks his teeth, dismissing me. "Man, shut up. I just thought I'd try some' new since you gon' be Unc real soon."

I howl laughing.

He points a finger at Bryan. "But *you* coulda stepped ya game up today."

"Nigga, I came from work," Bryan scoffs, glancing around, probably wondering why he's getting smoke.

"So? You can't dress a lil' better in the office? I mean, you coulda at least just tucked ya shirt in, B." He shakes his head like a disappointed father.

Bryan just sighs, rolling his eyes and sipping his beer. I laugh at them, relishing in their usual vibe already. Just what I needed to bring in 29.

Jaquade launches into a story about his week since he just flew in yesterday from a weeklong stay in Puerto Rico. He and a slew of other producers and artists stayed with a rapper at his vacation home. He can't disclose the artist but they're working on an album, one Jaquade says is like his magnum opus. Sounds like it'll be epic. Whoever it is, I can't wait to hear it.

I also can't wait to see Camesha. She told me she was going to get here as soon as she got off work. Still new in her position, she couldn't call out for the day to chill with me, which I understood.

As if I thought her up, the door opens, and she breezes in. The dining room is only but so big, so I stand, and her eyes immediately land on mine.

As I stroll toward her, my gaze drags from her head to her toes, admiring how she put herself together today. She brought this outfit to change into after her shift. I appreciate her effort.

Her hair is in her signature style: middle-parted, fluffy twist-out. A delicate gold necklace and rings adorn her. A burgundy dress falls down her body, flaring out mid-calf, revealing black red-bottom heels. A small gift bag flourishing with tissue paper hangs off her wrist while a chain strap purse dangles from her shoulder. And her nails are now red.

Up close, I can smell that orange creamsicle fragrance on her and see her lips are coated in that two-toned gloss thing I love. From her scent to her glossy lips, I'd say she's trying to distract me this evening.

I hug her, whispering in her ear, "You look and smell good enough to eat, baby."

Camesha laughs, but at this point, she knows I'm dead serious. One hit of her pussy, and I'm hooked. "Thank you, Tim."

I back up to see her face. "*And* you wearin' the hell out of my favorite color."

She glances down at herself coyly. "Glad you like it." She beams at me, cooing, "Happy birthday, handsome." Camesha cups my face and brings it down to hers for a few soft pecks, swiping gloss off my lips when she pulls back. "Or should I say *old man* since you almost 30 now."

I laugh, my eyes drifting to the gift bag. "You got me a gift?"

"Yeah, *but* you will wait to open it." She moves it out of my reach.

I kiss my teeth. "A'ight, fine. You get here okay?"

"I did. How was ya day?"

"Better now that you're here." I squiggle my eyebrows.

She rolls her eyes, giggling. "Okay, my cute cornball."

"C'mon." I grab her hand and take her to our table.

Camesha

Tim looks *scrumptious* in a black crochet shirt, ankle pants, and shiny loafers. His usual jewelry is shining, and he got a fresh haircut. He smells so damn good I can't even tell what it is. His whole vibe is giving sexy grown man. And I love that.

But I snap out of ogling him from behind as we approach the table with his friends. I tried to calm down my nerves on the drive over here by listening to soothing music, but that didn't help.

"Hey, can y'all pause the dumb bickerin' for a sec?" Tim says with a chuckle.

The men stand.

"This is my lady, Camesha. Camesha, these are my best friends. This is Bryan," Tim motions to the chubby-ish light-skinned man with a friendly face, "and Jaquade," he gestures to the dark-skinned guy with locs in a messy ponytail.

But I can barely focus on them as my heart swells at the word *lady*. Tim didn't call me his girlfriend, or his girl. I'm his *lady*. I love that. Feels like our relationship has more dignity. Especially given how we met.

"Nice to meet you guys," I greet with a smile, hoping my face looks relaxed.

"Likewise, Camesha," Bryan says, nodding.

"Yeah, glad we can finally meet you. Took Tim forever to introduce us," Jaquade says with a straight face, making me giggle. Tim warned me about his dry humor.

"Man, shut up." Tim moves, gesturing me to slide into the bench seat first like a gentleman.

"So, Camesha, when did his slow ass finally ask you to be his lady?" Jaquade asks before sipping something brown.

I snicker. "End of May."

Jaquade shakes his head, looking at Tim. "Damn, it took you a month?"

"A month?" I ask, glancing at Tim.

"Yeah, I told him to be straight up witchu back in *April*." Jaquade shakes his head again. "But at least he did it! Bryan went on a date recently and scared the girl off, talkin' too serious too fast."

Bryan sighs loudly, pinching the bridge of his nose. "God, I swear I'm never tellin' you anything ever again, Quade. You stay tellin' my business."

Unfazed, Jaquade just shrugs his shoulders and nurses his drink.

"What happened, B?" Tim asks.

Bryan tells the story of his date with a woman he's been messaging on a dating app for a couple of weeks. And when she finally had time to go on a date with him, she felt he came on too strong. But he just explained that he's ready to find his person.

A server comes over, asking for my drink order and if the guys have decided on something to start. I quickly peruse the menu and order the Lemon Ting cocktail.

Tim leans in to whisper in my ear, "I knew you'd order that."

"How?" I look at him.

"Cuz you my ting." Even *he* doesn't take himself seriously as he holds back a laugh.

A giggle tumbles out of me as I playfully slap his arm.

Jaquade orders the Wagyu Pie and Lobster & Crab Knuckle for the table then the server leaves. "But fa real, B, I'm sorry 'bout that. I know you were startin' to like her."

Bryan deadpans him. "Thanks, asshole."

Jaquade smirks.

Tim echoes Jaquade's verbal sentiment, and he and Bryan dap.

I clear my throat to speak, "I'm sorry, too, Bryan. That sucks. Sounds like she wasn't really ready for a man like you. What kinda women do you like?"

Bryan runs down the qualities he looks for in his dream woman and just like I suspected, she sounds a lot like my girl, Oluchi.

"Ya know what? I . . . *might* know someone," then Tim and I say her name at the same time. I whip my head to face him, my eyes wide open. "How'd you know?"

"When I met her, I felt like she and Bryan would vibe."

"Thanks, guys. I'd definitely be interested in meetin' ya friend, Camesha. Do you have a picture you can show me?" Bryan says, offering a bashful, crooked smile.

I open my phone and pull up a recent photo she sent the group chat when she went to a new hairstylist to get her usual silk press.

Bryan's eyebrows damn-near meet his hairline when he sees her. "She's beautiful."

Tim and I make eye contact, smirking. I say, "She is. I know she's open to datin' so I'll let her know you're interested."

"'Preciate it."

My drink and our small plates arrive as we chat more. Tim's best friends don't grill me like Nikki did Tim. Bryan naturally asks me questions—if I came to LA to chase a dream, about life in Columbia, my basic likes and dislikes. Seems like Tim has talked quite a bit about me and Bryan just wanted me to fill in some blanks. That makes my heart flutter as I slide my hand down to rub Tim's thigh underneath the table. His muscles tense up a little, but then he kisses my temple. I like that his friends don't tease him or make it a big deal when he openly gives me affection like mine did. I know that Simonique was just excited for me since it's been *years* since I've talked about a boyfriend. And Nikki . . . well, she's just a nut. But so is Jaquade.

One night after Tim and I had sex, he mentioned how he could see Jaquade and Nikki date, noting their similar personalities. But I immediately shut that down, saying Nikki needs someone to balance out her crazy ass. And meeting Jaquade today, that still holds true. If anything, I can see them clashing. I think his deadpan, nonchalant personality would get on her nerves. Whether he jokes or not, his face has the same neutral expression.

The small plates are delicious, then we order entrees. Bryan gets a spicy dish—point for him since Lu loves spice—and Jaquade asks for a burger—minus a point because Nikki would judge him for being "basic." Tim orders the fried chicken and when our food comes, he lets me try it. . . And oh my God, it immediately transports me back home. I don't cook fried chicken because it's so laborious, so the kind out here will suffice, but *this* one? It reminds me of Mama's recipe. I'll have to call her soon.

By the end of the evening, none of us have room for dessert. And several drinks in, we're also loose. Tonight has made me so full with happiness, too, seeing Tim have a good time with his best friends. He's a "jokey-ass nigga" when he's with me, but with them, he's at another level. Roasts, jabs, jones—they all dish them out. Well, mostly Jaquade and Tim as Bryan just takes it in exhausted jest.

"A'ight Camesha, it was lovely to meet you," Bryan says outside on the corner. Night is here and the air is balmy. "Do you hug or shake hands?"

Awww, I love that he asked. Another point for politeness! "A hug is cool." I give him a one-arm hug.

Jaquade says, "Yeah, ya dope, Camesha. I can see you and my boy mesh really well." He nods repeatedly, and, for some reason, I can tell he really means it.

"Thank you, Jaquade. It was great meetin' you guys." I shift my gaze between him and Bryan.

They both wish Tim a happy birthday again, exchanging handshakes, hugs, and more jokes before they go their separate ways. My man is standing behind me and makes his presence more known when he wraps his arms around my waist. "Sooo, how was that?"

I turn in his grasp and lock my arms around his neck. "Good. You guys are," I think of the word, "*cute.*"

Tim looks taken aback. "Cute?"

"Yeah. I can tell y'all been friends a long time. Y'all feel like brothers. Especially Bryan and Jaquade," I chuckle.

Tim rolls his eyes, chortling, "Yeah, them niggas. . . They stay goin' at it and Bryan *always* taps out. I be tryna tell him that if he goes toe to toe wit' Quade a lil' longer, he'd pro'ly stop. He does it cuz Bryan makes it too easy to rag." He leans in and kisses my nose. "Anyway, that food was *it*, wasn't it?"

I throw my head back and laugh. Tim chuckles before I feel his warm lips kiss and lightly suck my neck. Cupping his head, I lift mine up straight and he pecks my lips a few times.

"You gotcho spend-the-night bag, right?" Tim asks me all low and husky, resting his forehead on mine.

My pussy throbs at the possibility of what we would do at his house. "Mmm-hmmm."

A sly smile smears Tim's face. "Let's go then. Where'd you park?"

Tim

We arrive at my house a little after 10. I hop out of my Jeep and walk to the driver's side of Camesha's Venza. I open her door, watching her grab her purse and my gift from the passenger's seat. I haven't stopped racking my brain on what it could be since I noticed it earlier.

I get her duffel bag from her trunk and guide her inside, my hand along the small of her back. After I flip on the lights and close the front door, Camesha struts inside and places her purse onto the entryway table.

"Want anything?" I ask, dropping her bag by the door.

Camesha slowly faces me, a searing smile playing on her face. "You."

I drop my head to hide my grin . . . and my blush. "Is that right?" With careful steps, I approach her, my hands pulling her closer by her waist.

She nods, circling my neck with her arms, the gift bag now dangling by my head—*teasing* me. She tries to go in for a kiss, her hands already pressing my neck down.

But I resist. "Camesha, c'mon now, tell me what's in the bag? Ya killin' me here." I sound like I'm whining, but she got a nigga super curious.

She drops her arms and laughs, stepping back a bit. "You're right, it's gift time," she says. "You haven't mentioned doin' this yet, so I thought I'd do it." She hands me the gift bag and I low-key rip it from her hand with my eager ass.

I remove all the delicate tissue paper, unearthing a little box. Glancing up at her, a mischievous look is plastered on her face. "What's this?"

"Tim, open it," she giggles.

I pull the box out, flipping it over to examine it. And my mouth drops open.

"It's a second cellphone for work," Camesha's soft voice cuts through my surprise-induced silence. "Since you're always sayin' you wanted to separate ya life that way—Wait, you didn't already get one, did you?" Worry slips in her voice.

I reach for her hand to pull her to me, smashing my lips onto hers. I kiss all that gloss off her gorgeous mouth, her hands holding my jaws. When I pull back, I breathe out, "Nah, I ain't get another phone." I look down at the iPhone box before placing it on the little entry table by the door. "I *really* 'preciate you gettin' this for me. This . . . This is a *great* gift, Camesha. Thank you." My voice cracks a little at how practical it is. I've been meaning to buy a work phone for over a year, but I never made a plan to do it.

Now I don't have to because my lady handled it for me. *The handler is gettin' shit handled for him. . . That's crazy.*

Camesha grins, pleased. "You're welcome." Her thumb starts wiping my lips. We both have her lip gloss all over our faces, but I don't care.

Then I don't think—I just react, wrapping my lips around her finger. Her mouth falls agape, and a slight gasp escapes. With hooded eyes, I watch her watching me suck on her thumb. I pull Camesha closer to me and let her thumb go so I can devour her lips again. With our tongues involved now, we start groping one another—my hands sliding down to grip her ass, hers on my face and neck. My dick stiffens, rising in my pants as I hook my hands underneath her knees to lift her in the air. I ain't that strong but this woman makes me feel like Superman.

Our eyes flash open and Camesha yelps a little as I carry her toward my bedroom. She has a simmering glimmer in her brown eyes.

After crossing that threshold, I lay her down on the bed, my body stretching over hers. I kiss on her neck right below her ear—her spot—before pecking my way across the tops of her breasts. Her breathing is sporadic as she holds onto my head. In her left ear, I grumble, "As good as this dress looks on you, I need you to take it off."

Camesha pushes me off her and sits up. I slightly stumble backwards but catch my balance before leaning against my dresser. I watch her stand up slowly, her eyes trained on mine as her fingers pull down her dress's thin straps. My heart rate quickens as I bite my bottom lip in anticipation.

It's not like I ain't seen her naked—I have and it's *glorious*—but it just feels like something else is in the air. And not on no Phil Collins-type shit either.

With her straps down now, Camesha shimmies out of the dress. She's wearing a sexy-as-hell red lace strapless bra and matching panties. Her heel straps climb her leg, too. There's just something about this kind of shoe on her that just makes my mouth water, drives me crazy.

Oh, she went all out wit' my favorite color today—"Damn, C. Red draws, too?" my intrusive thoughts say.

Her face twitches, the sexy smolder faltering a little. She whines while giggling, "Yes, Tim. Now, stop makin' me laugh, I'm tryna be sexy."

I lick my lips, my eyes glued to her bronze-brown body in this red. The color contrast is a gift in and of itself. "You ain't gotta try, baby. You *are* sexy." My hands stretch out toward her waist as I start to approach her.

She holds her hand out like a crossing guard. "Stay there."

My eyes snap up to hers. I'm confused as hell, but I listen.

Camesha takes the few steps to me excruciatingly slow, hips swinging like she's trying to hypnotize me. She braces her hands on my chest to lean in close to my ear. My heart is knocking like the cops against my ribcage now. I don't know what she's doing to me, but it's clear she wants to be in control tonight.

Her tongue traces the shell of my ear, then flicks at my earlobe. I squeeze my eyes closed as I suck in a deep breath, my hands gripping the fuck out of the dresser's edge.

"C'mon, Camesha," crawls out all strained. My shit is hard as concrete in my pants now, the erection almost feeling too heavy. *Shit, I might nut now wit' all her teasin'.*

"I wantchu to relax, birthday boy," she says all low. I *love* it when her voice drops down to that register.

One of Camesha's hands glide down to my stomach before she lightly cups my erection. I hiss at the contact when she starts stroking me. She leaves my ear alone to press a long kiss to my cheek.

"Shit, C," I let out, my chest rising and falling too fast.

"I know, I know," she murmurs against my face. Her lips brush more kisses on my cheek and her hand grips me tighter and strokes me faster. "Tim?"

I don't know why she's talking to me like she ain't trying to fuck me up. "'Whassup?"

"Take these pants off for me, baby."

I open my eyes a little as my hands start fumbling with my belt. She removes her hand from my length and pulls back a bit, watching me. Just as I hook my hands into the waistband of my boxer briefs, Camesha's hand stops me. I remove my hands as her fingers curl into my draws. With my pants and underwear, she slides down my legs, my erect dick springing free, already leaking pre-cum.

Her eyes flicker up to mine before eyeing my piece. Unless I'm still tipsy, I could swear that she licks the seam of her lips a little before gripping the base of my shaft and sticking her tongue out. *What a view.*

When her tongue meets my tip, a hiss lurches out of me. My stomach contracts at the contact and I frantically lift my shirt over my head, flinging that motherfucker somewhere across the room. Camesha smiles at my nakedness.

And without warning, her plump, round lips wrap around my dick. I've always thought she has some sexy-ass lips and may have wet-dreamed about them before, but seeing and feeling her mouth on me like this already has me ready to bust.

"Fuuuccckkk," I exhale, my eyes half-closing. I'm tempted to bury my fingers in her hair, but I'm not sure if she'd like that.

I know she takes great care to maintain it, and I don't want to mess it up. So, I just keep gripping my dresser.

I watch as she bobs up and down my shaft, lips wetting me up. One of her hands grip me, following her mouth, while the other juggles my balls. Camesha's gaze flicks up to me as she moans, the vibrations around my dick making me contract my abdomen again. *Shit, at this rate, I'll have a six-pack by the end of this.*

It's been a minute since I got any head, but it sure do feel damn good to get some on my birthday.

"Gotdamn, Camesha." My face is all twisted up because of the pleasure.

My hips start involuntarily thrusting, chasing the nut building up. That just makes her go harder—sucking and jacking me off faster, her hair blocking the view. I move it to one side so I can keep watching her. My breathing gets out of control as I try to exhale the cuss words bubbling out.

"Baby, I'm 'bout to cum," I announce through strained pants.

In response, she pulls me out of her mouth with a loud *pop*. My eyes snap open wider, wondering what the fuck she's doing.

Before I can ask though, she starts stroking and twisting my dick with both hands, tapping the sensitive head on her tongue. I bite my bottom lip as I try to focus on her wet mouth.

Next thing I know, she shoves me back down her throat and my hips pump a few times before I bust. A string of cuss words marches out of my mouth at varying volumes. Through slitted eyes, I try to watch Camesha slowly suck me, cum and saliva coating me.

When I calm down a little and my breathing levels out, she pulls me out of her mouth again. She licks her lips and sticks her tongue out, showing me that she swallowed every single drop.

Fuuuccckkk. . . My mind can barely form thoughts.

An overwhelming gratitude builds up in me. And it's not just the amazing head, but her gift, the way she carried herself and interacted with my best friends tonight. Just *her* in general. It'd be cliché to say those precious words now after I came, but I think I feel them for real.

"C'mere," I say breathless, my hands cupping her shoulders to pull her up to her feet. "Gimme these sexy-ass lips." Wrapping my arms around her waist, I smush my lips to hers. We kiss ravenously, moaning into one another's mouths. My hands slip down into her panties to squeeze and separate her ass cheeks. She arches her back something serious as my fingers find her wet, swollen clit from behind. I walk us backwards until we fall onto the bed.

The kiss breaks a little and we take the moment to catch our breaths. Camesha's hand caresses the side of my face as she looks at me happy-drunk.

"You liked that?" she asks.

"Hell yeah." I dip down to peck her lips. "I need to taste you."

A smirk smudges her face as she begins to lift off the bed, her hips touching mine. I pull her panties down her smooth legs, leaving a trail of wet kisses behind.

I eat her out like she's my last meal on death row, making her grip my hair and scream my name. Afterwards, she rides me like a Harley. We flow through a few positions before we're absolutely, completely spent and knock ourselves out. *Happy muhfuckin' birthday to me.*

Saturday, August 4

Camesha

I blink slowly, my eyelashes crusty and sticking as sleep is thick behind my eyes like a heavy blanket. I glance around to orient myself, feeling well-rested deep in my bones.

I'm in Tim's bedroom. The Sun is peeking through the sides of his blackout curtains, slivers of light to brighten the dark room. His face is in the crook of my neck, light snores blowing from his nostrils. I feel his arm draped over my chest underneath the sheets.

I smile, reminiscing on last night. I might've planned to give Tim head for his birthday after I gave him his gift. And boy, the experience did not disappoint. I liked watching him unravel as I had him in my mouth with all the power. It was even sexier when he obeyed my commands.

Earlier at the restaurant and in the entryway of his home, he looked at me like he was ready to eat *me*—and I allowed him to later, and that was at another stratosphere last night—but I wanted to eat him first. He deserved it. And since he asked me about my meal prepping process a while back, Tim told me he's been slowly cleaning up his diet and started prepping his breakfasts. I could tell. He tasted good.

I lightly kiss Tim's forehead to wake him up. He stirs a little and pulls my body closer. He nuzzles his face deeper into my neck, making me titter at his chin hair tickling me. He looks so peaceful and at ease that I don't want to speak to wake him, so I plant a few more kisses to his forehead.

He groans, "A'ight, I'm awake." He cracks open an eye and mean-mugs me.

I chuckle, covering my mouth to not attack him with my morning breath.

"C'mon, we pass that." Tim puckers his lips, and I giggle, trying to dodge him in his own bed.

"I 'on't wanna smell or taste *my* mornin' breath, so I *definitely* don't wanna smell or taste yours," I squeal.

He starts tickling my sides, saying, "Damn. I—"

The sound of his phone ringing stops him from tickling me and talking. My phone is in my purse, which I remember leaving on the entryway table. Tim sits up in bed and turns on his nightstand lamp. I notice his back scars, evidence of me scratching him up last night . . . and other times.

He swivels his head around, I guess trying to catch his bearings and see where the sound is coming from.

"If they were in ya pants, ya pants are in front of the bed," I help.

"Right. Thanks." He gets out of bed butt-naked to recover his phone. His ass is all tight, making me remember how I held onto his cheeks last night when he was digging me out.

"Oh shit!" Tim shouts, making me sit up like Dracula coming up from the dead. I find him staring at his phone with enlarged eyes. "It's my mom."

"Your mom?" I exclaim.

Tim nods, still letting the phone ring. "She ain't pick up the few times I called her yesterday. We usually talk on my birthday. I guess she's callin' me now."

I swallow the spit in my throat and with wide eyes, I wait until the phone stops ringing.

"Well, I'm glad to see she's okay. I'mma call her back later today." Tim rounds the bed to sit his phone on his nightstand.

I let out a breath I didn't know I was holding in and my shoulders relax.

"You wanna hop in the shower wit' me?" Tim asks, nudging his thumb over his shoulder toward his en-suite.

A smile worms onto my face. "Are we *just* gonna shower?"

Tim holds his hands out and once I place mine in his, he pulls me out of the bed. "If you want to. Or we could go for," he glances up at the ceiling, silently muttering, "round five—*is* it round five? Some' like that."

I laugh, my hand flying to cover my mouth. "I wasn't countin'." I scurry to his living room to grab my toiletries from my duffel bag.

We go another round in the shower, then we clean one another. After the shower, I brush my teeth and complete my skincare routine. Tim gawks at all my steps as he just uses a cleanser and a moisturizer. I invested in a more customized regimen to keep my skin clear and flawless for hustle jobs. Perfection or close to it was expected and appreciated from clients.

Seems like as soon as we changed into similar outfits—shorts and graphic tees—his phone rings *again*.

My stomach drops at the possibility of it being his mother a second time. And if she's persistent, she would keep calling until he answers.

Tim retrieves his phone from the nightstand. "Now it's a FaceTime request?"

"What?" I want to make sure I heard him correctly.

"Since when did she get an iPhone?" he mutters to himself.

"Tim!"

"Yeah?" He looks up at me with furrowed eyebrows and tucked-in lips.

"You're answerin' that?"

"Yeah, why not? I mean, she knows 'bout you, Camesha. I talk about you all the time, baby."

My heart flutters at how sweet that is—But I get back down to business. "Wait, you're gonna put me on camera?"

Tim's eyebrows draw together with concern. "Yeeeaaahhh. . . Unless you 'on't want me to."

"It's just—you 'on't think it's too soon?" I clench my teeth trying to bare down on my nerves.

"*I* don't. But if you not ready, I 'on't have to put you on camera." Tim foots over to me in his crew socks, running a hand down my arm. "Whatchu wanna do, Camesha?" His gentle eyes search mine patiently, even as his phone's FaceTime tone continues.

"I-I 'on't know. I'm a lil' nervous."

Tim's lips perk up into a half-smile. "Don't be. She's chill. Hell, *my* silly ass gets on her nerves."

I laugh a little.

"I'll answer it and angle my phone so she can't see you and then I'll segue into introductions. How's that sound?"

I pause a little, the tone continuing, making me wonder how much longer before it stops. I nod and Tim smiles, bending down to kiss my forehead.

He grabs my hand and leads me out to the living room, so we can sit on his sectional for the call. He plops down and stretches his arm along the backrest. I sit next to him a few spaces away to make hiding me from the camera easier.

Tim hits the green answer button and soon his mother's face pops up. He inherited her gingerbread-brown skin and square-shaped face. Her hair is naturally kinky and styled in what looks like a pinned updo. "Damn boy, I was wonderin' when you was gon' answer me. I was 'bout to hang up and try again later," she immediately says, a hint of seriousness in her voice.

"My bad. I wasn't decent."

"Boy, you came outta me, so I done see you butt-ass naked before."

I clamp a hand over my mouth to keep from laughing.

Tim scoffs and chuckles. "You ain't see me naked as a grown man, Ma."

"Praise God!" she exclaims, her hands to Heaven. "Anyway, happy birthday, Timmy!" she coos in a baby voice.

Timmy. That's cute.

He beams, lines cupping his mouth and around his eyes. "Thank you, Ma."

"I can't believe I got a 29-year-old." She glances off to the side, a faraway look in her eye before tears brim and she covers her mouth. "Ya dad would be very proud of the man you've become, baby."

Tim glances down at his lap. Out of the frame still, I turn in my seat to hold and kiss the top of his hand. His fingers wrap around mine to let me know he feels me.

"Thanks, Ma." He clenches his jaw, probably to bite back tears. Then he clears his throat. "But look, why you ain't call me yesterday? I was actually off and was chillin' all day. You ain't pick up three times nor did—"

His mother smacks her teeth and shoots him a look. "Well, you see me able to FaceTime you now, don'tcha? I blocked you cuz I got me an iPhone yesterday. This is *my* gift to you. Now we can do this." She motions two fingers back and forth, referencing this call.

Tim laughs. "I do like this. But you really had me worried, Ma. You ain't have to block me though."

"Yes, I did cuz then you woulda seen the blue bubbles and know that I changed my phone."

"Touché." He nods, his eyes flicking to me subtly while his mother chuckles. "But Ma, I have someone I wantchu to meet."

My heart drops to my stomach. *I am* not *ready for this. Do I look like Tim and I just had sex? Is my hair okay?* He scoots closer to me and shifts the phone to include me in the frame now.

"This is Camesha, my lady," Tim says.

I manage a nervous wave and a smile. "Hi," my voice smaller and weaker than I intended.

Tim's arm that was outstretched on the backrest is now around me, resting diagonally across my back and his hand is on my hip, thumb rubbing slow circles to calm me down.

"Oh my goodness!" His mother's face brightens. "Well, Tim told me you were gorgeous, but you really are stunnin', Camesha."

I laugh, my nerves dissipating like cockroaches afraid of light. "Thank you so much."

"Ya welcome, sweetie. It is so nice to finally meet you." She beams at me, very warmly.

"You as well."

Tim squeezes me a little and I glance at him, finding him smiling.

"I see y'all look mighty cozy," his mother says, wiggling her eyebrows knowingly.

Can she tell we just had sex? I wonder, my heart rate quickening.

"Ma, please don't embarrass me," Tim cuts in.

"No, that's good. I'm happy you've found someone and are happy. I love knowin' ya not just out there workin' to the bone, but that you have someone to enjoy life wit', too."

My heart warms at that.

"Thanks, Ma. I definitely am." I can feel Tim looking at me before he runs his hand up and down my arm.

I try to fight my cheeks from blushing.

Mrs. Starks asks how we celebrated Tim's 29th birthday, and we tell her about the dinner. She asks how his best friends are doing and where Tim is on the decision to quit handling. She even asks me how my new job is going, shocking me that Tim told her that.

Tim goes all concerned son mode, checking up on Mrs. Starks's eating habits which she groans about. He asks about her book club and winery job, and she excitedly updates us on them, even asking me what kind of wine I like because she can ship some to me.

"Oh, thank you so much, Mrs. Starks."

"No problem, baby." She beams at me. "Alrighty, I'll let you young folks go. Don't know what else y'all got planned today but thank you for talkin' to me. Y'all treat each other right, hear?"

Tim and I simultaneously say "Yes ma'am."

She smiles. "Good. Again, it was so nice to meet you, Camesha. We'll have to meet in person soon, sweetie."

"Yes, I'd like that," I reply honestly with a nod.

"Ma, I love you," Tim says.

"I love you, too, Timothy. Y'all take care, okay? Talk soon."

Tim peace-signs his mother before ending the call. He drops his phone next to him. "See? That wasn't so bad."

I snuggle up to him. "No, it wasn't. Ya mom's really nice. And warm—Like *you*, actually."

"I told you I was raised right."

I laugh, wrapping my arm around his torso. "And you just been tellin' e'rybody 'bout me, huh?"

"Well," his hand tilts my chin up to look at him, "when you got some' good, you gotta let ya niggas know."

I lift an eyebrow, poorly stifling a laugh. "Ya *mom's* one of ya niggas?"

"Yeah," he chortles, "that's the homie fa sho. Just don't let her hear that. . . *I am ya mother, not one of ya lil' friends*," Tim imitates her voice—pretty well, actually.

I laugh, then cup his jaw and kiss him. Then it seems like I blink, and he's pushing me back onto the couch. His fingers find my shorts' drawstring inside the waistband.

I break the kiss, giggling at him touching my FUPA. "Sir, what are you doin'?"

"'Bout to have dessert for breakfast," he says matter-of-factly and very serious.

"But *I'm* hungry now," I laugh and whine.

"And I can make you some breakfast *after* I get my energy up first." He pulls my shorts down and flings them to the coffee table before he buries his face between my thighs.

Tim's lips and tongue on me makes me gasp as I nestle my hands in his hair.

15
Break, Pt. 1

Thursday, August 23

Tim

A scrawny woman leads me down the hallway to the studio Terrence White is using this afternoon. The deadline to let him know my decision on his job offer is fast approaching, so I called him yesterday, asking when we can meet to talk.

The woman does a courtesy knock before opening the door. The studio's lights are on, and I see Terrence wearing a navy-blue button-up with his sleeves rolled up, tailored chinos, and white leather sneakers. He's leaning back in one of the swivel office chairs with a notepad and pen in his hand, mumbling under his breath. *Kickin' it old school.*

His dark brown skin doesn't show that he's 55-years old. He's infamous for saying he owes that to eating right, exercising, and having *amazing* sex with his wife of 25 years. He's bald now with a goatee and even still sports that stud nose ring everyone went into a tizzy over years ago. His many female fans—old and young—still call him sexy, and even sexier because he openly loves his wife and, to our knowledge, has never cheated on her.

Terrence smiles before he stands to our matching six-foot height. "Hey, Tim!" He looks at the woman before she leaves.

"Thanks, Chartreuse." *Chartreuse, like the color?* I think before he continues, "My man!" He goes in for a dap-hug, and I oblige.

I've only met him once, but I remember his cologne. A few years ago, I remember Terrence collaborated with a niche perfumer to craft his own signature scent, and they sell it in exclusive batches every year.

"How ya doin', Terrence?" I say after we let one another go.

He closes the door and motions for me to sit. I drop down into the second chair.

"Man, just workin' this song out—,"

"Really?" my overly juiced ass cuts him off. He's *still* Terrence White and to get a sneak peek at his process would definitely be a treat. "I-I'm sorry—"

"It's okay, man," he chuckles before continuing, "But yeah, the other day I remembered some' my wife did when we first started datin' and it had song potential all over it. Now I'm tryna get the words out to match the melody that keeps loopin' in my head."

I nod, giddy with childish glee. "That's dope, man." Before I can stop myself, I sputter, "Ya know, I started writin' poetry again. So, if it'd be helpful, I can brainstorm witchu."

He snaps his back as he strokes his chin hair. "Damn, Rah and Otie said you were the best, but they didn't tell me you write songs, too? What *don't* you do, Tim?"

Terrence makes me blush, but I chuckle and lick my lips to play it off. "I mean, I used to write poetry *all* the time, but I just started writin' again a few months ago. About my lady."

"That's wonderful, Tim. Love'll do that to ya, man. It's the best inspiration." He glances away with a content expression on his face, like he's thinking about his wife. "But yeah, after we talk 'bout this job stuff, I'll see whatcha got. I actually kicked out my producer and engineer when Chartreuse said you were here. Wanted to give us some privacy to talk for a few minutes."

"'Preciate that, man."

He nods. "So, I'm happy you reached out, wantin' to meet *in person*. I hate havin' business conversations over the phone or, God forbid, on Zoom. Fuck that shit." Terrence's face is all screwed up like he smells something foul.

I can't help but laugh. "Yeah, I feel that." I clear my throat. "I ain't gon' lie, when you first told me you need an executive assistant on ya tour at ill Yamz's afterparty and that you were interested in *me*? . . I ain't think you were serious."

"You thought I was bullshittin', huh?" He doesn't sound hurt but amused as he tilts his head up and keeps eye contact.

I shrug. "I mean, ya know people say all kinds of stuff to you in this city. I've learned to take everything wit' a grain of salt, to not take a person seriously until they give you a reason to."

"That's smart. Saves you a lotta headaches."

Nodding, I lean forward, pressing my elbows into my thighs. "Yeah, so to work witchu—one of the legends in the game still doin' it consistently and keepin' it fresh—*and* to see the world wit' a fat, stable check?"

He throws his head back, laughing and lightly holding his flat stomach. *I* made Terrence White laugh.

"It's an amazin' opportunity, Terrence. . ." I don't mean to, but my voice falters since I'm unsure how to say this. I'm staring at the carpet, but I feel his attentive gaze. Clearing my throat, I look at him. "I've thought about it and talked to my friends, my mother, and my lady about it and . . . I think I'm gonna have to decline ya offer, Terrence." My nerves are real bad, vibrating underneath my skin.

He just looks at me and nods, a smile slowly lifting to reveal his famous naturally white teeth. My face fights a frown and furrowed eyebrows from coming on. "That's all right, Tim. I had a feelin' you'd say no." I try to jump in to stutter through an explanation, but he holds his hand up and my mouth snaps closed. "It's okay, man. I heard it in ya voice on the phone yesterday."

"You did?"

"When you've been in this business as long as I have, you learn to read people really well. Whether they're in yo' face or over the phone." He shrugs, leaning back in his chair and proppin' a foot on his knee. "And I get it, man, the tour is *six* months long. Shit, after 25 years of marriage, this is only the *second* tour I've convinced my wife to join me on. Now that our children are grown and she's retired, she's ready to see the world again. So, I get not wantin' to be away from ya lady that long either." He narrows his eyes at me, stroking his chin hair. "She doesn't work in the industry, huh?"

Damn, he's good. "Nah."

He nods. "How long y'all been together?"

"A few months. I've known her for 'bout a year now though."

A smile slowly curves onto his face. "Ah, some friends-to-lovers-type shit?"

I chuckle, thinking about Camesha and I's unique circumstances. If we go the distance like I hope, we'd have one hell of a meet-cute story to tell our kids. "Some' like that."

"That's beautiful, man. Nurture that, *especially* since it's so new. Distance can make the heart grow fonder like they say but it can *also* strain the connection. Pro'lems you didn't have before can crop up now cuz ya presence is missin'. My wife and I had so many petty arguments over the phone when I was on tours and when I'd return home for a quick break. I missed her and she missed me, but because I wasn't there, she was left to deal wit' shit by herself. She was stressed and exhausted and there's only so much I can do to handle it from thousands of miles away. Coulda been anything from house repairs, or the kids actin' up, or hell, she was just plain ol' *horny*! Phone sex don't hit *all* the time."

My eyes enlarge at him telling me that, but Terrence clearly speaks his mind.

"I say all'at to say that I understand you declinin' the job." He leans forward, holding his hand out.

We dap up and sit back.

His eyes zero in on me again. "What else on ya mind?" he asks.

Damn, are all my impendin' decisions just radiatin' from me? But I tell him how I'm thinking about not being a handler anymore. I tell him about my client Keyana Renay, an artist he says he's familiar with and admires for her "refreshin' honesty and her pen game," and how she wants to see if we can work together on a song.

Terrence just nods with raised eyebrows. "That's amazin', Tim. Sounds like you got a great support system so whatever you choose to do, I'm confident that you'll do well in it."

"Thank you, Terrence. I really 'preciate that. Fa real." I feel like I'm in a mentoring session, not a meeting where I rejected his good job offer. He's over here just being understanding and affirming the shit out of me. Something Pops would've done if he was here. . .

He was always a great listener and always knew what to say. He never said too much, but just enough for me to leave our conversations with his words marinating in my mind so I could commit them to memory and practice.

"Now, let's see see if you can help me write this bridge." Terrence picks up his pen and notepad.

I switch gears to my poetry mind as I roll my chair up to the mixing board so we can collaborate. "A'ight, but before I leave can we take a selfie? My mom ain't gon' believe I did this."

He laughs. "Fa sho. Shit, let's take the pic right now."

We take a few selfies, then he calls in Chartreuse to take photos of us standing in front of the mixing board. I hold up a peace sign and Terrence wraps an arm around my shoulder. *I'm definitely postin' this shit on my Instagram.*

Saturday, August 25

Camesha

I've finished laundry and meal prepping early, so I decided to treat myself. I drove to Fairfax for lunch and to hit up an upscale sneaker store. Tim likes to clown the few "basic" sneakers I own, and since he mentioned these Jordan 4s that just dropped—some collab he's been scoping out for months—I figured I'd buy us matching pairs.

Plus, it's my gift to him since he's exploring his professional options. I'm excited to see what the future looks like for him. If he pens anything with Keyana Renay like what he's written for me, then I believe he has a long career ahead of him in songwriting if that's what he wants.

I'm perusing the sneaker wall as I wait for my sales associate to return with my pair to try on. Since Tim already knows he's a size 11 in 4s, I'm carrying his box tucked in my armpit.

"I've seen you before. . ," I hear a deep voice with a Southern accent say behind me.

I freeze, a familiar heat crawling up my back like it has long claws.

The man snaps his fingers. "Yeah. *Cammie*, right?"

I squeeze my eyes shut at him calling me my old name.

"I mean, how can I forget this fat ass?" Then he whistles under his breath. I can feel his eyes boring a hole into me.

I shouldn't've worn these biker shorts and this cropped tee, I chastise myself.

He steps closer, making me feel his undeniable presence now and smell his loud-ass weed stench. "C'mon, shawty." Then he pulls on my arm, making sure I definitely feel him now.

I yank out of his grasp, whipping around to face him. "*Don't* touch me," I grit lowly, my tone sharp.

My eyes dart around to see if anyone's clocked what's going on. The store's fairly busy with enough eyes around for me to have witnesses. . . But *no* one's paying us any attention over here. Several yards down the wall behind the man, what looks like a mom and her teenage son are trying on shoes.

The man is Black and taller than me by a few inches. He's skinny with tattoos littering his arms. He's wearing a too-small white tee, several platinum chains, Amiri jeans, and sparkly sneakers. His baby dreads look in need of a retwist. His large hand is holding one end of a Jordan shoebox.

I don't remember him from whatever event he's talking about. If only he knew how many functions I went to where so many niggas looked like him. *Shit, I pro'ly didn't even have sex wit' him. . . I pretty much remember all those guys. Hard not to.*

The man is smirking at me like I'm flirting with him. "I like that feisty shit." He licks his dark lips, the store lights catching the iced-out grills in his mouth.

"You must have me confused wit' somebody else."

"Nah, nah, don't do that. Don't act brand new," he chuckles darkly, stepping closer. "I remember you bein' at my homie Lil Souf Man's surprise birthday party in the Hills."

That was, like, two years ago! Memory of that party materializes in my mind. I believe I only slept with one man at that party, the birthday boy. I still don't remember this guy.

"Souf was talm 'bout how tight yo' pussy was. And I was mad as hell that I couldn't fuck you that night. I ain't have my funds together back then and nobody wanted to spot a nigga some skrilla." A creepy smile snakes across his face, revealing more of his grill. "But I got money now, Cammie."

My heart is slamming against my chest and in my ears as I step back, but he follows me. I realize that my arm is crushing Tim's new shoebox. The perfect illustration for the weight of my past pressing in on me right now. *By the way, where the fuck is* my *shoes?!*

"How much you need for me to hit that?" He licks his lips, coming closer. Just no regard for my personal space or my negative body language.

"Look, I 'on't know who you think—"

He smirks amusedly. "Wow, okay. So, you on some whole new life-type shit, huh? I mean, I ain't mad atcha. We all gotta level up, right?" His eyes drag over my body, making my skin itch. "Shit, you was bad then and you *still* bad as hell now." He bites his bottom lip and rubs his bare chin as his eyes meet mine again.

"Miss, your size eight and a half," the teen clerk says behind me, sounding unenthusiastic. I hear them set the shoe box on the bench.

I hope I don't look like I'm cowering under this man's gaze and his closeness, but damn, it would be nice if someone would step in and ask if I was okay!

"Thank you!" I toss over my shoulder before facing this man again. I feel the girl leave to tend to other shoppers.

"You pro'ly got a man now, huh?" He pokes his lips out like he's impressed. "Whoever you wit' now, he a lucky nigga. *But* if you change ya mind, find me on Instagram. I'm good for a few rounds." He winks at me before leaving to get in the short line to pay for his sneakers.

I love how he didn't even tell me his username. *Does he think he's* that *popular that I would know who he is?* He's probably a part of Lil Souf's entourage and gets paid to do whatever he needs—also known as a gotdamn assistant.

I sit down on the bench to try on my shoes, to try to return to normal and not let my frayed nerves get the best of me. I slyly watch the man move up in the line. He pulls his phone out to scroll and when he glances up a few times, I snap my gaze to my shoes, trying to look unbothered.

But my heart doesn't stop thudding, and my shoulders won't relax until I watch him pay and leave out the glass doors with his shopping bag, walking past the store's windows. I push out a deep breath I was holding in, feeling so relieved like I just iced a sore spot.

I have earned every step forward that I've taken out of that life. And *no* one, especially no fucking stranger I don't remember from a party I worked years ago, will take that away from me.

The sneakers fit so I stand in line to pay an arm and a leg for mine and Tim's, but I keep telling myself to loosen my tight jaw, to slow down my erratic heart rate, to untwist my stomach. Inconspicuously, I glance around the store to see if I can spot any other people who want to pop up and remind me who I was for three years.

But thank God, the coast is clear.

By the time I make it to the safety of my truck, I'm exhausted on every level. And pissed. As I drive home, a thought flickers in my mind like a candle in a dark room: *How many more times will I have to encounter remnants of that life now that I've moved on from it? First, Greer and now* this *random guy?!—Not to mention that handler askin' Tim if I'd be interested in doin' porn.*

When I get home, I immediately strip my clothes to shower and scrub the confrontation off my skin. After moisturizing, I try my best to pop Tim's shoebox back into its original shape.

Around six, Tim shows up with some food from Hawkins House of Burgers and his spend-the-night bag. He asks if I can wait for him to shower so we can eat together since he came straight from an event at ill Yamz's childhood community center. This was a planned sleepover, but I almost forgot amidst everything that happened this afternoon.

When he quickly returns from the shower, I show Tim our new sneakers. He's so shocked and hype like a kid because I "copped this grail." His little sneakerhead-speak makes me giggle, it's so cute. He doesn't seem to notice the box's imperfections, but he thanks me by peppering my face with kisses and . . . eating me out so damn good. That takes my mind off the situation from earlier. But only for a few minutes.

After Tim cleans me up, we sit down to eat—thankfully, the food's still warm—and he tells me about Yamz's event and his moving speech to the kids.

Now full, we wrap up in a blanket on the couch in my living room to watch an action movie. Well, *he's* watching it and joking about how predictable the plot is. I laugh at the right places, but my mind is still in Fairfax, still with the man fixated on running back my past hustle. The weight of his confrontation sits heavy and low in my stomach. I hate that I haven't been able to shake it hours later.

Maybe I should hole up in my condo until people forget I was ever a vibe model and an escort. Or better yet, maybe I should move away from Los Angeles altogether—not to go back home, but to go somewhere else. Maybe San Francisco. I don't know anybody up there and that's a good thing. A fresh start for real. I'm sure the hospitality group has another sister property I could work at up there.

Either way, I should go before it gets worse, before the past invades other areas of my life, and things get too deep with Tim. Deeper than they already are. He's already become a fixture in my life, but maybe leaving right now, while it's still early, is for the best.

Maybe I'm overreacting, but who knows—I haven't left situations and people at the right times before. But what I *do* know: I don't think I can take any more moments like today where I have to swat the annoying gnats of my past.

"Camesha, you okay? What's wrong? You were spaced out for a second, baby," Tim says, breaking me out of my head.

I blink back to the present. Glancing at him, I find his concerned face with knitted eyebrows. "It's nothin'," I mumble and clear my throat.

"C'mon, you can talk to me," he says softly as he pauses the movie with the remote.

Oh shit, oh shit, oh shit, I panic.

16
Break, Pt. 2

Tim

Truth is, I noticed Camesha's energy being off the entire time I've been here. When she greeted me at the door, she smiled, and it didn't reach her eyes. But I didn't want to start interrogating her as soon as I got here.

After she gifted me the sneakers and I ate her out, that put a smile on her face—and mine—but that didn't change her energy. Then, I figured maybe she was hungry, which is why I opted for the burgers—something heavy and greasy to stick to our stomachs. But now that she's full, hunger clearly wasn't the problem either. I'm going to figure it out though.

Turning toward her on the couch, my eyes search her face for any tells of what's going on in that beautiful head of hers. "Did some' happen earlier?" I gulp to moisten my throat like that'll prepare me for what she's about to say.

Camesha eyes the blanket. I notice her breathing softly yet rapidly. "It's-It's nothin', Tim." It's *definitely* something.

I clench my jaw, watching her. I want to caress her thigh or hold her—something to let her know that I'm here, that she can trust me with this information. But I don't know if touching her is what's best right now. I've never seen her like this . . . so off, bothered.

"I can leave if you need some space to deal wit' whatever's goin' on," I offer.

A few times, she opens her mouth slightly and closes it, still avoiding eye contact.

Alrighty then, I think, pursing my lips. I take her silence as her wanting me to leave, so I unravel from the blanket to stand up.

"No, stay!" she says, grabbing my hand.

I sit back down and cover her hand with mine. "I'll stay, baby, but you gotta tell me what's goin' on. Hell, I 'on't know, maybe I can fix it or help you." I grin a little, hoping to thin her tension.

But it doesn't. Instead, it thickens. Camesha removes her hand from my grasp and shoots up to her feet. "You can't, Tim!" she groans. She begins pacing the living room, running her hands over her hair.

More than confused, I just sit and watch her with cautious eyes. "What can't I fix or help you wit'? Help me understand," I let out delicately.

Her breathing is ragged as tears start flowing.

My face ticks as something in me shatters, watching my lady break down. Antsy to help her, I slowly stand up and approach her. "May I hold you?"

Camesha stops pacing and nods. We meet each other halfway and she hooks her arms underneath mine to clutch my back as my arms circle her neck. I kiss the top of her hair a few times.

She lets me go and steps back, still avoiding my eyes.

As gently as I could muster, I ask, "Camesha, what's goin' on? Did some' happen?"

She takes a deep breath. "At the sneaker store, a man recognized me from a party I worked two years ago," she sucks up some tears, "and he-he—"

"*Did he hurt you?*" I cut in, my voice sharper than I intended, as my eyebrows pinch together. This is all tripping me up because I've never seen Camesha cry before. Now on top of that, if I hear that a motherfucker hurt her, too, I'm going to fucking lose it.

She shakes her head. "No. He grabbed my arm to get my attention. He kept invadin' my personal space and talkin' to me, tryna make me remember him. He kept tryna see how much—"

I blow out a loud breath to stay calm. I also didn't want her to finish that sentence. Unfortunately, I can connect the dots. *Muhfuckas are bold to do that in public when she ain't in that life no more—Shit, she ain't even move like that when she* was *hustlin'.*

"I-I can't seem to get away from Cammie," Camesha croaks out. "I just wanna disappear for a while. Figure my shit out."

"I'm so sorry, baby." I come forward to wrap my arms around her again.

She doesn't hug me back, which makes me frown. "And-And maybe it's best if I do it by myself," she says, her words muffled against my T-shirt.

I drop my arms from around her and back up. Nodding, I say, "Okay. I get it. But Camesha, ya know you 'on't have to do it all alone, right? That's what I'm here for. You can lean on me. I gotchu."

She tenses up a little like I said something wrong. "I know. And I know you care, Tim. It's just . . . hard to trust that. People have—," she chokes on her words as fresh tears spring up.

I run my hand down her arm in an attempt to soothe her. "You've been through a lot. But know that I'm not goin' anywhere. I'm here for you, fa real." My fingers lightly lift her chin, so she'd look at me.

She swallows, her wet eyes darting between mine before squeezing them shut. "I think I need to do this by myself."

Her words sting. My heart sinks a little. These shouldn't be my reactions because everyone processes shit differently. But I can acknowledge the unexpected hurt.

I let go of her chin. "Okay, I'll leave—But I wanna call or text you tomorrow to check up on you."

"No, like," Camesha swipes tears as they leak out of her closed eyes, "I wanna figure this out by myself," she sucks in a sharp breath, "*outside* of this relationship."

It feels like she just punched me squarely in my chest. In my heart. "Wait, what are you . . . what are you sayin', Camesha? You-You wanna *break up?*"

Her big, beautiful brown eyes open to look at me and she slowly nods her head. "I think I need to."

I shake my head repeatedly, feeling like the air in the room is thinning out as I start to hyperventilate a little. "We-We just gettin' started, baby. I know this is a tough time and I absolutely *hate* that for you. But this is exactly when we need to hold each other closer, *not* let go."

She drops her gaze, still wiping fallen tears.

"Don't do this." My voice sounds like I'm begging. I don't like that. I just don't understand why in the world Camesha wants to deal with this transition by herself when she doesn't have to. She basically said she has trust issues, but still, I could've sworn that she at least trusted *me* at this point.

She shakes her head and mumbles through her tears, "You deserve someone easy, Tim. Someone uncomplicated wit' lil' to no baggage. I've got several luggage sets of shit."

Anger rises up in me, twitching my face. "I don't care. I don't want easy. I *want* you, Camesha. *All* of you," I enunciate. "We all got baggage. We all got shit goin' on. I *met you* while you were hustlin'. That didn't stop me from wantin' you." My nostrils flare as I tighten my jaw. "Muhfuckas like that nigga at the store tryna remind you and suck you back into it *pisses* me the fuck off. I hate that people won't let you move on, like you ain't allowed to or some shit—" I cut myself off, noticing her looking at me now. She doesn't look scared, just stunned. Then I realize my tone escalated.

Bracing my jaw, I drag a hand down my face then blow out some air to calm down. "I'm sorry for raisin' my voice atchu. I just—" I interrupt myself again when I see her shaking her head like she's trying to keep more tears at bay.

But they fall anyway. I cup Camesha's face with both hands, my thumbs swiping away her tears. Her wet eyes look up at me and my heart breaks for her, seeing all the pain swirling in them. Pain she hasn't shared with me.

Camesha

Tim's facial features are soft yet pinched with concern. His jaws are flexing like crazy—I'm sure to calm himself down.

I avert my gaze as overwhelming anxiety and fear swells up inside me like bile, threatening to choke me. "You're too good, Tim. That scares me. I 'on't know how to be wit' a man like you," I say barely above a whisper. "Someone so kind and carin' and empathetic." Another wave of tears spill from my eyes.

He wipes my face, shaking his head. "I ain't *too good*, baby. No one is." Tim inhales deeply. "I'm a good person, but so are you, Camesha. You deserve someone bein' good to you. You deserve it all."

This tug of war is too much. I'm exhausted and I need space to breathe. I pry Tim's hands from my face. I don't dare look at him as he steps back because I know he'd look sad. I really *don't* want to hurt him.

I roughly wipe the rogue tears as I pace again, my mind spinning.

"Don't do that," Tim says firmly.

I stop in my tracks, whipping my head toward him as my eyebrows scrunch up.

"Ya gettin' in ya head, aren't you?" His voice has a slight edge, not mean, but unwavering. Like he's sick of me—or rather, my shit.

Tim gets closer, towering over me, not in an intimidating way, but like he wants me to focus on the fact that he's here. Hard *not* to focus on that. His presence has always been solid, grounding. "I can see it on ya face. Ya self-sabotagin'. Ya tryna push me away."

Damn, he read the fuck outta me like Nikki does, I think. But his voice, his curled-up lips, his wrinkled nose and eyebrows—it all reminds me of when we first hung out in his Jeep, and he was offended that I wanted to Uber home so he could work.

Tim's hands gently cup my face again, but I avoid eye contact. All this shit—Tim stepping back then getting close again, touching me—is going to make me crack.

"I 'on't wanna go anywhere. I'm here because I want to. Because I care about you." He pauses. "Camesha, look at me."

The soft firmness in his voice makes me snap my eyes to his.

"I'm here because I love you." One of Tim's thumbs caress my cheek.

I blink a few times like my brain short-circuited, unsure if I heard him correctly. *He* loves *me? How? Why?*

As if he read my mind, Tim repeats, "*I love you, Camesha.*" He clenches his jaw. "I've known for a while now. Shit, I think I fell in love witchu durin' all those months we texted." He chuckles. "No pun intended, but . . . let me have the chance to handle ya heart correctly. And because I'm *not* perfect, I'm sure I'll *mis*handle it even though that's not my intention. But if I do, please tell me so I 'on't do that shit *ever* again. Like I said from the beginning: I wanna do you right. I wanna be here for you. I can't do that if you push me away."

I feel like I'm going to burst. All of my concocted emotions will reach their boiling point soon enough and I will splatter all over my condo's walls. I can feel the exhaustion coursing through my body. This is all too much to process right now.

"I know it's still very early in our relationship and we're still gettin' to know each other to a degree . . . but I want you, Camesha. The real you. However you come. Baggage, past, flaws and all." He drops his hands from my face and steps back.

I immediately miss his warmth steadying me.

Sighing, Tim glances at the carpet. I can see the turmoil and exhaustion marring his face. A relaxing night turned stressful. "Camesha, I wantchu if you'll have me. But I'll leave if you want me to leave. I 'on't wanna press you—I just needed you to know how I feel." His voice is strained, and his eyes intently search mine. "If you truly feel like this—us breakin' up—is what's best for you to deal wit' all'at you got goin' on right now, that this is whatchu want fa real, I need to hear you say it." He clears his throat. "I'll respect ya decision."

Then like a raging sea calming down—hurricane averted—my wound-up body relaxes. From his intense eye contact to his closeness to when his large warm hands encased my face, forcing me to look at him, I realize how badly I needed to hear Tim say all of that.

I needed to hear him choose me like that. I'm an actions person, but it's as if I was blind to his actions the entire time. I always questioned his genuineness even though I desperately wanted to believe him.

I don't want to lose Tim.

I reach for him, wrapping my arms around his torso and pressing my cheek to his chest, inhaling the calming scent of him and his woody bodywash. He's stiff for a second, like I surprised him, but then he tightly embraces me, too.

So solid. So real. Tim is here. And he wants me. *All* of me.

"My intentions are purely good, Camesha—I promise. I 'on't wanna hurt you, baby. I wanna love you. *Let* me. I'm not goin' anywhere," he reassures me, then plants several kisses to my hair.

I needed to hear him state his true intentions even though everything he's done to this point has shown me them. Mama said trust your gut, but I wasn't listening. I was listening to my anxiety and fear—those terrible sons-of-bitches.

Something hot and overwhelming stirs up inside of me, like smoke coiling up a chimney. I untie my arms from Tim's body and pull his head down to smash my lips to his. He doesn't hesitate to kiss me back passionately, exhaling heavily through his nose. Our vulnerability and frustration dissolve into something deliciously spicy.

When we pull away, our foreheads resting against one another's, we catch our breath.

"I love you, too, Tim," I let out.

A smile tugs on his lips. "You do?"

I nod. "I do. But I was—no, I *am* scared." I squeeze my eyes shut, not to cry sad tears, but overwhelmed ones.

He swipes away some tears before softly pecking my eyelids, my nose, then my lips. "That's okay. But you 'on't have to be perfect or unafraid wit' me. Just be real. Let me be there for you cuz I'm right here. You 'on't have to carry everything on ya own no more. You hear me? I *got* you, Camesha."

And man, I finally, *really* believe Tim.

I hug him tighter. His heartbeat soothing, his warm body grounding me as his hands slowly glide up and down my back.

Tim

It's only a little after 8pm, but we climb into her bed, forgetting about the movie. That conversation exhausted the fuck out of us.

So *much* was said. I don't think I've ever laid out no shit like that to a woman I was dating before—Shit, I ain't never *felt* this way about a woman before. I needed Camesha to know how I feel about her and I wanted to make sure I left nothing out.

I'm kind of sitting up with my back against a pillow, but she decides to slide lower under the covers, laying her head on my stomach. I hold her close.

"Movin' to LA at 19 . . . was a lot. The culture shock hit me harder than I thought it would. I went from Columbia to Los Angeles, and I didn't realize how much of an adjustment it was gonna be. I 'on't think I really got used to it 'til I started hustlin' and needed to be someone else."

My eyes enlarge at that.

Camesha tells me how all that Southern warmth she was raised on didn't translate out here. "Because people were friendly and smiled, I trusted 'em way too easily. I believed their words over their actions. Had it backwards. I pro'ly coulda caught signs that shit might go down if I was payin' attention."

I brace my jaw, shifting in my seat.

Camesha shares a few stories from her early LA days—lessons, she calls them. I just listen intently, slowly rubbing her arm. But I'm not sure if it's to comfort her or me.

She tells me how she met people on Bumble For Friends and a bunch of dating apps. One situation happened her first year here: while still living out of motels, Camesha met a girl who she thought would be her first friend in LA. The girl swore she found them an apartment in Koreatown, but she disappeared after taking Camesha's half of the "security deposit."

She tells me about the clown-ass niggas she used to date, including an influencer I always see in the news for DUIs.

"People say they *gotchu*, that they have ya back and end up stabbin' it. People say they wanna help, but they're unreliable or it comes at a secret price. People lie, steal, ghost, flake."

Camesha exhales loudly through her nose, and I rub her arm slower. "I also learned that people can smell the green on you, so I kept my head on a swivel. I'm sure LA isn't the only city like this, but here, there are vultures just lookin' for a crumb to survive. Even if that crumb is on you. Or *is* you."

She adjusts her head on me. "After my first three and half years in LA, I sharpened up. I *questioned everything*—people's words, actions, their desire to *help*. My mama's voice got louder in my head," then she runs down all her sayings. She pauses and sighs before continuing, "And maybe the hardest one: 'Trust ya gut.'

"My gut has been wrong so many times that it feels like that muscle is weak. So, I 'on't rely on it all the time. I focus on what I can see and what I can control. That's why I rely on myself for the most part." Her voice gets smaller as she fingers a loose thread of her comforter. "Even wit' good friends like Nikki and Oluchi—shit, even witchu, Tim. . ."

My jaw locks and my stomach clenches.

Camesha sighs, "I'm still watchin'. *Waitin'* for people to turn on me."

I lick my lips as my chest tightens. I hate that for her.

"Nikki knows this and will call me out on it when she sees me spiralin'—like she did on July Fourth. She reassures me that she's not goin' anywhere." She pauses and scoffs, "I love her, but that heifer could use her readin' skills to fight crime or some'."

A laugh tumbles out of me as Camesha wraps her arm around my lap.

"I just misread so many people and situations that I really stopped trustin' myself. I didn't wanna keep makin' the same mistakes so, I got out before people got me." She looks up at me. "I actually succeeded in pushin' a man away. He was a good guy and we dated for a few months shortly before I started hustlin'. He wanted to get serious, and I wasn't ready for all'at."

I smirk. "Well, I'm glad I didn't fall for ya argument. Although not *very* convincin' cuz I saw whatchu were doin'."

"You did clock that, didn't you?" she chuckles, snuggling closer to me.

Camesha deeply inhales and exhales. "I was just broke, lonely, and vulnerable, Tim," she says quietly, "I lost myself even more when the whole reason I moved out here was to find myself, to figure out what to do wit' my life."

All of her words sink into me deep. The lessons explain a lot about her. Why she moves the way she does. Why her guard was always halfway up with me.

I kiss the top of her head. "I'm so sorry, Camesha."

"Thank you," she murmurs. Moments later, she softly says, "There's somethin' else I need to tell you, Tim."

My chest tightens and curiosity draws my eyebrows together.

Camesha sits up to look at me. "I've never told *anybody* this. Not ZZ, not my friends, not Simonique."

I swallow as if that will slow my increasing heart rate. "Okay. . ."

Camesha lays back down, cuddling me. I continue rubbing her arm, feeling her skin pebble with goosebumps. She inhales slowly before speaking, "My first year hustlin', I was hired to vibe at a rapper's album-going-platinum party." Pause. "So, later that night, the label owner requested me. I told him my rules, and we went upstairs to his office. He paid me all of it up-front. In cash." *Another* pause.

I swallow again, waiting for her to continue.

"I've always had rules. Not nearly as many as I had before I left the hustle though." Camesha sharply inhales. "But he-he—," she stops, choked up.

My jaw locks. My heart rams against my ribcage. But I have to calm down to hear Camesha. I don't want my nervous energy to make her go quiet. So, I lean down to press a long kiss to her hair, encouraging her to continue. To let her know that I'm right here.

Camesha sucks in a deep breath before telling me how this motherfucker didn't put on a condom and tried *twice* to make her give him head. But on his second attempt, she escaped.

I bring her closer to me, sharply breathing through my nose and looking up at the ceiling, thinking, *Thank God!*

No lie, throughout her story, it took everything in me to remain calm and *just* listen, not react. I'm just so pissed off that she went through that.

"The handler never even paid me the rest of my money for vibe modelin' that night," Camesha scoffs, like she's trying to gloss over what she just said.

Her fingers play with the same thread as before. "I later found out that the man was also on pills—Not that that matters." She takes in a deep breath. "After that, I got stricter. Made sure all clients wore condoms. Made sure clients weren't on hard drugs. Bought a self-defense kit to carry wit' me. And I started bein' nice to security at events." She pauses. "Cuz that night, I barely acknowledged 'em, Tim. They were all downstairs, spread thin. But I *really* coulda used some help back then," her voice cracks like she might cry.

Squeezing my eyes closed to restrain the tears pricking my eyeline, I rasp, "Camesha, I'm—"

"That's not it." She unravels from my arms and sits up to look at me.

My eyebrows scrunch up, worried, my heart beating so loud in my ears.

"At the time, he didn't have any allegations. But now? So many women have come forward—" Camesha's voice catches as she drops her head. "He hurt *a lot* of women. And in a way, he hurt me, too, but not like that," she says all low.

I almost jump in to tell her that just because he wasn't violent with her doesn't mean he didn't violate her, but she keeps going,

"What he did to those women? It just—It coulda *easily* been me, too." Her voice breaks and my heart breaks for her.

I suck in a deep breath and lean forward to collect her in my arms. She buries her face in my chest, clutching my waist, and bawls.

"Tim, it was Raw Math," Camesha's words come out wet and muffled against my shirt.

The way my heart plummets to my ass, I want to make sure I heard her correctly. "Wh-What?"

She backs out of our embrace, wiping her tears. "It was . . . Raw Math," she calmly repeats, but I can hear the tremor underneath.

My body freezes, even though I'm hot. With shock, anger, disgust. But they're all understatements.

Raw Math clearly doesn't know what no means and what boundaries are. That nigga violated Camesha's. And she's been carrying that alone for years.

This . . . This is just so fucked-up. I'm a little speechless but I *praise God* that Camesha's okay. As far as I can tell.

Camesha

I can see the mixed emotions playing on Tim's handsome face as the big truth I was withholding from him now hangs in the air like a chandelier swaying on a weak chain. I'm sure learning what one of his old clients did to his lady a couple years ago is a lot to process.

Even though my heart is shuddering and slamming hard in my chest, I also feel a serenity settle over me as my goosebumps fade. It's a weird feeling inside. But telling somebody—especially Tim—relieves the weight I've been holding for too long.

Tim bites down on his jaw so hard, I'm afraid his teeth might shatter. His eyebrows pinch together something serious. He twists his mouth up, like he's holding back words that want to come out.

Then I notice his eyes. They're almost *vibrating*, brimming with tears. He glances up at the ceiling as if to stop himself from crying. Seeing that makes my tears flow out.

Tim sucks in a deep breath and gathers me into another hug. "I'm so sorry that muthafucka did that to you, Camesha." His usually warm voice is now sharp and strained.

Still crying, all of my tears from the night now ingrained in his T-shirt's fabric, I nod my head.

"I fuckin'—," Tim cuts himself off.

I back out of his arms and wipe his escaped tears.

"Fuck. Him." He sniffles, clenching his jaws. "And that nigga doesn't get a pass cuz he was drunk and high."

"Of course not," I mumble. Something might be wrong with me because Tim's pissed voice is turning me on. *Settle down, ma'am.*

Tim removes my hands from his face and holds them between us. "I'm okay, baby. I'm okay. How are *you* though?" he croaks out.

A smile worms onto my face. "I actually feel much better," I chuckle and sniffle, too.

He smirks and brings my hands up to kiss my knuckles. He's still flexing his jaw.

I drop my head, looking at our hands. His engulfing mine. Safe. "I think I wanna go to therapy," I mutter.

I hear him take in a deep breath. "Whatever you wanna do, I gotchu, Camesha."

I lift my head to peer up at him.

"If you want, I can even help you find a therapist. Make sure you find one that you click wit'."

A grin tugs at my lips. "I'd like that. Thanks."

"Of course, baby." He leans forward to press a long kiss to my forehead. "I love you, Camesha."

"I love you, too, Tim."

17

I Got You

Camesha

After my breakdown in front of Tim a few weeks ago, we kept talking, crying, and laughing until we fell asleep in each other's arms. I'm not that heavy of a sleeper, but I think all those heavy-ass emotions, bawling my eyes out, and exposing my heart and past wore me the fuck out. That dusty nigga confronting me in public just showed me that even though I've moved on from that life, the past doesn't stay buried until it's addressed head-on. Which is why I'm glad I told Tim what Raw Math did to me.

In the morning, Tim made brunch and served it to me in bed. I didn't really want space anymore now that I got all that out, so I asked him to stay with me all day Sunday. We just streamed a church service from one of his favorite pastors, finally finished that predictable action movie, and he whipped up some dinner using one of the courtyard grills.

The following week, Tim made sure to call me every day after work. One day, he called on his way to a cypher that one of his clients was doing on a rooftop bar and this new nickname slipped out: I called him Tree. It fits Tim so well! He's tall, slim, and has been such a grounding presence in my life that Tree just makes sense. When I'm feeling goofy, I call him Timmy Tree, but he'll only respond to Tree now . . . reluctantly.

I have also been heavily leaning on my girls, too. I need Nikki's silliness and Oluchi's guidance more than ever—balance. We try to get together at least once a week after work or on the weekends.

This past Friday, we met up at Bassment 323. Nikki got us a table on short notice again, working her charm on Cassidy. When he checked up on us for the third time during our three-hour stay, his eyes lingering on Nikki like they usually do, she squirmed and smirked and I *thought* I saw her blush, but it was too dark to confirm. Lu and I made eye contact and, rolling her eyes, Nikki said, "A'ight, g'on and ask." We did and she confirmed that she's giving Cassidy a chance! I was so happy, and Lu exhaled a "Finally."

Nikki told us that she ran into Cassidy at the farmer's market one day. They talked and she discovered that "he's actually kinda handsome and funny"—her exact words. He's not her typical type—he's bald, has stubble, isn't ripped, and isn't toxic—but she said because she's getting older so why block her blessings because of a type? I agree. I wouldn't say I have a type, but I've never met anyone like Tim before. And what a blessing he's been.

Then Lu told us that she's interested in getting to know Bryan romantically. On Labor Day, my girls and I hung out with Tim and his boys at Jaquade's house. Without Tim's or my prompting, Lu and Bryan gravitated toward one other and chopped it up in a quiet corner of Jaquade's backyard. Like I suspected, Quade and Nikki were cracking on each other and arguing—not seriously, but still, it got tiring after a while, and Tim and I left them alone to go play with Mic, the dog.

But today, no hangout. Although with it being mid-70s and sunny all day, we could've done something.

I pull into a parking spot in front of my building, and several texts come through:

Lu (7:47pm):

> Bryan finally asked me out! ☒

Nikki (7:47pm):

> Yaaasss bitch!

Me (7:48pm):

> Yay! What are you gonna say? ☒

Nikki (7:48pm):

> It better be a yes, tf! I know that much

Lu (7:48pm):

> Of course, Nik ☒I think I like him ☒

Me (7:49pm):

> Awww, Lu☒

I smile big rereading our thread, waiting to see if either of them will send more rapid-fire responses.

Oluchi hasn't dated anyone in years, having been focused on building up her real estate career, so I'm happy she's giving Bryan a chance.

After gathering my stuff, I head inside my condo. Like I do most days after work, I immediately shower then change into some loungewear.

Tonight's prepped dinner is a Buddha bowl, so after assembling that, I sit at my dining table and turn on an episode of *Girlfriends*. I would call Tim, but I knew he'd be busy all day with the press tour of Rugged Rah and ill Yamz's deluxe version of *Black Like We Always Here*. When the project dropped, Tim played all 15 songs for me at his house, nerding out about all the "literary devices" and references they used. I just watched and listened to him talk, loving how much he revered their artistry.

Which is why I'm happy Tim's giving songwriting a try. He spoke to Keyana Renay, and she set up a writing session with him later this week. He's nervous about that but I'm so excited for him. If he can write me lovely poems, I'm sure he can help her write R&B songs.

With one episode down and my bowl empty, I curl up on my couch with some wine and watch the next one. Then at 9pm, my phone rings. *Wow, right on time.*

It's a FaceTime request from my mama. Since telling my folks about my new job and my regular work hours, we've decided to start scheduling FaceTime check-ins at least once a month. I pause my show and sit up before accepting the call.

My parents pop up on the screen, looking like they're sitting in the living room as the phone is probably propped up on the coffee table. Mama is snuggling into Daddy as his arm is around her. He's still wearing his custodial uniform, and she's dressed down, having always gotten home from work before him.

Besides my parents both having a pecan-brown skin tone, they look like they've gotten darker after being outside at all them cookouts I hear them going to. It seems like every time I text or call them, they're telling me they just got back from a function or been invited to one.

"Hey, guys!" I say, my face creasing. This is my first time seeing them since I went home for Simonique's graduation.

"Hey, darlin'!" Daddy says, his gap on display.

"Hey, baby!" Mama adds, beaming, showing her gap, too.

"Y'all look good." Looks like Daddy is growing out his salt-and-pepper hair per Mama's request and her latest wig is all voluminous and burgundy, courtesy of Lanelle.

Daddy blushes and glances away, and Mama says, "Thank you, honey. You look beautiful." Daddy nods in agreement.

"Thank you."

"So, you just got off work?"

"Few hours ago."

"Oh okay." Mama nods.

Daddy glances at Mama before jumping in, "So, Simonique tells us you have a boyfriend? Camesha, when were you gonna tell us?"

I fight the urge to roll my eyes and instead, I grip the bridge of my nose. *Of course, Nique ran her big-ass mouth.* I called her after my breakdown and told her what happened: how Tim expressed that he loves me and how I told him that I feel the same way, but I'm scared. She squealed, super excited for me, making me blush. Like Nikki, she affirmed that I deserve this love.

But I should've known that she was going to tell our parents. Besides my first relationship, which lasted from 11th grade up until I left for Los Angeles, I haven't told my parents about the other guys I dated. One, because they weren't serious to me, and two, because I don't want to share something that may not last. But Tim? He made it clear that he wants me long term. And I want the same with him.

I exhale, "Uh, soon. I wanted to wait to see if it was serious."

"Well? Is it?" Mama says, side-eyeing me in anticipation.

I look off coyly.

"Camesha," Daddy says firmly.

"It is." I laugh.

Mama's mouth drops open. "Ooo, well tell us about him! This yo' first boyfriend since Travis or just the second one *we* know about?" She clocks me. *Damn, am I just* that *easy to read or does e'rybody know me so well? Do I need to slip Cammie on to stay a tad mysterious?—No, no, no, we're not goin' back to her.*

"Yeah, tell us 'bout this young man," Daddy prompts, looking serious, an eyebrow raised, while Mama is sitting there all excited like Simonique did when I told her about Tim.

I haven't and don't plan on *ever* telling them about my hustle, so I keep it vague, saying I met Tim at a work event and how our first conversations were welcomed distractions.

Mama interjects, "He works at ya old hotel?"

"No, he's a handler for rappers and singers."

"A *what?*" Daddy asks, tilting his head.

I chortle. "He's, like, an on-call special assistant for several artists. He handles emergencies and puts stuff together like that party."

"Sounds like a busy man. He got time for you?" Daddy asks.

Mama playfully slaps his arm. "Clif!"

"I'm just sayin', LaWanda—if the boy on-call, when he gon' see Camesha and take her on dates?"

I miss this—Daddy watching out for me. He questioned the *hell* out of Travis when I first introduced them after Travis asked me to the homecoming dance junior year.

Giggling at their banter, I say, "Daddy, he makes time and he's good about textin' and callin' me. He's very reachable. Plus, he started takin' days off to rest and see me more."

"I know that's right!" Mama says, snapping her fingers.

Daddy nods and I continue the story, ending it with how we reconnected after the seven-monthslong award season, our first official date, and how Tim asked me to be his girlfriend by performing spoken word. Mama is impressed, cooing in awe, and Daddy is . . . happy for me, but skeptical.

"That's great, Camesha. Glad to hear someone's treatin' you right. I'd still love to meet him—ya know, get a feel for him and shit," Daddy says.

"Of course. But when you meet him, don't do him like you did Travis. He's not a *knucklehead*," I giggle.

"I'll be the judge of that, darlin'." He jabs a finger in his chest all serious. "But fa real, he sounds like a good dude—got his head on his shoulders. I can't promise I'll go easier on him since you still my baby and all."

I squirm in my seat, blushing.

"This is wonderful, honey. I'm happy for you. I can't wait to meet him," Mama chimes in, smiling ear to ear. "Have you met his family yet?"

"Yeah, I met his mom on FaceTime last month. She called after his birthday."

"Awww, that's nice."

I'm happy neither of them asked about his dad. I think that's something Tim should divulge when he's ready.

To change the subject, I ask, "So, how's Nique? She texted me that she started her new job, but I haven't been able to talk to her 'bout it yet."

Simonique and her friend Destiny moved into an apartment right outside of Columbia and spent time decorating and getting settled before they both started their new jobs after Labor Day.

With all her Clemson and business experience, Nique was able to snag a mid-level marketing specialist position at a niche advertising agency in downtown Columbia. Mama tells me that she loves her "big girl job." Her co-workers respect her expertise and appreciate her ideas.

Because she's acclimating to her new job, she's taking on less event planning clients, much to Montrell's dismay. I'm sure he's also upset because they won't be spending as much time together. Either way Simonique is making moves, and I couldn't be a prouder sister. I will have to send her a little something-something to show her.

My parents and I chat for 30 more minutes—updating me on extended family drama and nonsense at their jobs—before we end the FaceTime. I will definitely set up a call so they can meet Tim soon.

Thursday, September 20

Tim

I punch in the code Keyana told me over the phone, and her gates open up to a stone-paved driveway. I've been to her modern Mediterranean house a few times before for stuff—fittings, photo shoots, parties—but not in *this* way. After Camesha spilled the beans to her that I write poetry, Key hit me up about it a few times and I kept putting it off, too anxious to share my work with her.

Keyana and her songwriting partner, Corryn, pen all her songs—soft and savage, but always honest, sung in Keyana's velvety voice that have won her millions of fans, money, and accolades. So, I was surprised that *she* was impressed with the poems I shared and wanted to see if "we can make some magic happen" in a writing session. I can't lie, I'm sweating like I'm in that Texas heat, and my heart feels like it's competing in the Kentucky Derby, galloping hard as shit.

Just as I turn off the engine and get out my Jeep, my phone rings. I look down at it, seeing it's Terrence White. Furrowing my eyebrows, I answer, "Whassup, Terrence?"

"Hey, Tim! I catch you at a bad time?"

"I got a few minutes." I arrived 10 minutes early. *Nervous-ass nigga*, my inner self says.

"Cool, I just wanted to thank you again for ya help in the studio a while back cuz we're usin' that bridge you wrote for the song."

In shock, my neck extends, and my eyes enlarge. "Wait, fa real?"

"Yeah. I had to sit wit' it for a while—mull it over. But when I shared it with my team, they loved the song, but they *especially* kept callin' out ya bridge as some' that'll really resonate with my audience."

"Now I've sung to crowds, and I've won some things.
But nothin' feels better than wearin' ya ring.
All them stages, bright lights, fame, and gold
can't compete wit' the way you hold
my hand when life is heavy.
Ya love, steady and ready.
Girl, you taught me what it means
to be truly seen," Terrence sings in his buttery-smooth voice.

"Oh yeah, that definitely sounds amazin' witchu singin' it."

He chuckles. "Well, you wrote good shit, man, so I called to thank you, Tim. You might've helped me write a hit song. You will definitely get a songwritin' credit."

"What—Wow—Uh," my tongue trips me up. "Terrence, I—," I laugh incredulously. "Thank you, man. Thank you."

"Thank *you*. Be on the lookout for when our song hits the airwaves. My team and I will definitely call you to work out the credits and all the legal shit. I just wanted to share the good news witcha first."

My hand runs over my hair as I look around with enlarged eyes, like *is this real life? I helped Terrence White write a song. . . I have to tell Ma 'bout this.* She was hype as fuck when I texted her those pictures of us, so when I tell her this? She will definitely flip!

"This is definitely good—no, *awesome* news. I'm actually at Keyana Renay's crib right now for our first songwritin' session."

"Nice! See, ya where ya 'posed to be, Tim." I imagine him with a wide grin on his face, nodding his head.

"Thank you, man, I really 'preciate this. I'll watch my phone for y'all's calls."

He chuckles, "Great. Well, don't leave Miss Renay hangin'. Can't wait to hear what y'all put out."

"Shit, me neither."

He laughs before we hang up. And I do a victory dance in Keyana's motor court, face hurting from smiling so hard. After I compose myself, I walk up to her ornate wooden door and ring the doorbell. Moments later, I hear the locks disengage and the door swings open, revealing Keyana in an oversized graphic tee, leggings, fuzzy flipflops, and her hair in a messy top bun with a printed silk scarf around her edges.

"Hey, Tim!" She beckons me inside, welcoming me into a side-hug.

My smile widens. "Whaddup, Key?"

She closes the door. "I knew you were reliable, but my God, you're early."

"Just seven minutes early." I chuckle.

She shrugs. "You want anything?"

"Some water would be good."

She nods and I follow her to her kitchen. Keyana's house is Keyana to a tee: warm, sensual, and romantic. It's not too big for one person, but spacious enough to not feel crammed, letting her creative juices flow freely. After opening her fridge, she hands me a fancy bottle of Icelandic water.

"Bougie ass," I murmur as I uncap it.

"Shut up! Someone gifted me those," she laughs.

I chug some to drown my anxiety and cool off. She has the air blowing in here, but my nerves are flaring like I'm having a hot flash.

"You ready?" she asks, quirking up an eyebrow.

Looking at her over my bottle, I shrug.

Keyana giggles a "C'mon" before heading down the hallway until we're in her studio. Moody lighting, jewel-tone colors, and her favorite cozy materials: velvet and silk. A table is along one wall with office chairs pulled up to it. A curvy sofa lines the wall opposite the door. The mixing board faces the window into the dark booth.

I spin to get a good look around. "This is really nice. I 'on't think I've ever been in here before."

"That's cuz I just got it decorated the way I wanted."

"You really are in ya velvet season, huh?" I joke, using her album title.

"Absolutely." She sits in one of her office chairs.

I drop into a chair. "So, is Corryn joinin' us?"

"No, it's just me and you today. Wanted to see ya process without too many people around."

"I 'preciate that cuz this is already nerve-rackin' enough," I chuckle around the lump rising in my throat.

"*You're* nervous, Tim?" Her facial expression is open in surprise.

"Hell yeah, Keyana." I scratch the back of my head, looking at her with an arched eyebrow. "Do you know *how* many hit songs you got?"

She smiles humbly and glances at her lap, but I know she'd tell a motherfucker off real quick if they don't acknowledge that she been putting in work. She didn't sleep her way to her success.

"Ya pen game is sharp."

"I 'preciate that, Tim," her hands fly to her heart, "but don't sell ya'self short. You got skills and a voice." She pauses, tilting her head. "And were all the poems you sent me 'bout Camesha?"

"Yeah. . . She's inspired me these last few months to write again." Now *I'm* bashful, avoiding eye contact as my neck twitches just thinking about my lady.

"Awww, that's so cute! I'm so happy for y'all." She beams. "And when y'all wanna get married, make sure you invite me to the wedding since I *kinda* helped plan ya first date." She side-eyes me.

A big smile tugs at my lips. "Oh, fa sho. Shit, I might ask you to sing."

"Say less, I gotchu!" She points at me. "Well, I'm definitely eager to see what we can do in the next three hours." She scoots up to the table where there's some notepads, journals, and pens. *Ah, she's also old school.*

"Same." I clear my throat. "Look, I also wanted to talk to you 'bout some' else, Key."

Her eyes enlarge as she turns to face me. "Uh oh. What?"

I swallow, my hand rubbing my now tense neck. "I'm thinkin' 'bout not bein' a handler anymore. . ."

Her mouth morphs into an O shape. "Really?"

"Yeah. . . I 'on't know, I've always wanted to become an A&R, but now I'm rethinkin' that. And ya know Terrence White offered me the job to be his executive assistant on his next world tour?"

"Terrence White?! Fa real?" Her eyes get bigger.

"Yeah," I laugh, "But it starts next month, and it'd last for six. He was gonna pay me *very* well, but I turned him down."

"Awww." Her eyebrows meet.

"But check this out: when I met wit' him to turn him down, he was in the studio writin' a song. I offered some ideas for his bridge, and he just called me when I pulled up to tell me that he's usin' my lyrics."

"Tim!" She playfully slaps my arm like *shut up!* "That's *amazing*. When is the song comin' out?"

"Soon, so listen out for it."

"I will. So, why the hell are you nervous to write wit' *me*?" Keyana's hands fly to her chest again. "*You* wrote wit' the muthafuckin' legendary Terrence White! *I've* never done that."

I cackle, thinking back on that surreal experience. "I told him 'bout this session, and he said he's a fan of yours. He admires ya 'refreshin' honesty' as he called it."

She throws her hands up, eyes closed. "Oh my God, Terrence White is a fan of mine? Mama, I've made it." She fishes her pants pockets for her phone. "Nah, fa real, I gotta tell her. She *loooves* that man."

"I told my mom, too," I laugh, watching her feverishly tap out a text to her mother.

After she sends it, she sets her phone on the side of the table. "This is awesome, Tim—Wait, so when will you decide to for sure quit handlin'?"

"Depends on how well Terrence's song does and how well this session goes. So, let's make a hit so I can quit," I chortle.

"I gotchu." She smiles but it quickly falls. "But I ain't gon' lie, I'mma miss you handlin' shit for me. You *always* get stuff done so fast."

"I know, I'm the best," I shrug, making her laugh.

"You are! But I think if we write some' good, I might be able to keep workin' witchu. And shit, wit' a Terrence *and* a Keyana credit, you'll be way too busy to be a handler anyway."

I sit back in the chair, my thoughts spinning to weave an image of what my life could look like. Writing songs in studios with artists I admire. Attending award shows—*not* as a handler, but as a nominee. Spending more time with Camesha, my friends, and traveling back home to see my mom more. A slower pace of life—well, maybe. But life looks really good, really fulfilling in that vision.

"Let's get to work then." I rub my hands together.

Keyana smiles and, as if a mask falls over her face, she slips into professional mode. She tells me that last minute she decided the deluxe *Velvet Season* needed one more song—one about her needing her new lover to intentionally make time for her.

She opens up a journal, and I gather a notepad and pen. Keyana's very focused as she flips through her journal which she tells me holds her daily entries, lyrics, performance ideas, and anything else. After being in therapy, she says she carries one everywhere now.

Those three hours fly because it seems like I blink, and her doorbell is ringing. Her glam squad and stylist are here to prepare her for a label dinner.

We're both proud of what we came up with. We rightly called our song "Reservation." I can't wait for her producer to cook up a beat for this and hear her sing our words. I just feel honored that she wanted to work on her music with *me*, a whole noob.

Sunday, September 23

I'm sitting at my dining table, cleaning out my email while Camesha cooks dinner over the stove, using whatever ingredients I had. She slept over last night after our salsa dance class and bar hopping. She's playing her music through my Bluetooth speaker—some Cleo Sol, some Ari Lennox.

"Mmm, smells good over there. Whatchu makin'?" I ask.

"It's a surprise, Tree." She glances over her shoulder , wiggling her eyebrows.

I scoff at her new nickname for me and laugh. "How's it a surprise when you got all the ingredients in *my* kitchen?"

"Because you clearly 'on't know what I'm makin' wit' *your* ingredients, right?" She narrows her eyes at me.

I nod. "True."

"Just sit tight. I'm almost done, baby."

"Yes ma'am. . ." my voice trails off as my eyes focus in on a subject line.

It's a reply to a poem submission I sent three months ago. I didn't tell anyone—I just quietly submitted some poems to a few magazines on a whim to see if someone would want to publish me.

My heart races like I've never been rejected before. My body heats up with roiling anxiety.

I huff out a breath. It must've been loud enough over the music fading out because out of my peripheral, I see Camesha spin around, holding a kitchen utensil. "Tim? You okay?"

"Yeah," I rush out. But then I shake my head and tell her the truth, "Uh, no actually."

She sets the utensil down and pads over to me in her slippers. "What's wrong?" Her hand finds the back of my head, lightly caressing it as she looks at my screen.

"I got an email, respondin' to a poem I submitted to a journal months ago."

"You submitted a poem?" She whips her head to me, excitement brightening her face. "Why didn't you tell me, baby?"

"Wasn't nuttn to tell."

"Sure, there is, Tim. That's a big deal. You put ya'self out there. Is this ya first time doin' this?"

"I submitted a few poems at one time, but yeah," I manage to say over the lump growing in my throat.

Camesha resumes rubbing my head. "Well, I'm proud of you." She kisses my hair.

"Don't get too proud. I 'on't know what they said. I already got four other rejections." I exhale another big breath as the anxiety spins faster and wilder inside. I turn to peer up at her. "Actually, can you read it for me? I 'on't think I can do it."

"Of course." She smiles and bends to look at my screen. I turn my head, looking through the glass sliding door to my backyard. I hear her use the mouse to open the email.

"What's it say, Camesha?" I ask impatiently.

"It says that," she pauses, and I hold my breath, "they accepted ya poem," she softly says.

"What?" I damn-near yell, snapping my head to the screen.

"They wanna publish ya poem, Tim!"

I read the words for myself:

Dear Tim,

We're pleased to inform you that your poem "Resonate" has been accepted for publication in our upcoming Winter issue.

That's as far as I go before I stand up and wrap Camesha up in my arms. I pick her up and spin her around. She giggles in my ear as I attack her neck with kisses. "Ya boy's gonna be a published poet!"

I set her feet on the ground and give her a real kiss. We pull away and, with my face in her hands, she says, "*And* a songwriter. I'm so proud and excited for you, Tim"

"Thank you, baby."

With fall officially here, it's definitely a new season all right: from writing songs to publishing a poem... Man, God is showing out for real.

"And I need to read or hear this poem." She backs up, pointing a finger at me.

I chuckle, "*After* you feed me. I can't perform on an empty stomach, girl," I say, clutching my torso. Truth is, I made us a nice brunch a few hours ago, and while I'm not starving, I could definitely eat. Especially since she got it smelling hella good in here. *Big-back ass.*

"I gotchu." She presses a kiss to my lips before unraveling from my arms to head back to the kitchen.

"And *I* got you." I slap her ass, watching it jiggle in her joggers.

We've been saying that a lot to each other after we both bared our souls to each other last month after that nigga confronted Camesha in public. It's a simple affirmation, but a powerful one.

I got her. She got me. Period.

18
New Season

A Year Later

Camesha

After a few FaceTimes, I took Tim home with me last Thanksgiving for the first time and my parents fell in *love* with him. Mama catered to him with that Southern hospitality, making sure he was comfortable. Daddy tried to interrogate him. But just like when he met my friends and Nikki grilled him, Tim rolled with the questioning so well that Daddy let up and just enjoyed him. Shit, he made both of my parents crack the fuck up! Now, they ask about Tim all the time when we're not FaceTiming them together.

I spent that Christmas with Tim and his mom in San Antonio. Meeting her in person was great. She was pleased to have another woman in the house since it's always just been her with Tim and "her Gregory," as she called her husband and Tim's father. They both shared stories of Mr. Starks and it made my heart swell, hearing the love and respect they have for him. I wish I could bring him back just so they can love on him in the flesh, but I'm sure he's watching them in Heaven with the same amount of adoration they have for him.

December through mid-January was *very* busy at The Aubade retreat, too. I asked my manager Nile to low-key hold my hand through that time as I dealt with booking holiday parties, handling travelers, and even working out the kinks for guest performers. It was definitely a crash course on what the busy season looked like and how to handle it as the assistant service manager.

But once things slowed down, I got serious about finding a therapist. Tim helped me and, after two months of sessions to try some folks out, I landed on a woman whom I've been seeing ever since.

It's been a wonderful experience having Casey, someone whom I can dump all that I've been holding inside and she's able to help me sort through those puzzle pieces so we can make sense of the image they make. We've been addressing my past, my ideas around purpose and love, my feelings about my sex work . . . the Raw Math situation—everything. She even encouraged me to do school nervous. And to *at least* talk to Tim's interior designer friend.

Over the summer, I started a hospitality management certificate program. Baby steps to get the degree later if I find that that's necessary to continue moving up the ladder. Then I asked Tim to introduce me to his interior designer friend.

He invited her over to his house for dinner and I was so *shook* when I met Adama Hughes! I froze—actually starstruck because I watched her YouTube channel religiously for inspiration when I was decorating my condo. Tim's best-boyfriend points went up just because he knows her. He let us talk in private in the living room after dinner while he chilled on his back porch. I definitely gushed like a teenage girl, but she was sweet and answered all my questions.

So far, I'm able to manage everything: doing classwork after work and on weekends, if I'm not exhausted, I'm kind of

Adama's apprentice, shadowing and assisting her! She even asks for my opinion on stuff to gauge my design eye.

Plus, shortly after meeting Adama, I moved into Tim's house. He was so excited for me and wanted to support me while I studied for my certificate—cooking more, rubbing my feet as I studied, etc.—and he figured he could do that better if we lived in the same place. So, I decided to sell my condo and moved in with him since his house was bigger and it's closer to The Aubade. He turned his second bedroom into my office, so that I have a separate space to do my schoolwork when I want to.

But right now, I'm lounging on the sectional in the living room with Tim. We're sitting on opposite ends, our legs tangled up. I'm reviewing my typed notes while he writes on his notepad. I'm not sure if it's a poem or a song he's working on, but I enjoy our quiet working hours.

Tim

Camesha taps her foot against my thigh as her eyes scan her touchscreen laptop. Unbeknownst to her, I've been writing a song to the rhythm of her foot taps. The song's not for anyone in particular, I just like to do this every once in a while to stay sharp. I don't know if Camesha's aware that she can keep good rhythm for 45 minutes, but I'm sure it does something for her focus when studying.

I'm super proud of her for doing this program to level up in her hospitality career. One day without telling her, I got lunch at The Aubade *just* to watch her work. She looked so sexy in her uniform, gracefully moving around and ordering waitstaff. When she made her rounds to check on customers, she almost leaped out of her skin when she got to my little table.

Last year, the song I helped Terrence White write, "You Showed Up," did *very* well when he finally released it right before going on tour last October. I had to pull over on the freeway when I heard it on the radio for the first time and videotaped myself singing along to it. I sent that to my mom and posted it on my Instagram, mentioning how I'm one of the songwriters. The song did so well that he told me he added it to his setlist while he was on tour. It was his newest hit, but fans sang it like it was one of his older crowd favorites.

Keyana Renay's song "Reservation" sounded as good as I imagined it would with her singing softly over a sparse guitar beat. Women even started using the song as a sound for funny videos of them mouthing the lyrics to their partners, asking them to spend time with them. Keyana loved the new life her music was taking on, especially when she finally dropped that deluxe *Velvet Season*.

After both of those songs made waves and my name being attached to them made their rounds in the industry, my phone started going *off*. I'm talking emails and calls from some of my favorite artists' teams—and even my old handling client Amber Royce wanted me to write something for her! Other clients congratulated me on the success, and Zay Dubb$ jokingly said that he didn't know I was an "R&B nigga." I decided to tell clients I was done handling right before Camesha and I flew to be with her family on Thanksgiving.

Camesha's mom was sweet and hospitable. I could tell her dad didn't *want* to like me at first with all his questions and hard faces, but he eased up on me, and we chopped it up like old friends. Simonique was her usual crazy self, making me howl laughing the whole time. Camesha got a little jealous that me and her sister soon had inside jokes. I checked in with my mom throughout the trip since I'd usually spend the holiday with her, but she assured me that she was fine, hanging out at a friend's house.

Christmas with Ma was especially nice with Camesha there. Ma really enjoyed Camesha's company, and I loved being able to share more of where I came from with my lady, from stories about Pops to showing her places I used to hang out at in high school.

Coming back from the holiday travel, I hit the ground running with songwriting sessions. Meeting artists I love and have never worked with before to working with some I've met as a handler but now being reintroduced as a songwriter?.. Shit hit different.

When Terrence White returned after his tour was over, he hosted a huge wrap-up party at his mansion in Malibu. Camesha and I were able to meet his wife, his adult children, and other legends in the R&B game that I had to take pictures with.

Terrence enlisted me for a few more songs and released that album to critical acclaim a month ago. With my songwriting credits and all these pictures and videos with artists, my Instagram following has skyrocketed from 5,000 to over 25,000. It's just incredible—the rooms I'm able to walk in now, the opportunities I'm able to receive, the accolades I'm able to celebrate.

All because I fell in love with a woman who inspired me. I've just been thanking God nonstop for all of this.

I'm happy Camesha moved in with me, too. I love coming home to her or welcoming her with a hot meal and foot rubs when she gets off work. We still meal prep but, because I don't have to run ragged all over the place anymore as a handler, I can be at home writing and cooking more.

She's been *killing* it with Adama, too! I didn't want to force Camesha to meet her, but I just so badly wanted her to give her dream a chance. It made me giddy when she asked me to introduce them. Now, I just sit and watch her nerd out about a project when she comes home after shadowing Adama.

With all that Camesha's learned, she's upgraded the house's interior design and even helped me finish the backyard, so that

Jaquade's house isn't the only house fit for entertaining our friends.

Speaking of, Bryan and Oluchi are together! And Nikki has been on and off with Cassidy. If it was up to Cassidy, she'd be his wife by now, but I think Nikki still likes to play games. The man's patient, but not *that* patient, so I hope she's not taking advantage of him.

But anyway, sitting here, watching Camesha study with her curly hair in a half up-half down style, wearing one of my old hoodies, a thought hits me out of nowhere.

"What if we had a kid?" the words leave my mouth before I can stop them. I drop the notepad and pen on my lap.

She stops scrolling on her laptop and her gaze lifts to mine. She blinks. "Wh-Whaat?"

I shrug, trying to play it off even though my heart is fluttering like it's got hundreds of butterflies trapped in it. "I'm just sayin' ... *what if?* That wouldn't be crazy, would it?"

She stares at me wide-eyed with shock. Her mouth opens and closes a few times like her brain short-circuited.

I rub her calves, my mouth twitching to not laugh. "Relax. I'm not sayin' right now or anything. Just, ya know . . . in the future."

"Okay, yeah in the *future*." She blinks again, seeming to regain herself. "Where did that even come from?"

"You over there, lookin' all cute and studious, and it hit me."

She giggles.

I lean forward to caress her face with my thumb. "Shit, watchin' you kill it these last few months, I *know* you'd be a *great* mom."

Camesha looks stunned but then her face softens and red blooms under her brown cheeks. "You really think so?" she asks quietly.

"Absolutely. And ya definitely a better student than I was. Bryan helped me study, but I crammed way too much."

She busts out laughing.

"I'm serious, girl," I say while laughing, too. "God definitely helped me get my 3.4 GPA in college."

"You a mess," she chortles.

"I *was*. But you been cleanin' me up, C. Got me eatin' healthier, preppin' meals, takin' more time off, writin' again." I link our fingers and kiss the back of her hand.

She grins warmly. "But fa real, Tim, you think 'bout us havin' kids?"

I move her laptop to the coffee table before I grab her hands and pull her to me. We keep eye contact as she straddles my lap. Her arms circle my neck as my hands settle on her hips. "I do. Do you?"

She glances away, all cute. "Sometimes."

I lean forward and kiss her cheek a few times. "Ya know, when we have a kid, their name's gotta start wit' an A."

She tilts her head as a curious frown claims her mouth. "Why A?"

"So as a family, we could be CTA." I tap my chest. "Call To Action: Camesha, Tim, and Baby A." She told me a while back that she realized we're both hustlers in our own way, so CTA makes sense for our family identity.

Camesha blinks for a second before cackling like a cute hyena. "What is wrong witchu, Timmy Tree?"

"What is wrong wit' *you* for insistin' on that nickname?" I ask her, tickling her, knowing I'm not going to get a response. "But I'm serious though. CTA is unstoppable. Can't *nobody* fuck wit' us—we 'bout that action."

As her laughter dies down, she shakes her head. "Okay, but *don't* be tryna get me pregnant anytime soon wit' all'is CTA talk, Tim." She points her index finger at me.

"I gotchu." Smiling, I rub my hands up and down her back. "I'm just sayin' when the time comes, we gotta make it iconic."

"I hear you. But I ain't ready for all'at. I 'on't think *we're* ready for that right now honestly. No rush."

I smile at the callback to the poem I performed on our first date. My heart does a weird shock thing, but I ignore it. "But ya know what I *am* ready for and what name sounds even better?"

She sighs, but before she can answer, I clutch her waist to remove her from my lap and set her on the couch. Clenching my jaw to dissolve the nerves flooding in from all angles, I get down on one knee in front of her.

I pull the ring box I've been carrying around in my pockets for over a month. "Camesha . . . *Starks*." I swallow hard, my heart beating so loud in my ear. "Camesha Danielle Russell will you let me love you forever? Will you marry me?" I open the box to reveal the three-carat diamond ring that Nikki and Lu helped me pick out.

I FaceTimed Camesha's family a couple months ago to tell them my plans to propose soon and they *fervently* gave me their blessing. Mrs. Russell—or Mama Russell, as she told me to call her now—squealed louder than Simonique, which I didn't think was possible.

Camesha

My lips part but no words flow out. I can't breathe good. My chest is rising and falling too fast. My cheeks are hot, flushed.

Tim's just looking at me with wide eyes, hopeful and waiting. "Baby, I need you to say some'," he chuckles.

I hear him but his *big* questions keep replaying in my head, swirling like a tornado. *Did he-Did he. . . Did Tim really just ask me to marry him?* Me?

I shake my head quickly, trying to find oxygen and words, but everything's stuck in my throat. Tim's shoulders drop as his smile falls into a small frown, his jaw set like he's bracing for something.

"Sorry—yes, yes, yes, Tim. Of course, I'll marry you," the words tumble out all tangled with tears as my face scrunches up.

Relief and joy wash over Tim's handsome face as he smiles so wide. His shaky hand slides the gorgeous ring onto my trembling one. But it gets on. It's real.

Oh. My. God. Even though Casey and I have started dissecting my thoughts on love in therapy, that doubt—if love is something I can have—still creeps in sometimes.

I shoot up and, before he can even fully stand up, I pull Tim's face to mine. We kiss hard and messy, but it's perfect. His arms lock around my waist, holding me close like he wants me to know and feel deep down that I'm safe here with him.

I do.

We pull back, breathless, our foreheads touching.

"I love you, Camesha," Tim softly says, but there's so much impact in his tone that it makes my chest ache with joy.

"I love you, Tim," I let out, my voice breaking. A single tear slides down my face, but his thumb tenderly swipes it away. "So much. I thank God for you every day."

He kisses my temple. "Me, too, baby. And I actually wrote you a proposal poem, but I ain't gon' lie, I forgot it as soon as I decided to propose right now," he chortles.

A wet laugh leaps out of me. "That's okay. This was perfect, Tim."

He grins before pressing a lingering kiss to my forehead, grounding us both in this promising new season of life we're entering.

We embrace, just squeezing and rocking one another, the world fading away around us. I caress the back of his head and Tim presses me closer like he wants to live in my skin as much as I want to live in his.

God, I want all of Tim. And he wants all of me.

I deserve this love.

The tighter he holds me, the more I melt and the faster the fear and anxiety I'm beginning to understand in therapy roll off of me like boulders down a hill. I can relax into Tim, into this love and this joy, because I know that this man is genuine and has got me for real. Tim handles me and my heart with so much care. I can trust that reality.

We've never been about rushing, just going at our comfortable pace, but I *can't wait* to do life with Tim.

Acknowledgements

First and always, I thank God

For knowing my deepest desires and my wildest dreams. For speaking to me and guiding me.

For moving things around and creating space for me to bring this story to reality.

For the ability to create and the opportunity to pour myself into writing Tim and Camesha's love story.

For helping me achieve this lifelong dream of becoming a published novelist. I thank you, in advance, for when I share my other stories.

This year has been both incredibly fulfilling and joyful, but also challenging, exhausting, and lonely at times. Writing and preparing this book for publication was my *singular* focus. This story has lived in my head and in my heart since January 2025. From drafting, editing, receiving feedback, revising, rewriting, learning the entire self-publishing process and marketing *all while* working a full-time job and trying to stay healthy (I lost some weight, but I also have worsened sleep quality and suffered a tension headache) . . . to now have *Let Me Handle Your Heart* out in the world is an immense achievement that I give You the glory for.

Years ago, while writing my college application essays, my mom asked me, "What do you love that doesn't feel like work?"

I said writing. It's *never* been clearer to me because this year has solidified that writing stories is my purpose. There is absolutely *nothing* I want to do more than to take the stories that live inside me and share them with the world. So, thank you, God, for that gift and passion.

To my family

I thank my parents for always supporting and investing into every single dream I had. That is such a gift I do not take lightly. Unfortunately, not everyone is blessed with parents who want to see their child happy, thriving, and pursuing their dreams.

From buying young Josie fashion design software that I barely touched, to my dad and I co-writing a young adult science fiction novel when I was 10-12 years old. I've always been a storyteller, but I think that experience ignited the desire in me to really pursue writing. My dad will be the first to take credit for that, and while I might roll my eyes, I'll let him.

No one will ride for you like your mom, so I thank you for always being team Josie!

I thank my sister—my best friend—for listening to me ramble about stories and books over the years. Your unhinged, annoying sibling energy has uplifted me, made me laugh, and feel better many times. I also appreciate your encouraging words—a "That's cool, bud" goes a long way.

To my former English professors and classmates

You poured into me as a writer. You introduced me to stories and authors that have resonated and shaped me. You read and thoroughly critiqued my work, helping me sharpen my craft. I thank the English department at my alma mater, Stevenson

University, for nurturing and supporting me during some of my most formative years as a writer.

To my beta readers

Thank you for reading the early version of Tim and Camesha's love story. Special gratitude to Colette, Lanasia, and my mom for giving me generous and thoughtful feedback during that process. Your enthusiasm and careful attention really helped me shape the book that exists today.

To my editor, Megan Joseph

Thank you for your thorough feedback. The changes you suggested added more revising and editing rounds, but it was worth it. I cut what didn't serve the story and added more texture, depth, and emotional impact so that readers can resonate with it more. This book is better and stronger because of your insights.

To Whitney D. Grandison

Though we have yet to meet in person, I've been reading your work for over a decade. From Wattpad to traditional and indie publishing success, I really appreciate you being very generous with your journey, advice, and encouragement.

And to you, the reader

Thank you for taking a chance on my debut novel. It really means the absolute world to me.

I am not a new writer, just a new *author*. Thank you for being a part of this lifelong dream coming true.

I take Toni Morrison's famous words to heart:

> If there's a book that you want to read, but it hasn't
> been written yet, then you must write it.

And I intend to write *all* of those stories (trust me, there are many in the queue). This novel is only the beginning. I hope you come along for the ride.

Cheers to a thriving creative writing career!

All glory to God!

About the Author

J osie Hunter (she/her) is a Black writer from the DC, Maryland, Virginia metropolitan area. A graduate of Stevenson University, her short stories and poetry have appeared in their online magazine, *The Greenspring Review*, where she also won First Prize in Fiction for their 2020 COVID Creative Contest. In 2024, she was a quarterfinalist in the New York International Screenplay Awards. She shares reflections on writing, fiction, publishing, and creativity in her bi-weekly Substack newsletter called *Notes from a Work-in-Progress Writer*. *Let Me Handle Your Heart* is her debut novel!

When Josie's not writing, she's probably reading a good book, trying a new restaurant, or experimenting with ways to consistently exercise and improve her sleep. You can find her on her website at josiehunterlit.com and social media: @josiehunterlit on Instagram and TikTok.

NOTE:
It would mean *so much* to me if you left a rating and/or review on Amazon, Goodreads, and StoryGraph! Please tag me on social media reviews as well. Every rating, review, like, comment, and share really helps independent authors like me reach more readers. So, I thank you in advance for your continued support.
—Josie